# PRAISE FOR THE KEERA DUGGAN SERIES

## *Beyond Reasonable Doubt*

"A cunning master class in why you should always trust your lawyer, and what it'll cost you if you do."

—*Kirkus Reviews*

"Robert Dugoni once again demonstrates his complete mastery of the suspense/thriller murder mystery genre. Expertly crafted characters, impressively original story, and a fun read for mystery fans from start to finish."

—Midwest Book Review

## *Her Deadly Game*

"Fast-paced legal-intrigue gold that could be improved only by kicking off a new series."

—*Kirkus Reviews* (starred review)

"Twist-filled . . . John Grisham fans will be pleased."

—*Publishers Weekly*

"Justice has rarely been this compelling."

—Criminal Element

"*Her Deadly Game* is one of the best murder trial tales to come along in recent years. It's superb."

—*The Free Press* (Winnipeg)

"One of the best puzzle books ever! I raced through the pages, which are packed full of compelling characters and taut gamesmanship, desperate to learn the answer to this extraordinary thriller, which is both whodunit and how-dunit. I would follow Robert Dugoni anywhere."

—Lisa Gardner, #1 *New York Times* bestselling author

"I adore Robert Dugoni's legal thrillers, and *Her Deadly Game* is his best one yet. I loved Keera Duggan's strength and her heart, which shine through the pages, and I rooted for her every step of the way through this unputdownable story."

—Lisa Scottoline, *New York Times* bestselling author

"Absolutely riveting. A juicy tale that will leave readers hungry for more."

—Victor Methos, bestselling author of *The Secret Witness*

"Robert Dugoni has done it again—created a twisty puzzle-box story with one of the most satisfying, jaw-dropping endings I've read in a long time. Part murder mystery, part courtroom drama, and part character study of fascinating chess prodigy turned defense attorney Keera Duggan, *Her Deadly Game* will keep you reading late into the night."

—Angie Kim, international bestselling author of *Miracle Creek*

# HER COLD JUSTICE

# ALSO BY ROBERT DUGONI

*Hold Strong* (with Jeff Langholz and Chris Crabtree)

*The Last Line* (a short story)

*The World Played Chess*

*The Extraordinary Life of Sam Hell*

*The 7th Canon*

*Damage Control*

## The Tracy Crosswhite Series

*My Sister's Grave*

*Her Final Breath*

*In the Clearing*

*The Trapped Girl*

*Close to Home*

*A Steep Price*

*A Cold Trail*

*In Her Tracks*

*What She Found*

*One Last Kill*

*A Dead Draw*

*The Academy* (a short story)

*Third Watch* (a short story)

## The Keera Duggan Series

*Her Deadly Game*

*Beyond Reasonable Doubt*

## The Charles Jenkins Series

*The Eighth Sister*

*The Last Agent*

*The Silent Sisters*

## The David Sloane Series

*The Jury Master*

*Wrongful Death*

*Bodily Harm*

*Murder One*

*The Conviction*

## Nonfiction with Joseph Hilldorfer

*The Cyanide Canary*

# HER COLD JUSTICE

ROBERT DUGONI

Published by Thomas & Mercer, Seattle
www.apub.com



EU product safety contact:
Amazon Media EU S. à r.l.
38, avenue John F. Kennedy, L-1855 Luxembourg
amazonpublishing-gpsr@amazon.com

ISBN-13: 9781662524622 (hardcover)
ISBN-13: 9781662524639 (paperback)
ISBN-13: 9781662524646 (digital)

Cover design by Jarrod Taylor
Cover image: © Alex Gontar / Shutterstock

Printed in the United States of America

First edition

*To Mom.*
*My champion. My rock. My anchor.*
*I will miss you.*

# Prologue

***July 1985***
***Little Saigon***
***Seattle, Washington***

Seattle homicide detective Jack Thompson stepped from the Chevy Caprice onto the sidewalk at the corner of Twelfth Avenue South and South Jackson Street, the business center of what was now called Seattle's Little Saigon. People hustled from one grocery store or restaurant to the next, vendors enticing them in Vietnamese, English, and a mix of the two.

"Xin Chiào! Xin Chiào! Come. Look at produce. Fresh today."

"Vietnamese coffee. Best prices. You try."

Traditional Vietnamese music spilled from the businesses and mixed with the cacophony of voices, the hum of passing cars, and the hiss of brakes on the electronic buses hooked by trolley poles to a spiderweb of cables strung overhead.

Thompson reached back into the car and grabbed his suit jacket, slipping it on. He didn't bother to button his shirt collar or cinch tight the knot of his tie.

It was too damned hot.

A heat wave had hit Puget Sound. Temperatures had exceeded ninety degrees for three straight days, and the high temperatures were expected to continue.

His partner, Kyle Mitchell, a newbie to Seattle's homicide squad, adjusted his suit jacket with great care, not a wrinkle in the expensive fabric as he walked around the hood of the car to Thompson. The ten-year homicide veteran had been tasked with showing Mitchell the ropes. Mitchell still dressed to impress in tailored suits, shirts with monogrammed cuffs, and expensive ties. The rookie would soon learn the suit was just a uniform; no one cared how you dressed.

What mattered in this job were the results.

Mitchell unwrapped the foil and rolled a piece of spearmint gum into his mouth, chewing with that cocksure grin. In Ray-Ban Aviator sunglasses and short, gelled hair, he resembled a taller, more muscular version of the actor Tom Cruise.

"You ever been down here?" Thompson asked Mitchell.

A history buff, Thompson had read of the Vietnamese people's struggles before, during, and after the war, as well as their resilience and determination in America. As they had done in countless cities, they'd established a community in these few square blocks, first populated by war refugees after the fall of Saigon in April 1975. In what seemed overnight, more than a hundred mom-and-pop restaurants, markets, hair salons, jewelry stores, and professional offices overtook the area, a testament to their hard work despite their displacement, which limited their economic opportunities.

"Nah," Mitchell said with a dismissive headshake. "Had my fill when I served my tour. No desire to go back. Though I do miss the food. You?"

Thompson took in the savory aroma of pho and grilled pork, chicken and chili-infused beef fat, fresh basil and mint herbs, and the briny scent of seafood. "The wife likes to come down here to shop. Likes to be spontaneously exotic and buy things like jackfruit and rambutan."

They crossed the intersection to the strip mall of shops now distinguished by multiple police cars, one with its roof lights still swirling, and an ambulance. "My father says this area was once Seattle's jazz capital," Mitchell said. "Said Ray Charles and Quincy Jones played in clubs here."

"Different time," Thompson said.

A uniformed officer stood outside the glass door to the Tran Jewelry Market, one of several jewelry stores in the area, this one sandwiched between a movie-rental business—VHS videocassettes in the windows—and a grab-and-go Vietnamese deli offering bánh mì sandwiches. Thompson and Mitchell flashed their badges and shook the uniform's hand. The young man looked pale beneath his snap-back navy-blue police hat. The pavement had to be over one hundred degrees.

"You okay, Officer? You look a little pale," Mitchell said, his tone and grin baiting.

"I'm okay," the officer said.

"Make sure you're drinking water," Thompson said. "I've lost a few pounds just crossing the street."

"Will do."

"What do we have?" Thompson asked.

"Looks to me like two murders during a robbery." The uniform sounded tentative, and Thompson realized the quiver in the young man's voice, his pale complexion, and sweaty brow wasn't just from the heat but from what he'd seen inside the store. "A man and a woman." He gestured to his right. "The movie-rental store owner said husband and wife." He let out a burst of air, fighting to rein in his emotions.

"Take your time," Thompson said.

"It's pretty gruesome, Detective. A lot of blood and spatter and, in this heat, with no air-conditioning . . . the smell is . . . It's pretty bad."

"Okay. Just a few more questions, then I want you to find something to drink with sugar in it. A Coke. You understand?"

The young man nodded.

"Who's been inside the store other than you?"

"Just me and my partner. We checked the two people on the floor for a pulse. Pretty obvious, but we checked. Then we stepped back out and called it in."

"Medical examiner on the way?"

"I . . . I don't know."

"Why don't you find out? If the office hasn't been alerted, tell them to send someone out."

Thompson glanced over at the two paramedics waiting near the back of their ambulance. They seemed eager to get inside the store. Not happening. Paramedics were like elephants. They trampled crime scenes.

The senior homicide detective considered the stores in the strip malls on both sides of the street. "Any of the other business owners see anyone going in or coming out?"

The officer pointed to a sign on the door displaying the store hours. "Looks like they'd just opened, so . . . Not that anyone is saying. Not yet anyway. My partner is still talking to the other business owners."

"Where in the store are the two bodies?"

The officer turned to the storefront. "Just inside. Behind the display counter. A curtain separates the retail section from an area where they cleaned and repaired jewelry. Looks that way to me. There's also a living area—like maybe the owners spent a lot of time here."

"They're refugees. You can bet they did," Thompson said.

He handed Mitchell a pair of gloves, and they both slipped them on before stepping past the officer.

"Guy was pretty shaken up," Mitchell said, referencing the uniform and working hard to sound tough, but his smile was no longer so cocksure.

Inside, the temperature felt ten degrees hotter; air-conditioning was an unnecessary expense. It would be like working in a sauna. The glass in the long and rectangular display case had been smashed. Glass shards crunched beneath Thompson's black wing-tipped shoes. He stepped carefully around pieces of jewelry strewn amid the glass; the stones green, ruby red, and sapphire blue.

"Looks like they were in a hurry," Mitchell said.

Thompson took mental pictures. He'd have a photographer document and videotape the scene. He stepped around the end of the counter; more glass crunched. Mitchell followed, his Aviators now folded and clipped to his suit pocket.

Thompson smelled the killings, a sharp metallic odor, before he saw the bodies. From the sour expression on Mitchell's face, he smelled it also. Thompson pulled back the dark-gray blanket hanging by shower rings from a water pipe along the ceiling. Blood, a dark crimson, pooled near the head wounds of a man and a woman. It looked as if they'd been told to kneel on the worn tile floor, their hands tied behind their backs before the gunman shot them, and their bodies had pitched forward. Gruesome didn't begin to describe the carnage.

"Shit." Mitchell put a hand to his mouth, like he was fighting back bile. "Goddamn."

Thompson said, "If you're going to be sick, do it someplace where it doesn't contaminate my crime scene."

Mitchell turned away and worked another piece of gum into his mouth.

Thompson also felt sick, though not physically. These poor people had come to America to escape this kind of violence. He put that thought aside and documented in his head what he would have photographed and drawn to scale. The back room looked maybe twenty by twenty feet, the only light from a pane in a locked back door leading to an alley. And it did look like the couple spent a lot of time here. Maybe even lived here. He stepped to a rectangular Formica table in the center of the room. On it was an opened schoolbook, a piece of paper with math problems not completed, and a small pencil. Beside the paper was half a glass of some beverage and a plate on which lay half-eaten slices of mango and lychee. His sick feeling returned. He hoped to God a child had not been here, that these were remnants perhaps from a prior study session.

Thompson walked to where a second curtain hung, though not to the floor. Behind it, tucked against the concrete wall, he found a bed, a dresser with drawers, and atop the dresser, a small television set with a rabbit-ears antenna.

He turned, about to leave, then stopped when he spotted a piece of blue fabric sticking out from under the bed. He caught Mitchell's eye, then nodded to the garment. Mitchell released the strap over his .38 Special revolver, put his hand on the grip, and turned to the side, like a gunslinger. Thompson rolled his eyes and gestured with an open palm to stand down. He knelt and gently lifted the corner of a blanket, revealing more of the blue garment. A sweater. A plaid skirt. White ankle socks. Black Mary Jane shoes.

A school uniform.

A young girl crouched on her knees, the way Thompson had once crouched beneath his desk during Cold War nuclear bomb exercises. She lifted her head and looked up at Thompson with the frightened, uncertain eyes of a kitten abandoned too young by its mother.

Thompson turned his head to the right—the direction the girl had been looking. The two bodies, her parents, stared back at her with lifeless eyes.

# Part I

# Chapter 1

***Present Day—December 4***
***Seattle, Washington***

Frank Rossi turned the corner and slowed his 1969 Pontiac GTO, custom-painted British racing green; the exhaust pipes rumbling loud as a boat engine. Inconspicuous he was not—which wasn't a good thing when you were the last detective to arrive at a homicide scene.

"If you're going to be a bear, might as well be a grizzly," Rossi said.

He drove through what otherwise appeared to be a quiet residential neighborhood in South Seattle. The car's heater and defroster churned on high against the unseasonably cold weather. Early December in Seattle normally meant a lot of rain, but the twenty-three-degree temperature this morning foretold an early and long winter.

His partner in the Violent Crimes Section, Billy Ford, and their sergeant, Chuck Pan, stood on the sidewalk dressed for the cold weather in knit caps, down jackets, and gloves. Their breaths marked the air with wisps of condensation.

Rossi pulled the Pontiac to the curb and got out, feeling the numbing cold like a slap to the face. He slipped his navy-blue knit hat over his ears, then pulled on his lined leather gloves. Anticipating Ford's questions, he answered before his partner had the chance to ask them. "Yes, I was out late. And yes, I thought it prudent to come straight here and not go downtown and get a pool car."

"I was just going to say, 'Good morning, sunshine. Thanks for making us wait out in the cold,'" Ford said, voice raspy.

Rossi frowned and looked to Pan, who had initiated this party, waking both detectives with telephone calls. Ford and Rossi were the Violent Crimes team on call this week.

Rossi looked about. "We the first to arrive?"

"'We'?" Ford said.

"Give it a rest, Billy." Rossi knew from his earlier conversation with Pan that the crime looked to be a double homicide. The uniformed first responders had secured the house, a one-story rambler, and the detached garage. His Italian mother would have called the house a "baracca"—a small, unimpressive abode.

"Two dead bodies," Pan said, his breath continuing to mark the air. "A man and a woman. Home is registered to a John Lockett, age forty-three. The woman, according to identification, is Melissa Scott, age thirty-one."

"Girlfriend?" Rossi asked.

"Undetermined at this time," Pan said. "Though a reasonable assumption. Lockett was shot and killed in the garage. Scott looks to have been bludgeoned to death in the bedroom. It's ugly."

"Murder-suicide?" Rossi asked. It would be rare for a burglar to shoot one victim and bludgeon the other. The gunshot or the bludgeoning presumably would alert the second victim.

"Also undetermined," Pan said. "First responders said you'll find drugs and cash inside the house."

"Dealers?" Ford said.

"Also undetermined, though it's more than you'd expect for just recreational use. Neither victim has a record."

"Any gang affiliations?" Ford asked. He and Rossi had worked a narcotics rotation on their way to Violent Crimes. Gangs often ran drugs.

"Again, unknown at this time."

"Who called it in?" Rossi asked.

"Neighbor. Alex Cortez." Pan pointed to a house across the street. "A uniform is interviewing him."

"What was he doing at Lockett's house so early?" Ford asked.

"Lockett works the graveyard shift at an airfreight company out by the airport. He gets off around four. Neighbor said he and Lockett had agreed to meet at eight to work on the car in the garage."

"We'll want elimination prints," Rossi said to Ford.

"You run him?" Ford asked Pan, meaning the neighbor.

"One DUI, had his license suspended six months. Otherwise not even a parking violation." Pan looked back at the house. "If this was a drug hit, I'm not sure why the perps wouldn't have taken *all* the drugs and cash."

"To make it look like it wasn't?" Ford postulated.

"Not sure your garden-variety gangbanger is that forward thinking," Rossi said, subscribing to the theory that most criminals weren't rocket scientists. "They'd take the money and sell the drugs."

Pan flipped a page of his spiral notebook. "On a cursory inspection, first responders did not note any spent shell casings."

"The shooter picked up the shell casings?" Ford asked, though he meant his question to be rhetorical.

"Or used a revolver," Rossi said.

"Either could indicate a professional hit," Ford said.

"As could leaving behind cash and drugs, as well as the violent nature of the deaths," Rossi said.

Pan closed his notebook. "You know the drill."

"Too well," Rossi said. "MDOP been called?"

"Been called. Haven't seen anyone yet," Pan said. "CSI and ME have also been called. I've ordered patrol to cordon off the street at the turn up there. Rodgers and Hammerstein are your next up."

Hammerstein's real name was Doug Stein, but the nickname was just too hard for other detectives to ignore. As next-up detectives, he and Phil Rodgers would provide Ford and Rossi support by conducting interviews and scanning the crime scene.

Ford picked out gloves and rubber booties from the go bag at his feet and handed a pair of each to Rossi. "Rock, paper, scissors?"

"Fat chance, Bernstein. This is your symphony," Rossi said, meaning Ford would be the lead detective. They alternated.

"Is someone actually listening to classical music?" Ford asked as they walked toward the front door. The uniformed officer held the sign-in log. He looked half frozen.

"Watched the movie," Rossi said, referring to *Maestro*, which depicted the life of Leonard Bernstein. He removed his leather gloves and felt the bitter cold as he took the pen, clumsy in his hands, and scratched his name and badge number beneath Ford's.

"How was it?" Ford asked.

"Bradley Cooper did a good job, but they didn't play enough of Bernstein's music. At least the stuff I'd recognize."

"You see it with your new lady friend?"

Rossi handed the pen back to the uniform. "'Lady friend'? How old are you?"

"Can we call her a girlfriend?" Ford asked. "I don't really care, but Allysia would like to know. She thinks I'm withholding juicy gossip. She won't believe we spend all day together and I don't even know this woman's name."

Allysia was Ford's wife and the mother of their three boys.

"Tell Allysia I don't like to put labels on things."

Ford laughed as he slipped on his booties. He looked to the lowered garage door, then asked the uniform, "Is there another entrance to the garage?"

"Around the side." The officer pointed across the driveway, past two cars parked side by side. Frost covered their windows.

Ford and Rossi stepped around the cars to round concrete pavers leading to the door on the side. A second uniformed officer in a fur hat and long coat, which made him look like a Russian sentry, also held a sign-in log.

"Detached from the dwelling, so we thought we might need a second sign-in sheet," he said, sounding cold. The log was not just a way to monitor who went into and out of a crime scene; it also served as a deterrent. Those who crossed the line were required to file a report, which was the bane of every officer's existence, especially the brass.

Rock music spilled out the door, guitars and heavy drums—AC/DC.

"Assume the music was on when you arrived?" Ford asked the uniformed officer.

"It was," the officer confirmed. "We didn't touch the stereo in case it had fingerprints on the dials."

"Dials?" Ford said.

"It's old school," the uniform said.

Rossi and Ford stepped inside the garage, where it was noticeably warmer. "Thunderstruck" burst from tower speakers. Rossi also heard a hum followed by a click and looked up at a space heater attached to a wooden joist.

"I think we can turn the music off before it gives us both a headache," Ford said, pressing the power switch.

"That's AC/DC," Rossi said. "It's a classic." In his younger years he'd been a metalhead.

"I'm glad, at least, that you didn't call it *music*," Ford said.

A 1951 Packard, a sweet-looking ride with a pale-green body and yellow hardtop, took up half the garage. The hood was up. A light bulb in a protective cage illuminated the engine. Tools lay strewn about, a ratchet set on the grill, a tire iron on the garage floor.

Rossi gestured to the car. "That's worth some money."

"If it runs," Ford said. "Until then, Allysia would call it a large paperweight."

"Says the guy with a piano, half a dozen guitars, a violin, *and* a saxophone."

"All of which are used regularly."

The other half of the garage looked to have been converted into a rustic man cave. A flat-screen television, mounted to the wall studs, faced a brown leather couch and matching chair on a rust-colored carpet. Behind the couch was a well-used pool table, the green felt worn and bald in places. Face down on the concrete floor between the pool table and the car lay the body of a white male. Blood, a dark crimson, pooled from the back of his head, indicating the body had not been moved or otherwise disturbed. The man wore a grease-stained T-shirt and black Carhartt work pants.

"Focused on the car?" Ford said.

Ford deduced, as Rossi had from the gore and the blood spatter, that the man had been shot at close range. "The music was loud enough to have masked the killer's approach," Rossi said.

Rossi and Ford backed out carefully to await the CSI van carrying the team of detectives who would photograph and record the garage from a million different angles, dust for latent fingerprints, collect DNA, and otherwise examine the scene for forensic evidence.

They made their way back to the uniformed officer at the front door and changed shoe coverings before stepping inside the house. The interior was modest. The furniture dated and sparse. On a table, bags of pills and powders spilled from opened Blue Horizon Air Cargo packages, along with some cash. Rossi recognized the company name—an airfreight service out near the airport.

A shaken-looking officer motioned to a narrow hall with doors on each side. "Last door on the right."

Rossi and Ford stepped inside the bedroom, encountering the reason the young officer looked sickened.

Ford swore.

Rossi made the sign of the cross, another habit he'd inherited from his mother, who did so each time she passed a church or a wreck on the highway—or anything else unnerving.

The woman, presumably Melissa Scott, lay naked on bloodstained sheets, her limbs and body twisted and contorted.

"This looks like rage to me," Ford said.

"Or somebody leaving a message," Rossi said. "Either way, they got the message across."

# Chapter 2

***Present Day—Two Weeks Later***
***Seattle, Washington***

Keera Duggan listened to her oldest sister, Ella, go over the law firm's profit and loss statement for the year end, as well as providing projections for the upcoming year, and wondered if she could learn to sleep with her eyes open. Her flight back to Seattle from Rome, Italy, had been delayed. She didn't land at SeaTac Airport until after 1:00 a.m. By the time Keera crawled into bed it was nearly 3:00 a.m. She awoke severely jet-lagged.

The peaceful violin music Ella played on the speakers in her office wasn't helping either, fostering images of Keera's warm bed and comfortable down pillow. It was all Keera could do to keep her head from falling forward and slamming onto her sister's desk.

After defending Jenna Bernstein in a physically and emotionally draining trial, Keera had been burned out. Her father, Patsy, the founding member of the law firm Duggan & Associates, had insisted she take a break to refresh and recharge. Now she wished she'd stayed longer on the Italian island of Ischia. She missed the sweeping views of the Gulf of Naples and the Aragonese Castle, and the marina teeming with restaurants, each with a menu as tempting as the next.

The sporadic rain showers in Italy had discouraged the usual crowds, but Seattleites knew how to put on a Gore-Tex jacket and shoes and get about in the rain. The stores in the towns had been magical, playing Christmas music and decorated with festive ornaments and lights. Traditional treats like zeppole and struffoli tempted Keera on every block, and an impressive Christmas tree in Piazza Tasso had reminded Keera of the decorated trees her parents placed in the family home.

It had all been romantic.

The only thing missing was someone to share it with.

And enough money to make it last.

But it wasn't just dwindling funds that brought Keera home. For a trial lawyer, a vacation was a double-edged sword. The break was a much-needed respite from the daily grind and stress, but for each day away, work in the office built like seawater rising behind a dike plugged with the fingers of those lawyers left behind.

Patsy, a legend in the courtroom, no longer tried cases; a lifelong addiction to alcohol had finally caught up with him. He'd told his three daughters—Ella, the oldest; Maggie; and Keera, an "oops" baby ten years younger than Maggie—that after fifty years devoting his time and energy to his jealous mistress, he would now focus on their mother. Ella was best at running the firm, not a courtroom, and their associates were too green for most criminal trials, which were now Keera's domain, with Patsy serving as Keera's ombudsman.

It made Keera's and Ella's new reality even more impactful. The law firm's survival now rested with them, the two partners.

"Ella, is Keera with you?"

Keera's head snapped up at the sound of Maggie's voice through the speaker on Ella's desk. Maggie served as the firm's receptionist, paralegal, and alarmist. There wasn't a flame she couldn't turn into a blaze, given the chance.

"What is it, Maggie?" Keera asked.

"First, can you let me know where you are?"

Keera rolled her eyes at another Maggie power play. No *Welcome back!* or *How was Italy?* "I'm in Ella's office."

"Funny," she said, returning the sarcasm. "I don't have time to be hunting you down."

"Maggie," Ella said. "What is it?"

"Tall, Dark, and Handsome is here, and he needs to speak to Keera ASAP."

"Hopefully not standing at your desk listening to you," Ella said. Ella could get away with saying things to Maggie that Keera dare not utter.

"Give me some credit, please. I sent him to the conference room . . . since I couldn't reach Keera in *her* office."

Keera shook her head. To Maggie, she'd always be the annoying little sister who didn't do as told. "I'm on my way, Maggie," Keera said. Ella ended the conversation, and Keera asked, "I'm surprised she let him out of her clutches so easily. Does this mean she has a new beau?"

"I can't keep track. Nor do I care to," Ella said. "But given the pissy mood she's been in, I highly doubt that's the case. You know Maggie."

*Too well,* Keera thought. But you couldn't pick your family. "She could be pissy because I was in Italy, and she wasn't."

"True."

"Are we done here?"

"For the most part."

"Work our asses off, make as much money as possible, and take another vacation when I'm seventy-two like Patsy?"

Ella smiled. "You *were* paying attention."

Keera departed Ella's office and made her way down the hall to the conference room. She passed the offices of the two associate attorneys Ella had hired while Keera was knee-deep in the Bernstein trial. They worked dutifully at their desks. Associates were another double-edged sword. They took work off Keera's and Ella's desks and added to the firm's monthly billable hours, which generated revenue, but they also received a paycheck every two weeks, and Ella and Keera had to bring in business to ensure they earned it.

JP Harrison stood facing the view of the ferry dock and Elliott Bay. A ferryboat crossed to Bainbridge Island, leaving a V-shaped wake on the calm, slate-gray, winter waters. Tall, dark, and handsome did not adequately describe Harrison. With his British accent, he sounded charming, and his fashion sense shaved years off his fifty-three. This morning, he wore khaki chinos and a light-blue cashmere sweater that complemented his Black complexion and made him look elegant. On the back of a conference room chair he'd hung his navy-blue peacoat and a scarf. On the table rested leather gloves and a black knit beanie. It was hard to imagine that the firm's private investigator had once been a Seattle homicide detective.

Keera pushed open the door and entered. Harrison turned from the view. "To what do I owe the pleasure?" she asked.

Harrison gave her a grave smile. "I need a favor. A big one."

# Chapter 3

***December 4***
***Seattle, Washington***

Frank Rossi and Billy Ford stood on the concrete driveway going over their checklist on a laminated card they kept in their go bag. The list ensured they did not miss any steps during their investigation, and procedures were rigidly followed to prevent mistakes that could become the subject of a defense attorney's cross-examination or motion to dismiss.

The medical examiner's van had arrived, and Ford had spoken with King County medical examiner Arthur Litchfield, who now had control over both bodies.

The CSI mobile unit, a van containing specialized equipment, from petri dishes and sterile swabs to fingerprint and DNA collection equipment, had also arrived on scene. CSI detectives dressed in black cargo pants, black jackets with "CSI" across the back, knit hats, and leather gloves sipped from steaming cups of coffee while waiting to get inside the garage and the home. Billy had instructed the CSI sergeant on what he wanted in terms of forensic evidence, though the unit, formed in 2004, was now well oiled and didn't need much instruction on how to do its job.

The crowd of police personnel at the small house had attracted a crowd of its own, though the bitter cold had discouraged all but the hardiest neighbors from venturing outside. Most peered from behind windows.

Rodgers and Hammerstein, who had interviewed the neighbor who made the 911 call, approached Ford and Rossi on the sidewalk. The two looked as if they'd been plucked from central casting: Rodgers, young, good looking, and physically fit, and Stein, the gray-haired veteran with a paunch that evidenced his love of pasta. Rossi liked Stein, but Rodgers had a cocky demeanor that rubbed Rossi the wrong way.

"What did you find out?" Ford asked.

Stein told them the neighbor, Alex Cortez, appeared visibly shaken and repeated what he had told the 911 dispatcher, as well as the uniformed officers who had first interviewed him. "He and Lockett were friends. They fixed up old cars and sold them at classic car shows. He said they had agreed to meet at 8:00 a.m. to continue rebuilding the carburetor on a '51 Packard. He heard music playing when he walked into the garage but didn't see Lockett. He almost left, then saw the blood and stepped around the pool table and saw the body. He ran back to his house and called 911, then waited outside his home for the police to arrive. The shoe prints you see on the garage floor are his. He stepped in the blood before backing out."

"Did he know whether Lockett had been running drugs?" Ford asked.

"Says he didn't," Stein said.

"Did he sound honest?" Ford asked.

"Hard to tell. He might have been protecting his friend," Rodgers said.

"He provided elimination fingerprints and a DNA swab," Stein said. "He said we'd likely find his fingerprints all over the garage—on the car, the pool table. He was over here frequently working on the cars or to drink beer, listen to music, or to catch the Seahawks or Mariners games."

"Alibi?" Rossi asked.

"Asleep in bed with his 'old lady.' She confirmed."

"Any other neighbors come over regularly?" Ford asked.

"He said a neighbor down the street came one time, and some 'kid' Lockett worked with at Blue Horizon." Stein checked his notes. "A Michael Westbrook."

"Any other neighbors see or hear anything this morning?" Ford asked.

Rodgers shook his head. Stein said, "So far, no. They all claim to have been sleeping, and given the time—"

"And the freaking cold," Rodgers interjected.

"—that seems logical," Stein finished.

It also wasn't unusual for most citizens, unfamiliar with the sound of a gunshot, to mistake it for a car backfiring, a transformer blowing, or fireworks and not pay it any attention.

"No one saw any suspicious cars or people. No one loitering around the house," Stein continued. "If Lockett was dealing out of his house, the neighbors didn't know it."

"What'd he do for Blue Horizon?" Ford asked. "Cortez know?"

"Said Lockett supervised the graveyard shift, which is why he usually didn't get home until after four thirty in the morning," Stein said.

"It narrows the killing to sometime between 4:30 a.m. and 8:00 a.m., when Cortez found him," Rossi said to Ford. "We should have them take a drive by Blue Horizon and confirm all this."

"You want us to make a call?" Stein said.

Ford did.

Rossi said, "I'll call Joe Jensen at TCI. See if there are any traffic cameras between Blue Horizon and here. Do we know which of these two cars Lockett drove?"

"Neighbor said the Trailblazer was Lockett's," Stein said, pointing to one of the two cars parked in the driveway.

Rossi snapped pictures of the car and the license plate to transmit to Jensen. Then he said, "If Lockett was dealing, it looks like he was getting his product through Blue Horizon, at least from the packaging on the table. And if this was a hit, *somebody* knew that bit of information." He addressed Ford. "Maybe we find out if others at Blue Horizon could have been involved."

"Worth running down," Ford agreed. "Maybe we start with the kid he worked with who Cortez said had been over several times. What did you say his name was?"

"Michael Westbrook," Stein said. "Cortez said he lives close by. Couple of miles."

Rossi saw uniformed police officers remove a sawhorse to allow a black Tesla to drive toward the crime scene. It was not an SPD pool car. "MDOP?" Rossi asked, meaning a prosecutor from the prosecuting attorney's Most Dangerous Offender Program.

"Any bets?" Ford said.

"Not Walker Thompson. Heard he was out getting a knee replaced."

The car came to a stop, and the door pushed open. Anh Tran stepped from the car in blue jeans, a black V-neck sweater, winter boots, and a long wool coat.

"Batwoman," Rossi said to Ford.

At five foot eight, Tran moved with the grace and elegance of a fashion model but with a determined, no-nonsense, hard-to-read look. Rossi had never worked with Tran, but everyone in SPD and the prosecutor's office either knew her or knew of her. She was either infamous or famous depending on whom you spoke to. Orphaned at a young age after her parents were killed in a jewelry store burglary, Tran was raised by an aunt in Seattle's Little Saigon and had managed to pull herself up by her bootstraps. People in the PA's office and SPD related Tran's circumstances to the fictional Bruce Wayne, Batman, because of the similarities to the comic book character's tragic loss of his parents to a violent crime and his ability to rise from those ashes to devote his life to fighting for justice. It was an analogy Tran did not discuss but also did not discourage. She'd been with the PA's office prosecuting violent criminals for twenty years, and though many had suggested she run for higher office—the King County prosecuting attorney, even mayor—she'd declined, choosing to fight in the trenches, which only increased her aura as a crime fighter.

"Detectives," Tran said, condensation hanging in the air between them.

"Anh," Ford said. He filled her in on the investigation's status. "CSI sergeant has control of the scene at present and will let us know when we can get back in."

Tran seemed impervious to the cold, not wearing a hat or gloves, which made Rossi's fingers feel numb.

"Anything you need? Search warrants?" she asked.

"Maybe," Ford said. "Neighbor across the street says the victim, John Lockett, worked for Blue Horizon, an air cargo outfit based out at the airport. We found cash and heavy narcotics inside several Blue Horizon envelopes in the house. Initial review is heroin, fentanyl, oxy, and some weed. We've called for a hazmat team to handle the drugs."

"How much?" Tran asked.

"Still processing the scene, but more than for recreational use," Ford said.

"Where was it coming in from?"

"The Blue Horizon envelopes indicate Southeast Asia."

"I'll get a search warrant put together."

"Maybe he kept a locker or an office at work, a computer," Rossi said.

"I'll also reach out to the narcotics unit and the feds, see if they're working anything that might include Blue Horizon. You think the killings could have been a drug hit, then?" Tran asked.

"Too early to say, but it has similar characteristics," Ford said. "No shell casings found in the garage, meaning—"

"The killer used a revolver to kill the two occupants or picked up the shells," Tran said. "A professional."

"The girlfriend wasn't shot," Ford clarified. "She appears to have been bludgeoned to death. It's gruesome."

"Gangs fighting over territory will often make a killing particularly violent—a wife, sometimes children. No one is safe," Tran said.

Tran spoke from experience. She'd once worked as the prosecutor on SPD's Repeat Offender Program, also known as the "ROPE team." The unit's job had been to track paroled felons upon release.

After the ROPE team disbanded, Tran moved to the Most Dangerous Offender Program and sent a message of her own to those she prosecuted. If a suspect refused to plead, she would charge them to the fullest extent of the law and seek its harshest penalties. Detectives who had sat beside her in court said she had an evangelical fervor to her arguments, crafting theatrical narratives to explain mostly circumstantial evidence during her hundred-plus jury trials, a high percentage of which resulted in convictions.

"What about taking a drive out to the airport to talk with Blue Horizon?" Tran said to Rossi. "While the fingerprint and DNA analysis is happening."

Ford hid a grin, no doubt enjoying Tran telling Rossi what to do.

"I can do that," Rossi said. The joke was on Ford. Rossi was glad to get out of the cold.

Tran handed them each a card. "Anything comes up, let me know. If you need anything, call. I'm going to talk to the CSI sergeant and find out where his team is at and if he needs anything. Send me copies of any and all interviews. ASAP." She held out her hand. Ford shook it. "Gloves and booties," she said.

Ford looked embarrassed as he bent down and retrieved a pair of each, handing them to her. Rossi watched, doing a poor job of hiding his pleasure.

Tran turned on her heels and walked toward the officer standing sentry at the front door. The officer glanced at her, then shifted his eyes to Ford and Rossi. Ford nodded his consent, and the officer handed Tran the clipboard.

"Why don't you make a run out to Blue Horizon? I'll stay here and run the crime scene," Ford said.

"Great idea, Billy. You come up with that on your own?" Rossi said.

"Don't be a smart-ass."

"You're not one of those guys threatened by a strong woman, are you, Billy?"

"Shut up."

# Chapter 4

***Present Day***
***Seattle, Washington***

Harrison declined anything to drink and folded his hands in a prayer position atop the oak conference room table, an Apple watch and a gold bracelet on his left wrist, his nails manicured to perfection. His facial expression was anything but polished. He looked worn out, run down, a man who hadn't slept much and hadn't eaten well, which was not like him. The room held the nauseating odor of the lemon-scented wood cleaner Maggie sprayed over the table each morning.

"How was your trip?" Harrison asked. His question sounded dutiful and not from genuine interest.

"Heavenly," she said. "And too short."

"Just you?" he asked.

She'd briefly contemplated asking Frank Rossi to join her, but she ultimately decided against it, knowing it would have changed their relationship in a way that could not be unchanged. She feared getting carried away by the lure of romance amid the scenic Italian beauty. Frank remained a homicide detective, and she was now a criminal defense attorney. Not a good mix. Had she continued in the prosecutor's office where they'd first met, things might be different. But that was now water under the bridge.

"Just me," she said, then cut to the chase. "What is it? You look troubled."

"I am. My sister Tina's son, Michael, has gotten himself into trouble. She said it's like a bad nightmare they can't wake from."

"What kind of trouble?"

"He's in the Federal Detention Center in SeaTac," Harrison said. "He's been charged with being part of a drug ring smuggling in large quantities of fentanyl and other heavy narcotics. But I think that's the tip of a very deep iceberg, and it's going to get worse as this goes down."

Keera felt her eyebrows rise, a habit she'd inherited from her father. "Worse?"

"Did you hear about the double homicide in South Seattle about two weeks ago?"

"No. I just got back early this morning, and I've been in meetings with Ella."

"Two murders. John Lockett, forty-three, and his girlfriend, Melissa Scott, thirty-one. According to my sources, Frank Rossi and Billy Ford pulled the case. My sources are also telling me Lockett was smuggling large quantities of drugs into the state through an airfreight company he worked for as a graveyard-shift supervisor. Michael, worked for him at that same company."

"And the police think your nephew is somehow involved in the smuggling operation?"

"The night of the two murders, my sister's car had broken down. Michael took an Uber to work. John Lockett lived relatively close by, just a couple of miles. He gave Michael a ride home after their shift ended, right around four thirty in the morning. At some time that next day, Ford and Rossi knocked on my sister's door to talk to Michael. They'd gone to the airfreight company and learned Lockett had given Michael a ride home, secured a search warrant, and found two Blue Horizon packages in Michael's bedroom, one containing fentanyl and the other almost sixteen thousand dollars in cash."

"Were the envelopes opened?" Keera asked. The lawyer in her was already thinking of ways to challenge the warrant.

"No, but Rossi didn't take any chances. He must have phoned it in and got a second warrant to open the packages. Michael was arrested. He's been sitting in FDC on the drug charges. The federal prosecutor isn't offering a plea deal."

"You said you think it's going to get worse. Why?"

"At Michael's initial hearing, the prosecutor told the magistrate the investigation into the two murders remained pending, and additional charges a possibility. Until then, bail could not be considered."

Keera could see the worry wrinkles on Harrison's brow. She knew that being a former cop, like being a lawyer, came with its perils. Friends and family sought your help when they, or their relatives, were in legal trouble.

"They think Michael was somehow involved in the murders?"

"Lockett gave Michael a ride home within the ME's estimated time of death, I'm told."

"The last person to see him alive," Keera said.

"I have copies of the search warrants," Harrison said. "They sought handguns, and they sought Michael's work clothing and his boots."

"Blood spatter," Keera said.

"Has to be. Another thing, and it isn't good. When the detectives found the drugs and money in Michael's room he panicked. He said it was like the walls in the house closed in on him. He tried to run. They tried to stop him. It got physical."

Keera knew that would not play well with the detectives, or a jury—if it got that far. "How physical?"

"It took several detectives and uniforms to put handcuffs on him."

It also made Michael look guilty. Maybe he was. She had to ask. "Do you think he's guilty, JP?"

"Of murder? No. Of running drugs, I don't know . . ." Harrison gave a frustrated headshake, then sat back. "He's had a few run-ins with the police. Misdemeanors for selling dime weed bags when he was in high school. But that seemed to be in his past. He was attending classes at the community college and working to help pay the bills at home. There's no father in the picture, Keera. I've tried to be around for Michael and my sister, but my schedule doesn't always allow for it. She's done her best, but . . ."

Keera heard regret, maybe guilt.

"Rumor is going around SPD no one has been arrested for the murders because the prosecuting attorney intends to proceed by way of a grand jury."

Prosecutors occasionally convened grand juries to determine if sufficient evidence existed to charge a defendant with a crime. The proceedings were secretive. Only the prosecutor presented evidence. The defense did not have the right to know about the proceedings, be present, or access grand jury evidence or testimony from witnesses. In short, the defense would never know what might have persuaded the grand jury—if it returned an indictment.

"And you think they will convene the grand jury to determine if enough evidence exists to charge your nephew with the two murders?"

"I can't think of any other reason. That and the federal prosecutor's statement at Michael's first appearance, and the fact that no one else has been arrested. And . . ."

Keera waited for an answer that didn't come right away. "And . . ."

"The prosecutor handling the two murders is Anh Tran."

Keera sat back from the table. She'd never met Tran, but she knew of her from her years in the PA's office. Tran had a reputation as a no-nonsense prosecutor with a resume to prove it, and a penchant for getting convictions from little more than circumstantial evidence—evidence that required a jury to find the existence of a fact by inference, rather than from direct evidence such as an eyewitness's testimony or a gun with fingerprints. If Tran was the prosecutor, they could expect the charges to be extreme—and the consequences for JP's nephew grave.

Keera let out a held breath. It did sound like a nightmare, and she could understand why Harrison was visibly distraught. "You want me to meet with your nephew? What's his full name?"

"Michael Westbrook. It might be easier to meet first with my sister, Tina." Harrison sighed. "She works for a janitorial company that cleans offices at night and gets some additional hours as a cashier at a local grocery store. Listen, I can pay your fee. I'll take a second mortgage on my home if need be."

Keera shook her head and raised her hand. "Let me talk with your sister first. Then I'll talk to Michael and try to determine the lay of the land."

Harrison told Keera he'd arrange a meeting with his sister at her home in South Seattle. Keera would have Maggie determine visiting hours at FDC-SeaTac and make calls to contacts she still maintained at the prosecutor's office to see if anyone knew anything.

It would also be an excuse for her to call Frank. She hadn't seen or spoken with him since she'd invited him to sit down and eat breakfast with her after Jenna Bernstein's sentencing. Not that she hadn't thought about him each night she ate alone in Italy.

She walked Harrison from the conference room to the lobby. Maggie, thankfully, was not at her desk. Harrison hit the button for the cage elevator. Keera listened to it hum and rattle as it rose to the third floor.

"I'm sorry to foist this on you your first day back from your vacation, Keera."

"Don't worry about it," she assured him. "Let's hope, though, that this is something that can be quickly resolved."

JP grimaced. He knew better.

After JP left, Keera returned to her office. She looked out the windows at the same view he had been staring at in the conference room.

Criminal matters rarely resolved quickly.

And if Anh Tran was involved, the matter rarely resolved favorably for the accused.

# Chapter 5

The following day, Harrison met Keera at the office, and she followed him to Tina Westbrook's home, not far from South Seattle College. Maggie had learned that the Federal Detention Center near the Seattle-Tacoma Airport limited non-attorney visitors to certain times on the weekdays and weekends. If Keera became Michael Westbrook's attorney she'd have nearly unlimited access to visit him. Until then, Harrison had his sister call the facility and put Keera's name on Michael's approved visitors list, and Keera instructed Maggie to file the online paperwork for the visit.

Tina Westbrook's home was a one-story rambler with gray shingle siding that matched the color of the low-hanging morning cloud cover. A white Toyota, an older model, sat in the driveway beside a postage-stamp-sized patchy front lawn and a single rhododendron bush. Christmas lights hung in haphazard loops from the gutter, and a small undecorated Christmas tree stood on a table in the front window.

The cold snap, producing near-freezing temperatures, continued, with no rain or warming in the forecast.

A woman answered Harrison's knock, and he held the screen door as he leaned in to kiss her cheek, then introduced Keera. Tina Westbrook invited them into her home with the same Liverpool accent Harrison had never been able to completely shed. Their parents, Beatles fans, had named him John Paul Harrison after three of the Fab Four who came from their hometown. Harrison liked to say he was lucky they'd left out the drummer, Ringo Starr.

They sat in a small living room on a leather couch, Tina across a coffee table, seated in a wing chair.

Tina had made a lemon-scented tea, and the pleasant aroma filled the room. She'd also set a plate of butter cookies on the coffee table. Keera accepted a cup of tea, but after gorging on incredible Italian pasta and other dishes, including desserts, she did not need Christmas cookies.

On the floor beside the undecorated tree sat an unopened cardboard box—*Christmas Ornaments* written in black marker on the side. This would not be a merry Christmas.

On the mantel above the fireplace, framed photographs of Tina and a large young man stared back at them. "Is that Michael?" Keera asked, standing and moving to the mantel.

Tina turned to see the photographs. "Yes. He was always bigger than the other boys."

In one, Michael wore a red graduation cap and gown. In another, a yellow-and-white Little League uniform; in a third, a football uniform. He towered over the others in the pictures. No wonder it had taken multiple officers to subdue him. Missing from the mantel were pictures of a husband or a father.

Keera returned to the couch. Tina said, in a quiet voice, "Thank you for coming." She was an attractive woman; Keera could see the family resemblance to Harrison in the oval shape of her eyes, and their color, green, and her nose. "JP talks very highly of you." Tina used a napkin to wipe tears from her eyes. "I'm sorry. I told myself I wouldn't cry, but I just feel like my world is coming apart."

"It's okay," JP said. "You have every right to be upset."

Keera noticed JP's accent became more pronounced talking to his sister. "Maybe you can start by just telling me what you know?" Keera hoped the task might help to calm Tina.

"I don't know what happened," she said. "That's the problem. I wasn't at home when they took Michael away. The public defender said Michael was charged with possession of narcotics, but he can't, or he won't, tell me much else. He says the prosecution is waiting for an investigation to conclude."

"Let's start with that day Michael went to work," Keera said. "I understand the car wasn't working?"

"We only have the one to share. On nights Michael works, I ride with another woman to my job so Michael can get back and forth. He attends classes at the college during the days. That day the car wouldn't start, so he took an Uber to work, but his coworker gave him a ride home after his shift."

"And you weren't home when Michael returned?" Keera asked.

"No. I work evenings and usually return home around six in the morning."

"What time does Michael typically get home?"

"About four thirty, unless he works overtime. But he did not that night."

"Was he home when you arrived home?"

"I assume so, but his door was closed. When he works, Michael sleeps until noon, then attends afternoon classes at the college. He'd gone to his class when the police first came and asked to speak to him."

"Did they say why they wanted to talk to him?"

"No." She shook her head. "I asked them, but they said they needed to talk to Michael. They did ask if Michael worked at Blue Horizon at the airport, and when he would be home. I sent Michael a text asking him why two detectives had come by the house looking for him."

"What did he say?"

"He said he had no idea, but that he would handle it."

"The men who you spoke to, were these uniformed officers or detectives dressed in casual clothes?"

"Casual clothes. One, a Black man, was very tall. He did most of the talking."

Billy Ford, Frank Rossi's partner, was six foot eight. "What did the other detective look like?"

"About six feet, broad shoulders. Italian name. Like that wine."

"Frank Rossi?" Keera asked.

"That's it. They left cards. I put them on the mantel."

"Were you home when they came back to the house to talk to Michael?"

"No. I work a second job a couple days a week as a cashier at a local grocery store, had already left for that job."

JP had given Keera copies of the two search warrants on the drive over. "Michael had the two packages I told you about on the floor in his room," he said.

"They said one package contained fentanyl," Tina said. "Michael does not use fentanyl. And he doesn't sell it."

"How did Michael explain the packages?" Keera asked.

"He said John Lockett asked him to hold them for him," JP said. "He wasn't hiding it. I don't know why he didn't call me when the police showed up, Keera. When I asked him, he said he didn't have anything to hide."

"When I arrived home, the police wouldn't let me in," Tina said. "They had a hazmat team in special equipment and said fentanyl can be dangerous even in small amounts. I asked an officer where Michael was, then I called JP and told him what had happened."

"As I told you, we haven't been able to get much from the public defender," JP said. "He said whenever he asks the prosecutor, he's told the State investigation into criminal charges remains pending."

"My son is a good boy, Ms. Duggan. He works hard and attends classes at the college. He is not a drug dealer. When I told him John Lockett and his girlfriend had been murdered, he wept. That boy wept. He did not know. And he did not do it."

JP got up and wrapped an arm around his sister's shoulders. He spoke to Keera. "He's scared, Keera. I can see it in Michael's face."

Keera had seen terrified looks on the faces of some of her clients, but it was not always possible to know if they were scared because they had been falsely accused or scared because they'd been caught.

# Chapter 6

After speaking with Tina Westbrook, Keera drove to FDC-SeaTac. JP had offered to go with her, but she had counseled against it. While he worked for the firm as a PI, the attorney-client privilege did not automatically extend to third-party consultants. It wasn't worth the risk.

Black steel fencing surrounded the facility. Reinforced steel-and-concrete wings extended on both sides of a rectangular, central monolith, all a uniform pale gray. Male and female prisoners were separated in the two wings. The building windows were narrow and positioned high up on the walls, no doubt to dissuade escape attempts.

Inside the monolith, Keera made her way through administrative processing and red tape before an officer escorted her to a private attorney-client room in the area reserved for legal visits. A few minutes later, the door opened and a guard escorted Michael Westbrook into the room. As the photographs on Tina's mantel had documented, Michael was tall, like his uncle, but heavyset. He shuffled into the room wearing a khaki short-sleeved shirt over a white T-shirt, long pants, white socks, and rubber slip-on sandals. Michael looked worried and, as was common with new inmates in prison, his head was on a swivel.

He started to speak, but Keera raised a hand, indicating he should wait until the guard had left the room. When the door shut, Michael placed both palms on the table and leaned across it into Keera's space. She pulled back.

"Are you the attorney my uncle told me about?" He spoke in a rush, his voice higher pitched than Keera anticipated.

"I'm Keera Duggan, yes. JP asked me to talk with you."

Michael paced, flexing his hands repeatedly and continuing to speak in a rushed voice. She wondered if the young man could be having a panic attack. "You got to get me out of here, Ms. Duggan. This is a mistake. I didn't know what was inside the packets John gave me to hold for him. He said they were gifts for Melissa."

Keera raised a calming hand. "Michael, I'm going to need you to take a deep breath and try to calm down. We're not in any rush here. I can stay until nine tonight if necessary."

"I shouldn't be in here." He continued to pace and to flex his hands, balling them into fists. He looked like he could take the room apart. "I shouldn't. I shouldn't be in here."

"Michael. Come sit down."

He looked at her as if he'd forgotten she remained in the room. "What?"

"Sit down, Michael," she said gently.

The young man sat but looked to be having trouble catching his breath. "I can't breathe."

Panic attack. Keera had experienced a few when she'd been competing in chess tournaments.

"I want you to take slow, deep breaths with me. Can you do that?"

"What?"

"Take slow, deep breaths with me, Michael. Through your nose. I'll count to ten."

She took a breath through her nose, counting to ten, and exhaled through her mouth, again counting to ten. Michael joined her, and eventually he calmed.

Keera said, "You need to understand that nothing is going to happen today. I'm sorry, but the legal system moves slowly, and I can't file any papers or pull any strings to get you out. Not today. I need you to start from the beginning and tell me what happened so I can better understand the frustration you're experiencing. Can you do that?"

Michael slumped in his chair like a man who'd just run a long distance, exhausted. His voice softened. "What do you want to know?"

Keera opened her laptop to take notes. "Tell me how you knew the victim, and what happened on that particular evening."

"John and I worked together. That's where we met."

"At Blue Horizon, the airfreight company?"

"That's right."

"How long had you worked there?"

"About a year. It was part-time work while I took classes at South Seattle College. We needed the money. My paycheck helped my mom with my room and board, and I needed tuition money for when I finished my prerequisites and went to a university. I screwed around too much in high school playing football and got in with a bad crowd, but that was all in the past. I had some work to do at the community college, but I was getting it done."

"You have some misdemeanors on your record."

He shook his head. "I know. Selling dime weed bags at school. Like I said, I made bad decisions. I screwed up my grades, but that was all behind me. You have to believe me."

"Anything other than arrests for selling dime weed bags I need to know about?"

"No."

"Okay. How long did John Lockett work at Blue Horizon; do you know?"

"I don't know. He was there when I got the job. So, longer than me."

"Did you know him before you worked there?"

Michael shook his head. "No. He lived a couple of miles away, but I'd never met him. He was my supervisor on the graveyard shift. A lot gets transported overnight."

Keera knew the airlines were like hospitals, open 24-7, 365 days a year.

"Were you friendly with John Lockett?"

"Yeah, I mean . . . He'd invited me over to shoot pool and watch the Mariners and the Seahawks a few times."

"Inside his house?" Keera said. Not good news.

"No. He has a detached garage where he works on old cars with the neighbor. He put in a television, pool table, a sound system."

"When was the last time you were there?" Keera had learned that Lockett was killed in his garage, and she worried Michael's DNA or fingerprints had been found there.

"Maybe a week or so."

"So how many times total had you been over there?"

Michael made a face, like he was fighting a headache. "I'd say a dozen."

"Did you know John Lockett dealt drugs?"

"No," he said, and he vehemently shook his head. "I had no idea."

"Okay. You didn't see any drugs when you went to shoot pool or watch the games?"

"A joint one time; you know? But I wasn't doing that much anymore."

Lockett had been forty-three, Michael twenty-one, which raised an obvious question. "Why did he invite you over, Michael? You guys are what, twenty years apart in age? Did he say?"

"No." A soft headshake. "Just invited me to shoot pool one morning after work. His girlfriend made us breakfast."

Keera wondered if maybe Lockett had been grooming Michael, seeking to gain his trust to perhaps hide drugs and money for him—or to serve as a distributor. Michael indicated he and his mother needed the money, which Lockett might have known. It would have made such an offer tempting. "You need to understand that anything you tell me, and that I tell you, is privileged during this conversation, though I'm not yet your attorney. Do you understand what that means?"

He nodded. "The attorney-client privilege; right?"

"That's right. So, you need to be perfectly honest with me about everything."

"Okay."

"Tell me how you ended up with a package full of fentanyl in your room."

Michael told Keera about the car not starting. "I didn't want to spend the money, but I ordered an Uber to get to work."

"We can prove that; right?"

"Yeah. I used the app on my phone. And they sent a receipt to my email."

"Okay. So how did Lockett end up giving you a ride home?"

"I was in the lunchroom at work telling somebody about the damn car breaking down and John overheard me. Like I said, he fixed old cars. He asked me what the car had sounded like. When I told him, he said it sounded like the starter had gone out, and he could look at it for me. He also said he'd give me a ride home after our shift, given how close we lived to each other."

"What time did your shift end?"

"Four a.m."

"And what happened then?"

"Nothing. I mean, I walked out with John to his car, and we were just talking about stuff . . . Just sort of making conversation."

"What way did you drive home?"

"We took Air Cargo Road to 518 to 99 to Marginal Way. I can get you the street names."

"Did he drive you straight home or did you take any detours?"

"Straight home."

"What time did you get home?"

"He dropped me off right around four thirty."

"Did he take a look at your car for you?"

"Nah, it was too dark and cold to be messing around with it. He said he'd come by on the weekend when it was light, and he had more time."

"Okay. Tell me about the packages the police found in your room."

"Those weren't mine." Michael sat up and Keera sensed him growing agitated again. "John gave them to me when he dropped me off. He asked me to hold them for him. He said they contained birthday presents for his girlfriend, Melissa, and he wanted them to be a surprise, so he didn't want them anywhere around the house or garage where she could find them. He said he'd pick them up from me when he came to work on the car."

"Did you look inside either package?"

"I couldn't. Both envelopes were sealed. I literally just dropped them on the floor with my uniform and crawled into bed."

"Your mother wasn't home when you got home?"

"Not yet."

"Did you see anyone when Lockett dropped you off?"

"What do you mean?"

"The newspaper delivery person. Someone out walking their dog or maybe jogging? Anyone at all."

He shook his head. "No one. I mean, I just went inside the house and went to bed. The next morning, I went to class—"

"How'd you get there?"

"It's not that far. I walked."

"Okay, what happened next?"

"I got a text in class from my mother. She said two police detectives came to the house looking for me, but they wouldn't say why. I knew she'd be upset and that she'd worry, so I told her I'd handle it when I got home. When I got home, I was chilling on the couch watching television and contemplating calling them."

"How were you getting to work that day?"

"I wasn't working that day. The job was part-time, couple days a week unless they were getting a large shipment in and needed extra bodies."

"The two detectives who came by, were they Billy Ford and Frank Rossi? Tall Black man and an Italian-looking man," Keera said.

"Yeah. That was them."

"Tell me what happened."

"They knocked on the front door with a uniformed officer and asked my name. I asked if they were the detectives who came by earlier and what they wanted. They asked if they could come in."

"Did you let them?"

"I didn't think I had much choice."

"What did they ask you?"

"They asked if anyone else was home and said they were there to execute a search warrant. I said, 'For what?' and the Black detective told me I could either wait inside or in the back of the police car. I kept asking what they wanted, and the other detective handed me the search warrant and said it gave them the right to search the entire home."

"They didn't say why?"

Michael shook his head. "Not at first. They asked if I knew John, and I asked what searching my home had to do with John. And then a light bulb went off, and I remembered the two packages he'd given me, and I started wondering if it had something to do with them. I started sweating and getting hot. I told them how I knew John, and my voice it . . . it caught a couple times, and the detective, the Italian one, he looked at me like he heard it and . . ."

"And that you knew why they'd come."

"Yeah."

"What happened next?"

"They wanted to know when I'd last seen John, so I told them he'd given me a ride home that morning. They asked about the car and if I'd ever been to John's house, and I told them that I had hung out a few times shooting pool and watching games. I kept asking them what they were looking for, but they wouldn't say."

Keera typed rapidly, then looked up at Michael. "What happened after that?"

"They searched the house, and two other detectives searched the car," he said. "They went into my room and the Black detective came out holding my Blue Horizon uniform. The other detective had the two packages."

"What did they ask you?"

"The Black detective asked if it was the uniform I wore to work that morning, and when I said 'Yes,' he put it in a bag. The Black detective said something to the other detective about the packages being in 'plain view.' They took photographs of them. Then he asked me about them."

"What did he ask you?"

"He asked if either package was mine."

"What did you tell him?"

"I told him the truth. I told him John gave them to me that morning to hold for him, that he didn't want Melissa to find them in his house."

"Did the detectives have a response?"

"Not to me. One photographed the packages with his cell phone, front and back, and asked me if he could open them."

"Did you give them permission to open them?"

"I said they weren't mine, so it wasn't my permission to give. I said they should ask John."

"What did the detectives do?"

"The Italian one said he was going outside to make a phone call."

Keera knew from experience that Rossi had likely called Tran, and that he'd asked her to obtain further authorization to open the sealed packages. Though the packages were in plain view, making the need for further judicial authorization debatable, Rossi and Ford were conservative; they weren't going to make that call and potentially be wrong, especially with Tran as the MDOP. "Did the other detective eventually come back inside?"

"At some point he showed me another search warrant and said it authorized him to open the packages. And that's what he did. He pulled out a clear plastic bag filled with white pills. The Black detective said, 'Is this fentanyl?' and I said I had no idea, that it wasn't mine, and then they started telling everyone to clear the house and making more calls and talking about getting in a hazmat team."

"What did they find in the other envelope?"

"The other one had money inside. I don't know how much. I was shocked. I had no idea."

"You have no idea why John gave them to you?"

"Only what he told me."

Keera looked the young man in the eyes, searching for any tells when he lied. A lifetime of competitive chess tournaments had honed those skills.

"Did you know John Lockett was dealing drugs?" she asked.

"No." Michael sat back, shaking his head. "That's the truth."

"Were you distributing the pills for him?"

"No," Michael said more emphatically. He sat forward, forearms resting on the table. "I swear, Ms. Duggan. I had no idea." He looked and sounded sincere, but so did many of Keera's clients, most recently Jenna Bernstein, a sociopath who could lie through her teeth. "John told me the packages contained birthday gifts for Melissa and asked me to hold on to them. And I believed him."

Keera typed more notes, the keys on the keyboard rapidly clicking. "What happened after the detective opened the packages?"

"The Black detective read me my rights. I was so scared . . . It felt like the walls were collapsing on me. I couldn't breathe. And I was sweating. I wanted to get outside where it was cold. I told them I had to get outside. They said not to move, but I couldn't help it. I shouldn't have, but I ran," Michael said. His voice trailed off and his eyes became glassy. He let out a burst of air, then inhaled deeply as if on the verge of passing out and struggling to get his emotions in check.

Keera could get a doctor to explain panic attacks as the reason why Michael had run. "Take your time," Keera said.

He wiped at tears rolling down his cheeks, his voice soft. "I knocked over the police officer and the other detectives jumped me. I didn't know what was happening. I kept yelling at them that the packages weren't mine. They put me in the back of a police car and processed me at the King County jail, then put me in a cell for the night."

"When did you call JP?"

"First chance I got. Two marshals arrived the next morning and drove me to the federal courthouse for an arraignment. My mom and JP were there. I had a public defender I met when they brought me into the courtroom. I didn't even have a chance to talk to her. She told me when the judge asked how I plead, I should answer 'Not guilty.' I didn't even know the charges, Ms. Duggan."

Keera had pulled the charging papers, which alleged conspiracy to distribute a controlled substance—possession of fentanyl with intent to distribute; but as JP had said, that now appeared to be just the iceberg's tip.

"I did what she said. I thought I'd be released on bail, but the prosecutor told the judge the quantity of drugs indicated an intent to distribute and that other state crimes were still being investigated. I didn't even know John and Melissa had been killed."

"Who told you?"

"JP, when he came to the jail after the hearing." Michael sat back. "Are you going to ask me if I killed John and Melissa?"

"No," she said. Michael looked confused, as did most of her clients. She explained, "My job, *if* I defend you, is to defend you whether you're innocent or guilty."

"I'm not guilty, Ms. Duggan. I didn't kill John. He was a friend of mine. And I didn't kill Melissa." He was becoming agitated again.

"When John Lockett drove you home after work, you went to bed?"

"Yes."

"You didn't turn on the television or get something to eat?"

"No. I had to get up at eleven to go to class so, as I said, I just took everything off, dropped it on the floor, and climbed into bed."

Keera looked at her watch. They'd been talking for more than two hours. She went over the items the police took from the home, including Michael's Blue Horizon uniform—navy-blue pants and a striped denim shirt—and the work boots he'd worn that night. Working part-time, he only had the one uniform. Keera knew they would test the uniform and shoes for blood spatter. They possibly also wanted his work boots to compare to any impressions found inside or outside Lockett's house. Michael had been fingerprinted and ordered to provide a DNA swab, and it was likely he'd left a fingerprint or his DNA.

"Anything else you can think of?" Keera asked. "Doesn't matter whether you think it's insignificant or not."

"When can you get me out of here?"

"I don't know, Michael. The federal drug charges against you are serious, and I haven't yet seen any information on the two murders."

"But I didn't even know what was in those packages."

"I believe you, but that doesn't mean the police, or the prosecutor, believe you. Put yourself in their situation, Michael. Two people have been murdered, one a drug dealer. They found packages in your room containing a heavy narcotic and a substantial amount of cash. And right now, you're the last person they know of who saw John Lockett alive."

"You think they're going to charge me with their murders? But I wasn't even there." He sounded incredulous.

Given the federal prosecutor's statement that bail would be premature pending additional investigation into the State crimes, and rumors that Tran had convened a grand jury, Keera suspected Tran was evaluating the strength of her evidence to determine if she had enough for the grand jury to issue a probable-cause indictment.

Keera would have time to deal with that later.

"I'll file papers asking for a bail hearing and request you be released pending further federal proceedings, but I'm not optimistic that request will be granted. Barring that, there isn't much we can do except wait. I'm sorry, Michael."

Following her meeting with Michael, Keera called Harrison from the FDC parking lot and updated him.

"One thing that stands out," she said. "If Tran had forensic evidence linking Michael to the crime—a gun found in his possession, blood spatter on his clothing, DNA, even a shoe print, anything—she wouldn't be taking this to a grand jury. She's won a lot of cases with a lot less evidence."

"Then why is she?" Harrison asked.

"I suspect she's going to bootstrap the police finding fentanyl and the money in Michael's possession as the motivation for the murders. She's taking it to the grand jury to determine if they buy that argument enough to return with an indictment."

"It's the bludgeoning of Melissa Scott that gets to me," Harrison said. "I heard an expert once say that in a moment of anger or passion, we're all capable of pulling a trigger and almost immediately regretting it. But to beat someone to death . . ." Harrison blew a breath into the phone. "That requires a cruelty most humans don't possess. Michael does not have that in him."

But the grand jury, and the subsequent jurors who would be empaneled in any trial, did not know Michael the way JP knew him. They did not have an impression of him formed over a lifetime. They would know him only from the snapshot Tran presented in the courtroom, and more often than not, she made juries believe that snapshot was the whole person.

"Where do we go from here? What do I tell Tina?" Harrison asked, sounding forlorn.

"Tell her I'm going to file a request for a bail hearing."

"A federal judge won't agree to bail. Not when the pending crimes are a double homicide."

"No, he won't. But Tina doesn't need to know that. Just tell her she needs to be patient. I'm hoping my request will light a small fire and maybe speed up a decision from the State."

"Can we hope the grand jury won't find enough for an indictment?" he asked, but Keera didn't answer that question. It had been rhetorical anyway. With Tran as the prosecutor, "hope" quickly went out the door.

Keera disconnected the call and slid behind the wheel of her car. The interior was as cold as an icebox. She started the engine and felt the heater kick on, then slipped on sunglasses to deflect the December sun's glare. As she waited for the car to warm, she used the time to debate how to greet Frank Rossi. This was exactly the reason why a relationship between the two of them would never work; Keera would have to refrain from representing anyone Frank investigated due to a conflict of interest. And he'd be placed in an awkward position within the department each time she represented a defendant SPD believed guilty. Unflattering comments were not infrequently exchanged in the detective cubicles about defense attorneys.

On a more personal note, she did not want Frank to think she was using him to get information she shouldn't otherwise have. But if she was going to represent Michael Westbrook, it was her job to gather as much information as she could, from whatever sources she could.

She punched in Rossi's business cell phone number. Detectives kept two—one for business calls and one for personal calls, and she had both of Rossi's numbers.

"Frank Rossi."

"Frank, it's Keera Duggan." He hesitated long enough that Keera almost spoke over him.

"You're back," Rossi said without emotion. "How was Italy?"

Now it was Keera's turn to pause. She should have just said *Fine*, but she couldn't get the word out fast enough.

"Maggie told me you spent time on the Amalfi Coast; right? Said it was last minute, that you needed a break after the Jenna Bernstein trial."

Keera fumed. Maggie had no business telling anyone her personal business, but that was for another conversation. What intrigued her was why Rossi had called the law firm and not her cell phone, though given her own rationale for calling his business number, she suspected she maybe knew why. "Did you call for any specific reason?" she asked.

"I can't remember why I called," he said, now sounding dismissive. "Probably something to do with Bernstein. What can I do for you?"

End of discussion. Back to business. "You're aware that Michael Westbrook is JP Harrison's nephew?" Keera said.

Rossi paused. "I wasn't. Does this mean you'll be representing him?"

"I don't think he's been charged . . . yet; has he?" she asked, fishing.

"Federal case. The drug charges, I mean," Rossi said. Did he really mean the federal drug charges, or did he know something, had slipped, and tried to cover it up?

"Undetermined at this time, but I did tell JP I'd make a few phone calls to find out what's happening, and why his nephew didn't make bail," she said.

"Serious federal charges would be my guess. Fentanyl. A lot of it. Talk to the federal prosecutor."

"I'm told the federal prosecutor indicated to the judge that state criminal charges are pending."

"Wouldn't know. I wasn't there."

"But given the circumstances . . ."

"I think you can figure it out," Rossi said. Curt. To the point. Abrupt.

"I also heard Anh Tran is the prosecutor."

"Billy Ford is the lead detective on this one, Keera. If you have questions, it might be best if you spoke to him."

"Okay," she said. "Rumors—"

"I don't talk rumors, Keera. You know that also. Talk to Billy. I got to run."

He hung up.

Keera sat back and lowered her phone, staring out the windshield, thinking about the breakfast they'd shared after the Bernstein trial. It had felt to Keera like more than breakfast. Had Rossi thought so also? Was he upset she'd gone to Italy without telling him? Or that she hadn't called him during her time away? Or was he just doing his job and deflecting the inquiries of a defense attorney? She chided herself for thinking it was only her decision whether to move the relationship to the next step.

Maybe Frank Rossi had already made that decision for himself.

And for her.

She debated calling him back. Apologizing. Asking him if he wanted to grab a bite somewhere. They could do that, couldn't they? Just agree to never talk about their work?

Maybe. But at the moment, work was all Keera had.

And Rossi's dismissing her was a painful reminder of that fact.

Frank Rossi hung up the phone and gave the conversation a moment of thought, notably that Keera had called his business cell phone. He wondered if it was personal. She was fishing for information about Westbrook and didn't have a personal reason for calling him. They'd had breakfast after the Bernstein trial. He'd thought maybe they had a chance at a relationship, that Keera was opening the door that morning. When they'd worked cases together, their conversations had always been easy, without awkward pauses. They'd each simply enjoyed the moment—so much so that Frank had decided after that breakfast that he wanted to make it clear he wasn't interested in an occasional meal. He wanted something more. He'd called Keera at work, but his call got kicked to Maggie at the front desk, who told him Keera was "on her way to Italy to get away and recharge." She'd left without even bothering to call him.

Had she gone alone or with someone? Rossi didn't ask. He didn't want to know.

But who went to Italy alone?

# Chapter 7

Neither Keera nor Harrison intended to sit on their hands until the grand jury returned its verdict. The following morning, they drove back to South Seattle hoping to talk to Tina's neighbors, in case anyone had seen or heard Lockett's car pull up and Michael arrive at home. Depending on the ME's estimated time of deaths, it could be significant. She would also talk to Lockett's neighbors and find out what they knew. Somebody had called 911 and alerted the police. In addition, she and Harrison would clock the distance between Michael's and Lockett's houses, in case the State argued Michael ran to Lockett's house after he was dropped off.

"Not likely," Tina said as they sat again in her living room. "Michael has asthma. He's dealt with it his whole life."

"Treated?"

"He has an inhaler."

"I'll need those records and the name of his doctor."

Keera asked Tina to put together a list of her neighbors, the houses they lived in, how well Tina knew each, and if she had spoken with any about recent events. If nothing else, it would give Tina something to do.

While Tina did so, JP and Keera drove to Lockett's home to speak to his neighbors. Inside JP's car, he said, "What did you know of Ms. Tran?"

Keera suspected it was a subject Harrison had not wanted to discuss in front of Tina.

"Patsy said she's pretty much as billed," Keera said.

"You know the circumstances of her background, then?"

"I know more *of* her—what she went through. It's impressive that she graduated with honors from UW and went to law school."

"And came back to Gotham City to fight crime?" Harrison said.

"I've heard the Batman references also."

"I know she's a bit of a legend at the PA's office, and she earned the respect of many officers at SPD, but I remember her a little differently," Harrison said.

"How so?"

"More infamous than famous. She was the prosecutor on the ROPE team."

Keera shook her head. "Not familiar with the ROPE team."

"Before your time," Harrison said. He explained the Repeat Offender Program was a team within the narcotics unit that tracked convicted felons after their release on parole.

"You're right. I never heard of it."

"That's because it never existed, at least not on paper. The group's purpose was to fly under the radar and not attract attention."

"Because they used questionable tactics?" Keera surmised.

"They called those tactics 'proactive.' They didn't wait for the paroled felon to commit a crime. They'd pull them over on some small infraction, like expired tabs or a taillight being out, and argued probable cause to search the car. If they saw something like a baggie or a pipe, they'd bust the felon."

"Are you saying they didn't always have probable cause?"

"I'm saying Tran always got the search warrants the team needed."

"Meaning?"

He shrugged. "I just know the guys in that unit loved her because she didn't sit at a desk in her office and was willing to bend the rules when necessary. And she had guts. She'd go out with them on raids. Even carried a gun."

"Seriously?" Keera asked.

"Seriously. The guys making a bust didn't have to wait to secure the warrants they needed because she was right there with them. And if they busted the person, she convicted him, which always makes a cop feel good."

"Like shooting fish in the barrel she built," Keera said. "I thought she *earned* her reputation."

"Oh, she earned it. Don't get me wrong. She had an incredible conviction rate."

"But?"

"But the unit disbanded after accusations of racial profiling and questionable search-and-seizure tactics. The Justice Department investigated. Rumors of questionable search warrants and of ROPE team members planting drugs could not be proven, but the DOJ report insinuated that had been the case."

# Chapter 8

***March 2010***
***Little Saigon***
***Seattle, Washington***

Anh Tran watched water cascade down her car's windshield and heard the raindrops pecking on the roof of the car. The weather wasn't cooperating, but in this instance that wasn't a bad thing. The darkness, wind, and rain would mask the ROPE team's approach to the building. She exited the vehicle with her leather briefcase pressed to her hip and hurried to the unmarked van parked in the lot behind the building. The mom-and-pop stores in the strip mall had closed for the evening, and most owners had gone home. At midnight, in this weather, anyone out was up to no good.

The side panel on the van slid open before Tran arrived, and she quickly ducked inside. Settled, she lowered the hood and shook rain from her Gore-Tex jacket. "It's torrential," she said. The officers, in black cargo pants and bulletproof vests, had warmed the interior, and she smelled the sour odor of their perspiration. A few in the unit carried the M4A1, a variant of the AR-15. Tran had a Glock 9 millimeter holstered on her right hip, and she had taken a plethora of classes to not just fire it, but fire it well. She carried it everywhere she went.

Three nights earlier, ROPE team members, dressed in SPD patrol uniforms, had pulled over Tommy Phan, a convicted drug runner operating in Little Saigon. Phan had been released from prison after serving time on felony drug charges. The traffic stop had been for a failed taillight. The team member had used the opportunity to slip a tracking device under the rear bumper of Phan's car, and the team had been tracking everywhere he went for the past seventy-two hours. Phan epitomized those displaced Southeast Asians with limited economic opportunities who had turned to crime to survive. Tran understood their circumstances but could not accept their choices.

After roughly ten minutes, the panel on the van again pulled back, and a Vietnamese man climbed inside. His soaked hair hung to his shoulders, and water dripped from his goatee. He'd spent months setting up what was hopefully going down tonight, a bust of a shipment of heroin, cocaine, and prescription opiates.

The undercover narcotics detective let out a held breath. Anh could see the operation's strain on the man's face. After months of undercover work, he did not want to let Tommy Phan slip away.

"What do you have?" she asked.

He shook his head. "I didn't see anything out in the open."

She felt the air in the van cool. "Tell me what you saw."

"One of Phan's guys met me out front and asked me if I had the money."

"What did you tell him?"

"I told him I wanted to see and sample the product to know what I was getting. He said I had to bring the money first."

"Is Tommy Phan there?"

"He's in an office upstairs off a wooden staircase."

"You saw him?"

"No. I know from past experience. He's always there."

"Did you see drugs on the premises?" the ROPE team sergeant, Alan Brenner, asked.

Again, the officer shook his head. "There's a curtain across the store separating retail from the back."

"We don't have probable cause," Brenner said. "Shit."

"Hold on," Tran said, unwilling to give up so easily. "When you walked in, the man you met walked out through a separation in that curtain; right?"

The agent looked at her.

"Right?" Tran asked again.

"Right," he said, sounding uncertain.

"And when he pulled the curtain back to come out, you saw into the back room; right?"

The undercover agent looked at her, then at his ROPE team officers, who resembled large dogs before being fed. "Yeah. Yeah, I could see into the space," he said with what sounded like growing confidence.

"And you saw packages on a table; right?"

"Yeah?"

"Yeah?" Tran said, asking again.

"Yeah. I saw packages."

"Packages that, from your extensive undercover experience, looked to you like blocks of heroin or cocaine; right?"

"Yeah," the agent said, this time with more conviction. "Yeah. They did."

Tran looked up at the ROPE team sergeant. "Let me type this up," she said and pulled out her laptop. Twenty minutes later, she transmitted the agent's affidavit supporting the search warrant. She knew the judge on call. It was just a matter of dotting i's and crossing t's to keep a defense attorney from successfully challenging a probable-cause finding.

She disconnected. "We're good to go," she said.

The officers in the van smiled. They had carefully choreographed how this raid would go down. Brenner said, "We'll take it from here, Counselor. Thank you."

"The hell you will. I'm going with you."

"Going with us?" the sergeant said. "You sure about that?"

"Sit here and miss out on all the fun? I'm sure." Tran pulled back her coat and revealed the Glock on her hip.

The sergeant looked to the rest of his men. "Someone get the counselor a vest and a ballistic helmet, and let's rock and roll."

◆ ◆ ◆

The morning after the successful takedown and arrests, Tran stepped off the elevator at Police Headquarters in downtown Seattle. Sergeant Brenner greeted her. At five foot eight inches, he was built like a gymnast, with large shoulders and forearms.

"Where are they?" Tran asked, referring to Tommy Phan and Tuấn Le, Phan's attorney.

"We put them in the soft interrogation room." Less intimidating than other interrogation rooms at SPD, it resembled a conference room more than a cell.

"At least I won't need an introduction," Tran said. She and Le had sparred on several occasions. Tran had always won, but Le kept getting clients because Vietnamese drug dealers, like many immigrants Tran knew, felt more comfortable with an attorney who could speak their native tongue and understood the nuances of their culture.

"Let me know if you need anything," Brenner said outside the soft interrogation room. Then he left her.

Tran entered the room.

Tuấn Le sat at the table beside his client. Both men looked relaxed. Even managed smiles. "Giấy phép khám xét của bạn is bullshit," Le said. *Your search warrant is bullshit.* There wasn't a Vietnamese word for "bullshit."

English was not Le's first language. He was more comfortable speaking Vietnamese. Tran was not here to make him or his client comfortable.

"Is it?"

"No way your undercover officer saw drugs on the premises from where he stood. Not possible."

"Judge seemed to think so."

"Lies. He lied in his affidavit to establish probable cause. We can prove. We'll have the warrant thrown out on a motion to suppress, and the evidence as quả của cây độc."

"Fruit of the poisonous tree? You could bring that motion," Tran said. "Seems to me you have before, and you lost. You'll lose again, and Mr. Phan will be looking at decades behind bars. He'll be an old man before he gets out again."

Phan gave her a sidelong glare.

Le looked at her, like a poker player wondering if his competitor for the money pot was bluffing.

"Something you and your client should know about me by now, Tuấn. I don't bluff. Does your client want to take that chance?"

"What are you offering?"

"Offering? I'm not offering anything. I came here to listen. I was told Mr. Phan had something he wanted to say."

Again, Le and Phan studied her, no doubt looking for a crease in her armor. They wouldn't find one.

"I guess not." She stood.

"Wait," Le said. "What if Mr. Phan were to have information?"

She looked at Phan. "What kind of information?"

"Information that can assure you convict the men distributing the drugs," Le said.

"I'm not interested in small potatoes."

"No small potatoes. Very big potatoes."

"I'm listening."

Le said, "He gives you names and information, and in exchange, he goes free."

She smiled. "Can't do that, Tuấn."

"These are big names," he said emphatically.

"He gives me names and information. If I convict these big names, I will advise the court of Mr. Phan's substantial assistance helping the prosecution and seek to get his sentence reduced. Best I can offer."

Le looked to Phan, and the two men turned their heads, speaking Vietnamese softly. After a minute, they separated.

"How long?" Tuấn asked.

"I'll recommend a plea of five to ten."

Phan scoffed. Le shook his head. "Too long. These are *really* big names."

"Will Mr. Phan provide the names now so I can independently determine how big?"

"I told you, *very* big."

"I'd like to decide for myself." She'd call in the narcotics team and the federal agencies to consult.

Le and Phan again turned their heads, this time whispering for nearly a minute. Le turned back. "Okay. Mr. Phan will give you names but no information. Then you come back with a better offer. One thing, though."

"What's that?"

"You don't use Mr. Phan's name. You use his name and he's a dead man. You don't tell anyone where you got your information."

"I can live with that. *If* the information is as good as Mr. Phan leads me to believe. If it isn't, I'll throw the book at him."

Le smiled. "You'll see. You'll look like a big shit in Seattle. Very big shit."

# Chapter 9

***Present Day***
***Seattle, Washington***

As they clocked the mileage between Westbrook's home and Lockett's home, taking two different routes, Harrison continued to explain to Keera that Tran, and the ROPE team, on which she served as prosecutor, took down several of the biggest narcotics distributors in Seattle's history.

"Where'd she and the team get the information?"

"Don't know. But those convictions are what put her and the ROPE team on the map, which put her in the public eye, which was when some newspaper reporter at the *Seattle Times* did some digging, uncovered her past, and labeled her Batwoman. She became a star. And I'm told Tran offered no quarter to the guys the ROPE team arrested," Harrison said.

Keera knew prosecutors who used similar tactics. They'd throw every charge they could into the complaint or criminal indictment and seek the harshest penalties when those arrested refused a plea. "Guilty until proven innocent," she said.

"Though most never got that chance," Harrison said. "Before Governor Inslee abolished the death penalty, Tran offered a murder suspect life without the possibility of parole. If he declined and went to trial, Tran sought the death penalty."

"And often got it, according to Patsy."

"I'm not sure what she offers now," Harrison said.

"PA won't plea Murder One charges, especially if it involves multiple homicides."

"That doesn't leave you a lot of room."

It didn't. Nor did it bode well for Michael. And that was largely the reason for the pit in Keera's stomach that would likely be there for the months to come and throughout the trial. It was why it was so difficult to represent someone you knew—or someone related to someone you knew. It became personal.

The shortest and most direct route from Tina's home to Lockett's was 2.2 miles. A good runner could make it to the house in under twenty minutes. A bad runner not as fast, but certainly double. JP was unaware if Michael ran. Given Tina's revelation that her son had asthma since childhood, that did not seem likely.

"He could have walked," Harrison said. "That's what Tran will argue."

"Maybe, but I can then argue it unlikely a very large Black man, his clothes blood splattered, walked casually through the neighborhood without being seen. Doesn't seem likely; does it?"

John Lockett's house and detached garage remained sealed with police tape. Blinds had been lowered on the windows to keep the curious from looking inside. Keera would coordinate an inspection with her own experts. She'd document the crime scene with video and photographs so as not to be surprised at trial. Her team would also look for DNA and fingerprints belonging to persons other than Lockett, Melissa Scott, and Michael. It was the classic SODDI defense—Some Other Dude Did It. Keera had been giving this a lot of thought since her first meeting with Michael. If CSI or her experts found a fingerprint that was within IAFIS—the Integrated Automated Fingerprint Identification System maintained by the FBI, meaning the person had a conviction on his or her record—Keera could point her finger at that person, and if they didn't have an airtight alibi, argue reasonable doubt to the jury. If the fingerprint was not in IAFIS and could not be matched to a particular person, she would still argue the SODDI defense. She'd suggest smuggling drugs was an inherently dangerous business, and either a rival had found out Lockett was dealing, or persons for whom he had been smuggling drugs determined he had been skimming product, money, or both, and killed him. She'd argue Lockett had temporarily passed the two packages on to unsuspecting Michael so they would not be found in his possession, should someone accuse him.

Reasonable doubt.

Maybe.

She was getting ahead of herself.

First things first. Harrison had managed to obtain the name of the neighbor who found Lockett's body and called 911. Alex Cortez lived across the street and one house down from John Lockett. Harrison and Keera parked at the curb and stepped from the car. Keera would let Harrison do the talking. Witnesses could get skittish answering a lawyer's questions, fearing they'd be subpoenaed to appear in court.

Cortez answered the door wearing sweats and a Kobe Bryant Los Angeles Lakers purple-and-gold jersey pulled tight over a blue sweatshirt. He looked understandably suspicious and didn't invite them in, despite the cold weather. Keera heard the television in the other room and smelled the lingering odor of cigarettes.

"Mr. Cortez?" Harrison said.

"Yeah." He sounded brusque but also curious.

"I'm JP Harrison. I'm a private investigator. This is Keera Duggan. We're hoping to talk to you about the morning you found your neighbor, John Lockett, and called 911."

Cortez folded his arms and rested them on his protruding stomach. He was short, with a crew cut and trimmed goatee he stroked. "I already talked to the police and gave multiple statements," he said. "You can read those."

"I appreciate that, Mr. Cortez, and I appreciate that you're busy," Harrison said. "But this case has significance to me personally. Michael Westbrook is my nephew."

"Michael's your nephew?"

"That's right."

"Oh. Shit. Sorry, man. Good kid. I liked Mike."

"You knew Michael?" Harrison asked.

"Oh yeah. We met a couple of times at John's." Cortez motioned vaguely to the house across the street.

"What was Michael doing over at John's?" Harrison asked, playing dumb.

"Just shooting some pool, drinking beer, watching the Seahawks with us. Or the Mariners. You know. Hanging out. John had fixed up his garage for hanging out."

"Would you say John and Michael were friends?"

A shrug. "I only met Mike a couple of times. He and John seemed friendly with each other though, but I mean, there was an age difference and all."

"That's what makes me curious; why Michael would be at Mr. Lockett's house—given the age difference," Harrison said.

"They worked together," Cortez offered and gave another shrug. "I don't know."

"I know they worked together, but like you said, didn't seem a likely pairing," Harrison said. Keera knew he was hoping to get more.

"Unless Michael was working for John," Cortez said. "You know?"

"I don't."

"I mean they're saying in the paper and on the news that John was dealing drugs. So . . . maybe that was the connection."

"Did you know Mr. Lockett was dealing drugs?"

"Me? No." Cortez shook his head. It didn't look like an act. "No, man, I didn't know. Just speculating, because, you know, I'd heard Mike had a bag of fentanyl in his house." Cortez sounded convinced.

Keera could expect the same from most jurors, unless she could figure out how to let them know Lockett told Michael the package was for Melissa Scott, and he had asked Michael to keep it for him. Even then, some jurors would find that explanation dubious. Michael said he'd told this to Ford and Rossi when they'd come to search his home and hoped it was in their police report.

"Where did you hear that?" Harrison asked.

"I don't know. Maybe I read it in an article in the paper or on the internet."

"During the times that you were with Michael and John, did you get any sense that Michael was working for John?"

"How do you mean?"

"Did they ever talk about product coming in, or—"

Cortez started shaking his head before Harrison finished the question. "No. Like I told the detectives who were here, I didn't know John was dealing that shit. I knew he had weed. I mean, we smoked a few joints together, but I wouldn't have been around him if I had known he was dealing fentanyl. That shit kills people, man. I don't need to be around shit like that. But, I mean, I also wasn't always over there when Mike was there, so . . ."

"How do you know Michael was there when you weren't?"

"They worked nights together, him and John. I work the day shift at United Rentals, so I wasn't always here when Michael was there after work."

"So you're just making an assumption. You don't really know," Harrison said.

"My old lady told me she'd seen Mike over there, I think a couple of times. She'd say, 'I seen that big kid over at John's house today.' Something like that."

"It sounds like your wife didn't approve of Michael being at John's."

Keera wondered if Cortez maybe knew more than he was saying; that he knew Lockett was dealing but didn't want to get involved.

"No. No, I didn't mean that." He backtracked. "She was just making like an observation; you know?"

"How many times did she see Michael over there when you were at work?"

"I don't know. Is it important how many times?"

"It could be," Harrison said.

"Hang on." Cortez turned and yelled inside the house. "Theresa? Come to the door. Some people are asking more questions about what happened to John and Melissa."

"Police?" a woman shouted back.

"Just come to the door. I don't have time to explain it."

A barefoot Hispanic woman walked into the room in cutoff jeans and an extra-large sweatshirt slipping off her shoulder.

"Here, talk to them." Cortez stepped back from the door frame so Theresa could step forward.

She turned and scowled at Cortez. "You're letting all the heat out, and our bill is already too high."

Not to mention Keera was freezing and assumed Harrison was also.

"Come on in," the woman said, though it didn't sound welcoming.

Harrison and Keera stepped inside. Theresa shut the door. The house was cozy and warm. Keera smelled bacon, but also coffee and an even stronger cigarette odor.

Theresa looked between Harrison and Keera. "What did you want to know?"

Harrison explained what Cortez had just told them. Theresa pulled back long brown hair, twisted it into a ponytail with a band she had over a wrist, and made a bun atop her head. "I don't know how many times. I'd say maybe half a dozen. Not a lot."

"Did you ever ask John or Michael about it? Ask either of them what Michael was doing there?"

"Not my business to ask them," she said dismissively. "Grown men can do what they want."

"Mr. Cortez and I were just discussing that the relationship seems a bit, well, odd, given the age disparity between John and Michael," Harrison said.

"Seemed like it to us, too, but I guess not so much now."

"Meaning what? Michael's arrest?"

"Yeah. I mean, if John was selling drugs like the police say, then Michael was likely working for him; right? I mean it makes sense."

Keera knew it was the type of circumstantial evidence Anh Tran would use to imply to the jurors that Michael was working for Lockett, and his statement that Lockett told him the packages held gifts was just an excuse.

"You're just speculating, right? You don't know that Michael worked for John."

"Call it whatever you want," she said with a dismissive shrug. "I'm just saying it seems like it. I mean, why else was he going over there? And why would he have all that fentanyl? Could be why he killed them."

The statement seemed to upset Harrison. Before he could respond, Keera stepped in. "What makes you think Michael killed them?"

"Well, it's obvious; isn't it? I mean, he had the package, and he was over there a lot. And someone killed John and Melissa; right? Seems like a lot of coincidences; you know? Who else would have killed them?"

Many jurors believed a defendant had to be guilty of something if hauled into court, though the tenor in the general public had changed somewhat with recent events making some jurors less trusting of police and the judicial system.

"Did you ever see any animosity between Michael and John?" Keera asked them both.

"I didn't," Cortez said.

"I didn't either," Theresa said. "In fact, one time Michael was over there helping Melissa in the yard."

"What kind of help?" Keera asked.

"Yard work. He cut back the branches on those plants in the front and mowed the lawn for her. That kind of stuff. Like I said, they all seemed friendly."

"This was recent?"

"Not in this cold weather," Theresa said. "End of fall is what I can recall."

"What time did you go over to the house on the morning you found the body?" Keera asked Cortez.

"Like I told the police," Cortez said. "It was right around eight o'clock."

Keera asked him why he'd gone over, and Cortez told her about him and John buying vintage cars, fixing them up, and reselling them. He told her how he had quickly backed out from the garage after seeing Lockett's body on the floor, and that he had never gone inside the house. Given that Cortez had found the body, and that he lived across the street, Keera knew he would be on Ford and Rossi's radar. He claimed to not know Lockett was dealing, but that could be a lie and the vintage cars an excuse for his being over there.

"That's something I hope to never see again," Cortez said, shaking his head.

"What about your other neighbors? Were any of them friendly with John and Melissa?"

Cortez and Theresa looked at one another and both gave a shrug. "I don't know, man," Cortez said. "People around here all get along; you know? Now . . . not so much. Everyone is like, *Damn, that could happen to me*; you know?"

"You never saw any of your other neighbors go over to shoot pool or watch a game?" Keera asked.

"Not really. No."

"Jerry," Theresa said to Cortez.

"That was just the one time," Cortez said.

"Who is Jerry?" Keera asked.

"He lives down the street," Cortez said.

"What's Jerry's last name?"

"Garcia. Like the singer for the Grateful Dead."

"He was at John Lockett's?"

"Just the one time," Cortez said again. "The Seahawks were in the playoffs, so John invited him over. I don't think it was his thing, though."

"Football?"

"The Seahawks. He grew up in Pittsburgh. He's a Steelers fan. And I haven't seen him over there since that one time or heard John say anything more about him."

"Are you aware of any animosity John had with any of the neighbors? Arguments or disputes?"

Cortez and Theresa considered each other, then shook their heads. "Everyone was just sort of live and let live," Theresa said.

"What about cars driving up during the day or at night?" Harrison asked. "Did you ever witness anything like that?"

"No. Nothing like that," Cortez said. "It's like I said, John seemed like a stand-up guy. We had no idea about the other stuff."

Keera looked at Harrison. He shook his head, indicating he had no further questions. They thanked Cortez and Theresa, handed them business cards, and encouraged them to call if they thought of anything else. On the walk back to his car, Harrison said, "She's going to make those arguments; isn't she? Tran's going to argue that was the reason Michael went to the house, why he had the package, that he was dealing for Lockett. It makes sense too; doesn't it? I mean, they worked together at Blue Horizon."

Keera wasn't going to lie. "She'll make the arguments, if it comes to that." She pulled open the car door and got inside. Harrison quickly started the motor to get the heat going but didn't immediately drive off. "But something doesn't sit right with me," Keera said.

"What's that?" Harrison looked over at her.

"Lockett giving Michael the package to hold for him sounds like a guy worried; doesn't it? And if he was worried, who was he worried about, and why?"

"He could have thought maybe the feds were on to him," Harrison said. "And he was testing the waters, seeing if Michael would hang on to a package for him."

"Maybe, but he still had drugs and money in his house. But we should find out one way or the other," Keera said.

"I'll make a call to some contacts and see if the feds had anything working. That much fentanyl, it could very well have been on their radar. Should we talk to Jerry Garcia?"

"At some point. But let's get back and talk to Tina's neighbors before it gets too late. Maybe somebody saw Michael coming home that morning." She was struggling to stay optimistic for JP's sake, but she also could imagine Anh Tran standing before a jury making the same arguments Theresa had just made, and, as Theresa had said, those arguments made sense.

Keera would have to be just as convincing.

# Chapter 10

After picking up the list of neighbors Tina had cobbled together, Keera and JP went door-to-door while it remained light out. People got funny when strangers knocked on their door after dark. Harrison checked off those neighbors not at home and would try to talk to them another time. None of the half a dozen neighbors they'd spoken with had any helpful information. No one seemed reluctant to talk, and most expressed sympathy for Tina Westbrook, but they hadn't been awake that early to see or hear anything.

Finished for the evening, Harrison and Keera spoke on the sidewalk outside Tina's home, discussing what next and feeling the darkness and the cold settling in.

An older-model Prius drove toward them and slowed as it approached. The driver, a young Black woman, gave them more than a curious stare before she turned the car into the driveway directly across the street.

Keera and JP had knocked on the door earlier but got no answer. They had deduced that if anyone had seen or heard anything, it was more likely someone within the house across the street.

The young woman stepped from the car and glanced again at Keera and JP. It was the suspicious look you'd give two people you either hadn't seen before in your neighborhood—or who you suspected would try to talk to you about the person who lived across the street and had recently been arrested. Keera looked at JP and could tell from his expression he was thinking the same thing.

They stepped off the sidewalk into the street and slowly approached the young woman as she retrieved what looked like a heavy backpack.

"Excuse me?" Keera said. She didn't tell Harrison she'd take the lead. He knew it instinctively from the years they'd worked together.

The young woman turned to them.

"Hi," Keera said, smiling.

"Hi," the young woman said, looking and sounding apprehensive.

"I'm Keera Duggan. I'm an attorney representing Michael Westbrook. This is JP Harrison, Michael's uncle. I assume you know what has happened to Michael?"

"Some people in the neighborhood have been talking about it." The young woman, who Keera estimated to be early twenties, about Michael's age, spoke in a soft voice. She was dressed in casual clothes, black spandex pants, and a gray pullover hoodie several sizes too large with "SSC" scrawled on the front.

"What have they been saying?" Keera asked.

"Well, I've really only heard from my mother and father. My mother saw the police here one afternoon and said Michael was taken away in handcuffs."

"Is your mother home?" Keera looked at the well-maintained house. The wood siding had been recently painted a blue gray, the trim white. In the yard, an English hedge separated the lawn from flower beds, rhododendron plants, rosebushes, and others.

"No. She and my father are both at work."

"Were you home when the police came?"

"I was at school."

"Do you go to South Seattle College with Michael?" Harrison asked.

"No. My boyfrie . . . I go to Seattle University. I'm studying nursing."

"But your mother was home when Michael was arrested?" Keera asked to confirm.

"No, not home. I mean . . . I think my mother heard about it from Mrs. Westbrook . . . I don't really know."

Odd. She seemed to be backing away from her earlier statement.

"What did your parents tell you they had heard?" Keera asked.

A small shrug. "Just that Michael was arrested, and Mrs. Westbrook said the police were accusing him of dealing drugs."

"Can I ask your name?" Keera asked.

"Jada Davis."

"How old are you, Jada?"

"Almost twenty-one."

"That's about the same age as Michael." She looked to Harrison for confirmation. He nodded. "Did you and Michael know one another, living across the street from one another and being the same age?"

"Of course. We grew up together. Went to the same schools, but we don't hang out, not so much anymore." She put her free hand into the pouch of her hoodie. The other held the strap of her backpack. "Is this going to take long? I really need to study. I have a test tomorrow."

It, too, seemed an odd comment from someone who called Michael a friend and knew he'd recently been arrested.

"We won't keep you long," Keera said. "We're just trying to help Michael. To do that I need to ask a few tough questions. Do you know if Michael dealt drugs?"

"You said you're representing Michael?"

"That's right."

"So why don't you ask him?"

Keera smiled. "We did."

"What did he tell you?"

"We're hoping to confirm some things. Did you ever know or hear of him selling drugs?"

"Is what I tell you confidential? I can't, like, get Michael in trouble or be called to testify or anything; can I?"

"As I said, we're just learning as much as we can, Jada," Keera said without answering the young woman's question.

"Do dime bags of weed count?"

"You mean a bag containing ten dollars' worth of weed?" Harrison asked. "Did Michael sell those?" He knew Michael had. So did Keera.

"When he was in high school. I mean, it isn't a big deal; right? A person can buy weed in a cannabis store now. But I don't know if he was still selling or not. As I said, we don't really hang out and we go to different schools. So . . ."

A thumping beat permeated the silence. Another car drove down the block, the music increasing in volume as it approached and drove past, then fading.

"Who did Michael get the weed from that he was selling in high school; do you know?" Harrison asked.

Jada had a habit of shrugging the shoulder not burdened by the backpack. "I have no idea."

"Did you know the name John Lockett?" Keera asked.

"No. How much trouble is Michael in?" The question sounded sincere.

"At the moment he's in pretty big trouble," Keera said, though it didn't seem like Jada Davis had heard about Michael being charged with murder or about the fentanyl. "That's why we're talking to his neighbors, gathering as much information as we can that might be helpful."

"As I said, we really didn't hang out much after high school. We aren't enemies or anything. It's just that Michael dropped out of school for a while, and I had a lot of school and other commitments. I haven't really talked to him too much the last couple years. So, I don't really know anything."

"I imagine, going to nursing school, that you're up late studying with all the math and science courses nursing requires," Harrison said.

"Sometimes," Jada said.

"Is your room in the front or the back of the house?" Harrison turned and looked at the windows facing the street, curtains drawn.

"My room is right there." She pointed to a window that faced the street.

"Do you ever see anything late at night, while you're studying?" Harrison asked.

"Like what?"

"People out late or up early walking their dogs or maybe exercising? Maybe the newspaper delivery driver comes by?"

She exhaled. "Not that I can think of." She looked at her phone. "I really need to study. This is a big test."

"Sure," Keera said. She and Harrison each handed her a card. "If you think of anything. Maybe something we didn't ask you, or maybe something that comes to you later, will you call and let us know?"

Jada had her head down, looking at the names on the cards. She looked up at Keera and seemed to pause, as if about to say something more. "Sure," she said. Then she walked inside her house.

"That seem a little off to you?" Harrison asked as they walked back across the street to his car.

"Didn't sound like they were close friends. Not any longer."

"She also didn't sound anxious to help Michael out."

"Thought so, too, but . . . Maybe she can't," Keera said.

"Wouldn't she at least be curious about what kind of trouble her friend is in?" Harrison asked.

Keera said, "We need to find out where Michael was getting his weed supply when he was selling the dime bags. Let's hope it wasn't John Lockett."

"I'll check with Michael," Harrison said.

"You still have a contact in the DEA?"

"Still do."

"Get in touch with him. Find out if they had anything working on John Lockett or Blue Horizon. If he was importing that much product, they might have been."

"Already set it up."

# Chapter 11

Midday the following day, JP Harrison parked his 1972 Verona-red BMW in the lot beside Keera's office, not wanting to risk parking it on the street in Seattle's Pioneer Square. He'd walk to the Salumi deli, a long-established sandwich shop that used to attract a line of customers snaking down Occidental Avenue and around the corner onto South Jackson Street. How much longer the sandwich shop could remain in business seemed less and less certain with each block Harrison walked. Covid, and the resulting work-from-home trend that had started as a necessity and somehow become a God-given right, along with the rapid rise in Seattle's homeless population, had caused a mass exodus from the neighborhood. It had once been Seattle's first business center, home to banks, professional offices, craftsman shops, restaurants, and warehouses. "For Lease" signs greeted Harrison in the ground-floor windows of several historic redbrick buildings.

He stepped around tents and tarps lining the sidewalk. Garbage overflowed from a receptacle on the street corner. At the base of one bin lay an abandoned, well-worn pair of shoes he thought illustrated the area's slow, prolonged death. A pink trolley car rumbled and clanged along South Jackson Street; the seats inside empty, like the buildings he passed.

It made Harrison even more curious why Alexander Kuznetsov had chosen Salumi to meet. Nostalgia, perhaps. He and "Kuz," as everyone referred to the DEA agent, had eaten at the shop frequently when they'd worked joint drug cases, back when Harrison worked in the SPD narcotics unit. Though Harrison was ten years older, the two had become fast friends, sharing a love of music, vintage cars, and red wine. Kuz, now a senior DEA agent, had been friendly on the phone but became quiet when Harrison mentioned the double homicide in South Seattle, and he suggested they meet.

Harrison deduced that Kuz had to be careful about what he said and who was around to hear him. Harrison was no longer a Seattle police officer. Even if he had remained on the force, there were certain things the feds would not discuss with their state counterparts.

As Harrison approached from the east, Kuz turned the corner at King Street, approaching from the west. The DEA's office was on Fifth Avenue, up the hill from Pioneer Square. Kuz, of Russian heritage, reminded Harrison of a Cold War–era Soviet KGB officer. His long black leather jacket swayed with each step taken. A black knit cap covered his bald pate, and he stepped confidently in straight-leg blue jeans and black, square-toed boots. But Kuz had been born in the United States, which made him more red, white, and blue than Harrison, who'd immigrated to the States from the UK as a boy with his parents and his sister.

Kuz got that familiar, crooked grin, and rubbed his hand over the stubble on his chin as his eyes took in Harrison's white pants, blue peacoat, knit hat, and red scarf. "You can dress like a flag, but you'll always be a Brit to me, unless you've managed to drop that faux accent of yours."

"I'll have you know the British flag was red, white, and blue long before America existed, and the ladies still love this faux accent as much, if not more than, this outfit." Harrison gestured to a Band-Aid along the side of Kuz's nose near his right eye. "What happened to you?"

"Ah," Kuz said, touching the strip as if he'd not remembered it was there. "My dermatologist keeps cutting and scraping. Basal cell carcinoma."

"Serious?"

"Is there a non-serious cancer? Just a few spots."

Kuz gripped Harrison's hand and yanked him forward as if pulling him off balance in a judo match. He wrapped Harrison in a bear hug. "You never call. You never write. How have you been, my friend?"

"I'm well," Harrison said. "No complaints. You? Other than the basal cell?"

"As well as a man with a wife and three teenage daughters can be."

"Teenagers already?"

"Most men put in man caves. I want to add one of those outdoor showers. It might be the only way I ever get in one." Harrison smiled. Kuz's daughters were his pride and joy. "You're still dressing like a fashion model, I see."

Harrison looked around at his surroundings. "I feel a little out of place."

"A little? I'm surprised people haven't stopped to salute you. Come on. Let's beat the rush."

Harrison laughed. They were the rush.

Inside the deli, Harrison ordered a spicy sopressata with provolone, garlic spread, and pickled peppers. Kuz also ordered the sopressata but chose finocchionna and mozzarella with the works, including roasted onions.

"No onions for you," he said. "You must have a date."

Harrison shook his head. "Nah, I'm just old. They give me indigestion."

"Shit, you *are* getting old," Kuz said.

"Tell me about it."

When Kuz reached for his wallet, Harrison raised his hand. "This one is on me."

"You wouldn't be bribing a federal officer; would you?"

"Would it work?"

"Every time."

They took a seat at a small metal table at the window and stretched their legs on the terrazzo tiles while they waited for their sandwiches.

Harrison sipped from a bottle of water, Kuz from a Dr Pepper. "I need the caffeine," Kuz said. "Not all of us are retired. How's the PI biz?"

Harrison smiled. "Which brings up the reason for this clandestine meeting."

"Can I assume this discussion is for your ears only?" Kuz asked.

"Always, Kuz. Just looking for a little background to hopefully get me digging in the right area."

"The problems is, you might be digging in a graveyard, my friend."

"You got my attention."

"John Lockett had been on the DEA's radar for months."

"Yeah?" Harrison said, cautious but excited by this bit of news.

"We've known for several months he was smuggling drug shipments into the country through Blue Horizon."

Harrison knew the implication if the DEA had an operation in progress but had not yet acted on it. "But Lockett was just a cog in the wheel?"

"The importer. Not the money man."

"Who was he bringing in the product for?"

"Don't know. That's what we'd been working on. Now we may never know, and some people are not happy about it."

"Why does the DEA think Lockett was just the importer?"

"Lockett didn't have the kind of money or the distribution in place for the shipments coming in through Blue Horizon. That required someone with a lot more resources."

"Someone in Seattle?"

"We were operating under that premise. Somebody higher up the food chain, but who stayed well insulated and unknown."

"Any idea who might have killed him?"

"If you believe everything you read, it was the kid, Michael something."

"No way, Kuz."

"You sound certain."

"Michael Westbrook is my nephew."

Kuz's eyes widened. "Oh shit. I'm sorry. I didn't know."

A man from behind the counter set their sandwiches and chips on the table. Neither man made a move to pick up his lunch.

"How did he get mixed up with Lockett?" Kuz asked.

Harrison told Kuz what he knew, about Michael working with Lockett at Blue Horizon and Lockett befriending him, inviting Michael over to the house to drink beer, shoot pool, and watch sports.

"He drove Michael home the other night when Michael's car broke down, and he asked Michael to hold a couple of packages for him. Said they were gifts for his girlfriend that he didn't want to leave around his house."

"Bad luck for your nephew."

"Indeed, but maybe it wasn't bad luck," Harrison said.

"I'm all ears."

"What if Lockett did it deliberately? What if he was worried someone might come looking for the two packages?"

"Who?"

"You guys come to mind. Or maybe this unknown boss."

"I don't think Lockett knew about our investigation. Like I said, we kept this closely wrapped."

"Okay, so maybe his unknown boss."

"That's higher up the food chain than I am currently privy to," Kuz said. "But if Lockett sensed he was about to get hit, why wasn't he better prepared for it?"

"I had the same thought and a possible explanation," Harrison said. "Hear me out. What if Lockett was skimming product and/or money from the guy he was importing for, and each shipment he set a package aside to sell?"

Kuz gave that a moment of thought, then said, "It's plausible. And it would explain why he paid for it with his life. And your nephew was just, what then, in the wrong place at the wrong time?"

"Maybe so. Maybe Lockett tried to set him up as the person skimming, and whoever did kill Lockett just got lucky Michael was

Lockett's fall guy, or that Michael was in the wrong place at the right time. With a suspect arrested for the two murders, there would be no further investigation; right? The killer or killers walk."

"Again, could make sense."

"What more can you tell me about the DEA's operation?"

"Blue Horizon flies in a lot of its cargo from the Southeast Asian market, and we assume the drugs were hidden within legitimate shipments. We had Lockett, and we were beginning to piece together his network, but as I said, we lacked the person's name at the top."

"And that's why you didn't move on Lockett?"

"Taking down Lockett wasn't going to stop the flow of drugs. To kill a snake, you have to cut off its head. You know that." Kuz picked up half his sandwich. "Who's the PA?"

"Anh Tran."

Kuz gave a low whistle. "And the hits just keep on hitting," he said. "Does your nephew have a private attorney or a PD?"

"Private. Keera Duggan."

Kuz grinned. "The Irish Brawler's daughter? I'd like to be in court for that fight."

"I wish I wasn't. If I don't get Keera some evidence she can use to fight back, Tran will crush her and send my nephew away for the rest of his life."

# Part II

# Chapter 12

***May 1986***
***King County Superior Court***
***Seattle, Washington***

Detective Jack Thompson felt as nervous as he had the first time his wife went into labor. Helpless. He and his detective partner, Kyle Mitchell, had worked nonstop for months to gather sufficient evidence to convict Andrae Ollson—a drug dealer, addict, and drifter—of the Tran Jewelry Market murders. They did not find Ollson's fingerprints inside the store, nor had they recovered the murder weapon. They had found a witness. The owner of the market across the street from the strip mall had seen Ollson in the area on a couple of occasions days prior to the murders. And when Thompson and Mitchell eventually arrested Ollson and searched his person, they located a piece of jewelry from the Tran Jewelry Market inventory. Ollson, however, said he found the jewelry in an alleyway close to the store, even directed them to that alley. When Thompson and Mitchell searched it, they found an additional piece of stolen jewelry, which Ollson's defense counsel had hit hard during cross-examinations as proof Ollson was telling the truth.

Why else would Ollson have given them the information?

Without further confirming evidence, the prosecuting attorney, Robert Steinman, suggested to Thompson that Anh Tran's testimony might be their only remaining hope of a conviction—if she could identify Ollson as the man who killed her parents. Thompson had resisted that option. He'd done everything he could to protect the young girl from having to testify in court about what happened to her parents on that horrible morning, but he, too, knew Steinman was running out of options. And hope.

Ollson would walk.

He felt guilty that it had come to this. He'd had nightmares of that crime scene from Anh Tran's vantage point hiding beneath the bed. He could only imagine her nightmares. The second-to-last thing he wanted to do was to make Anh relive that horrific moment. The very last thing he wanted was for Ollson to walk free from that courtroom.

He and Steinman had brought in a child psychologist to evaluate Anh's mental status and to determine if the pressure of her testifying could result in any long-term mental health issues, something Thompson would not put the young girl through, no matter if they lost this trial. The psychologist concluded Tran's reliving the episode would not be any more emotionally scarring.

Thompson showed Anh a series of mug shots of various men who looked similar to Andrae Ollson. She had studied the photographs at great length, looking them over carefully before she pointed to the picture of Ollson and identified him as the "bad man" who made her parents kneel on the ground, then fired his gun.

With no other option, no other concrete evidence, Steinman decided, and Thompson agreed, the State needed to put Anh on the witness stand.

King County Superior Court judge Marcus Bennet had denied the prosecution's motion to allow Anh to testify via closed-circuit television or, alternatively, in a closed courtroom without the defendant, Andrae Ollson, present. Bennet ruled that Ollson's Sixth Amendment right to confront witnesses gave him a strong presumption the prosecution could not overcome. Judge Bennet did, however, allow Anh's aunt, now raising the young girl, and the child psychologist to sit at the State's counsel table to offer their emotional support.

Thompson had worked hard to help Anh understand the legal proceedings and to ensure she would feel safe. He'd even brought her into the courtroom ahead of testifying, so she would know what to expect and to help reduce any anxiety. But now, following a lunch break, as he waited for Steinman to call Anh, his stomach churned, and his nerves felt frayed.

Steinman approached the podium after Judge Bennet took the bench, and Thompson had to resist an impulse to stand and call the whole thing off. The prosecutor advised the court that the State would call Anh Tran to the witness stand. Thompson and Mitchell had also spread the word to the Vietnamese community, and they had packed the courtroom with friendly faces to support the young girl and to ensure justice was done for the brutal murder of two of their own.

The courtroom door opened. Anh entered holding her aunt's hand. Her aunt looked more nervous than Anh. The little girl, now seven, walked in wearing a plaid skirt and a white blouse with a rounded collar. Her black shoes clicked on the linoleum floor as she made her way to the witness stand, playing with a strand of hair freed from a pink bow. She was tall for her age, with long limbs.

As Anh's aunt led her to the witness chair as they had practiced, you could have heard a pin drop inside the courtroom. The aunt and psychologist took their seats at counsel table beside Thompson.

Judge Bennet leaned toward the witness chair, his face benevolent and his voice friendly. "Hi there," he said.

"Hi," Anh said, looking up at him with an unsure smile.

"Can you tell me your name?"

"Anh Tran."

"Nice to meet you, Anh. How old are you?"

"I'm seven years old. How old are you?"

Bennet smiled, as did others in the courtroom, and, for a brief moment, Thompson's nerves eased.

"I'm sixty-two," Bennet said. "Do you know why you're here in court today?"

"Yes."

"Why are you here?"

"To answer questions."

"That's right. Before the attorneys ask you any questions, I need to ask you a few questions to make sure you understand some important things. Okay?"

Tran shrugged. She'd tucked her hands under her thighs and swung her legs beneath the seat. "Uh-huh."

"Do you understand that I'm the judge here in court?"

"Uh-huh. That's why you're sitting up high and have on the black cape."

Judge Bennet smiled, as did others in the courtroom. "This is called a robe. And I'm sitting up here on what is called a bench."

"It looks like a desk."

The judge nodded. "It does; doesn't it?" Another smile. "Anh, can you tell me what it means to tell the truth?"

"It means saying things like it's a desk, not a bench."

Several jurors chuckled, and Anh looked out at the gallery. Thompson smiled but watched anxiously.

"And what is it called if someone doesn't tell the truth?" Judge Bennet asked.

"That would be a lie."

"And what happens if someone tells a lie?"

"They get in trouble."

"Right." Bennet held up his pen. "Now, can you tell me what color this pen is?"

"It's blue."

"Great! And if I said this pen was red, would that be the truth or a lie?"

"That would be a lie."

"Wonderful. Where do you live now?"

"I live with my aunt, Linh Nguyen."

"And is your aunt here in court today?"

"Yes."

"Can you point to her?"

The little girl removed her hand from under her leg and pointed to her aunt.

"Thank you. I think you're ready to answer the lawyers' questions. And if you want to take a break to have a sip of water or for any reason, will you let me know?"

"Yes." Anh picked up her glass with both hands and took a sip of water, then set the glass back down on the table beside the witness chair.

Judge Bennet looked at Steinman, who approached. Thompson's insides churned. He felt himself sweating beneath his shirt and tie.

After preliminaries, Steinman gently brought Anh back to that hot day in July. "Do you remember what you did that day?"

"Uh-huh. I went to school."

"What did you do after school?"

"I went to the jewelry store to have my snack and do my homework."

"Do you recall what homework you had?"

"I always have math and spelling."

"Did something happen that day that wasn't like the other days when you went to school, then went to the jewelry store?"

"Yes."

"What happened?"

"Somebody started yelling and breaking things."

"Was this at the jewelry store?"

"Yes."

"Did you see the person yelling and breaking things?"

"No. I was behind the curtain."

"Did you hear the person yelling?"

"Yes."

"And did you hear the person breaking things?"

"Yes."

"Did it sound like a man or a woman yelling?"

"A man."

"What happened after you heard the man yelling and breaking things?"

"My mother came behind the curtain and said, 'Giấu! Giấu!'"

"Is 'giấu' a Vietnamese word?"

"Uh-huh."

"And what does 'giấu' mean?"

"It means 'hide.'"

"And did you hide?"

"Yes."

"Where?"

"Under the bed."

"Did you see what happened next from under the bed?"

"Uh-huh."

"What did you see?"

"The bad man made my mother and father kneel on the ground. Then he shot them, and they fell over, and they died."

"I'm sorry, Anh. Is that bad man who shot your parents here in the courtroom today?"

Anh stopped and looked at the defense table. "Uh-huh."

"Will you point to him?"

Anh pointed to the defendant, Andrae Ollson.

"Let the record reflect that the witness has pointed to the defendant, Andrae Ollson," Judge Bennet said.

"No further questions," Steinman said.

Thompson let out a held breath. The little girl could not have done better.

"Mr. Wentworth?" Judge Bennet said.

Seymore Wentworth, the public defender, had a reputation for not always playing by the rules in successfully getting his clients off. He was short and balding, which was unfortunate given the odd shape of his head, covered by only wisps of stray hairs. His suit looked a size too large, the jacket sleeves extended past his wrists, and the pants bunched at his shoes. It was a carefully chosen costume, and Wentworth did everything he could to give the jurors the impression of a beleaguered public defender. But Thompson knew Wentworth came from money. He served as a public defender because he believed the judicial system disfavored the poor.

He walked to the lectern and spoke in a friendly voice. "Hi, Anh," he said. "I'm also going to ask you some questions. Is that all right?"

Anh again shrugged. Her legs swayed. Judge Bennet said, "Anh, you have to use your voice to answer Mr. Wentworth, just like you've been doing. Okay?"

"Okay."

Wentworth repeated the question and Anh answered, "Yes."

"Anh, that day in the jewelry store was not a good memory for you; was it?"

"No."

"I imagine you have tried very hard to forget it; am I right?"

"Yes."

"And were you able to forget it?"

Anh's brow furrowed. Then she said, "Yes."

Thompson felt his stomach quiver.

"You had forgotten all about it; is that right?"

"Counsel." Judge Bennet leaned forward and used his hand to tell Anh to wait. "Given the age of this witness, I'm going to ask you to ask open-ended questions and not suggest answers to her."

"Certainly," Wentworth said. "My apologies." He turned to the little girl. "Anh, did you forget all about the incident in the jewelry store?"

"Yes."

"When did you remember it again?"

"When Ms. Concorde helped me to remember it."

"And who is Ms. Concorde?"

Anh removed her hand from under her leg and pointed to the child psychologist seated beside Thompson. Wentworth noted it for the record. "Now you said you went to the jewelry store after school; is that right?"

"Uh-huh."

"Was that in the morning? The afternoon? Or the night?"

"The afternoon."

"And you did your homework there?"

"And had a snack."

"And had a snack. Yes. Did the room where you were doing your homework have any windows?"

"No."

"Was there a window in the back door?"

"I don't remember."

"Okay. Can I show you a picture?"

"Okay."

Wentworth stepped forward holding the photograph so Anh and the jurors could see it.

"And where is the door with the window?"

Anh pointed and Wentworth noted it.

"And is that a curtain covering the window?"

"Yes."

"Can you point to where you hid in this picture?"

Anh pointed to the bed across the room from the door at the back of the store, which led to the alley, and Wentworth again noted it for the record.

"Now, Anh. Do you see the blanket that is pulled down on that bed corner?"

"Yes."

"Did you pull that corner down?"

"Yes."

"You did? And where in the room did the bad man make your parents kneel?"

Anh again pointed.

Wentworth paused for a moment, so the jury had time to consider that the room had been poorly lit, particularly the area where Anh had hidden, and that her view was likely obstructed by the blanket.

"When you were hiding, Anh, did you close your eyes tight?"

"Um. I don't know . . ."

"Okay. That's fine. I want to ask you just a few more questions. What did Ms. Concorde do to help you remember what happened that day?"

Anh looked up at the ceiling. "Um, she had me play games using dolls."

"And did she have a doll of the bad man?"

"Yes."

"And was the doll white, like the man sitting at the table who you pointed to earlier?" Wentworth pointed to Ollson.

"Uh-huh."

"And did he have dark hair, like that man sitting at the table?"

"Yes."

"And what did Ms. Concorde call the doll?"

"The bad man."

"And did she help you to remember what the bad man did?"

"Yes."

"Did she tell you what the bad white man with the dark hair did?"

"Uh-huh."

"What did she tell you?"

"She said the bad man shot my parents."

Again, Wentworth paused, and Thompson knew the defense attorney would argue to the jury that Anh had not remembered on her own but rather had been coached on what to remember. He felt the air in the room releasing like one large exhale.

"And after Ms. Concorde showed you the doll of the white man with dark hair and said he was the 'bad man,' did Detective Thompson show you some photographs of bad men?"

"Yes."

"Can you point to Detective Thompson?"

Anh did. Thompson gave her a small, tight-lipped smile.

"Did Detective Thompson show you pictures of bad men and ask you to point to the picture of the bad man who shot your parents?"

"Yes."

"Okay, and did Detective Thompson show you one picture at a time or more than one?"

"I don't remember."

"That's okay. When you were looking at the pictures, were you looking for a man who looked like the doll that Ms. Concorde showed you? Were you looking for a bad white man with dark hair?"

"Yes."

"Can I show you some photographs of some bad men who have white skin and dark hair?"

"Yes."

Wentworth approached and put six photographs on an easel facing the jury. "Are these pictures of bad white men with dark hair like the pictures that Detective Thompson showed you?"

"Yes."

"Is one of these a picture of the white man with dark hair who you saw shoot your parents?"

"Um." Anh leaned forward to study the pictures. Her brow wrinkled in thought. Thompson felt the entire gallery also lean forward, urging the young girl to pick the photograph of Andrae Ollson, bottom row, center.

"Take your time, Anh," Judge Bennet said.

Agonizing seconds ticked by, the courtroom deathly silent. Finally, the little girl said, "I think . . ." She looked at the defendant, then back to the photographs. "I think maybe this one."

Wentworth held up the picture for the jury.

It was not Andrae Ollson's photograph.

# Chapter 13

***Present Day***
***Seattle, Washington***

Keera tried, but the federal prosecutor remained reticent about discussing anything specific concerning the charges except for what was already in the complaint. Keera had made a few court appearances, and she'd filed a motion to set bail, which the prosecutor opposed, and the court declined to grant. Rumors persisted of an empaneled grand jury, but she could get little information from her sources in the prosecuting attorney's office or from Patsy's sources.

As she turned the calendar to February, she made another fruitless call to the federal prosecutor. Then she hung up and called the King County prosecuting attorney's office, a number still embedded in her memory. She asked again to speak to Anh Tran, expecting to get Tran's voice mail. Prior calls had either not been returned or were returned by a first-year lawyer working with Tran who told Keera he could neither confirm nor deny the rumors of a grand jury, which meant one had been empaneled.

This morning, however, to Keera's surprise, Tran not only took her call but invited Keera to meet at McCoy's Firehouse Bar & Grill, which was just around the corner from Keera's office on Second Avenue and South Washington Street.

Before leaving the office, Keera checked her appearance in the bathroom mirror and debated whether to put on makeup. She hated to admit it, but the aura of Anh Tran made her nervous. She decided against makeup, wanting to present a confident business package.

◆ ◆ ◆

Keera entered the brick-façade building just after noon. She'd never eaten at the restaurant, often opting to dine at the Paddy Wagon, conveniently located on the ground floor of her firm's building. It was quick and easy, which was usually paramount given her hectic schedule.

She removed her knit hat and gloves and shoved them in her jacket pockets. Various vintages and colors of fire helmets, jackets, and a massive collection of shoulder patches from fire stations around the world hung on the walls above narrow, red-leather booths. The glass shelves behind the bar, lined with bottles of alcohol, and an assortment of colored beer taps added to the ambiance. The music was loud but not obnoxious. Lynyrd Skynyrd sang "Sweet Home Alabama." She passed tables with plates of food: bacon burgers, sandwiches, and steaks. French fries. More food than Keera could eat in a sitting.

Tran sat at a booth with a thick bacon burger, a mound of fries, and a tall glass of beer. Given the hour, on a weekday, the beer surprised Keera. As did the fact that Tran looked focused on a flat-screen television hanging above the bar. The television was currently playing a University of Washington basketball game from the prior night. Keera only knew because her father had attended the game and had been talking about it in the office earlier that morning.

Keera approached and Tran glanced at her, then directed her attention back to the game. "They've had leads of ten and twelve but haven't been able to put them away. Now Michigan is within five. Are you a fan?"

"I should be. The Mariners' and the Seahawks' stadiums are within walking distance of the office, and the games often dominate our office conversation, but no, not really."

"I love all sports," Tran said. "I love competition. I'm watching what I missed last night while I was working." She extended a hand. "Take a seat." It sounded like an order, not an invitation.

Keera removed her coat and threw it into the booth, then sat.

"You want me to call the waitress over? Food is good here," Tran said, her eyes still focused on the game.

"If I eat that much at lunch, I'm pretty much done for the day. How do you do it?"

Tran didn't look to have an ounce of fat on her. Her face was lean, and her arms, bare beneath a blue sleeveless shirt—despite the cold weather outside—well toned. Her long dark hair showed traces of gray and was pulled back off her face in a tight ponytail.

"I run five miles most days, four to five days a week—rain, sleet, or snow. Even when I'm in trial. Relieves stress. That, and I've always been lucky to have the metabolism of a jackrabbit. You run also?"

"More for self-preservation than anything else. I'm not blessed with the same metabolism, so . . ."

The waitress approached and Keera ordered an iced tea, declining a menu. The music changed to a Garth Brooks song. It sounded like "Wild Horses," but Keera wasn't certain. Music was like sports; she had only a tangential interest.

At a commercial break in the game, Tran said, "I was sorry to hear you left the PA's office. You were on a fast track." Keera didn't think Tran had ever noticed her. They'd never spoken. "And I can't understand why you did. Miller Ambrose is an ass; you should have stayed and gone over his head and got him fired. That was a mistake by you."

No pulling punches. Opening round one with reference to Keera's failed relationship that caused her to leave the office was a sharp left hook. "I was young and stupid," Keera said.

"Weren't we all once. You're not married?" She looked to Keera's left hand.

"Nor are you," Keera said.

"True. But I'm what, ten, twelve years older than you? Mine's by design. I don't have time for a relationship, nor the desire to go through the whole dating ritual to weed my way through the losers, retreads, and has-beens. Most guys are intimidated by a woman who isn't interested in a serious relationship, and I like my alone time."

"I can understand that."

"I know. That's why I said it." Tran dipped a french fry in ketchup and ate it. "I knew you'd be a good trial attorney."

"Why is that?"

"You're Patsy Duggan's daughter. If you have his innate instincts and fight . . ." She shrugged. "You kicked Miller Ambrose's ass in the Vince LaRussa trial, and you ran circles around Walker Thompson to get Jenna Bernstein a result she didn't deserve. Those were two good outcomes."

"Thank you." Tran had clearly researched Keera or had someone do it for her.

"Not going to happen for Michael Westbrook, however."

The bluntness of Tran's statement, and her confidence, again caught Keera off guard, though she was making some of her own observations. Tran presented herself as the image Keera had heard so much about—the no-nonsense crime fighter who didn't pull punches and had a flair for the dramatic. It was hard to say whether Tran's presentation was an act—a first impression meant to intimidate—or her true self. It didn't matter. At the moment Tran could afford to be cocky. She was holding all the cards.

"No?" Keera said.

"No." Tran took a pull on her beer.

"Tell me why not?"

Tran eyed her, as if evaluating her and ultimately determining Keera wasn't going to beat her in court. Tran ate another french fry.

"Westbrook and Lockett worked together at Blue Horizon. Lockett was importing drugs, mostly from the Far East. Westbrook helped him to distribute those drugs to the people Lockett supplied."

Keera didn't think this was a fact as much as blustering. "You have evidence to prove Michael was acting as a distributor?"

"I think it will become self-evident." *Not an answer,* Keera thought. "Anyway," Tran continued, "Westbrook concocted a reason for Lockett to give him a ride home from work, said his car had broken down."

"Maybe it had."

Tran again ignored the response. "Lockett just had a package of fentanyl come in, and Westbrook decided he'd kill Lockett and Scott and make it look like a drug hit by a competitor. He even left behind drugs and money as props for the detectives to make such a deduction."

"And all this came to him because his car broke down?" Keera asked, being sardonic.

"I'll convince a jury he was considering this for a while. He just needed the right opportunity."

Keera said, "You can prove all of this?"

Tran smiled. "I've proven a lot more with a lot less."

"Sounds thin."

Tran put her paper napkin on the table. "Here's something you should know about me, Keera. I don't bluff. It's why I suck at poker. When I have a full house, I bet it all. I have a full house. And you're not holding four of a kind, a straight flush, or a royal flush."

Keera felt her competitive juices kick in. "My father used to like to bet the ponies. One day he took me to the Emerald Downs racetrack. Just the two of us. He gave me five dollars to bet and told me how the odds worked. The first couple of races, I mimicked my father's bets. He bet the odds. He bet on the horse with the best odds to win, to place, and to show. I made a lot of money for a young girl. When the last race came, I wanted to bet on the horse with the longest odds to make the most money. My father didn't try to talk me out of it. He told me it was my decision; that the people that made the odds didn't know everything, that they could be wrong. He said that until the race had finished, anything was possible. So, I bet. The horse was named Cipriani, and it went off at fifty to one."

Tran gave her a quizzical look. "And you lost?"

"No. I won. And I never forgot what my father told me about odds and about how, despite those odds, the horses still had to run the race. He said, 'Until the race is finished, you never know who's going to win.'"

Tran's look became a condescending smile. "Well, you're going to get your chance to bet again." She looked at her watch. "This morning the evidence you call thin went to a grand jury. I'm asking for an indictment of your client on two counts of murder in the first degree and robbery in the first degree. I'm going to get it. It's the reason I'm here, having a beer and a burger." She paused, perhaps expecting Keera to respond. She didn't; the news didn't come as a complete surprise. "When you walk out that door, Keera, the race will be over. I won't discuss a plea."

Keera's turn to smile. "Here you just made a point of telling me you were a lousy poker player because you could never bluff, and then you go and bluff. The PA's office never offers a plea in a first-degree murder charge. Not since the state abolished the death penalty. You'll seek life in prison. We were going to try this case whether I walked out the door or not; weren't we?"

"Your client could plead guilty."

Keera smiled. "As my father said, you have to let the horses finish the race to see who wins. When will the complaint be filed?"

"As soon as the grand jury comes back." She looked again at her watch. "I'd guess by day's end."

"Then I'll see you at the arraignment. Thank you for meeting with me, and for your candor." Keera slid from the booth, grabbed her belongings, and moved toward the door.

"Keera?"

She turned.

"Did your father ever tell you how often those long shots actually win?"

"No. I figured out that answer on my own."

"That it's almost never?"

"That there is always the possibility."

# Chapter 14

Billy Ford entered their bull pen near day's end. He was dressed in a charcoal-gray suit, his knotted tie loose and the collar of his shirt unbuttoned. He looked beat. For the past two weeks, Ford had returned to his cubicle each afternoon to fill in Rossi on the grand jury proceedings. He tossed his knit hat and leather gloves on his desk. Then he slung a briefcase onto his chair and dropped it with a thud. "Colder than a monkey's ass out there."

"I think you mean a witch's—"

"I know what I mean. It's cold. Bone-chilling cold."

Rossi smiled and checked his watch. "You finished for the day?"

"The judge sent the grand jury to deliberate. I was with Tran."

"What are your thoughts?"

"Tran is as good as billed. She could make a silk purse out of a sow's ear, as my mother liked to say, but we all know we're light on hard evidence. No gun. No weapon he used to bludgeon the woman to death. No blood spatter on his clothes or in the drain in his bathroom."

"How did she explain it?" Rossi asked.

Ford gave an exaggerated shrug. "She intimated Westbrook dumped the gun in a garbage bin in the neighborhood and burned or buried the clothes he'd been wearing."

"But there's no evidence of that either," Rossi said.

"I know."

"And given that we confirmed the starter on the car was bad, he couldn't have gone far to bury the gun or the clothes anyway."

"She argued he changed clothes and shoes when he did the killings."

"Where'd the gun come from?" Rossi asked. They'd found nothing on all the usual sites.

"She argued guns are a dime a dozen and can be purchased almost anywhere now, despite tighter federal regulations."

"Circumstantial," Rossi said. "We told her that."

"Not the package of fentanyl and envelope of cash we found on the floor of his room," Ford said.

"If he dumped the gun and his blood-spattered clothes, why wouldn't he have at least tried to hide the fentanyl and the money?"

"Tough to dismiss, for sure." Ford scratched the day-old growth on his cheek, then shook his head the way he did when he was exhausted. "And arguing a robbery as motivation for the killing is something the average juror can understand."

"What did she say about the money and drugs left behind in the house?"

"That it was calculated. To make it not look like a robbery but a hit."

"So then it comes down to the two packages in his bedroom, Westbrook's fingerprints and his DNA found in the garage and the house, and the testimony of the two prison informants?" The informants had come forward to let Tran know they had information about the two killings, and she'd had Ford and Rossi interview them both at FDC-SeaTac.

"Pretty much."

"How'd the grand jury respond to the informants?"

Ford shook his head. "We'll find out . . ."

"You don't sound convinced."

Ford sat on the edge of his desk. "I'm as skeptical of jailhouse snitches as you. But I don't think the grand jury gives a rat's ass what I'm skeptical about."

Rossi shared Ford's frustration. Police were judged on their arrests and on gathering enough evidence for prosecutors to convict those arrested, which created an incentive to do what was necessary to secure that conviction, including using questionable witnesses, something Ford and Rossi would not do.

Like Ford, Rossi had an inherent lack of trust of informants in general, and specifically with respect to the two at the Federal Detention Center who came forward against Michael Westbrook. Since the war on drugs had led to longer prison sentences, and the Sentencing Reform Act abolished federal parole for those serving those long federal sentences, providing information to the government had become a way to shave years off their sentences, and possibly earn an early release. Rossi and Ford believed it created an underground market that permitted the State to trade leniency for information, giving informants an incentive to lie, and possibly leading to wrongful convictions.

"When do you expect the grand jury back?"

"Soon. Tran believes that, and I agree. If I read them correctly."

"Then we better get geared up. This is going to be a brawl with Keera Duggan representing Westbrook and him being JP Harrison's nephew."

"That does change things; doesn't it?" Ford said.

"If she brawls for people like Vince LaRussa and Jenna Bernstein, imagine what she'll be like if she has a personal interest in the case."

Ford shook his head and stared past Rossi. "The Irish Brawler's daughter against the Queen of Circumstantial Evidence."

Ford's voice had that tone Rossi knew well. "It certainly won't be boring." When Ford didn't respond, Rossi said, "Something else bothering you?"

"Another young Black man about to be tried for murder based on questionable evidence. Wouldn't be human if it didn't bother me."

"The fentanyl and money aren't questionable, Billy. Nor are Westbrook's fingerprints and DNA, or his admission to the informants."

"If they can be believed. But let me ask you something. If Westbrook was white, would we be rushing to a grand jury like this? Going this fast? Why won't Tran wait and let us do our jobs?"

"You sound like you're giving the closing argument Matthew McConaughey gave in *A Time to Kill*."

"Would we?" Ford persisted.

"I hear you, Billy."

"All the same, no, you don't, Frank." He raised a hand before Rossi could respond, not that Rossi was about to say he understood what it was like to be Black. Billy grew up in Texas and, from what little he had shared with Rossi, Billy knew racism firsthand. Direct evidence. Rossi only knew racism from what Billy and other Black friends had told him—circumstantial evidence, at best, and never as good as direct. "You never got a stare from someone because of your skin color, Frank."

"No, I haven't."

"You've never been questioned by the police for walking down the street. Never were stopped and told to remove your shoes and socks and empty your pockets because you were Black and just had to be a drug dealer."

"Never have, Billy," Frank said.

"It's easy to blame a Black man for crimes, and even easier to convict."

"You're right, Billy. And I don't disagree that we're light on direct evidence in this instance, but we told Tran all of this, and she is determined to go forward."

"And that's what is going to happen, Frank. We're going to go forward, because Tran can spin a web better than Charlotte. But that doesn't make it right; does it?"

"I don't know what's right in this instance," Rossi said. "But what I do know is this time there'll be someone across the courtroom who can spin just as strong and intricate and compelling a web, and a closing argument to explain it. You and I have both witnessed Keera's abilities in the LaRussa and Bernstein trials. Maybe, somewhere in the middle, a jury will find justice."

"Maybe," Ford said. Though he didn't sound convinced.

# Chapter 15

Anh Tran wasn't bluffing, at least not about filing the grand jury indictment late that afternoon. The indictment against Michael Westbrook included two counts of first-degree, premeditated murder; one count of robbery; and another count of burglary—unlawfully entering Lockett's house.

Michael and his mother were in no position to pay Keera's hefty fee, and Keera couldn't stomach Harrison taking out a second mortgage on his home to do so. Her worry had been unnecessary. Ella had already prepared for scenarios like this. When Patsy had been in his prime, his reputation, built in the trenches, attracted more clients than the firm could handle. Ella had the foresight to know that Patsy's alcoholism, and the destruction it wrought, would eventually lead to his decline and prevent him from being in those trenches—or the rainmaker he once had been. Upon becoming the firm's managing partner, Ella had filed a certification of compliance with the court. It allowed the firm to serve as a criminal case public defender, should an indigent client request one, and the county would pay the firm's fee. It meant, in essence, that Duggan & Associates was already in the court's queue.

Upon Tran's filing the indictment, Ella had taken the bull by the horns and filed a notice of appearance, listing Keera as lead trial counsel and Patsy as second chair. She'd also moved to have Michael Westbrook declared indigent, per the guidelines established by the Revised Code of Washington. Given that Michael was charged with two counts of first-degree murder, and Tran would seek the ultimate punishment—life without the possibility of parole—and since Keera had the requisite experience to defend such clients, neither Ella nor Patsy could see a judge denying Michael's request and possibly give him a potential avenue of appeal, should he need one.

The day after the firm's certificate had been accepted and Keera had been appointed to represent Michael, the clerk called and advised her the case had been assigned to Judge Ima Patel, and that Michael would be arraigned in her courtroom at a time that coincided with the judge's calendar.

"Will Judge Patel serve as the trial judge as well?" Keera had asked the clerk. Judges did not usually serve in both capacities, but since this case was proceeding by a grand jury indictment, Patel had that option.

"She will," the clerk said.

Keera had appeared before Patel once as a defense attorney and several times when she had been in the prosecuting attorney's office. She had a cordial but cool relationship with the jurist, which she largely attributed to Patsy. Patsy and Patel had sparred numerous times when Patel had been a prosecuting attorney, and their battles had been contentious. It didn't help Keera that Patsy had not always fought cleanly, though always within the rules.

It wasn't a great draw for Michael Westbrook.

Keera would have to tread carefully.

Along those lines, Keera told Michael and Tina Westbrook she would not seek bail. They had no chance that Patel, or any other King County judge for that matter, would consider bail in a case of double homicide. Keera making such a request would only give Tran the opportunity to discuss the heinous and brutal murders in open court with the press in the gallery, and to argue that Michael posed a danger to the public. It would be an easy win for the prosecution.

Instead, Keera would request to have Michael moved from FDC-SeaTac to the custody of the King County jail to give him better access to his legal team. Keera's office was located down the hill from both the jail and the courthouse. Again, given the serious charges against Michael, Keera thought it highly unlikely Judge Patel would deny her request. And Patsy always said it was better to start with a win, of any kind, than a loss.

The following morning, Keera arrived early to the office to finish preparing for the arraignment, though she anticipated the hearing would be over quickly. As Keera made her way to her office, a light spilled onto the hall carpet from the crack beneath the door to Patsy's corner office. Her father had always arrived in the office early when he'd been practicing full-time, but since becoming her ombudsman, he came in later and snuck out earlier. She knocked and pushed open his door. Patsy sat with his feet propped on the corner of his desk, a green Tiffany lamp illuminating papers in his hands. He wore an open-collared dress shirt, slacks, and slippers. He looked at Keera over reading glasses resting on the tip of his nose.

"Hey, kiddo."

"What are you doing in this early?" Keera asked.

"Old habits are hard to break."

Her father looked well rested after his six-week stint in a rehabilitation facility in Eastern Washington. The bags under his eyes were not as pronounced, and he had lost weight through his face and his neck. He also had retained a bit of a tan, having gotten out more often to walk the golf course, including several nine-hole rounds with his wife. "Golf and your mother," he often said now, "not the law, are my jealous mistresses." In the background, classical music softly played: violins, cellos, and a flute. Music helped him concentrate. Keera also. She could smell the coffee wafting from the mug on his desk and the faint odor of all those celebratory cigars Patsy smoked following each victorious jury verdict.

"And you just happen to be in early on the day of Michael Westbrook's arraignment?"

He gave her a mischievous smile. "Is that this morning?"

Keera smiled.

"Just wanted to be a good ombudsman and make myself available," he said. "Any questions?"

"I think I can handle it."

"Who's your judge?"

"Ima Patel. For the arraignment and the trial."

"I'ma From-Hell," Patsy said, which was what many in the defense bar called Patel. The jurist knew her nickname and didn't appreciate it. Patsy lowered his feet. "Not a great draw, but I suspect Ima will treat you fairly—for no other reason than she won't want to appear biased against you or your client because she hates me."

"Not exactly reassuring, Dad." She took a seat positioned across the desk. "Let me ask you something. Did you ever go up against Anh Tran?"

"Half a dozen times."

"And?"

"It was a hell of a show. She's not afraid to push the envelope in her courtroom theatrics nor in the conclusions she wants the jurors to draw from the circumstantial evidence she introduces."

"Sounds like you."

"We had some epic battles. You'll have to be prepared to give the jurors just as compelling a show with just as convincing arguments. But do not get so sucked into her case. Try your own case. Have a game plan going in and execute that game plan, or she'll have you on the ropes throughout the trial."

It was advice Patsy had given Keera before chess tournaments—to play her game—and it had more often than not worked. "I'll remember that."

"Another thing. She won't produce evidence that is questionable unless the court orders her to do so. So be sure to create a record of having asked for everything."

"I'll let Ella know."

Ella's designated role when Keera was in trial was to file and respond to trial motions, a skill at which she was very good. Trials were no longer supposed to be games of hide-and-seek the evidence, as they'd once been, though certain attorneys were more recalcitrant than others about turning over expert reports and documents relevant but damaging to their case. Under the United States Supreme Court case *Brady v. Maryland*, the prosecuting attorney was legally required to provide the defense with access to *all* discoverable evidence, including exculpatory evidence that could exonerate the defendant or impeach a prosecution's witness.

"You look nervous, kiddo. That's not like you. Never knew you to be nervous before a chess match or a trial."

"I think the grand jury has me a bit unnerved. Tran has already had a trial run and knows what evidence and what arguments are convincing and what aren't."

"True, but since she didn't have to worry about objections or cross-examinations, the grand jury's findings could also give her a false sense of confidence."

"I've met with her. It doesn't sound like it's false."

Patsy lowered his feet. "Tran tries to intimidate through her record and her demeanor. She pushes plea agreements and, if not taken, she overcharges at trial and seeks the longest possible sentence. That can also work against her."

Keera well knew that Patsy had become a defense attorney because he believed prosecutors had too much sway in the criminal justice system. He frequently complained that prosecutors ruled with near absolute power, not only deciding whether to bring charges but what charges to bring. Overcharging was just one abuse of that power. Another was penalizing a defendant who refused to plea and exercised his constitutional right to make the prosecutor prove the charges to a jury. Withholding or hiding potentially exculpatory evidence was yet another form of abuse, as was the particularly egregious practice of manufacturing evidence. Seeking redress from the courts was also difficult. To prove misconduct by the prosecutor required clear and convincing evidence. And courts were quick to find the prosecutor had made a "mistake" and conclude the mistake was "harmless error" that did not impact the defendant's constitutional rights or the trial's outcome.

"It's the reason our battles were epic. I was never intimidated by her threats and pushed her to prove the charges in court."

"Yeah, but you've had hundreds of jury trials. I haven't."

"We all have to start somewhere, kiddo. And contrary to popular lore, I didn't win them all. I just fought like hell to protect my clients' constitutional rights. You do too. Don't equate a lack of experience to a lack of talent. You're just as talented as Tran, perhaps more so. I'd say the outcomes in both the LaRussa and Jenna Bernstein trials prove your mettle."

"Thanks, Dad." She appreciated the pep talk, but she also couldn't divorce the fact that this was her father as well as her mentor. Keera got up to leave, then turned back. "You weren't planning on coming with me this morning; that isn't the reason you're in dress clothes; is it?"

"I'd like to, kiddo. I loved that stage, but I think it would send the wrong impression to both Patel and Tran. You can stand on your own two feet. The suit is because Ella wants to use me as a show pony today to bring in two potential white-collar clients."

Keera left the office and bundled up for the walk from Pioneer Square to the courthouse. As she climbed the hill, her breath marked the cold air. Unlike her past two trials, which generated significant public interest, no line of reporters or civilians eager to get a seat in the courtroom gallery awaited her. She walked into the courthouse unnoticed, but got a rush of adrenaline nonetheless, and realized she was more like Patsy than she cared to acknowledge. She, too, loved the stage and loved playing to an audience.

She made her way across the marbled foyer and rode the elevator to the second floor. As she made her way to Ima Patel's courtroom, voices reverberated off the marble floors, walls, and columns.

A young woman waited outside Judge Patel's courtroom and approached as Keera neared. She introduced herself as a reporter for the

*Seattle Times* and held up her cell phone. "Ms. Duggan, I understand you will be representing Michael Westbrook."

Keera wasn't completely anonymous.

"Can I get a statement?" the reporter asked.

"My client is innocent and looks forward to proving his innocence in a court of law."

"I understand he was indicted by a grand jury."

"Many defendants are indicted by a grand jury and proven innocent at trial. The grand jury system does not allow a defendant or his counsel to put on evidence or witnesses, or to cross-examine the prosecution's witnesses. It's a one-sided process and the outcome therefore circumspect."

"Anh Tran indicated justice would be served in this courtroom. Any comment?"

Keera was surprised Tran would speak to the media prior to a trial. Most prosecutors didn't discuss a case until after a verdict had been entered. Then the press was handled by the King County prosecuting attorney. "I agree with the prosecutor. Justice will be served."

Keera pulled open the outer door to the vestibule, stepped in and opened the interior door to the courtroom, and slipped inside. Judge Patel's courtroom was dated, with yellow-spined legal books shelved along one wall. Attorneys made arguments from behind two tables resting on worn black and white checkered flooring that made Keera think of a chessboard—and the attorneys and their clients as chess pieces. This was her comfort zone. A carved wooden backdrop resembling the façade of the United States Supreme Court building framed Patel seated on her elevated bench.

Patel listened to an argument by a prosecuting attorney Keera knew from her time in the office. The defendant, wearing a red jumpsuit, sat at the defense table with his attorney. Keera quietly greeted JP Harrison and Tina Westbrook, seated in the gallery, then sat and glanced around the courtroom, which would be her home for several weeks. She did not see Tran and wondered if it was deliberate, another tactic to intimidate.

The legal matter finished, and marshals escorted the defendant from the courtroom. A moment later, Patel's clerk stood in the well below the bench and said, "Number two on the calendar. State of Washington versus Michael Francis Westbrook."

Keera stepped to the counsel table closest to the jury box and directed Tina and Harrison to the first pew behind her. She noticed several people in the gallery open laptops or take out a reporter's notebook and pen. Was it the case? Tran's involvement? Keera's developing reputation? Regardless, this case would garner at least some attention.

"And is the prosecutor here?" Patel asked.

A young man Keera had not met, but whom she had spoken to on the phone, moved to the State's table. "Your Honor, the prosecutor, Anh Tran, is trying a case this morning before Judge Valle. I'm Deputy Prosecuting Attorney George Thomas. I will handle the arraignment—"

The door to the courtroom opened, and Tran sailed in with elegant, purposeful strides. She wore an all-black pants suit, her dark hair pulled back, ponytail bouncing. The only thing missing was her black Batman cape and mask. The young attorney dutifully stepped aside. He didn't look the least bit surprised by Tran's dramatic entrance, which made Keera think it had been staged.

"I'm sorry to keep the court waiting, Your Honor. I hope it has not been inconvenienced."

"We were just getting started, Ms. Tran. I understand you were finishing up trial in Judge Valle's courtroom?"

"I got here as quickly as those ancient elevators would allow, Your Honor. The prosecuting attorney's office considers this a very important case, and it is my intent to give it my full attention."

"The court appreciates your diligence."

Keera barely managed to keep her breakfast down.

Patel turned her attention to Keera. "Good morning, Your Honor. Keera Duggan of Duggan & Associates appearing on behalf of the accused, Michael Westbrook. I can attest that the elevators worked just fine this morning, and that I, too, consider this an important case and intend to give it my full attention."

She smiled.

Patel did not.

In her peripheral vision, Keera saw Tran smirk, as if Keera were an insolent child.

Patel said, "Thank you, Ms. Duggan. The clerk has entered a notice of appearance on behalf of Ms. Duggan of Duggan & Associates. I note that Patrick Duggan's name is atop on the pleading. Will he be appearing for the defense?"

Keera wasn't certain of the question's purpose and therefore did not directly answer it. "That has not, at this time, been determined, but he does remain a partner in the firm."

Patel turned to her bailiff. "Is the defendant here?"

"He is, Your Honor."

"Bring him in, please." The bailiff left the courtroom.

Two correctional officers escorted a handcuffed Michael Westbrook into the courtroom from a door at the back. He wore the khaki-colored FDC uniform. Keera was reminded again of Michael's size; the correctional officers looked small beside him. The jury would also notice. She made a mental note to have Michael wear clothing in court that would try to minimize his size.

Michael gave a faint smile to his mother and to JP, then turned around so an officer could remove the belt chain and handcuffs. Keera put a hand on his shoulder and leaned close. Michael bent to allow her to whisper in his ear. She'd do it frequently after a jury was empaneled. She wanted those in the courtroom to know Michael was not to be feared, a technique her father had taught her.

Tran said, "Defendant is present and in the custody—"

Keera interrupted Tran. "Your Honor, the defense acknowledges receiving the charging document and waives a formal reading of those charges. The defendant is prepared to enter a plea."

Patel shifted her attention to Michael. "Mr. Westbrook, are you prepared at this time to enter a plea?"

Keera had rehearsed this with Michael the prior afternoon. He spoke in a clear voice. "I am," he said.

"How do you plead?" Patel asked.

"I plead not guilty," Michael said.

"Does the defense wish to discuss the issue of bail?" Patel said.

"The State opposes bail," Tran began. "This is a double—"

"The defense at this time does not seek bail but reserves the right to do so at a later date," Keera said, and again felt the room deflate. She would not give Tran a chance to play to the gallery. She approached the clerk and handed her the first of two multipage documents prepared by Ella. She also handed a copy to Tran, who smiled upon reading the caption.

"The defense has filed a motion requesting that the defendant Michael Westbrook be remanded to the King County jail during the trial of these State charges. Mr. Westbrook should have unfettered access to defense counsel. The King County jail is within walking distance of my firm. FDC-SeaTac is half an hour away, on a good traffic day, which seems to be less and less the case here in Seattle."

"Ms. Tran?" Patel asked.

"The State does not object."

"Mr. Westbrook will be remanded to the King County jail pending the outcome of this trial."

Keera handed the clerk the second motion and again provided Tran a copy. "The defense also requests the State produce all discoverable evidence within the prosecuting attorney's file, including all exculpatory evidence, and the Seattle Police Department's full investigative file, including but not limited to discovery of all police reports, witness statements, physical evidence, expert reports, and *Brady* material. The defense also understands this matter was presented to a grand jury and requests those transcripts." Keera was pushing the boundaries seeking the grand jury transcripts, but it is where she wanted Tran's focus.

It worked. "The State objects to defendant's request for any grand jury materials," Tran said quickly. "Grand jury proceedings are confidential, and the defense has not articulated a particularized need that would constitute good cause for production."

"Absent a showing of good cause, the request for grand jury transcripts or evidence is denied," Patel said.

It was a loss, but Keera had expected it. "The defense reserves the right to renew its motion upon a showing of good cause," she said.

"Noted," Patel said. "When can the State have the other discovery materials to the defense?"

"Two weeks," Tran said.

"Your Honor, the underlying deaths upon which these charges are based took place two months ago, and the State has already presented its evidence to a grand jury. Surely it can provide the defense with those materials just as readily as they were provided to the grand jury."

"Your Honor," Tran said. "The State did not present the prosecuting attorney's file or SPD's file to the grand jury. We will need time to review and redact any and all work product materials."

Keera said, "In that case, Your Honor, the defense would request that the State provide it with a list of any and all documents withheld or redacted and its basis for doing so." Again, Keera wanted to preemptively put the court on alert should she have to later argue that the State had not met its discovery obligations.

"Two weeks sounds sufficient," Patel said. "As does the defense's request of a log of documents withheld and on what basis. Are there any other issues to address at this time?"

"The defense has filed a motion for a court order granting access to the crime scene," Keera said.

"The motion is granted and I have signed an order. Please coordinate access with the Seattle Police Department and the prosecuting attorney. Anything else?"

"No," Tran said.

"The defendant waives his right to a speedy trial," Keera said. She would need as much time as possible to prepare for this trial.

"So noted," Patel said. She set a case-scheduling conference, rapped her gavel once, and said, "This matter is adjourned."

Keera spoke briefly with Michael before correctional officers led him away. As Tran passed behind her, the prosecutor stopped and turned. "Your clients waived their right to a speedy trial in both LaRussa and Bernstein. I expected you to do so today as well."

Keera smiled at the thought of her father having beaten Tran several times. "My father taught me to never be in a rush to win," she said.

# Chapter 16

A week after the arraignment, Keera had been busy working her other cases. She'd had a three-day trial and various other court appearances—and little help. Doug Glant, one of two associates Ella had hired during the Jenna Bernstein trial, had brought in two white-collar criminal cases, CEOs being investigated by the FBI and the United States Department of Justice. Glant had worked in the Criminal Division within the Department of Justice and had experience with white-collar criminal defense, though not a lot of trial experience, should either case progress that far. Ella and Patsy helped him as the two cases moved through the system, generating much-needed revenue for the firm, but leaving little spare time for anyone to help Keera. Ella said Patsy was in his glory, and that maybe teaching young lawyers how to position cases for trial was his new forte.

The door to Keera's office opened without a knock and Maggie marched in, which was her habit. "Come on in, Maggie. I'm not on the phone with the queen of England or anyone important."

"The queen of England is dead. Charles is now the king. You are really out of the news loop."

Keera couldn't tell if Maggie didn't get sarcasm, was being facetious, or was just being Maggie. "What is it?"

"Do you want the information I found on Michael Westbrook?"

Keera had asked Maggie to get a copy of Michael's criminal record, then make arrangements with SPD and the PA's office for her, JP, and her experts to get into John Lockett's house. "I would appreciate that very much."

She handed Keera a document. "Michael Westbrook was arrested twice for the unlawful delivery of a controlled substance. The first time he was directed to and completed a drug diversion program. The second time he was convicted of a class C felony, fined one thousand dollars, and served thirty days in the King County jail."

Keera sighed. He had a felony record for dealing. Not what she wanted to hear, though unlikely Tran could get the conviction into evidence. Tran would argue Michael's prior conviction was relevant to prove he had a penchant for dealing drugs, which explained the fentanyl in his possession. But that was a reach. It had nothing to do with the real issue before the jury—whether Michael was a murderer. Keera would argue what little relevance existed was greatly outweighed by the potential prejudice to Michael.

"You have the inspection of the crime scene on your calendar?" Maggie asked.

Keera looked at her watch. "In roughly two hours, yeah."

Maggie started for the door, then turned back. "By the way, first-Sunday dinner this weekend. You're no longer out of the country, so you'll be there."

"You could never afford it."

Keera could have said any number of unkind responses, but she took the high road her mother had so often called "the road to heaven."

"I have it on my calendar, Maggie. I'm bringing dessert."

"Bring something good. It's my birthday."

Keera glanced at the date on her computer. "No, it's not."

"My birthday falls in between the Sunday dinners this month and next month. Mom said we'll celebrate it this Sunday." More likely Maggie had made the suggestion, and their mother went along to keep the peace. "Ooh, get a Cafe de Olla from Simply Desserts."

"Not likely. Those cakes are eighty dollars."

"Well, don't buy something at the supermarket that's all dry with fake frosting that tastes like wax."

"I'll be sure not to," Keera said, making a mental note to stop at the local market and look for the driest, waxiest cake she could find.

Keera wanted time outside the office and away from her desk phone before the inspection. She also needed to get to the King County jail to talk to Michael Westbrook about his prior felony conviction. The walk up the hill to the jail would serve both purposes.

Outside, she wrapped her wool scarf around her neck, pulled on her gloves, and started across Occidental Square past the empty Paddy Wagon patio.

She walked up South Washington Street to Second Avenue, and turned north, her mind considering questions to ask Michael. She crossed the street to the eastern sidewalk, continuing on autopilot, having made the walk dozens of times. A siren echoed in the canyons between the high-rise buildings, causing her to look back over her shoulder. By the time she'd turned forward, she'd nearly walked into a couple exiting Shawn O'Donnell's American Grill and Irish Pub.

"Excuse me—" she said. Then, "Frank?"

Frank Rossi stopped himself before he'd knocked Keera over, reaching out to ensure she didn't fall. Beside him stood a blonde woman in fashionable attire—high-waisted blue jeans, a black turtleneck, leather jacket, and ankle boots that gave her an edgy look. So, too, did her makeup. Keera, by contrast, felt frumpy, dressed for the crime scene inspection in unappealing blue jeans, tennis shoes, and her well-worn black down jacket. She wore no makeup and had pulled her hair back in a frazzled ponytail.

"Hey . . . Keera," Rossi said, sounding almost as if he had forgotten her name.

Keera recovered, somewhat. "Didn't mean to run you over, Frank. I guess I wasn't paying attention to where I was going."

"A lot on your mind these days, I'd imagine," Rossi said, sounding like he, too, had partially recovered, though he still looked and sounded awkward.

"Too much," she said. The woman watched the interaction with interest. She didn't wait for Frank to introduce her. She stuck out her hand. "Hi. I'm Amy."

"I'm sorry. Where are my manners?" Rossi said.

"Yes, Frank. Where are they?" Keera said.

"Keera, this is Amy." He offered nothing more than her first name.

"I gathered that when she said, 'Hi, I'm Amy.'" She gave him a thin-lipped grin. She had no intention of making this encounter any easier on him, though she realized she had no right to torment him. They weren't dating. That had been her choice; hadn't it?

"Keera is a criminal defense attorney now. We used to work together when she was in the prosecuting attorney's office." *Now. Used to.* Definitely creating distance.

"Switched sides?" Amy said.

"Something like that." Keera feigned looking at her Apple Watch. "I have to run. I have to speak with a client in the county jail." She gestured to her outfit, as if to explain her drab garb before she stepped away. "Good to see you, Frank. Nice to meet you, Amy."

She took off up the block telling herself not to turn back, not to look like she cared. But she did. Maybe Amy was why Frank had been dismissive on the phone and she hadn't heard from him. Maybe he was already getting on with his life. Good for him. Really.

She on the other hand remained stuck in neutral, too busy at work to even contemplate a social life. She got asked out, not infrequently, but not by anyone who interested her. Maybe that needed to change. Maybe she needed to be less picky, though certainly not like Maggie, who went through boyfriends as quickly as a marathon runner went through shoes. Maybe she had to rethink her mantra that the only thing worse than being lonely was being miserable with someone.

She turned on James Street and started up the hill to the jail at a quickened pace. Yeah, she wore tennis shoes and not cute ankle boots, but at least she wouldn't get blisters on her feet, which was something.

# Chapter 17

After meeting with Michael and confirming he had no other convictions, Keera met with her experts outside John Lockett's house half an hour before she was to gain access. She needed time to reiterate what she wanted from each expert, without anyone from the prosecutor's office listening. Getting into the house so long after the murders was a disadvantage, but her videographer/photographer would, at least, document the scene as is, then compare the video to the photographs and video taken by CSI the day of the killings. They might find something different that she could use. It didn't happen often, but it was always worth a look.

Primarily, she wanted her experts to ensure the PA's experts had a basis for the opinions they would offer at trial, and this would help Keera formulate cross-examination questions.

JP was not yet present, but he'd also direct the experts inside the house, having worked a two-year forensics rotation at Park 90/5 before becoming a homicide detective. He had investigated more than two dozen murders.

After meeting with her experts, Keera stepped back to consider her notes, as well as a laminated detective's cheat sheet. Frank Rossi had given her the checklist when Keera worked at the PA's office and had filled in for an MDOP prosecutor. That's where she and Frank had first met—at a homicide scene. An inauspicious start, if she and Frank were to ever have a relationship.

Shortly before the agreed-upon meeting time with SPD, a car pulled to the curb and parked. George Thomas, the young prosecutor at Michael Westbrook's arraignment, stepped out and approached, reintroducing himself.

"Yes, I recall you were going to handle the arraignment," Keera said. "Just before Anh Tran soared into the room to save the day."

"Are the detectives here?" Thomas asked, deflecting.

One of Keera's experts pointed to the street. "Looks like they just arrived."

"I'd like to get each of your expert's names," Thomas said, fingers pressed to his cell phone keyboard.

"You will—when, and if, I disclose them," Keera said. "Until then who they are is my work product. You certainly have every right to be here, but you have no right to speak to any of my consultants."

Thomas, looking sufficiently chagrined, stepped back.

Billy Ford and Frank Rossi exited an SPD pool car, a black Ford. Keera had not expected Rossi to attend the inspection, given Billy was the lead detective. She wondered if he'd changed his afternoon plans after their awkward meeting.

"Hey, Billy," she said, ignoring Rossi for the moment. "The gang's all here. I understand you're lead?"

"I'll let you in. You know the parameters, Keera. Do I need to repeat them to you or your team?"

"Not to me, but feel free to tell my team," she said. "I don't want any objections at trial."

"I didn't know Westbrook was JP's nephew. For what it's worth, I'm sorry."

"Thanks, Billy."

Ford stepped away with Keera's experts to discuss legal issues and protocols. He wouldn't control their work, but he would closely monitor them. Rossi remained behind, and Keera had the sense he wanted to say something.

"You going to listen in?" Rossi asked, nodding to Ford and the group surrounding him.

"Heard it before," she said, watching Ford.

"Yeah, I guess you have." Neither Rossi nor Keera said anything more for what seemed a long, uncomfortable moment. Then Rossi said, "Sorry if that was a little awkward at lunch today."

She glanced over at him and almost smiled. "Awkward?" she asked as if she had no idea what he meant.

"The meeting on the sidewalk."

"Oh. No. We're good, Frank."

"Yeah?" he said, not sounding convinced.

"Yeah," she said. "I am anyway."

He smiled. "Me too."

"Good." *Such a guy,* she thought. *He really does think things are good between us.*

Keera stepped to Ford and her experts, who were slipping on gloves and shoe coverings. Ford addressed Keera. "Where would you like to start, the garage or the house?"

"The garage," she said.

Ford led the others to the side of the garage and peeled off the crime scene tape that had sealed the door shut. Keera's videographer videotaped Ford doing so. Thomas, having missed the opportunity, quickly grabbed his phone. Keera thought he was going to ask Ford to reenact the moment.

Keera had instructed her videographer to go in before the others to document the scene. Then she turned to Billy. "Any ETA on when we'll get your investigative file?"

"It's in the prosecutor's hands," Ford said.

"The file or the decision to turn it over?"

Ford grinned.

Keera looked at George Thomas.

"I don't know," he said, and she believed him. He lowered his gaze and typed on his phone.

"When did you send your file over to the PA?" Keera asked Ford.

"Don't answer that," Thomas said, looking up from his phone. "Attorney work product."

"*When* he sent it over?" Keera asked.

"If a communication accompanied the file."

Keera didn't push it. She knew what she needed to know. Tran had the detective's investigative file. She'd contact Tran when the court's two-week deadline expired.

Ford and the videographer/photographer went inside the garage.

Rossi took a step forward, then looked back at Keera. "You going inside?" he asked.

"I'm waiting for JP."

He gave her a smile. *Such a guy.*

At half past the hour, Harrison parked in the street and spoke to Keera about his lunch meeting with his contact at the DEA's office, confirming the feds had been looking into Lockett, which Keera believed was as good as finding an unknown fingerprint. It was another twist on the SODDI defense. A federal agency like the DEA pursuing Lockett added a certain air of authority to the argument. Jurors could be persuaded that where there was smoke, there was fire. In the absence of direct evidence, this case was going to depend heavily on the prosecuting attorney's arguments to spin the circumstantial evidence into a coherent legal theory and logical conclusion. Keera's theory would at least have some basis in fact.

To subpoena a DEA agent to testify about an investigation would require Keera to comply with the Touhy regulations, which were named for a Supreme Court decision in which an inmate had sought testimony from the agent in charge of the Chicago FBI office. The agent objected to the subpoena, citing a Department of Justice regulation prohibiting the agent from revealing sensitive information. Federal agencies, anticipating similar legal problems and not wanting to leave the outcome in the court's hands, enacted regulations to govern the release of such information.

Harrison said, "My contact said the Touhy regs require a letter to the assistant attorney general of the Criminal Division summarizing the testimony and documents we want. He said it can be a long process, so not to wait."

"I'll get Ella on it," Keera said.

And on a Friday afternoon, Keera was grateful to end the week on a positive note, faint as that note rang.

# Chapter 18

Sunday afternoon, Keera drove to her parents' home in Madison Park after stopping at a local bakery and picking up a blueberry tart—Maggie's favorite—and some candles. She'd actually brought two desserts—the first, just for Maggie, was a plastic cake she'd found at Magic Mouse Toys in Pioneer Square. The cake looked real, even had slots to insert candles, but it deflated with a noise her niece and nephews were sure to get a kick out of. Maggie not so much. She'd have her nephew set the cake in front of Maggie before Keera brought out the blueberry tart.

She didn't bother to park in the street to ensure an early getaway from what she had once referred to as the insane asylum. She'd dreaded these dinners for years, but her mother had decreed them to be sacrosanct; you couldn't miss one unless you were hospitalized, traveling out of the country, or six feet underground. But ever since her father's return from the rehabilitation clinic in Eastern Washington, the dinners had become tolerable, even enjoyable. Her mother no longer allowed alcohol, not even wine or beer, which Shawn, Keera's eldest brother, had loudly protested. Absent alcohol, her father's dry, Irish humor was on full display, and Keera no longer felt as though she sat on a nuclear warhead waiting for the bomb to detonate.

Her mother's alcohol ban suited Keera just fine. She'd largely quit drinking, though she did have an occasional glass of red wine with her meals while in Italy. Had she been an alcoholic or heading down that path? She didn't know, but alcohol had certainly been a reason for her poor decision to date her boss, Miller Ambrose. Giving up alcohol had not been difficult, although after particularly strenuous days, she did miss the soothing calm her glass of Dewar's had offered.

Keera pushed open the front door and walked inside her childhood home. The smells emanating from her mother's kitchen comforted her the way a blanket warmed her. She could smell the stuffed chicken and homemade bread rolls cooking in the oven. Her other siblings would bring salad, mashed potatoes, and corn on the cob.

Her mother was not in the kitchen, nor were her sisters. The dining room table was half set. That was Maggie's regular family dinner chore. They all knew Maggie "volunteered" to set the table so she didn't have to spend time or money making or buying a dish. But they had all also learned not to go down that path with their sister. As Shawn liked to say, "Happy Maggie, no naggie."

Keera called out, "Hello?"

"In the den," her mother said. Her voice sounded rushed, anxious. Keera thought immediately of her father, that he'd suffered a heart attack or a stroke, some medical emergency. She set the tart and plastic-cake boxes down and hurried into the den, finding her family seated, some on the armrests of chairs, their eyes riveted on the flat-screen television.

"We're watching the Notre Dame–Connecticut basketball game," her father said.

"I thought you'd had—"

Shawn raised a hand. "Shh!"

Ordinarily their mother forbade them from turning on what she called "the idiot box" and interrupting her Sunday dinners. She'd apparently made an exception for Keera's, Ella's, and Patsy's alma mater playing a game against the two-time defending national basketball champion. Under a minute remained to play in the game, and Notre Dame had the ball, down two points to Connecticut.

Notre Dame's guard pulled up at the three-point line and released a shot. The net rippled.

"That's a three," Patsy yelled amid the high fives. "We're up by one."

Connecticut did not call a time-out, hurrying the ball up court as the seconds ticked down. They got the ball to their big man down low. He turned, with five seconds on the clock, and banked in a shot, putting Connecticut back up by one.

"Time-out. Time-out," Ella yelled.

But Notre Dame did not call a time-out. The center quickly inbounded the ball to their guard, who was racing up the court with time expiring. Three. Two. One. He let fly a shot just past half court, with no time on the clock. The family watched as the ball arced across the court toward the net.

"It's good," Patsy yelled, just before the announcer shouted, "Notre Dame wins. Notre Dame wins."

A chorus of cheers and high fives followed among the crowd, except for Michael's wife, Isabella, whom he had met in rehab. She didn't know a basketball from a soccer ball and didn't care. Maggie sat looking perturbed, likely because this was supposed to be her birthday dinner and she the center of their attention.

When the celebration ended, their mother said, "Maggie, finish setting the table. Ella, get your salad ready. If my chicken is dry, you can blame Notre Dame."

As her siblings departed, Patsy said, "Keera. Hang on a minute."

Keera held back.

"I've been up to my eyeballs with the two white-collar criminal cases," Patsy said.

"Ella says you're enjoying it."

"Maybe I'm proof you can teach an old dog new tricks. It feels good to be of use again."

"You'll always be of use, Dad."

He waved off the compliment. "How is the case with Tran going?"

"I haven't seen much of her yet. She's delegated a lot to her young associate. We got into the crime scene. Lots of fingerprints and DNA. I'll know if it means anything soon. And I should have SPD's file shortly. I'm guessing the photographs will be gruesome. I'm told Lockett was shot in the head, likely at close range, but the most unnerving scene was in the bedroom where the girlfriend was beaten."

"Do you think your client has that type of violence in him?"

"I don't know, Dad. Nothing surprises me anymore, though I can't think of what would have been Michael's motivation."

"That's not what I'm asking. You have to decide whether your client has that violent behavior in him. Not everyone does."

She understood. "What caught my attention was that the house was torn up—books knocked off shelves, cabinets and dresser drawers opened, closets ransacked, clothes strewn about."

"Someone looking for something?"

"That's how it appeared to me and to JP. And JP has a contact at the DEA who says the feds had been investigating Lockett for months, but Lockett wasn't who they were after."

"They wanted the entire organization."

"The money man or men paying to bring in the shipments."

"That could be useful," Patsy said.

"It could if I can get it into evidence. JP and I were spitballing an argument."

"Let me hear it."

"What if Lockett was skimming drugs or money from the shipments and worried someone might have found out? It would explain why he gave Michael the packages to hold for him—and his bullshit excuse. It might also explain Lockett's relationship with Michael; why he had him over to the house."

"He wanted to gain his trust to hold the packages for him," Patsy said.

"Michael swears he didn't know what was in either package. Of course Tran will argue he did, and that Lockett was grooming Michael to distribute for him but Michael had other ideas."

"Make it look like a professional hit and sell the drugs himself," Patsy said.

"I could argue either the killer was someone in the organization who learned Lockett was skimming drugs or money, or perhaps a competitor for the same drug territory—someone who found out about Lockett's shipments and wanted to send a violent message."

"If you can get in enough evidence to make the arguments. What do you think really happened?"

"I don't think Michael knew anything. I think Lockett just wanted to get the evidence out of his house—whether that was because he was ripping off his bosses or because he feared a hit." She shrugged. "Who knows?"

"Hey," Maggie yelled down the hall. "Mom said, '*Everyone* at the table.' We're waiting on you two."

Keera rolled her eyes. "She must be anxious to open her presents."

"If it makes her happy," Patsy said, "then I'm happy."

"We're all happy, Dad."

Keera and Patsy took their usual places at the long table, with red candles adding a touch of elegance. Her two nephews and niece sat at the far end, animated and boisterous. Though Ella and Maggie did not have children, the family was growing, and the dinner conversation was getting more and more lively.

As dinner finished, Keera helped her niece and nephews clear the table, their assigned chore. Her nephew Nicholas looked at her and gave her a wide-eyed, conspiratorial nod, which she acknowledged. He moved into the kitchen to get the cake.

Her brother Michael said, "Keera, I want to hear about Italy."

"Wait. Wait," Maggie interrupted. "Before Keera hogs the floor, *again* . . ." She gave Keera a condescending smile. Keera returned it. "I have an announcement."

"Here we go," Shawn said.

Maggie scowled at him.

"Enough," their mother said. "What's your announcement, Maggie?"

"Well, it just so happens that I'm seeing someone and it's serious. I really think he could be the one."

Those seated at the table paused for a second before Michael said, "Okay, Keera, tell us about Italy. Isabella and I are thinking about going next May."

"I don't want to go to a foreign country. I won't understand anything anyone is saying," Isabella said. "Can't we just go to Cabo?"

"Uh . . . Isabella, you do know Mexico is a foreign country; right?" Ella said.

"Not really. It's just across the border."

Maggie slammed her fist on the table. The remaining dishes and glasses shuddered. "Seriously? Is no one interested in the man who could someday be my husband?"

"Whoa," Shawn said under his breath. "Naggie Maggie is back."

"Shawn," their mother said.

"Of course we're interested, Maggie," Patsy said, pacifying her.

"Isn't this the third family dinner where she's announced a new boyfriend could be *the* guy?" Shawn said under his breath.

"I'm losing track," their brother Michael agreed.

"Like either of you divorcés should be giving marriage advice," Maggie shot back.

"Go ahead, Maggie. Tell us about your new beau," their mother said.

"No," Maggie said, now looking and sounding insolent. "Not if you're all going to be like that."

"I didn't say anything," Ella said.

"Exactly. I never get any support from you or from the princess over there."

Keera had been about to pick up another plate but stopped. "What did I do?"

"Don't act innocent. Blabbing on about Italy."

"I haven't said two words—"

"What's his name, Maggie?" Patsy asked again.

"Just forget it."

At that moment, Nicholas came into the room, the candles burning brightly on Maggie's plastic cake. He'd placed it in the red tart box to make it look authentic. Keera moved to stop him, but not before Nicholas and his sister broke into "Happy Birthday." The others joined in.

This was not going to be good.

After the song, Maggie, smiling and momentarily pacified, blew out the candles, picked up her fork, and stabbed at the cake. The pressure valve released with a loud farting noise. Everyone but Keera and Maggie burst out laughing. Even their mother had to lift a napkin to cover her face.

Maggie looked up and glared at Keera.

If looks could kill.

# Chapter 19

Monday morning, Keera returned to the office to find SPD's case file on her desk. Timing was everything. The pretrial conference before Judge Patel was that afternoon, and Anh Tran did not want to be dragged on the carpet for withholding discoverable material and missing a court deadline. At the same time, she didn't want to give Keera a lot of time to digest the file and determine if and how it might be deficient before they met with the judge. Keera had her assistant quickly make two working copies and messengered one of them to JP Harrison. Then she asked Maggie to hold her calls, shut her office door, and dug in.

As she progressed through the file, she sensed the evidence was lighter than she had expected and wondered if everything had been produced. This was not unusual. Attorneys produced discovered evidence up to the date of the request and refrained from having their experts put their thoughts or conclusions in written reports so as not to tip their hand before trial. Attorneys also were not obligated to produce documents that contained their theories or impressions—considered their work product. In Keera's experience, most prosecutors didn't hide the ball, but they also didn't tell you where to find it. They withheld any document or scribbled note that they could argue included some internal attorney thought. And while they would disclose witnesses to whom they'd spoken, they wouldn't disclose what those witnesses had to say, as that included the attorney's impressions of the conversation. JP Harrison and Keera would have to hunt the witnesses down and interview them.

A knock on Keera's office door interrupted her thoughts. She looked to the clock on her desk. She'd been going over the file the entire morning and had to leave for court soon. "Come in," she said.

Harrison stuck his head in. He looked eager to talk. "You still going over SPD's file?"

She nodded. "Did you get the chance?"

"Soon as I got it." He stepped in and closed the door. "Had to come in and give you my impressions before you head to court." He looked at his watch as he moved to a chair at the round conference table, removed his peacoat, and slid it on the back of a chair, revealing blue jeans, an untucked black polo shirt, and winter shoes. He rarely wore socks, even in the cold months.

"The evidence seems weak," he said, sounding optimistic. "Does it seem that way to you?"

Keera smiled. "Maybe, but Tran will argue she is only obligated to produce what she has at present, and not where she might be going or what she might later obtain."

"Yeah, but she went to the grand jury with this?"

"Right, but I don't for a second believe this will be all the evidence at trial. Patsy says we can bet on it."

"Did you notice neither Ford nor Rossi made a recommendation to prosecute?"

"I wouldn't expect a recommendation to be in this file," Keera said. "Would I?"

"Not overtly, no. But there is no indication, anywhere, that they, as the investigating Violent Crimes team, were moving toward murder charges against Michael before Tran took the evidence to the grand jury. I suspect they felt, as we do, that the evidence in here isn't enough, that they needed more to ensure a conviction."

Keera knew from her years in the PA's office that investigating detectives were often consulted on whether a particular individual should be prosecuted based on the evidence they had gathered. A suspect could only be tried once. Double jeopardy prevented the State from retrying a person found innocent. For that reason, the prosecution often waited until SPD had all their ducks in a row before charging, despite public outrage at the delay. But the final decision to charge rested with the prosecutor, who had to consider not just the evidence but, as Keera was now doing, legal rules on the admissibility of the evidence and what might be excluded. The prosecuting attorney also had to consider public perception. Two people had been brutally murdered in a residential neighborhood. Keera wondered if the rush to name Michael Westbrook was in part due to pressure on the PA's office to bring someone to justice.

"Which could be why she took the case to a grand jury," Keera said. "In fact, I suspect that's the reason she did."

Harrison paced past the windows in Keera's office. "What I take away from this," he said, stopping long enough to tap his finger on the file, "is Rossi and Ford spoke to employees at Blue Horizon, who told them Lockett had given Michael a ride home after their shift at around 4:30 a.m." Harrison had also spoken to the employees.

"Which fits within the ME's estimated time of the murders," Keera said.

"Exactly. Then they found the packages in his bedroom and figured they had their guy. They arrested him for possession with intent to distribute and burglary, but really already concluded he committed the murders. The file doesn't indicate they seriously considered any other suspects," Harrison said.

"Michael was the logical suspect," Keera said, continuing to play devil's advocate. "Especially when his fingerprints and DNA turned up in the garage."

Harrison stopped pacing and moved back to the desk. "There's no indication the neighbor . . ." Harrison flipped through his notes. "Alex Cortez, was considered a suspect, and *he* found the body in the garage."

Harrison had a valid point. "Do you think Tran's reputation could have intimidated Billy and Frank to focus on Michael?" Keera asked. "To quickly come up with a suspect?"

"The detectives all know Tran's reputation, so it's plausible." He took a breath. "What did *you* get from the file?"

Keera checked her watch, then reconsidered her laptop notes. "The blood spatter droplet sizes indicate Lockett was shot at a close distance with a high-velocity bullet. Melissa Scott was bludgeoned to death by as many as a dozen blows, but—" Keera flipped to a page in the police file and was about to read from the police report, but Harrison could not wait.

"'No blood, rips, or tears were found on Michael's work clothes or his shoes,'" he said, reading from the police report Keera had copied and sent over to him, which he'd marked with numerous colored tabs, as was his habit. "How could he have killed them and not got any blood on his clothes? They checked them forensically. The clothes came back clean."

"I suspect Tran will argue Michael changed his clothes and his shoes."

"Okay. Then what did he do with the clothes he had on?" Harrison asked.

"Tran will argue Michael had ample time to dispose of his clothes and shoes," Keera said. "As well as the gun."

"His car was broken down, Keera. He couldn't have driven anywhere to discard anything. Which means they'd have to be somewhere close. So where are they? You can't burn shoes or clothes in a fireplace without leaving trace evidence, and nothing was found buried in the yard."

"That's a good point," she said, typing another note.

"As for the gun," Harrison said. "When forensics did not find any shell casings, Rossi and Ford hypothesized the gun was a .38 revolver, but ballistics identified the bullet as a 9-millimeter hollow point. Meaning it would do maximum damage and deform upon impact, making it extremely difficult for ballistics to match the bullet that killed Lockett to a particular gun, if a gun had been found. Which it has not been.

"Nine-millimeter revolvers are not common, unless you really know guns, and there's no evidence Michael has ever even owned a gun. None. The lack of a shell casing, if the gun was not a revolver, means the killer picked up the casing; that he knew the casing was a way to match the bullet to a gun. Again, sophisticated stuff that Michael did not know."

Keera typed rapidly. This could all support an argument of a professional hit.

"The inability to find the murder weapon is another reason Rossi and Ford would have been cautious," Harrison continued. He flipped additional pages, scanning the text. "And another thing. Toxicology explains why Scott didn't wake up when Lockett was shot."

"She had enough drugs and alcohol in her system to put a bull to sleep," Keera said.

Harrison flipped more pages. "Did you read that Michael offered to take a polygraph test—"

"—which I can't get into evidence," Keera said. The Washington Supreme Court had deemed polygraphs to be too unreliable to be admissible.

"Maybe not, but if a suspect made that offer in one of *my investigations*, I would have definitely taken him up on it. The results might not be admissible, but most suspects don't know that, and if a suspect failed the test, the failure could have been used as a pressure point to get a confession. If he passed the test, then I know I need to look elsewhere. My point is, there's no reason to turn him down."

"Unless Tran didn't want that potential ambiguity."

"Exactly."

Keera considered her notes and said, "I can put on Cortez and his girlfriend to testify that Michael was over at the house and the garage, which would explain why his fingerprints were on the pool cues and the table, but that's a bit of a double-edged sword. I can see Tran arguing Michael used the visits to scope out the home, gain Lockett's trust, and find out where he kept the drugs and the money."

"But if that were the case, if Michael knew where the drugs and money were kept, then why was the house torn up?"

"Tran will argue Michael used it as a diversion, to make it look like a professional hit."

JP paced again. "What about our experts?"

Keera said, "Blood spatter expert and latent fingerprint examiner both confirm what the State's experts concluded," tapping the file on her desk. "Including finding fingerprints of unknown persons in the garage. Nothing else earth shattering." She looked at her watch. "I have to get to court." She still needed to change her clothes. "Have you visited Michael lately?" she asked. Keera had tried to see Michael once or twice a week, but recent other case fires had kept her away. "How's he doing?"

"I took Tina over on Saturday, but it's rough. It's really hard on her to see him like that. And it's hard on Michael to see his mother in pain."

Keera nodded. "Don't tell Michael anything about the police file. Not yet. I think we both agree it would be premature, and it isn't everything the prosecution has or is working on."

The courthouse bustled with energy, people hurriedly walking and talking in the halls and the foyers. Attorneys in suits sat with clients on hallway benches speaking in hushed tones. Keera rode the elevator to Judge Patel's courtroom. The same *Seattle Times* reporter who had greeted Keera at the arraignment awaited her, as did a television crew. Seemed the case was picking up steam in the media.

Keera politely declined any comment and stepped inside, approaching the clerk sitting in the well talking with the court reporter and the courtroom bailiff. "Yes, Ms. Duggan. Judge Patel will be with you as soon as Ms. Tran arrives."

Keera looked at her watch. It was already after three o'clock. She wondered who was running this case, Tran or Patel. She took her seat at the defense table and continued to scroll through her laptop notes, wondering what, if anything, she could be missing. After several minutes, Tran, whose office was in the courthouse, entered the courtroom and advised the clerk of her presence. She then turned to Keera. They exchanged curt pleasantries.

"I trust you received the investigative file?"

"Just this morning," Keera said. She decided to poke the bear a bit, as her father would. "Not much in the way of direct evidence. I thought with you having taken this to a grand jury, the file would have more weight to it."

Tran smiled. "It had enough heft for the grand jury to come back with an indictment."

Now she fished. "I sense there is more out there. I did ask for all evidence."

Tran shrugged, unconcerned. "I sense we'll both keep working," she said without answering the question.

Judge Patel entered the courtroom, this time without fanfare or a proclamation from her bailiff. She climbed to the bench and said, "Ms. Duggan, Ms. Tran, let's get started."

Correctional officers brought in Michael dressed in his red King County jail scrubs. At trial he'd be in civilian clothing. As with his arraignment, Michael looked apprehensive. When he neared Keera noticed his right eye was discolored and nearly swollen shut.

"Are you all right?" she asked.

He nodded.

"Michael, what happened?"

"It's fine," he said in a tone that indicated it wasn't fine.

"Ms. Duggan?" Patel said.

Keera looked to the judge.

"Can we get started?"

"Yes, Your Honor."

Patel went through the charges and denied Keera's motion to have the burglary and theft charges dismissed. Ella had argued no evidence existed of a broken doorjamb or window, nor that Michael had stolen the packages from Lockett. Tran argued the packets being in Michael's possession constituted circumstantial evidence of a break-in and burglary, and the jury should decide what that meant, after hearing all the evidence.

"We'll let a jury make those decisions," Patel agreed. "Has there been any talk of a plea agreement?"

"No, Your Honor," Tran said.

"None," Keera said.

"Will there be any?" Patel asked.

"The PA's office will accept a plea of guilty," Tran said.

"The defense will accept a dismissal of all charges," Keera said.

"Then let's get down to business."

Patel went through other discovery issues. As a matter of procedure, and at Patsy's suggestion, Ella filed motions requesting all evidence that could exonerate Michael, known as *Brady* motions. "What about witness lists and statements?" Patel asked when prompted by Keera.

"The State continues to compile its list of potential witnesses and will provide a copy to the defense counsel at the appropriate time," Tran said.

"Your Honor, the State had sufficient witnesses and evidence to take this matter to a grand jury; surely the State can provide the witnesses' names to the defense."

"Ms. Tran? The defense has a point."

"The State hasn't decided which witnesses will testify at trial. We continue to speak with certain individuals about their testimony and their availability for trial. I would propose that both sides agree to identify witnesses expected to testify each afternoon before the next day of trial, as well as a summary of what the witness has to say."

"That sounds reasonable," Patel said. "Ms. Duggan?"

Keera sensed she wasn't going to get more out of Patel. "Agreed."

"What about physical evidence and scientific evidence?" Patel asked.

"SPD's investigative file has been turned over," Tran said. "The State is evaluating other material, redacting attorney notes, strategies, and impressions. What remains will also be turned over. And some experts continue to perform work and have not yet issued reports."

As Keera had suspected.

"Is there anything else to discuss before I set this matter for trial?" Patel asked.

Tran said there was not.

"I need a moment," Keera said. She sat beside Michael and lowered her voice. "If you're being abused, I can see about having you moved. Do you want me to try to get you moved someplace safe?"

Westbrook looked at her. "Moved where, Ms. Duggan? Back home?" He shook his head.

Keera stood. "Nothing further."

"Then we will set trial for a date in September. Please confer with the court clerk to find a mutually agreeable date to avoid conflicts. With that, we are adjourned."

◆ ◆ ◆

Following the hearing, Keera went quickly to the King County jail, meeting Michael in an attorney-client conference room. Michael walked in with the same hangdog look he'd had in court.

"Michael, what happened to your face?"

"I walked into a door."

"Michael—"

"What?" He raised his voice and looked angry. "What do you want me to say? What are you going to do? Where am I going to go? I'm here. I'm in jail. There's no place for me to go."

"If someone is hurting you, I can see that he's separated from you."

"For how long?" Michael said calmly. "Can you separate me from everyone? Everyone thinks I killed John and Melissa. They want to see how tough I am. JP told me to keep my head down, and I'm trying. He told me not to take their bait, and I'm trying not to. He said it would only make matters worse."

"What happened to your eye?"

Michael shook his head. "This is my reality, Ms. Duggan. Maybe for the rest of my life. This is what I have to look forward to. No holidays. No family. No life. Just me and a bunch of murderers, rapists, and drug dealers."

"Michael, you can't lose hope."

"Hope? Guys in here are telling me I have no hope. They say the prosecutor is going to chew us up and spit us out."

"I'm not going to let that happen, Michael."

"You told me up front you can't guarantee anything. You didn't even want to know if I was guilty or innocent. I'm just another client to you. I get it, Ms. Duggan. I understand."

"You're not just another client, Michael. You're JP's nephew."

Michael walked to the door.

"Are you thinking of taking your life, Michael?" It was a question she had to ask.

He knocked on the door to signal the guard.

"Michael? Are you thinking of taking your life?"

The door opened. Michael stepped out, then looked back. "That's the saddest part; isn't it? I don't even have a life worth taking."

The door shut behind him.

Keera hurried from the room and retrieved her phone from the storage locker, making a call to JP before she stepped outside the facility. She told him of Michael's black eye and everything Michael had said. "I'm worried he's going to do something, JP. I'm worried he's giving up, that he's thinking of taking his own life."

JP said, "Okay. Where are you now?"

"I'm just leaving the jail."

"I'm on my way. I know the guy who runs the jail. He and I attend the same church and he's a good guy. I'll make a call and get Michael put on twenty-four-hour watch and have him alert the guards to the abuse."

"What can they do about it?"

"I don't know. Let me call. I'll also ask about getting Michael treated for depression."

"What about Tina? Should we tell her?"

"She's already sick to death, Keera. I'm not going to add this to her list of worries. Stay there. Get me back in to see Michael. In the interim, I'll make those calls."

When JP arrived, Keera met him on the sidewalk outside the jail.

"Michael's going to be moved," JP said. "And he'll be put on twenty-four-hour watch and seen by the doctor. They also think they know the abuser, and he's being moved out to Monroe tomorrow morning."

"Is it enough?"

JP rubbed a hand over his face. "Let's hope it is," he said.

# Part III

# Chapter 20

On a clear September morning, Keera packed her legal binder and her laptop in her briefcase for the first day of trial. Everything to be admitted into evidence, including exhibits, would be projected from the laptop onto the court's computer system and screen. She removed her navy-blue blazer from the back of her chair and slipped it on. Then she took a deep breath and let it out in a burst. She'd awoken at 5:00 a.m. with nerves, more than normal for the first day of trial, and she hadn't been able to shake them. Was it because Anh Tran would be seated at the table beside her? Perhaps. Keera couldn't help but wonder what theatrics might come or what additional evidence the State might seek to introduce, and whether she'd be prepared.

Or were her nerves because, through her numerous meetings with Michael Westbrook over these past nine months, she had seen him for what he was, a truly scared young man? JP had managed to get Michael treated for his depression and his anxiety, and the guards had done a better job keeping him safe.

Was she afraid of letting down Michael?

JP?

Certainly.

The stress and strain had worn on Keera and those in the firm from whom she had enlisted help, most notably Ella. They had all spent long days and nights getting ready, doubling and redoubling their efforts to cross-examine the State's witnesses and to prepare their experts and their direct witnesses for when Keera put on the defense's case. Keera had lost eight pounds. JP, too, looked to have lost weight and, for the first time Keera could recall, he had developed bags under his eyes that had not gone away.

Pretrial motions had been civil, for the most part. Tran had been professional and razor sharp both in her arguments in her legal briefs and during her courtroom oral arguments. It had pushed Keera and Ella to be just as, if not more, prepared. They had been relatively satisfied with Judge Patel's rulings.

She was also pleased with the jury she had chosen. She'd used a jury consultant for the first time in her career, a man of color who helped her phrase her questions to encourage jurors to express any biases rather than give "socially desirable" answers. He told Keera she didn't necessarily want Black jurors but jurors who understood what it was like to be a person of color in the judicial system. Her goal was to pick jurors who could understand her argument that the State had rushed to charge Michael because he was Black, without her directly saying so.

Dictating against that argument would be Billy Ford, SPD's lead detective, and a Black man. Ford would sit at the State's counsel table beside Tran throughout the trial's duration.

The jury consultant had advised Keera to pick mothers, people who could empathize with Tina Westbrook, who Keera would seat prominently in the gallery's first row. Keera had told Tina to greet Michael at every opportunity.

JP had taken his sister shopping for off-the-rack suits, slacks, and sweaters for Michael. Keera cautioned against Michael wearing anything that looked expensive or tailored. She told JP she also didn't mind if the clothing was a bit too large, which would make Michael look smaller, a visual reminder, perhaps, that he was just a cog caught in the very large criminal justice wheel.

Keera had one more thing to do before walking to court to give her opening statement; something she did at the start of each of her trials.

She walked the hallway to the corner office, knocked twice, and opened Patsy's door. Her father waited for her at the chess table, the chess pieces hand carved from walnut and maple. A gift from an appreciative client. Playing chess had always helped Keera to relax and to focus on her strategy. It reminded her to trust her instincts. Her father had done much the same thing when he tried cases, and Keera had been told, more than once, that she was a chip off that block.

"How do you feel?" her father asked.

"Nervous."

"Nerves are good. It means you're focused."

"More than normal."

"There is no normal. Just remember, it's not about winning. That, you can't always control. It's about performing your best." She'd heard these words before. "This will be a marathon, not a sprint. Don't overreact to the good days or the bad days. Don't get too up or too down." She'd heard these words also.

She removed her blazer and sat across the table from Patsy. Her father always chose the dark chess pieces. His online chess name was the Dark Knight. Keera also played chess online and occasionally at the tables in Occidental Square when she needed fresh air to clear her head. Her online name was Seattle Pawnslayer.

Keera moved first. She advanced her pawn to e4.

"You feel good about the jury?" her father asked, moving his knight to a6.

"As good as one can feel, I suppose." She moved a second pawn forward to d4, to control the center of the board. It was impossible to keep every juror an attorney wanted or to excuse every juror she did not want, not with the opposing side fighting to do the same, and each side having a limited number of challenges. "The jury consultant is pleased."

Her father moved a pawn to d6. Patsy had never used a jury consultant. He chose jurors based on his gut, asking only if he could convince that juror. Given his track record, his gut had rarely been wrong. But this was a different time now.

Keera moved her knight to f3, starting her attack.

Her father moved his bishop to g4.

"I still think Tran is holding back," she said. "That she has something else, another piece of evidence or a witness." Keera moved her bishop to c4.

"Any idea who or what that could be?" Patsy moved a second pawn forward to e5.

Keera shook her head. She moved her pawn from d4 to e5 and took his pawn.

"You're on guard for it, though. And you're good on your feet, kiddo. What did I always teach you?" He moved his pawn and took her pawn at e5.

"Expect the unexpected and you won't be surprised."

"With Tran there is always the unexpected."

"That's what has me worried."

"I wish I could go into battle with you, kiddo. I'd like to watch, but . . ."

"But?" Keera said.

He smiled. "I know you'll make me proud, but sitting there, unable to do anything to help, would be too much like watching you in your chess tournaments all those years ago. I'd be more nervous than you. Besides, you don't need me."

"I'll always need you, Dad." She moved her queen all the way across the board to d8.

"Thanks, kiddo. But in the courtroom, you stand on your own two feet."

Her father slid his rook to d8 and took her queen.

Keera stared at the board. A feeling of panic and uncertainty built inside of her. How had she made such a fatal mistake?

Focus. She moved her knight to e5, taking Patsy's second pawn.

Patsy moved his rook to d1.

"Checkmate," Patsy said, sounding almost apologetic.

They had a deal. Neither would pull punches in their chess matches. Neither would let the other win; though Patsy had always found a way to let Keera win on the first day of each of her trials—to build her confidence.

Not this time.

She could be sure Tran would also not let her win.

# Chapter 21

Keera arrived in court early, part of what her father called his Muhammad Ali tactics. Her father, a great fan of the boxing legend, once told Keera that when Muhammad Ali fought George Foreman in Zaire, Foreman tried to intimidate Ali, a major underdog after Foreman had dismantled every other boxer in the heavyweight division. Foreman had made Ali wait in the ring before Foreman entered the arena. The move was intended to intimidate but had badly backfired. Ali, ever the showman, used the time to whip the crowd into such a frenzy that when Foreman finally entered the ring, the fans were loudly chanting in Lingala, "Ali, bomaye!"

"Ali, kill him!"

Patsy believed arriving early in court gave Keera time to become comfortable in the place where she would compete for the next few weeks. He told her to make friends with the judge's staff; that it would make Keera feel like she had allies. He taught her that trials, like boxing matches, had ebbs and flows. Her opponents would land some blows, maybe even knock her down. The goal was to win each day, but when victory wasn't possible on a given day, he taught her to cover up, absorb the blows, and survive to fight another round. The fight, Patsy said, could change with a single blow, but she had to be on her feet to deliver it.

Never give in.

Never back down.

Never concede defeat.

Twenty minutes after Keera arrived, JP walked in with Tina. Keera asked how she was holding up. Tina shrugged. Keera directed her to the first pew, within the jury's view. Harrison would also remain in the courtroom. Keera would not call him as a witness in this case.

Reporters and spectators filled the gallery. They wouldn't stay for the trial's duration, as some had for the Vince LaRussa and Jenna Bernstein trials. LaRussa and Bernstein had been celebrity defendants whose trials sold newspapers. Michael would, sadly, be considered just another person of color accused of a crime. The reporters would come for the opening statements and closing statements, and for the jury's verdict. They might come if there were fireworks, but they wouldn't stay for the mundane or the complex.

Try as she might, Keera couldn't think of a way to get those seated in the gallery to begin chanting "Keera, bomaye!"

Minutes before nine o'clock, the courtroom door swung open. Anh Tran entered, along with George Thomas, who carried a Bekins box. Billy Ford, Frank Rossi, and a woman Keera recognized to be a victim services specialist—a liaison to the deceased's relatives during the trial—directed more than half a dozen men and women to the first and second pews behind the State's counsel table. These were John Lockett's and Melissa Scott's families. Parents and siblings, relatives. They, too, were intended to make an impression, to remind the jury that Lockett and Scott would be missed. The men and women sat in the gallery looking sorrowful and anxious.

Keera would need to be careful. She'd have to get into evidence that John Lockett was a drug smuggler and establish it as a dangerous profession, but not go so far as to intimate his life somehow meant less.

Tran greeted Keera, but nothing more. The prosecutor looked all business this morning. She wore a tailored white jacket and skirt and navy-blue shirt. All that was missing from the "good guy" ensemble was a white cowboy hat. She wore little makeup and just small stud earrings for jewelry. No doubt she wanted to give the impression of an underpaid state employee seeking justice for the victims and for their families.

At precisely 9:00 a.m., the court bailiff stepped through the doorway behind the judge's bench and announced Judge Ima Patel's arrival. The courtroom dutifully stood as the judge entered and climbed steps to her bench. Keera could feel the energy that always emanated on the first day of a trial, as if an electric charge passed through those in the courtroom.

"Be seated," Patel said from atop her bench. "Counsel, are there any matters to discuss before we begin today?"

"No," Tran said.

"No," Keera agreed.

"The correctional officers will bring in the defendant."

Two correctional officers escorted Michael into the courtroom through a door to the far left. His hands were handcuffed to a belly chain at his waist. He wore a white shirt, blue tie, and gray slacks. Harrison had selected the perfect outfit. Michael looked like a young prep student, and his size was not nearly as imposing. When Michael reached his position beside Keera, the officers removed his handcuffs and belly chain. Tina leaned forward and kissed his cheek.

"Ms. Westbrook," Patel said, her voice calm and understanding, but also firm. "I have to instruct you not to have any physical contact with your son while he is in the courtroom. I'm sorry. I know it's hard. But defense counsel should have explained this is a security issue."

Keera had. Then told Tina to ignore the rule and to interact with Michael.

"I apologize, Your Honor," Tina said.

"The court understands he is your son," Patel said, then redirected her attention. "Now, Mr. Westbrook, do you understand that you are in King County Superior Court for criminal proceedings, namely the first-degree murder of John Lockett and the first-degree murder of Melissa Scott?"

"Yes, Your Honor."

"You have the right to be present throughout these proceedings, but it is not an absolute right. Should you do anything to disrupt these proceedings, this court has the authority to have you removed and to continue the trial in your absence. Do you understand?"

"Yes, Your Honor."

Judge Patel looked out over the partially filled gallery. "The court has the authority to have the court marshals remove anyone who is disruptive to these proceedings. I trust that will not be necessary. With that understanding, the bailiff will bring in the jury. Remain standing."

Keera leaned over to her client. "How do you feel?"

"Nervous," he said.

"Good. Let the jurors see your nerves. Look at them when they come in, but don't stare—and don't smile." She had given him these instructions in the King County jail.

Moments later, the jury filed in from a doorway at the back of the courtroom. A few jurors looked to Michael, whom Keera had introduced during jury selection. They moved to their designated chairs and picked up notepads and pens. For the next ten minutes, Patel welcomed the jurors and explained their vital role in the legal process, emphasizing their duty to act impartially in their evaluation of evidence, not to discuss the proceedings outside the courtroom, and to refrain from conducting any independent research and from reading newspaper articles or watching television accounts. When finished, she discussed the purpose of opening statements, cautioning that the attorneys' statements were not evidence but rather outlines of what each side expected to prove during the trial.

With those preliminaries completed, she turned to Anh Tran. "Ms. Tran, does the State wish to make an opening statement?"

Tran stood. "The State does, Your Honor."

They were underway.

Tran strode to the lectern without notes or a laptop. She gave the jury space and deference and thanked them for serving. "In voir dire, I told you this case is about the brutal, premeditated murders of John

Lockett and Melissa Scott in the early morning hours of December fourth of last year. The State will prove to you, beyond all reasonable doubt, that the defendant"—she pointed for emphasis—"Michael Westbrook, did, with malice and forethought, commit these crimes."

With that Tran introduced herself, George Thomas, and the members of Lockett's and Scott's families, many of whom were crying.

"Judge Patel has instructed you to keep an open mind and to consider all the evidence before rendering your verdict. The State welcomes your doing so. The State will provide you with physical and scientific evidence that will prove Mr. Westbrook had both the opportunity and the motive to kill John Lockett and Melissa Scott."

George Thomas put up a photograph on the court's computer screen, one Keera had approved in pretrial proceedings. Tran pointed out Lockett's home in relation to Tina Westbrook's home. She explained that Lockett and Westbrook worked together at Blue Horizon, and the duties each performed. "On the evening before the killings, the evidence will show that Mr. Westbrook took an Uber to work because his car would not start. The evidence will also show that Mr. Westbrook sought out Mr. Lockett at work for a ride home after their shift ended at 4:00 a.m."

George Thomas removed the neighborhood sketch from the computer screen and put up a picture of Lockett's garage, converted into his man cave. Keera had also agreed to the introduction of this photograph.

"The evidence will show that the defendant and Mr. Lockett and Ms. Scott were friendly, that the defendant was at Mr. Lockett's home on multiple occasions, shooting pool in his garage and watching sports on his television and performing chores for Ms. Scott. They shared beers and, on occasion, smoked a little weed."

She paused. "Now, I also must advise you the evidence will show that Mr. Lockett was importing drugs, hard drugs, and using his supervisory position at Blue Horizon to facilitate his smuggling operation. The evidence will show Mr. Lockett imported fentanyl, heroin, and other heavy narcotics, and that Mr. Westbrook was one of Mr. Lockett's distributors and that when arrested he had in his possession a Blue Horizon package containing fentanyl and another containing sixteen thousand dollars in cash."

Keera had wondered if Tran would make this argument. Now, it was out in the open. No evidence linked Michael to distributing the drugs but for the packages in his room. She thought it a lawyer's trick—Tran had to admit her victim was a drug smuggler and sought to soil Michael's reputation at the same time to soften that blow.

"The evidence will also prove that at roughly eight o'clock the following morning, less than four hours after Mr. Lockett arrived home, his neighbor, Alex Cortez, walked across the street to Mr. Lockett's detached garage. The two men had agreed to meet at that time to work on a 1951 Packard they had purchased together and were fixing up and intended to sell. It was Mr. Cortez who discovered the body of John Lockett on the garage floor and called 911. Experts will testify that Mr. Lockett and Ms. Scott were murdered between four thirty and seven thirty that morning. Experts will testify Mr. Lockett was shot in the head and Melissa Scott was bludgeoned to death. The medical examiner will also testify that both deaths were homicides.

"The Seattle Police Department dispatched Detectives Billy Ford and Frank Rossi from its Violent Crimes Section to the crime scene." Ford stood at the table, and Rossi in the gallery, as Tran introduced them. "You will hear more about the detectives' investigation of these crimes later during the State's case.

"The evidence will also show that through their investigation, Detectives Ford and Rossi secured warrants and searched the home where the defendant, Michael Westbrook, lived with his mother. Detective Ford will testify they searched the defendant's bedroom and found the two packages I previously described, and that when confronted, Michael Westbrook became violent and tried to flee."

Keera glanced at the jurors. Several scribbled on their notepads. A few made sporadic notes. Others glanced at Michael. But all listened intently.

Tran went on to detail the brutal murder of Melissa Scott. "She was not shot. You will hear testimony from the medical examiner that Ms. Scott was struck more than a dozen times with a heavy object."

Tran continued for another thirty minutes, discussing the State's charges, specifically the first-degree murder charges and what each meant. Then she paused and considered each juror. "The State is confident the evidence will convince each of you, beyond all reasonable doubt, that the defendant, Michael Westbrook, murdered John Lockett and murdered Melissa Scott. The State will ask you to render a guilty verdict to the charges of murder in the first degree as to both victims."

Tran thanked the jurors and returned to her seat.

Patel gave the jurors a short, ten-minute recess. After they had departed the courtroom, Michael Westbrook leaned over and whispered to Keera, "That stuff she said isn't true."

"As I told you, Michael, what she says and what she can prove are two separate things. Don't get worked up about everything the prosecutor or a witness has to say. Remember, this is going to be a long process."

"I don't know how much lying I can take," he said.

"Remain calm, especially with the jury present. Any display of anger will play into the prosecutor's hands."

"Okay," he said. "I'll try to meditate."

JP had hired a coach for Michael who had taught him meditation and self-hypnosis, techniques that had helped Michael get through the long and monotonous days in jail.

Patel returned to the bench and asked the bailiff to escort the jurors back into the courtroom. When they were all seated again, Patel said, "Ms. Duggan, does the defense wish to offer an opening statement at this time or defer?"

"The defense is eager to offer an opening statement, Your Honor."

Keera moved to the lectern. She, too, did not bring notes or her laptop. She greeted the jurors, introduced herself, and Michael and Tina Westbrook. Then she said, "As Judge Patel instructed, what the

State's attorney just told you is not evidence. It's what the State hopes the evidence will prove. Until then, it's just Ms. Tran's opinion.

"In our legal system, opinions are not facts. Now, about the process. You should know the State gets to put on its witnesses and its exhibits first. The State will, as counsel said, call witnesses to that stand." Keera pointed to the empty witness chair to the right of Patel's bench. "And she will ask those witnesses numerous questions. I will have a right to cross-examine these witnesses on behalf of my client. I will do so in some cases, but I might choose not to examine another witness. You should not read anything into my decision to cross-examine or not cross-examine a witness, nor should you conclude that my not questioning a witness means I agree with what he or she said. I will not be able to call a witness until after the State has completed its case. We," she said, turning to Michael, "ask you to be patient, and to withhold forming any opinions until after you have heard *all* the witnesses testify and have seen and considered *all* the evidence. Michael and I are confident, contrary to what the prosecutor intimated, that you will not find him guilty beyond all reasonable doubt. Michael and I are confident that after you have considered all the testimony and all the evidence, you will find him not guilty. Because he is not guilty."

Tran stood. "Objection, Your Honor. Improper opinion of counsel."

"Sustained. The jury will disregard defense counsel's opinion."

They could disregard it, but as Patsy had taught Keera, it was more important they heard her say it, with conviction.

# Chapter 22

After Keera had returned to her seat beside Michael Westbrook, Patel invited the State to call its first witness. Tran stood. According to the list of witnesses Tran had provided to Keera the previous afternoon, the State intended to start the trial with Billy Ford, the lead detective. Keera knew something was up at Tran's first utterance.

"Your Honor, with apologies to the court and defense counsel, the State must regrettably call a witness out of order this morning because of a scheduling conflict. To do so, the State respectfully requests, pursuant to the Supreme Court case *United States ex rel. Touhy v. Ragen*, that this court clear the courtroom."

Keera glanced over her shoulder at Harrison, who looked as stunned as Keera felt.

The night before, in the firm conference room, Keera and Harrison had discussed Keera's intent to call a DEA agent to open Michael's defense, establish the DEA's investigation, and intimate to the jurors that something nefarious had happened that had nothing to do with Michael Westbrook and everything to do with Lockett dealing drugs. Keera intended to then follow that witness with her experts who found unknown fingerprints inside Mr. Lockett's garage, and ultimately argue those fingerprints belonged to his enemies, which explained why Mr. Lockett gave Michael the two envelopes—to hide them from those individuals.

With these neat dominoes falling in succession, Keera felt she would be a long way toward reasonable doubt.

By calling a DEA agent to open the State's case, Tran clearly intended to undermine Keera's strategy. She would at least soften, but perhaps even eliminate, the blow Keera intended to deliver. This was the vintage Tran Patsy had warned her about—unpredictable and unafraid to skirt rules and ignore professional courtesy.

Keera stood. "Your Honor, pursuant to this court's order and counsel's agreement, the State submitted its list of the witnesses it intended to call today. Those are the witnesses the defense prepared to cross-examine. I am assuming from counsel's Touhy request that the proposed witness is not on that provided list. We haven't gone a single day without counsel ignoring a court order, not to mention professional courtesy. I was in my office at six o'clock this morning and in this courtroom well before 9:00 a.m. and never did counsel attempt to contact me to indicate this change in the order of witnesses."

"This conflict came to my attention early this morning." Tran sounded apologetic, though Keera wasn't buying that she had an ounce of remorse. This strategy was premeditated. "The State was equally surprised and unprepared for this development. But this witness is important to the State's case and therefore we have endeavored to oblige the witness's schedule by calling him out of order. Your Honor, may we approach the bench?"

Patel agreed and turned on white noise so their conversation at the bench would not be heard by the jurors. Patel leaned forward to look down at them. "Who is this witness?"

"Special Agent Jordan Parker, with the Drug Enforcement Agency," Tran said.

"And what is the purpose of calling Agent Parker?"

"To establish that John Lockett was working for a criminal enterprise importing drugs through Blue Horizon, and that the DEA was investigating that criminal enterprise, including Mr. Westbrook's potential involvement."

In other words, Tran would attempt to turn Keera's argument on its head before Keera ever had the chance to make it.

Patel turned to Keera. "Were you aware of the DEA's investigation?"

"I was aware of it, Your Honor. I did not expect to have to cross-examine an agent this morning. There is no agent identified anywhere on the State's witness list. Furthermore, the defense will stipulate that Mr. Lockett was working for a criminal enterprise, making this witness unnecessary."

"Did you anticipate calling the agent in your case in chief?" Patel asked, indicating to Keera that the judge would have little sympathy.

"I had not made a definitive decision, pending the State's presentation of *its* case in chief."

"Your Honor, this is trial," Tran said, now sounding condescending. "Calling witnesses out of order has happened in just about every one of my two hundred-plus jury trials. These things come up from time to time and can't be predicted. The State just learned that Agent Parker is leaving the country tomorrow and won't be back until the trial is concluded." In other words, the matter was not of her doing. "Ms. Duggan has acknowledged she knew of the DEA's investigation and even anticipated calling an agent in the defense's case. Therefore, I fail to see how my calling the agent out of order creates any prejudice."

"Out of order?" Keera said. "He isn't on the State's list of potential witnesses to be 'out of order.' This isn't the State accommodating a witness. It's an orchestrated sneak attack to open trial. If this has happened in each of the prosecutor's two hundred jury trials it only establishes a pattern of improper conduct."

"I resent—"

Patel quickly raised her hand and spoke through a clenched jaw. "Ms. Duggan, address your comments to the bench and do not engage in personal attacks. Not in my courtroom. Not like your father."

"And I resent that comment, Judge. My father is not trying this case. I am. Judge me. Not him." Her adrenaline had kicked in and just like that, her nerves were gone. Keera was now in fighting mode.

Patel paused. Then started what sounded like an apology before catching herself. "I . . ." She exhaled. "I agree with the State. The defense knew of the ongoing investigation. Therefore, I don't see the prejudice. Let's get moving. I want to limit these sidebars and not keep my jury waiting unnecessarily."

"I'd like a standing objection on the record to this witness being called out of order," Keera said, a veiled and unconvincing threat that it could be an appellate issue.

Patel issued her instructions to the bailiff to clear the courtroom of all spectators but for the defendant and the jury, the members of which now looked even more curious about who the State intended to call and what that witness would have to say.

Keera spoke to JP before he left the courtroom. "Get ahold of your contact at the DEA. See if you can find out anything."

"Already on it," he said, lifting his phone and stepping out the courtroom door.

"Call your first witness," Patel said after the room had been cleared.

Tran stood. "The State calls Agent Jordan Parker."

The bailiff exited the courtroom and returned with a tall, lean man who looked to be in his mid- to late forties. Keera and the jurors watched Parker stride toward the witness stand looking very much like a clean-cut federal agent, with gelled, short hair, a conservative blue suit, white shirt, and a paisley tie. He looked at ease taking the oath to tell the truth, unbuttoned his suit jacket, sat, and crossed his legs. Tran took him through half an hour of preliminary questions, including his years of service with the DEA.

"Now, Special Agent Parker, would you tell the jury what you told me in our conversation this morning?"

"I told you that if you wanted me to testify it would have to be this morning because I had just learned I would be leaving the country on special assignment and did not know my date of return."

Tran thanked him. "Would you tell the jury about the investigation you were leading concerning John Lockett?"

"I was the agent investigating John Lockett and a criminal enterprise for which we suspected he worked. Specifically, my investigation revealed John Lockett imported heavy narcotics from Southeast Asia through his employer, Blue Horizon." His answer sounded smooth and unrehearsed, though of course he'd been coached on his answer.

"Would you explain to the jurors the specific nature of your investigation?"

Parker went through the DEA's investigation, how it had tracked the shipments of narcotics, and how Lockett intercepted those packages upon their arrival. He told the jury the investigation of Lockett had been ongoing for eight months and what inroads the DEA had made into the criminal enterprise.

"Had you made any arrests?"

"Not at the time of the two murders, no."

"Why not?" Tran asked.

"Because we had not yet learned for whom Mr. Lockett was importing the drugs, and for us to stop the illegal flow of drugs into this country, it is important to learn who is running these organizations, and who has the money."

"You were looking for the head of the snake, so to speak?"

Keera looked up. Harrison said those were the words his DEA contact used, and Keera had intended to use them in her direct examination.

"If you don't cut off the head, the snake keeps operating," Parker said.

"Now, in your investigation, did you have any concern, or reason to believe that Mr. Lockett's life could be in danger because he was doing anything to upset those he worked for?"

"We had no such information that was the case, and therefore, no concerns."

"Were you concerned another criminal enterprise had knowledge of Mr. Lockett's criminal activities, and that Mr. Lockett's and Ms. Scott's lives could be in danger?"

"We had no such information and no such concerns."

Again, Tran had just attacked two of Keera's central arguments in her defense of Michael Westbrook. Keera briefly closed her eyes, her mind scrambling for any thought of how she could pivot when it was her time to do so.

"Were you investigating the defendant, Michael Westbrook, as someone also working for the criminal enterprise?"

"Mr. Westbrook was on our radar, yes."

"Will you explain why?"

"Mr. Westbrook worked with Mr. Lockett at Blue Horizon and spent time at Mr. Lockett's home after work hours."

"Had you reached any conclusions whether Mr. Westbrook was a part of this criminal enterprise?"

"We had not reached any conclusions."

"Was Mr. Lockett's home under surveillance?"

"Periodically. But because the home was in a residential neighborhood, we had to be careful not to be obvious, give ourselves away, and have Mr. Lockett contact those he worked for."

"Were you monitoring Mr. Lockett's text messages or emails?"

"Mr. Lockett, we believe, used burner cell phones to conduct his business, making it difficult to monitor his telephone calls and his text messages."

"Thank you, Special Agent. No further questions."

Tran returned to her seat and crossed her legs.

Judge Patel said, "Ms. Duggan?"

Keera had been scribbling furiously. She did not panic. She'd been in this position before, defending against an opponent's unexpected move, like Patsy's attack on her queen this morning. Maybe that had been a good thing. The key was not to rush, to take her time to examine the board and to consider each potential move, and which move would be the most effective. She also thrived on adversity, and she was determined not to let Tran's ploy succeed, to find a way to land some blows of her own.

She set down her pen and stood, notepad in hand. She had to be careful how she phrased her questions, making the jury conclude as she wanted them to conclude, regardless of the agent's answer.

"Did you suspect Mr. Lockett's neighbor, Alex Cortez, of being a member of this criminal enterprise?"

"He was another person of interest."

"Because he also spent time in Mr. Lockett's garage; correct?"

"Yes."

"And Mr. Lockett's relatives here in court today, his parents and his siblings, and his friends. They, too, were also potential suspects, correct?"

Parker paused. For the first time he did not look like the polished witness Tran had presented. "No."

"No?" Keera asked, deliberately sounding surprised. "But didn't they also spend time at Mr. Lockett's home?"

"I don't know. I assume they did."

"Anyone who spent time at Mr. Lockett's home or his garage was a suspect; wouldn't you agree?"

"Not necessarily."

"No? What distinguished them from someone like Michael?" she said gesturing to Michael.

"Mr. Westbrook also worked at Blue Horizon."

"So every employee who worked at Blue Horizon for Mr. Lockett was a suspect; right?"

"No. Because they didn't also spend time at Mr. Lockett's home."

"But you did suspect Mr. Cortez, and he didn't work at Blue Horizon; did he?"

"We did, and he did not."

"I assume you did not reach any conclusions as to Mr. Cortez either?"

"No, we had not."

"You were just spitballing; weren't you? You didn't have any evidence Mr. Westbrook or Mr. Cortez were part of any criminal enterprise; did you?"

"The investigation was ongoing."

"For eight months," Keera said with emphasis. "And after eight months of investigating Mr. Lockett and this criminal enterprise, you had no solid evidence that Michael worked for Lockett; did you?"

"As I said, he was a person of interest."

"Answer my question, Agent Parker. After an eight-month investigation you had no evidence Michael worked for or was distributing drugs for Mr. Scott; did you?"

"We did not."

"Was there anyone else who you suspected of being a member of this criminal enterprise that you were still investigating after eight months?"

"We had a list."

Keera raised her eyebrows for the jurors to see. "A list? How many names were on the list?"

"Perhaps a dozen."

"A *dozen* potential members of a criminal enterprise importing hard narcotics into this country who you were investigating; is that right?"

"Importing and distributing, yes."

"And did your extensive investigation reveal if a member on that list had any animosity toward Mr. Lockett?"

"We had no information Mr. Lockett was in any danger."

"That's not what I asked you, Agent Parker. Did you know if any person on your list held any animosity toward Mr. Lockett?"

"We did not."

"So one or more persons on that list could have had animosity toward Mr. Lockett. You just don't know; do you?"

"Objection." Tran stood. "Calls for speculation."

Keera welcomed the objection. "I'm not asking him to speculate. I'm asking this seasoned investigator who ran this extensive investigation if he'd learned of anyone who the DEA had identified as potentially having animosity toward Mr. Lockett."

"This is cross-examination," Patel said. "I'll allow the witness to answer."

"I do not know," Parker said.

"Then you had no information that Mr. Westbrook had a beef with Mr. Lockett; did you?"

"We did not."

"And you had no information that Mr. Lockett was in any danger from Mr. Westbrook either; did you?"

"No."

"I assume during your career at the DEA that you have investigated other criminal drug operations?"

"Several."

"Fair to say these are not 'upstanding citizens' running these organizations?"

"I would say they are not."

"They are engaged in criminal activity importing hard narcotics that are worth a lot of money; correct?"

"Correct."

"Narcotics worth in the millions of dollars in some instances?"

"In some instances."

"I would also assume, and I would suspect you would agree from your extensive experience, that the importing of drugs is an inherently dangerous business?"

"Any time you have drugs that can generate large sums of cash, it is inherently dangerous."

"And that danger could come from persons within the same organization, who might be upset should, say, a shipment go missing, or come up short; correct?"

Tran stood. "Objection, Your Honor. There is no evidence of what counsel is implying. Agent Parker has already testified he was unaware that Mr. Lockett or Ms. Scott were in any danger. Counsel is asking this witness to speculate."

"This is getting far afield from this agent's personal knowledge," Patel said to Keera.

Seeing the direction Patel was leaning, Keera responded in a manner to get across her intent. "Again, I'm asking this drug enforcement agent, who has years of experience investigating criminal drug enterprises, if, in his experience, these organizations are dangerous to the persons involved."

"And he's testified that he was not aware of any danger to Mr. Lockett or Ms. Scott," Tran said.

"The objection is sustained."

"Did your investigation reveal that Mr. Lockett was skimming product from this criminal organization and selling it on the side?"

Tran nearly jumped to her feet. "Objection, Your Honor. Speculation, again."

"Sustained."

"Your Honor," Keera said, seeing an opening and doing her best to sound innocent, "given the defense had no opportunity to prepare for this surprise witness, I would request some leniency to explore what this witness does and does not know."

Now it was Patel's turn to look chagrined. "I'll allow some leniency," she said.

Keera looked to Agent Parker, who said, "We had no information Mr. Lockett was skimming product."

"He could have been. You just don't know one way or the other."

"That is what 'we had no information' means," Parker said.

Keera had made her point. "I assume you learned of Mr. Lockett and Ms. Scott's murders at or around the time they occurred?"

"I did. I learned from local law enforcement."

"And upon learning of Mr. Lockett's and Ms. Scott's deaths, did you suspect they could have been killed by someone within the criminal enterprise, or by perhaps by a rival criminal enterprise?"

Tran again stood, like a kid on a pogo stick, which is what Keera intended. She wanted the jurors to think Tran was attempting to hide information. "Same objection. Counsel is ignoring the court's prior ruling."

"Your Honor, I'm asking this witness for his initial impression upon learning of the two murders."

"The objection is sustained. The jurors are to disregard counsel's speculative question."

They could disregard it, but they'd certainly heard Keera's implication. Under the circumstances, her cross-examination wasn't great, but it was also the best Keera was going to do.

# Chapter 23

Keera returned to counsel table battered but still on her feet and in the fight. Tran followed Agent Parker with the 911 emergency dispatcher. She played Alex Cortez's call in the courtroom. Cortez sounded duly upset on the phone.

Keera had not anticipated asking the dispatcher any questions but had a thought as Tran sat. She approached the dispatcher, who wore her SPD uniform. "Mr. Cortez told you he had gone into the garage; correct?"

"Yes," the dispatcher said.

"In the tape recording, he said that he 'quickly went in, saw the body, and hurried back outside.'"

"That's what he said."

"Presumably then, he only saw the body for just a very brief moment."

"I don't know."

"But in that 911 call Mr. Cortez did say Mr. Lockett had been 'shot'; correct?"

"That's correct."

"He didn't say Mr. Lockett was bleeding, that he'd been hit in the head, that he'd fallen and hit his head. He said he'd been 'shot.'"

"He said he'd been shot."

"Did he tell you how he knew Mr. Lockett had been shot, as opposed to suffering some other injury that caused him to bleed?"

"No. He just said he'd been shot."

"Did he tell you he had tried to alert Ms. Scott about Mr. Lockett's death?"

"No."

Keera looked puzzled. "He didn't say he ran to the front door and banged on it in an attempt to tell the woman living with Mr. Lockett that Mr. Lockett had been shot?"

"He didn't tell me that, no."

Keera scratched her head. She hoped she'd given the jurors something else to think about.

Following the dispatcher, Tran called Alex Cortez. Cortez appeared in black slacks, tennis shoes, and a colorful blue-collared shirt. He looked and sounded nervous, but Keera also sensed he enjoyed being the center of attention. At Tran's prompting, Cortez spoke of spending time with Lockett, and about how they had purchased, fixed up, and sold several vintage cars. He discussed that he and Lockett had agreed to meet at eight in the morning, how he had walked to the garage, heard music playing, and what he saw.

"You told the 911 dispatcher that Mr. Lockett had been shot. Did you know he had been shot?" Tran asked, giving Cortez a chance to explain before Keera could cross-examine him and intimate to the jury that Cortez had been the shooter.

"I didn't know for certain. I mean, I saw him on the ground and blood all over and the back of his head . . ." He paused to catch his breath. "Man, it was rough."

"Take your time, Mr. Cortez."

"I just assumed John had been shot."

"Did you try to tell Ms. Scott what you saw in the garage?"

"No. I was pretty upset; you know? I just ran home and told Theresa what I'd seen, and she told me to call 911. So that's what I did."

After establishing the basics, Tran said, "How often did you go over to Mr. Lockett's home to shoot pool and watch sports on his television?"

Cortez's brow wrinkled. "I don't know. Just every so often. It was a nice place to hang out if, like, my old lady was trying to put me to work." He smiled and several jurors smiled with him.

"Did you ever see the defendant, Michael Westbrook, at Mr. Lockett's house?"

"You mean his garage?"

"Yes, his garage."

"Oh yeah. Mike was over there a number of times when I was there. I don't know how many, but I seen him maybe, like, five times."

"What did you observe Mr. Westbrook doing at Mr. Lockett's garage?"

"He was just hanging out. He said he lived a couple miles away, and he and John worked together so . . . They were friendly, I guess."

"Were they friends?"

Cortez smiled. "See, that's what the police were asking me, but I don't really know how to answer that; you know? I mean, Mike is a lot younger than me and John, so I didn't know the reason for the two of them hanging out together. Mike was just there."

Tran was intimating that Westbrook had an alternative reason for being there, a business reason.

"Did you ever ask Mr. Lockett or Mr. Westbrook that question? Why Mr. Westbrook was there?"

"Nah. I figured it wasn't any of my business, and Mike wasn't hurting nothing, you know? He was all right." Cortez made eye contact with Michael and nodded.

"Were you aware Mr. Lockett was smuggling drugs through his employer, Blue Horizon?"

Cortez emphatically shook his head. "I didn't know nothing about that; no."

"Did you ever see any drugs at Mr. Lockett's house?"

"Weed, but that's legal now so . . ." He shrugged.

"Did you see Mr. Westbrook smoke any weed at Mr. Lockett's house?"

"Yeah, one time. No big deal. Mike was over twenty-one. Old enough to make his own decisions."

Tran turned to Keera. "Your witness."

Keera approached. "Mr. Cortez, you never witnessed Michael Westbrook and Mr. Lockett argue; did you?"

"Argue? Nah. They seemed to get along all right. They'd fu—" He caught himself, looking embarrassed. "Sorry. They'd mess around with each other sometimes about something on the television, or if they were shooting pool, but that was just in fun."

"Ribbing each other?"

"Yeah."

"They seemed friendly to you?"

"Yeah. Sure."

"No disputes or arguments you ever witnessed; right?"

"I didn't see any."

Keera also knew Tran had no direct evidence Michael knew the contents of the packages when he had agreed to hold them for Lockett. Her next line of questioning was intended to undermine Tran's implication he had known. "You said you didn't know John Lockett was smuggling drugs and distributing them; correct?"

Another deliberate headshake. "I didn't know nothing about any of that."

"You lived across the street and were over at the garage frequently to work on cars and play pool and watch games; right?"

"Yeah. That's right."

"You and Mr. Lockett were even in business together—selling the cars you fixed up; right?"

"That's right."

"And Mr. Lockett kept his drug smuggling hidden even from you; right?"

"I guess so."

"You never saw any suspicious cars pulling up to the garage; did you?"

"No."

"You never saw people on foot going into or leaving the garage who you didn't recognize from your neighborhood; did you?"

"I didn't notice. Wouldn't have been none of my business anyway who John chose to hang out with."

"Would you say John hid the fact that he was a drug smuggler well?"

"I guess he did. I didn't know, so . . ."

"And Michael never said anything to you about John maybe doing something illegal; did he?"

"Michael? No. Not to me."

"As far as you knew, Michael also didn't know John was smuggling drugs; right?"

"He never said nothing to me about it."

"Do you own a gun, Mr. Cortez?"

Cortez didn't immediately answer. His eyebrows furrowed. Keera had caught him off guard, as intended. "Why are you asking me that?"

"Just answer the question, Mr. Cortez," Judge Patel said.

He turned to the judge. "Why is she asking me that?"

"That isn't something the attorneys have to tell you or me. Please answer the question."

His look hardened. "Yeah, I own a gun."

"A 9-millimeter handgun?" Harrison had found Cortez's permit on file with the Department of Licensing.

"Yeah," he said, starting to sound defiant, which is what Keera wanted.

"Is that for protection? Competitive shooting?"

"I'd say protection."

"Did John Lockett also own a handgun?"

"Yeah, he owned a few guns."

"Also for protection? If you know."

"I assume. I don't know."

"You never talked about going target shooting with Mr. Lockett; did you?"

"No."

"Did the police who came to talk to you after you called 911 ask you if you owned a gun?"

"Are you saying I killed John?" Cortez squinted hard at Keera, as if he had a headache. He turned to Patel. "Is she saying I killed John?"

"Again, just answer the question, Mr. Cortez," Patel said.

Cortez shook his head. "Not that first time they came to talk to me. But they came back and asked me."

"How long after the killings did the police come back and ask?"

"Couple days, I think. Maybe the next day."

"And did you turn over your gun to the police?"

"Yeah, because I didn't kill nobody with it."

"When the police came that morning and took your gun, they didn't ask for your clothing; did they?"

"What?" Cortez looked visibly upset. "No. Why would they?"

"They didn't test your hands for gunpowder residue either; did they?"

"No."

"And the police never searched your home pursuant to a search warrant; did they?"

"What? What the fuck are you saying?"

Keera stood resolute.

Patel said, "Mr. Cortez, just answer the attorney's questions, and refrain from the use of profanity in my courtroom."

Cortez shook his head like a chastened young man. "No. The police never searched my home."

"Thank you, Mr. Cortez."

The police had found a bloody footprint in the garage that belonged to Cortez. It was further ammunition for Keera to argue the police, or the PA's office, had rushed the investigation, that they hadn't considered Cortez.

Following a brief redirect to rehabilitate Cortez, Tran called his girlfriend, Theresa Espinoza. Espinoza entered the courtroom in blue stretch pants, a white shirt, and sandals. She looked like she was chaperoning a school trip, and she did not sound the least bit anxious.

Tran established where Espinoza lived and her relationship with Cortez, then asked, "Were you friends with Melissa Scott?"

"Not really. We'd say 'hi' and stuff if we saw one another, but we didn't hang out or anything. Not like Alex and John hung out."

"Do you work?"

"Yeah, I work at the local Walmart."

"Do you work during the day?"

"Yes. My schedule floats, so I might be off Sunday and Monday one week or Monday and Tuesday. Like that."

"Did Melissa Scott work?"

"She did, but I didn't know what she did."

"She worked outside the home?"

"I think she worked from her house. She told me that one time. Said she worked from her house and was on a lot of Zoom calls, but I don't really know the details."

"Why did you think she worked from her house?"

"Because I'd see her at home when I was home during the week. She'd maybe be out sitting in a chair working on her laptop or doing stuff around the yard, and I'd say, 'hey.'"

"Did you ever see Michael Westbrook over at the house during the day when Melissa Scott was home?"

"Yeah, I saw him a couple of times."

"What was Michael Westbrook doing on the times that you saw him?"

"One time he was doing yard work, cutting down tree limbs and mowing the lawn. Another time I saw him on a ladder cleaning out the gutters."

Michael had told Keera about the few times he'd performed yard work and other chores at Lockett's home to make spending money.

"Did you ever see him with Melissa Scott?"

"No. Not really."

"Do you know if John Lockett was home on those occasions when you saw Michael Westbrook at his house during the day?"

"One time, I didn't think so, because I didn't see John's SUV in the driveway. But I don't really know."

"No further questions."

Keera approached the lectern. "Ms. Espinoza, was Michael being paid to perform jobs at the Lockett house?"

"I assume he was. I mean, I don't think he was working for free."

"Didn't you ask him if he'd perform some yard work at your house?"

"That was one time when I wanted to remove a couple of stumps from the backyard and needed someone with a pickax and a shovel to dig out the roots."

"Did you hire Michael?"

"No. Alex didn't want to spend the money. He said the stumps weren't hurting anything."

"No further questions," Keera said.

Patel looked at the clock. It was too late to call another witness. After a few housekeeping matters she recessed for the day.

In the hall outside the courtroom, Keera spoke to Harrison when his sister went to use the restroom. "You speak to your contact at the DEA?"

"He didn't know anything about Agent Parker testifying this morning."

Keera took a deep breath. While she'd thought it an odd coincidence, maybe she just wasn't giving Tran enough credit. Tran certainly would have determined if any federal agencies were investigating John Lockett. She'd likely anticipated Keera's arguments. Making the first move, as in chess, it was always the goal to control the center of the board. Tran had certainly done that.

Keera had to let it go. She needed to prepare for Billy Ford, who was the first witness on the State's list for tomorrow morning.

Unless that also changed.

She walked down the hill to her office. The summer sun remained high and reflected brightly on Elliott Bay, millions of diamond crystals. Traffic backed up on the city streets, commuters in cars waiting in lines to get on the I-5 freeway, others walking briskly, chattering. Keera remembered the days when Seattle had little to no traffic and no smog, back before the crowds found it. The wind had picked up, and Keera heard a low howl echoing through the buildings, mixing with the car engines, an occasional honk, and the roar of buses stopping and starting.

Keera cut down the alley leading to South Washington Street. She looked across the parking lot to Occidental Square and its London plane trees, so pretty with their full leaves. She watched a woman exit her father's three-story building. Maggie. Keera rechecked her watch. Ordinarily, Maggie rushed to the elevator as soon as the clock struck five. For her to remain past five was unusual. Ella could have asked her to stay late, but Ella avoided that when she could.

It was too far for Keera to call out, and Maggie had turned away from her. A dark-haired man stepped out the door behind her. They joined hands and walked across Occidental Square, away from Keera.

Ah, the infamous new boyfriend—the one whom Maggie had mentioned months ago at the family dinner. Must have come to pick Maggie up for a date. Keera would know soon enough. She was always eager to let everyone know she had a boyfriend and where they went and what they did.

Keera didn't have that luxury. More and more, she was becoming her father, and law her jealous master. And tonight would be another late night at the office.

# Chapter 24

The following morning, Billy Ford cut quite a figure in a dark-blue suit. At six foot eight with a lean build, he looked like a professional athlete, but Keera knew Ford was anything but athletic. As Ford acknowledged, he couldn't put a basketball through a hoop if he was sitting on it. Ford's talents lay in music, at which he was more than adept. He played multiple instruments—piano, guitar, saxophone, clarinet, and others—and he could play almost any song if he heard just the first few notes. Ford also had a talent for summing up people in a word or two, and he was usually spot-on. He'd once called Keera a "prodigy." Keera's word for Ford was "virtuoso."

From atop the elevated witness stand, Ford towered over the jury like a redwood, giving him an air of authority. Keera would have to somehow chop him down during her cross-examination.

Tran ran Ford through the preliminaries, allowing him time to settle in and get comfortable, and for the jury to get comfortable with him. In his baritone voice, Ford discussed his years working as a detective in SPD's various units, most recently in the Violent Crimes Section. He talked about the two years he worked a CSI rotation and his familiarity with the various forensic fields, and he discussed his years in the Violent Crimes Section.

"When you arrived at the crime scene, what was your understanding?" Tran asked, making the rehearsed question sound off the cuff.

"I have no understanding when I arrive at a crime scene," Ford said. "That's by design. I go into each investigation with an open mind and let the evidence dictate my understanding."

A good answer that also did not sound rehearsed. It was.

Tran put a diagram of Lockett's garage on the courtroom computers created by the CSI team using the total station surveying equipment, which re-created the crime scene to scale. She then walked Ford through each stage of his investigation, from sending in a videographer and photographer to sealing closed both the garage and the home.

Tran did not try to protect the jury from the violence Ford, Rossi, and the CSI team encountered in the garage and in the bedroom that morning. Keera had made pretrial objections to gruesome photographs Tran sought to introduce, arguing they were more prejudicial than probative, but Patel had her mind made up. She ruled, in essence, "It is what it is." She wouldn't sugarcoat the crime scene for the jurors.

Ford was on the stand for almost four hours, including an hour after the lunch break. It was midafternoon when Tran sat. Keera took her time walking to the lectern, hearing the coughs and movement of those seated in the gallery behind her. She wouldn't approach Ford except to hand him exhibits, maintaining a respectable decorum. She enjoyed cross-examining detectives like Ford and Rossi because she knew she would get straight answers to her questions.

"Detective Ford, you spoke to the neighbor, Alex Cortez, at some length the morning that he discovered the bodies; correct?"

"That's correct."

"But you didn't ask him whether he owned a handgun that morning; did you?"

"I didn't ask him during that initial conversation; no."

"You were here in court when Mr. Cortez said he owned a 9-millimeter handgun; were you not?"

"I was here."

"So, you don't know if that handgun had been recently fired on the morning that you arrived at the crime scene; do you?"

"I do not. We did, subsequently, take the handgun."

"How long after the murders did you do that?"

"It was several days."

"You didn't check Mr. Cortez to determine if he had any gun residue on his clothing or his hands the morning he called 911; did you?"

"No."

"You testified on direct that you had CSI's firearms and toolmarks division check to determine if the gun had been recently fired."

"I did."

"But that was several days after John Lockett was shot, correct?"

"That's correct."

"In which time the gun owner could have cleaned his gun; correct?"

"Objection, speculation," Tran said.

"Sustained."

"Did you ask Mr. Cortez whether he cleaned the gun?" Keera asked.

"He said he didn't."

"You didn't ask the National Integrated Ballistic Information Network to shoot Mr. Cortez's weapon and determine if the bullet shot matched the bullet that killed John Lockett; did you?"

"That was not possible."

Keera feigned ignorance, though Tran had broached the subject on direct. "No? Why is that?"

"The bullet that was recovered from Mr. Lockett's skull was too damaged for forensic examination."

"I see. I believe you said during your direct examination that the bullet was a hollow-point bullet."

"Yes."

"And you said hollow-point bullets tend to fragment upon impact; do they not?"

"They can, yes."

"Did you ask Mr. Cortez if he owned any hollow-point bullets?"

"He said he did not."

"This was when you confiscated the gun several days after the shooting?"

"Yes."

"Again, Mr. Cortez would have had time to dispose of any hollow points if he had owned any, correct?"

Tran again objected the question was speculative, but this time Patel overruled her.

"He could have. Again, he said he never owned any," Ford said.

"Because the hollow point fragmented upon impact with the body, you could not determine if that bullet came from *any* particular gun; could you?"

"We could not."

"Mr. Cortez was the first person on the crime scene; was he not?"

"Other than the killer," Ford said. Touché.

"Mr. Cortez left a bloody shoe print on the garage floor; didn't he?"

"He did."

"You confiscated his shoes and had the soles examined to confirm his shoe left the bloody shoe print you discovered in the garage; right?"

"That's right."

"How far from the decedent's body did you locate that bloody shoe print?"

"It was five feet ten inches."

The medical examiner and blood spatter expert would testify that Lockett had been shot at close range, within six feet. Keera could now argue Alex Cortez, arms extended with gun in hand, got within that range.

"When you spoke to Mr. Cortez, did he have any blood on his clothes?"

"He did not appear to have any blood on his clothing."

"You discussed forensic serology examination of clothing on direct examination. Will you explain it to the jury?"

"It is a process of analyzing the clothing microscopically for blood and other bodily fluids that might have come from the decedent."

"You never asked Mr. Cortez for the clothes he wore when he went to Mr. Lockett's home, so you didn't have them inspected microscopically for blood or any other bodily fluids; did you?"

"We did not."

"You never searched Mr. Cortez's home to determine if he had bloody clothes anywhere in the house; did you?"

"We did not."

"You don't know if he changed his clothes from when he went to Mr. Lockett's garage the morning he called 911 and when he spoke with you that morning; do you?"

"I don't know."

"You didn't have your CSI team investigate Alex Cortez's sinks and showers for blood in the traps; did you?"

"No."

"You don't know if he had a stack of envelopes from Blue Horizon in his house when you spoke to him that morning; do you?"

"I don't know."

"You testified you've never found the 9-millimeter handgun that fired the bullet that killed John Lockett; correct?"

"We have not."

"Mr. Cortez told you he went to Mr. Lockett's home at eight in the morning after Mr. Lockett had worked until 4:00 a.m.; didn't he?"

"That's what he said."

"Did that seem odd to you, Detective?"

"Mr. Cortez said Mr. Lockett did not require a lot of sleep."

"You and your partner, Detective Frank Rossi, initially believed the weapon used to kill John Lockett was a revolver because you did not find a shell casing in the garage; didn't you?"

"It was a working hypothesis."

"I assume another working hypothesis was the killer had picked up the shell casing after the gun ejected it; right?"

"That's correct."

"In your experience as a homicide detective, for a killer to pick up the shell casing would indicate some degree of sophistication by the killer; wouldn't it?"

"I don't know what's sophisticated anymore. With all the police and CSI shows on television educating criminals on how we process crime scenes and collect evidence, it's making our job more difficult."

"So, you're saying it's possible someone without a violent criminal history could have walked into the garage, shot Mr. Lockett in the head, then, in the heat of this horrific moment, stopped and said to himself, 'I better pick up the shell casing because the police could use it to match the shell casing to the gun that fired it'? Is that what you're saying?"

"I'm saying it's possible."

"The fact that you didn't find a shell casing could also indicate the killer was a professional and this was a professional hit; couldn't it?"

"What do you mean by 'professional hit'?"

Keera was prepared and almost thanked Ford. "Someone paid by, or who works for another, and is told to kill someone, and the killing is characterized by methodical planning, discretion, and efficiency to avoid detection."

"It could be possible."

"No one saw anyone enter or leave the garage before the shooting; did they?"

"Not that we discovered."

"No one even claimed to have heard the gunshot; did they?"

"No one did."

"No one spotted a car parked near Lockett's home at the time of the murders; did they?"

"No."

"And you didn't find a shell casing. Would you consider that methodical planning by the killer?"

"It could be methodical planning, and it could be sheer dumb luck."

"You testified the house 'looked ransacked' to you." Keera put up a picture taken inside the home showing opened cabinets and closets, cushions pulled from furniture and strewn on the floor, a coffee table and end tables turned over. "You testified that it looked to you like someone was searching for something inside the home?"

"It did look that way."

"You and your partner, Frank Rossi, interviewed my client at his home; didn't you?"

"We did after we learned from Blue Horizon employees that Mr. Lockett gave Mr. Westbrook a ride home that morning."

"My client confirmed Mr. Lockett gave him a ride home from work; didn't he?"

"He did."

"He told you his car had broken down and wouldn't start; didn't he?"

"He did."

"You also impounded that car and subsequently determined the starter had gone out and the car wouldn't start; didn't you?"

"We did, and yes, that's what we learned."

"So my client was also honest when he told you his car wouldn't start?"

"He was."

"You obtained Michael's emails and text messages; didn't you?"

"Yes."

"And you confirmed that he took an Uber to work that evening; didn't you?"

"Yes."

"So again, he was honest."

"About taking an Uber to work; yes."

"You didn't find any emails or text messages between Mr. Lockett and Michael on Michael's telephone; did you?"

"No."

"You didn't find any emails or text messages on Michael's cell phone concerning his distributing drugs for Mr. Lockett; did you?"

"No. But he could have used a burner phone."

"Did you find any evidence that Michael had purchased a burner phone?"

"No, but the phone could have been given to him."

"Did you find a burner phone when you did a thorough search of Michael's home and bedroom?"

"No."

"When you went to my client's home, you did so armed with a search warrant; correct?"

"Your client was the last person we could document as having been with the deceased that morning, so yes, we had a search warrant."

"Did you find a revolver?"

"No."

"Did you find a handgun of any kind?"

"No."

"Did you find any hollow-point bullets?"

"No."

"Did you find any bullets of any kind?"

"No."

"Did your investigation include paper trails that my client purchased a gun from somewhere?"

"We did not locate any paperwork that he purchased a handgun."

"I'm sure you also checked all the other ways a person can get a handgun without a permit, like eBay, or Craigslist, Etsy, OfferUp, Facebook, or Marketplace."

"We did and no, we didn't find evidence that he had done so."

"And you didn't find any evidence he'd ever purchased or obtained bullets?"

"Same answer. We did not."

"When you arrived at my client's home with a search warrant you found the two envelopes in Michael's room, correct?"

"That's correct."

"The two envelopes were sealed shut; weren't they?"

"They were both sealed."

"When you asked for permission to open the envelopes what did my client tell you?"

"He said the packages didn't belong to him and therefore he could not give consent."

"Did he say who owned the packages?"

"He said they belonged to Mr. Lockett, and that Mr. Lockett asked the defendant to hold on to them."

"Did my client say why Mr. Lockett wanted him to hold the packages?"

"He said Mr. Lockett asked him to hold them because they contained birthday presents for his girlfriend, Melissa Scott, and Mr. Lockett didn't want her to find them."

"Did he tell you he didn't know the contents of the packages?"

"He did say that."

"Reasonable answer given that the envelopes were sealed; isn't it?"

"You're assuming Mr. Lockett did in fact give your client the packages. We didn't make that assumption. We assumed your client took them."

"Without first checking if anything in the envelopes was worth taking?"

"He could have been the person to seal the envelopes, to support his position that Mr. Lockett asked him to hold them."

It was another good answer. This wasn't Ford's first rodeo.

Nor was it Keera's. "In your working hypothesis, did you stop to consider that Mr. Lockett gave Michael Westbrook the two envelopes because he suspected someone was going to come looking for them and ransack his house?"

"We thought it more likely the killer ransacked the house and garage and took the packages."

"You testified on direct that during the execution of your search warrant my client became violent and attacked the police officer watching him and tried to flee."

"He did."

"Did you ask anyone whether Michael could have had a panic attack given the circumstances?"

"I didn't, no."

Keera would put on Michael's doctor to discuss panic attacks.

"During the scope of your investigation you spoke to people who worked with my client and with John Lockett. Did any of them tell you they'd ever seen the two men argue?"

"No."

"Disagree?"

"No."

"Did Mr. Cortez tell you he'd ever witnessed them argue or disagree?"

"No."

"How close is John Lockett's home to Tina Westbrook's home?"

"Roughly two-point-two miles, correct?" Ford said.

"And you speculated that after Mr. Lockett gave my client a ride home, Michael then ran from his house to Mr. Lockett's garage. Shot him. Picked up the shell casing. Went inside and killed Melissa Scott, ransacked the house, stole drugs and money, sealed them in envelopes, then ran back to his house with blood on his clothes and carrying the gun and the envelopes?"

"Yes."

"On direct examination you testified you found blood spatter inside the garage and inside the bedroom. And you testified that the blood spatter in the garage extended as much as six feet from where the decedent died?"

"Correct."

"And three to four feet from Melissa Scott's body in the bedroom?"

"That's correct."

"The blood spatter expert concluded from the droplets' shapes and sizes that the killer shot Mr. Lockett within six feet; did he not?"

"That was his conclusion."

"You testified on direct that you confiscated my client's work uniform, which you found on the floor of his bedroom, along with his work boots; didn't you?"

"We did."

"And you had his clothing microscopically tested, but those tests did not reveal any blood spatter or other bodily fluids on his clothing; did they?"

"They did not."

"Similarly, you did not detect any blood spatter on his shoes; did you?"

"No. We did not. But he could have discarded the clothes and shoes he'd been wearing."

"Hmm. Could have . . . So, you don't know."

"Not for certain."

"And his car wasn't working—we've established that; haven't we?"

"It was not."

"You did a thorough search around the house for bloody clothes, a burner phone, and a handgun; didn't you?"

"We did."

"And didn't find them anywhere; did you?"

"We did not, but it was garbage day in that neighborhood. He could have discarded the articles of clothing in various garbage cans, which were then taken to the landfill. The gun as well."

"And run home in his underwear? Or naked? Carrying a gun and two packages?"

"He could have discarded them after he got home."

"But you found his work clothes, his only pair of work clothes, on the floor of his bedroom."

"He could have changed when he got home, killed Lockett and Scott, then discarded those clothes."

"Did you check the landfill for bloody clothes, a cell phone, and a 9-millimeter handgun?"

"We did have the landfill checked."

"Didn't find anything; did you?"

"We didn't find anything."

"Detective, let me ask, as an experienced Violent Crimes detective, would it make any sense for a suspect to meticulously pick up the shell casing at the murder site, meticulously dispose of the gun, meticulously dispose of the burner phone, and meticulously dispose of the bloody clothing, but leave the two packages containing fentanyl and a large amount of cash in the open on his bedroom floor?"

Ford paused. "I'd say it was unusual, but I'd also say, he wasn't going to dispose of the fentanyl, which he could sell for cash, or the sixteen thousand dollars."

"Detective, an experienced Violent Crimes detective such as yourself will sometimes recommend to the prosecutor whether a particular individual should be prosecuted for a particular crime; won't you?"

"My job is to gather evidence, interview witnesses, and assess the strength of the case. The decision to prosecute rests with the prosecuting attorney."

"But you do on occasion offer your opinion on the strength of a particular charge, such as a charge of murder in the first degree; don't you?"

"If asked."

"Were you asked in this case?"

"No," he said. "I was not."

Keera gave him an inquisitive look. "Interesting."

# Chapter 25

At day's end, Keera went for a long run. Harrison drove Tina home, then met Keera back in the conference room. Keera had showered and changed into sweatpants and a sweatshirt, but she had trouble cooling down. She'd pushed herself harder and run farther than usual, along the piers, past the sculpture park, to the grain silos and back. Running helped her relieve stress, got her endorphins pumping, and freed her mind. It also triggered her appetite. She was starving.

She entered the conference room using napkins to wipe persistent perspiration from her forehead and temples. Maggie had ordered Greek food for the trial team's dinner.

"How's Tina holding up?" Keera asked JP as she opened a Styrofoam box and cut a chicken gyro in half. The other half of her plate she filled with Greek salad. The aromas of garlic, onions, olive oil, and lemon made her mouth water.

"Like a paper rose in a rainstorm," Harrison said, picking at his salad with a plastic fork. "Your cross today of Ford was excellent, by the way. As good as your father's in his day."

"I'm pleased with it." She lifted the gyro to her mouth, then, reading the expression on Harrison's face, lowered it. "You don't look pleased."

"I'm just waiting for the next shoe to drop."

"Meaning?"

"There has to have been something else, Keera. Something more that convinced Billy and Frank to go forward."

"Such as?" She took a bite. The onions and tzatziki sauce tasted heavenly.

"I don't know. That's what makes me nervous."

"Patsy said Tran relies on circumstantial evidence and uses argument to fit all the pieces together." She talked and chewed at the same time, using a napkin to be discreet. "That could be what she hopes to do here."

"You think she can?"

"Let's just say I'm also remaining on guard. Okay." She put her sandwich down. "We have another long night ahead of us. Tomorrow Tran is putting on her forensic experts: ballistics, DNA, fingerprint, blood spatter, and toxicologist. So we have work to do." She pushed the Styrofoam with half the gyro across the table. "Eat."

Frank Rossi leaned back in his chair as Billy Ford entered their bull pen, his tie undone and his collar unbuttoned. Rossi had not been in court today, having other matters to attend to, and it took a moment for his eyes to adjust after staring at the computer screen all afternoon. "You look sufficiently beaten up," he said to Ford, then smiled. He knew Keera had crossed Ford this afternoon, and Rossi had been in that ring before.

"I *feel* sufficiently beaten up." Ford rotated the chair at his desk and fell into it, facing Rossi, his legs outstretched, his body slumped against the backrest. Overhead, the flat-screen televisions played news station chatter. In a cubicle close by, someone had ordered Indian food. Rossi could smell the curry.

"Are you back on the stand tomorrow?" Rossi asked.

"Tran hasn't decided if she wants to ask me anything else after Keera's cross-examination. We just spent an hour discussing it and prepping our experts for tomorrow."

"How did your testimony go?"

Ford gave a small shrug. "It went."

"And Keera's cross?"

"What you'd expect from the Irish Brawler's daughter. She scored some points; that's for damn sure. Didn't miss what you and I have been talking about—no gun, no blood-spattered clothing, no known motive, no other suspects. She finds a small gap in the evidence and runs a truck of reasonable doubt through it."

"Just like her father used to."

"She thinks we rushed to judgment." Ford waited a beat, then said, "Did we, Frank?"

"Wasn't really our call, Billy. Tran wanted to move forward, and she believed she had enough to convict. That's her call. More times than not, she's been able to swing a guilty verdict. I wouldn't bet against her in this case either."

Billy didn't answer right away, staring down at the carpet between his knees.

"Something else?" Rossi asked.

"I'm just wondering . . ."

"About?"

Ford looked up, made eye contact. He sounded almost apologetic. "She doesn't seem to know what's coming. Keera, I mean."

Rossi sat back, not sure how he felt. A part of him, the detective, felt good about it. Another part . . . the part that still cared for Keera . . . couldn't help but feel the way Billy sounded.

But this was Tran.

Within the rules, but skirting the edges, and ruthless.

# Chapter 26

Tran opened the morning with her forensic fingerprint analyst—a well-educated and experienced crime scene expert. The woman looked younger than her forty-four years, with an upbeat personality. She testified to finding multiple fingerprints inside the garage and home from as many as eight different people. Elimination prints taken from Lockett, Scott, Cortez, and Michael Westbrook helped to identify all but half a dozen fingerprints in both the garage and the house. Those unidentified prints couldn't be matched to fingerprints in IAFIS, meaning the people who made them didn't have criminal records.

"And you can't tell us how old these unknown fingerprints were; can you?" Keera asked.

"There are methods being developed to estimate the age of a fingerprint, but at this time, no. I really can't tell you when the fingerprint was left."

"They could have been left one minute before the murder; couldn't they?"

Tran stood. "Objection, Your Honor. Speculation."

"Overruled. I'll allow it."

"Or one month before the murder," the expert countered.

Tran followed her fingerprint analyst with Barry Dillard, head of the Washington State Patrol Crime Lab's firearms and toolmarks division. Dillard's work was impeccable. Keera wasn't going to poke holes in it. She'd have to try to score points another way.

Dillard confirmed the bullet extracted from John Lockett's skull was a 9-millimeter Luger, the most widely used 9-millimeter cartridge, and popular with both military personnel and civilians.

Tran then asked Dillard a series of questions that explained why Ford and Rossi's inability to find the missing murder weapon was somewhat irrelevant—an argument she would surely make in her closing to undercut Keera's attack.

"When a 9-millimeter round is fired into the back of a person's skull, the bullet can undergo significant deformation and fragmentation due to the dense bone structure and the impact forces involved," Dillard testified. "The muzzle distance from the skull is also a factor. The closer the muzzle, the greater the deformation." Dillard used a video to explain how the tip of this particular hollow-point bullet, upon striking the skull, flattened or "mushroomed." "As the bullet further penetrated the skull, it then fragmented into smaller pieces due to the skull's density and the bullet's velocity."

"Were you able to send this bullet to the NIBIN?" Tran asked.

"No," Dillard said. "The deformation and fragmentation made that pointless."

"I assume, Mr. Dillard, that if the round is widely used that means it is also readily available?" Tran asked.

"It is. It can be purchased in any gun and accessory store, as well as from online retailers."

Tran sat.

Keera, having already confirmed with Ford that his investigation did not reveal any evidence Michael had purchased a gun or ammunition from any source, declined to ask Dillard questions.

Tran followed Dillard with the State's toxicologist, a scarecrow of a man who testified in a monotone voice that he'd analyzed the grisly tissue samples and bodily fluids. He also detailed the levels of alcohol and narcotics in Melissa Scott's system, which Tran would use to explain why Scott, perhaps mercifully, never awakened to the blows that killed her. Scott's relatives cried and blew their noses in the gallery.

Again, Keera asked no questions.

She had prepped Michael Westbrook on her strategy to not ask questions of certain experts but sensed him getting upset sitting beside her. Criminal defendants sitting through the State's presentation could be like children in church, anxious for it to be over. But they still expected their attorney to fight and win every battle.

"Certain experts she will put on this morning won't hurt us," Keera had explained to Michael. "They'll provide scientific evidence that can't be refuted, and I can use their testimony when I give my closing argument and make it look as though I'm using the State's experts against it."

Following lunch, Arthur Litchfield sat in the gallery with a folder in his lap. Litchfield had arrived in the King County Medical Examiner's office after Keera departed the PA's office. He was one of half a dozen forensic pathologists now on staff, a medical doctor with specialized training in pathology and forensic pathology. Litchfield had a monk's ring of brown hair and wore round glasses in need of a good cleaning. His gray suit hung from his slender frame; the shoulders, like his glasses, flecked with dandruff. His shirt was loose around the collar, like a man who had recently lost significant weight. He wore brown oxfords and, when Tran called him to testify, he started for the witness chair in a rush but had to pause to tie a shoelace. Once he had done so, he moved swiftly to the witness stand, as if eager to testify—but more likely eager to get his testimony over with so he could get back to work on other cases in his office.

With the aid of gruesome photographs, Tran walked Litchfield through his visual examination of the two bodies. He testified Lockett had died from massive trauma resulting from the single head wound. He classified the death as a homicide. He testified Scott died from trauma caused by no less than twelve blows administered with a blunt-force object that struck her head, neck, and upper body. Keera noticed several jurors wince, grimace, and drop their gaze from the photographs.

Litchfield told the jury, in his professorial tone, how he had used a rectal thermometer to obtain the temperature of each body, as well as made a small incision in the upper right abdomen into which he had inserted a thermometer into the liver to obtain a more accurate core body temperature. This information allowed him to estimate the times of death more precisely.

"The general rule is the body loses about one-point-five degrees per hour until it reaches an ambient temperature. Considering other factors like the environment, the temperature in the home, the amount of clothing worn by the decedent, and the decedent's body size, I estimated the time of death of both victims to be within three to five hours of my examination."

"So sometime after four in the morning, and before you arrived and took control of each body at roughly 9:00 a.m.?" Tran asked.

"Actually, we know the neighbor arrived at the house at 8:00 a.m. and found the body. So sometime between 4:00 and 8:00 a.m."

"Did any other factors influence your estimate of time of death?"

Litchfield explained rigor mortis to the jury, the muscles stiffening within two to four hours after death due to chemical changes in the body. "The stiffening starts in the smaller muscles such as those in the face and neck and progresses to larger muscle groups, peaking at around twelve hours and lasting up to forty-eight hours. I also noted livor mortis—"

"Would you explain livor mortis for the jury?"

"Livor mortis is the pooling of blood in the body's lowest parts due to gravity after the heart has stopped pumping."

"And when does livor mortis begin and end?"

"It begins roughly thirty minutes to four hours after death and becomes fixed after eight to twelve hours."

"Why are rigor mortis and liver mortis significant?"

"Both further evidence the estimated time of death, and both can provide evidence as to whether the body has been moved or repositioned after death."

"And what did you conclude as to John Lockett?"

"I confirmed both my estimated time of death and that his body had not been moved or repositioned."

"And Melissa Scott?"

"The same conclusions."

"Did you collect any trace evidence from either body?"

"From Mr. Lockett I recovered gunshot residue from the back of his head, as well as bodily fluids, and fibers from his clothing."

Tran again used the courtroom computers to put up photographs and had Litchfield narrate the collection of the trace evidence and the locations inside the garage.

"And from Melissa Scott?"

Litchfield did the same, cataloguing each recovered fiber and strand of hair.

Tran said, "What bodily fluids did you collect from the decedent, Melissa Scott?"

Litchfield detailed how he had collected blood and urine to analyze for the presence of drugs and alcohol, as well as bile from the gallbladder. "I also collected semen or seminal fluid from the decedent's vaginal cavity."

"And what is seminal fluid?"

"Seminal fluid is secretions from a male's seminal vesicles, prostate gland, and bulbourethral glands. Those secretions include sperm cells as well as seminal plasma that support the motility of sperm cells."

"Is it indicative that Ms. Scott had sexual intercourse recently?"

"Within one to three days of her death. I can't be more precise."

"Other than the vaginal cavity, did you detect the seminal fluid anywhere else?"

"Yes, on the bedsheets."

"Using this diagram, can you show us where on the bedsheets you collected the seminal fluid?"

Litchfield identified four different areas where he noted seminal fluid, three of which were on the side of the bed opposite from where

Scott's body had been found and presumably belonged to Lockett. An X marked each area.

"And what did you do with the trace evidence you collected?"

"It was sent to the forensic laboratory."

"For what purpose?"

"DNA analysis."

Tran established the chain of custody for the trace evidence, then sat.

Keera had received Litchfield's report earlier and had been through it. Nothing in it had surprised her, though she knew it was deliberately short and precise. She spent a half hour running Litchfield back through his testimony, getting him to admit he was more of an evidence collector than an analyzer. Then she asked, "Did it appear to you that the decedent, Melissa Scott, had been sexually assaulted either before or after she was killed?"

Litchfield said he did not find evidence of sexual assault. "I did not detect any bruising, lacerations, or other trauma to the genitalia, nor did I detect any such injuries to other body parts indicating a sexual assault."

Keera thanked Litchfield and requested the court dismiss but not release him, subject to her calling him as a witness in the defense's case in chief.

Keera ended the day feeling as though she had scored a few more points and was confident enough to send Harrison home with Tina. She told him not to come back to the office, to reenergize and to eat something healthy. She planned to do the same.

Before returning to her office, Keera took a detour to the King County jail to meet with Michael, as had become her norm when not pressed for time. She would have stopped at a local restaurant and brought in food to share, but that was not allowed.

She got past the red tape and waited in an attorney-client room. After several minutes, Michael arrived, dressed again in his prison uniform.

"Hey," he said. "Did you want to talk about something?"

"I just wanted to see how you were holding up."

Michael sat. "Okay. It all still seems so surreal to me. I think I'm going to wake up and find it was all a nightmare."

"Sometimes it seems surreal to me too."

"Really?"

She nodded. "I never thought I'd be a lawyer when I was a young girl."

"What did you want to be?"

"A professional chess player."

"Were you any good?"

She smiled. "I was. Very good."

Michael smiled with her. "Yeah? Look at you, smiling. Why didn't you pursue it?"

"Things happen, you know."

"So why did you go into the law?"

"When I was a little girl, I can remember my mother and father talking about his cases, about his trials, the shenanigans that he pulled in court and, more often than not, got away with. He made it sound fun."

"What kind of shenanigans?" Michael said, clearly not eager to go back to his cell.

"Well, the one I remember most clearly was the story he told me about when he started out and was having trouble getting clients. Then he represented a man, another lawyer, suing to get his parrot back."

"His parrot?"

"Not just any parrot, but a hyacinth macaw. It had cost the man a lot of money, and it had flown out the window when the cleaners left the window open. The man was devastated. He'd had the parrot for more than twenty-five years."

"Twenty-five years?"

"They can live to be seventy. The parrot had become like a family member."

"Did he get it back?"

"He searched all over the city and finally found it at a pet store. He suspected someone had found it, didn't know what to do with it, and turned it in. The pet store owner, knowing how valuable the bird was, wouldn't give it back unless the man bought it. So, the man came to my father, and my father got an injunction preventing the store from selling the parrot until the court determined its rightful owner."

"How could they do that? I mean, if one guy says one thing and the other says something else, how could they prove who was lying?"

"That's where the story gets interesting. The man told my father the parrot mimicked human speech and sounds, and my father could prove it was his bird if he could put the bird on the stand to testify."

Michael smiled, a broad grin Keera had not seen since first meeting him. "What happened?"

"My father called the bird to the witness stand."

"Get out. Really?"

"He didn't say it was a bird. He just listed the bird by its name on the witness list and called out that name in court. He didn't want to give the opposing side the chance to object before they got to court. Then he went into the hallway and walked back in with the bird in its cage."

"What happened?" Michael asked, laughing.

"Of course, the other attorney objected, and the people seated in the gallery started buzzing. My dad had let it leak to those he knew in the courthouse that he was going to put a parrot on the stand, so the gallery had filled. He wanted to put pressure on the judge to at least let him try to examine the bird. It worked. The judge allowed it."

Michael's grin broadened. "You're making this up."

Keera put up a hand, as her father used to do when telling her the story. "If you don't want to hear the rest of it . . ."

"No. I do. Okay, how did the bird take the oath to tell the truth?"

"As I said, according to my dad, the owner was also an attorney, and he used to watch all these legal shows on television with the bird in the room, and he had taught the bird things like how to take the oath to swear to tell the truth, the whole truth, and nothing but the truth."

"Shut up," Michael said, laughing. "Come on. Seriously?"

"My dad told me the bailiff gave him the oath and the bird said, 'I do.'"

"Oh man. Your dad is too much. A bird?"

"Well, the owner had also told my dad that when he left during the day he'd turn on the television to keep the bird company and the bird, Pete—"

"The parrot's name was Pete?" Michael asked. "Pete the Parrot?"

"It was. The man said Pete watched reruns of old shows during the day and had learned to whistle the tune to *The Andy Griffith Show.*"

"What's *The Andy Griffith Show*?"

"It's a show, well before your time and mine, but according to my dad, it went something like this." Keera whistled the opening tune to the show. "My father asked the parrot, 'Pete, do you want to watch Andy Griffith?' That was the main actor in the show. At first, Pete didn't do anything. My father repeated the question a second and third time, and just when he thought Pete was not going to do anything, he whistled the show's tune."

"And your father won?"

"The judge ruled in his client's favor, the owner got Pete back, and the story of Pete the Parrot ran in the *Seattle Times* the next day and on the news that night. After that, my father's career took off. He had more clients than he knew what to do with."

Michael smiled. He might have wondered if the story was really true, as Keera had, or if, perhaps, it had just been a story a father told his daughter at bedtime, but he didn't ask Keera. He looked content to not know the answer. "Thanks, Ms. Duggan. I haven't laughed like that, well, in a long time."

Keera nodded. "You're welcome, Michael." She checked her watch. "I better get back to the office. I have some work to do tonight."

She knocked on the door for the correctional officer. The door opened and Michael stepped out, but he stopped and turned back. "Maybe we can find a parrot to testify on my behalf, huh?"

"You never know, Michael. You just have to stay optimistic."

Keera hurried down the hill to her office. When she'd gotten older, she stopped believing in the story of Pete the Parrot and thought it was like Santa Claus. Her mother had always been close lipped on the subject, and Keera decided it was just a father's tale until, one day, she was in the attic and found some of her father's old scrapbooks containing articles on his earliest cases, and damned if she didn't find the *Seattle Times* article on Pete the Parrot and his testimony in court. From that day forward, she never doubted what her father told her.

Keera stepped from the cage elevator and made her way to her office. She activated her computer and checked her email and found several from George Thomas, Tran's minion. The first listed the experts the State intended to call in the morning. She opened his second email, this one with no explanation. Just an attachment. Another "Tran bomb," as she had labeled the late-night missives. She opened the attachment, a report from an expert.

And the other shoe, the one JP Harrison had been waiting to drop, hit the ground. Hard.

# Chapter 27

The following morning, Keera remained calm when Tran called Dr. Emily Carter to the witness stand. The night before, Thomas had attached Carter's completed forensic evidence report and her conclusions. Keera's initial instinct was to object in court before the jury was seated and argue that the delay in production was prejudicial to the defense—and another instance of Tran skirting the rules of evidence.

But that would get her nowhere.

Tran would argue this was the nature of trials. She'd say she had delivered the completed report as soon as she had received it. Based on the State's received stamp in the document's right-hand corner, Keera couldn't accuse Tran of a fabrication, but she had no doubt Tran had spoken to Carter on numerous occasions and knew exactly what to expect in her report, maybe even told her to hold off putting her conclusions in writing until Tran asked for them. Either way, Patel, once a prosecutor and trial attorney, would have little sympathy for Keera having to work long into the night.

A senior DNA analyst in the Washington State Patrol Crime Lab, Carter was in her forties, just five foot three and petite, but with an athletic build. After taking the oath to tell the truth, she sat with her report in her lap. She adjusted a plaid jacket and matching skirt, getting comfortable. Reading glasses dangled from a chain around her neck, but they made her look more fashionable than old.

Carter had impressive credentials, and Tran, wanting the jury to know how impressive, painstakingly walked Carter through her study of biology at the University of Washington and obtaining a master's degree in forensic science from UC Davis. Carter specialized in forensic criminalistics and forensic DNA. She had more than a decade of practical experience working with law enforcement on criminal investigations, conducting DNA extraction, quantification, amplification, and analysis. She had published twelve papers on various forensic DNA topics.

As Tran proceeded with her direct examination, Keera felt like she sat on a keg of gunpowder, that the fuse had been lit, and the flame inched closer and closer to the barrel. She'd been up very late, not having slept much, if at all. She'd called Harrison, and the two returned to the King County jail and spent a long hour with Michael Westbrook. She did her best not to chastise the young man, tell him she had warned him about his not being honest. At this point, berating him would do little good.

As her father liked to say, she needed to cover up and hold on until her head cleared from the blow. But this blow felt like a Mike Tyson left hook.

Tran's questioning, and Carter's testimony, was necessarily tedious, going over the maintenance and calibration of lab equipment to ensure accurate performance, and documenting and preserving the trace evidence submitted to the crime lab to ensure strict chain-of-custody protocols.

With every passing minute, the burning fuse inched closer to the keg.

Keera had admonished Michael not to react, to maintain his composure. She told him she wanted to paint a picture for the jury that she had this under control and was not worried.

She didn't.

And she was.

Westbrook looked to be on edge. Though he folded his hands in his lap or on the table, Keera noticed his fingers had paled.

Tran started first with hair samples recovered from the garage, and Carter walked the jury through the process of extracting DNA from those samples. She had an easy way about her—the way some teachers could take a complex process and simplify it but not make the recipient feel uneducated. Carter testified she focused on several different colors and textures of submitted hair samples, choosing those with the root still attached, which allowed for the collection of nuclear DNA. She then explained how the hair was cleansed of contaminants and the root separated from the shaft, then treated with a lysis buffer to break down the cells and release the DNA. Once the DNA was released, it was extracted using chemical methods.

"In this instance I used phenol and chloroform to isolate the DNA from proteins and other cellular debris."

"What happens next?"

"The DNA is purified for analysis. This is a multistep process that is essentially washing and binding the DNA." Carter then explained each step for the jury and related it to the different stages in a car wash.

"When the DNA comes out, shiny and clean, we quantify it to ensure there is a sufficient sample for analysis and to determine its purity." Again, she explained this in greater scientific detail, though careful not to overwhelm the jury. "Once the DNA is quantified, we amplify it—basically that means we copy it several times to be sure we have enough to test. When tested, the sample can be destroyed. We don't want to take any chances."

"And then?" Tran asked.

"Then," Carter said, "we determine if the extracted DNA matches a known profile."

"How do you do that?"

"We examine specific DNA regions known as 'short tandem repeats' or 'STRs.' These DNA regions vary greatly among individuals."

"What are the chances two people could have the same STRs?" Tran asked.

"Absent the two people being identical twins, the odds of two individuals having the same STRs would be in the billions."

"And what did you conclude with respect to sample G-2?"

"I concluded the DNA belonged to the decedent, John Lockett."

"And what are the chances the sample belonged to someone other than John Lockett?"

"One in a billion."

"And what did you conclude with respect to hair sample G-4?"

"I concluded that sample belonged to the known sample obtained from Alex Cortez."

"And what are the chances the sample belonged to someone other than Alex Cortez?"

"One in a billion."

This was not a surprise given Cortez testified he'd been to the garage many times and his fingerprints had been found there.

"And what did you conclude with respect to hair sample G-5?"

"I concluded the sample belonged to the known sample obtained from Michael Westbrook."

"And what are the statistical chances the sample belonged to someone other than Michael Westbrook?"

"Again, one in a billion."

The fuse burned closer.

"The forensic medical examiner, Arthur Litchfield, also provided you with trace evidence found on or within the body of Melissa Scott; didn't he?"

"He did."

"And if I can draw your attention to sample V-3, can you identify for the jury what that sample is?"

"That is a sample obtained by gently inserting a sterile swab into the decedent's vaginal cavity. The swab was then placed in a sterile container, labeled, and preserved for further analysis."

"What did you determine to be on the sterile swab?"

"I determined the sample was seminal fluid."

"Sperm?"

"Yes."

"You performed DNA analysis on that sample?"

"I did."

"Using the same process previously described?"

"In essence. I extracted the DNA from the semen sample through a process called 'differential extraction,' which separates the sperm cells from other cells in the sample. Then I quantified how much DNA was present, amplified the DNA, and separated the amplified DNA fragments by size to create a DNA profile."

"Are you able to determine if the sample contains multiple semen contributors?"

"We can. During the extraction phase a buffer containing a detergent and an enzyme called 'proteinase K' is added to the sample. This step breaks open all cells except sperm cells. Those cells are separated and collected. The remaining sperm cells are then broken open again using more stringent conditions and certain chemicals," which she named. "This releases the DNA from the sperm cells. The extracted samples are purified using organic solvents to remove proteins and other contaminants, leaving clean DNA for analysis. The DNA is amplified, separated, and compared to known profiles."

"And were you able to identify a known profile?"

"The DNA belonged to John Lockett."

"Did you locate a second profile?"

"No."

"Turning to the bedroom in which the body of Melissa Scott was found. You analyzed several hair samples obtained from that location also, didn't you?"

"I did," Carter said.

"Turning your attention to sample BR-7, was your analysis on that sample the same as the analysis you previously described to the jury regarding hair samples?"

"It was."

"And did you reach a conclusion with respect to BR-7?"

"I concluded the recovered sample, BR-7, matched the known sample obtained from Michael Westbrook."

It was a short, quick blow, but it struck the defense flush in the face. Keera did her best not to look hurt. Tran had just placed Michael within Melissa Scott's bedroom.

"And what is the statistical probability the hair sample did not belong to Michael Westbrook?"

"One in a billion, maybe more."

"Why more?"

"At law enforcement's request, I ran the sample a second time and came to the same conclusion."

"The trace evidence analyst catalogued where the team found each sample; did she not?"

"She did."

"And as for trace evidence sample BR-7. Where was that sample found?" Tran asked.

"According to the trace evidence analyst's report, sample BR-7 was collected from the sheets in the bed."

"In the bed where the decedent, Melissa Scott, was found?"

"Yes."

Tran put a diagram on the board and noted the location where the trace hair sample BR-7 had been found in the bed.

Another blow. Another direct hit. Tran now had placed Michael within Melissa Scott's bed. Still the fuse burned.

"Turning your attention to trace sample BR-14. Can you tell the jury where that sample was collected?"

"That was a sample also collected from the bedsheets where the decedent Melissa Scott's body was found."

"And what was it?"

"Seminal fluid."

"Did you analyze that seminal fluid using the techniques you've previously described?"

"I did."

"And did BR-14 generate a known DNA profile?"

"It did. The DNA profile matched the DNA profile for Michael Westbrook."

The burning fuse had reached the keg. The gunpowder exploded. The jurors looked stunned. In the gallery behind her, Keera heard gasps and other noises, loud enough that Judge Patel rapped her gavel twice.

"And what are the odds that the DNA profile does not belong to Michael Westbrook?"

"One in a billion," Carter said.

Tran, an experienced litigator, paused as if to consider exactly what that meant, and to let the jurors do the same. It meant hard evidence. Not circumstantial evidence, but hard evidence that Michael Westbrook had not just been in Melissa Scott's bedroom but had ejaculated and left his sperm on her bedsheets.

Tran had just blown up Michael Westbrook's defense, and the explosion had left him and Keera reeling.

# Chapter 28

Keera entered the attorney-client room at the King County jail, JP Harrison at her side. For the first time she could remember, she wasn't sure what to say to her client.

Keera had done her best on cross-examination of Emily Carter, but it had been an uphill battle, and the jurors' facial expressions and body movements indicated she had not been effective. She couldn't attack Carter's credentials or her science—or the conclusions she had reached. Her concern now was how to *explain* her findings. She focused instead on other trace evidence provided to Carter and submitted for DNA analysis, but for which no known DNA profile matched. The SODDI defense. Some Other Dude Did It. Keera was beating the same tired horse, and she sensed the jurors were equally tired of it.

As mad as she was at Tran for providing Carter's final report at the last minute, and at Judge Patel for allowing its introduction without giving Keera the chance to digest it, she was fuming at Michael Westbrook for not telling her the truth, for not telling her he had a sexual relationship with Melissa Scott. She had told him she could deal with almost anything if she had time to prepare for it.

She didn't.

And she hadn't. Not in this instance.

She thought again of her chess match against her father on the first day of trial, how she hadn't seen his attack before it was too late. Check. Then she'd made a second mistake. Checkmate. But it hadn't been just two moves. It had been the entire game. She had dismissed her lack of attentiveness to being preoccupied with the trial, but that didn't diminish the fact that she had not played her game, then did a poor job anticipating Patsy's moves. She wondered if it was an omen. If her skills had slipped. She should have been better prepared for what had happened in court, though she could not think of anything she would have done differently. Arguing against conclusive DNA evidence was like arguing the Seattle skies in February were not gray. It only made you look blind to the evidence.

Michael shuffled into the room having changed into his red jail surgical scrubs, white socks, and sandals. They did not exchange greetings or questions like "How are you holding up?" They each knew how the other was holding up. Not well. And by their fingertips.

Michael slumped into a chair at the table, looking defeated.

"Sit up," Harrison said.

Westbrook did so.

"How did your sperm get on Melissa Scott's bedsheets?" Harrison asked, voice still calm.

"How?"

"How, Michael? Tell me how. And do not lie to me."

"I didn't lie."

"Bullshit," Harrison said, raising his voice. "Keera told you to be honest. She told you she could prepare for the worst if she knew what was coming. She told you she can't help you if you're not honest. I won't ask her to help you if you're not honest." Harrison pointed an index finger at the young man. Keera had never seen him this angry. "That's her reputation when she stands up in court and makes statements on your behalf, and you've just undercut her credibility with the jurors. How long had you been screwing around with Melissa Scott?"

Michael looked like he had a walnut lodged in his throat. "Several weeks."

"A month?"

"More than a month."

Harrison shook his head. "Is that why you were at the house when John Lockett wasn't home?"

"It didn't start out that way."

"Tell me how it started."

"Melissa called and asked if I could come over and help her with a few things in the yard. Things that needed to be done. She said John didn't like to do yard work."

"She called you on your cell phone?"

"Yeah."

Harrison took out a small notepad and took notes. They'd need to go over those cell phone records and find those calls.

"Did she say Lockett would not be home?"

"No. I didn't know until I got there."

"And you said 'yes'; why?"

"To help her out."

"Bullshit. No twenty-one-year-old goes over to an attractive woman's house eager to do her yard work. Did you suspect she had another intent?"

Michael took a deep breath and exhaled. "I guess so."

"Tell me why?"

"It was just the way she looked at me when I was over there. She'd touch my arm, then dismiss it and say she was just very tactile."

"That she didn't mean anything by the touch?" Harrison said.

"That's what she'd say. When I was playing pool or watching the television, she would give me these looks when John was distracted working on the car. She'd play pool and brush up against me. She'd hold the pool cue and . . ." Michael hesitated and looked to Keera.

"And act like she was giving it a hand job?" Harrison said.

"Yeah. Things like that. But it was subtle. I knew if I said anything . . ."

"She would deny her actions had any sexual implications, and that you were just imagining what you wanted to see."

"That's what it felt like."

As Michael gave his answers, Keera deduced where Harrison was going. Keera had a working argument that Lockett had been trying to gain Michael's trust. She could argue Scott's seduction was intended for the same reason. They were using the young man.

Unfortunately, Tran would argue that the teasing finally became too much and Michael reached a breaking point, thus the brutal nature of Melissa Scott's murder.

"So how did it progress to you ending up in her bed?"

"She asked me to help her with the yard work. Said she would pay me. When I arrived, John was not at home. Things happened from there."

"Who initiated it?"

"She did. She invited me inside and made it clear she would be alone for several hours."

"Did you have intercourse?"

"Not that first time, or even the second, but later, yes."

"Where in the house?"

"The garage."

"And her bedroom?"

"A couple of times when John was at work, but I always wore a condom."

"Not always, apparently," Harrison said.

"That wasn't intercourse."

"She gave you a hand job? When was that?" Harrison asked.

Keera heard the anger in Harrison's voice, though she sensed it was anger directed at Melissa Scott.

"Just a day or two before the murders."

"Do you understand why I'm asking you these questions?"

"Yes."

"Do you?" Harrison leaned forward. "Do you know what Anh Tran can now argue, Michael? She'll argue Melissa Scott teased you until you broke, that you beat Melissa to death, then ejaculated on the sheets."

The young man looked stunned. He leaned away from the table. "What? No. No, JP. That's sick. I wouldn't do that."

"It doesn't matter what you say; Keera told you that from the outset. The jury doesn't know you. They won't give you the benefit of the doubt. What matters is what Keera can and cannot prove, and what the jurors will infer from the evidence."

"Can't you prove that I didn't do it; that it was old?"

Harrison looked to Keera.

She shook her head. "I talked to our expert. Accurately determining the length of time that the sample has been on the sheets is a challenge. The degradation of DNA is impacted by environmental conditions, exposure to light, heat, moisture. It's not feasible with current forensic techniques."

"What do we do?" Michael asked, sounding and looking alarmed.

"I don't know. I'm still thinking this over," Keera said.

"Will there be any other surprises, Michael?" Harrison asked.

"No," he said, shaking his head.

"You're sure?"

"I swear."

And then, Michael sobbed—a young man in physical and emotional pain who was quickly reaching the end of his rope. Keera wanted to console him. She wanted to tell him everything was going to be okay, but she didn't know it would be, not any longer. Michael Westbrook was a long shot, at best, to win this horse race. She'd told Tran the story about Cipriani winning because she could not bear the thought of walking out of that restaurant defeated.

It was a good story.

But it wasn't true.

She'd been the one bluffing.

Cipriani hadn't won that day.

He'd spit his bit and come in dead last, teaching Keera a valuable and painful lesson about long shots. You didn't bet when you didn't have the horse to win. You'd lose everything, as Keera had lost all the money she'd won in the earlier races that day, those many years ago.

This time it would be Michael Westbrook who lost.

And he would pay for it the rest of his life.

When Keera returned to her office, she found yet another Tran bomb in her email—one Tran intended to come at the conclusion of the State's case and leave a strong impression on the jury as Keera put forward the defense's case. Keera sighed and considered the list of witnesses the prosecution planned to call at trial the next day. Then she picked up the phone, calling Harrison.

"We got more problems," she said.

Neither would get much sleep again this night.

# Chapter 29

Keera met Harrison outside the courtroom ten minutes before nine the following morning, having spent the early morning hours again speaking with Michael. Harrison looked like Keera felt, spent and disheveled, as if he hadn't slept much, if at all. The dark circles under his eyes seemed more pronounced. She didn't realize how accurate she'd been when she told Michael and Tina Westbrook this trial would be a marathon. She felt as though she'd already run twenty miles, with the hardest miles to the finish line still in front of her.

Tran had them on the ropes and was raining blows. This morning, she'd seek a knockout. Patsy had told Keera not to get sucked in to Tran's case, but Keera couldn't get off the ropes. Each time she tried, Tran landed another blow, and Keera had to cover up—and fight to survive.

"What do you have?" Keera asked Harrison.

The prior evening's witness list had included the names Laurence Holmes and Glenn Ellis, inmates at FDC-SeaTac during Michael's incarceration there, before he was moved to the King County jail.

"Not a lot," Harrison said. He provided her with what he could uncover about both men. When their names appeared in the prosecution's file as witnesses, Harrison had attempted to speak with them at FDC-SeaTac, but both men had refused his overtures.

Michael told Keera that Glenn Ellis had been his cellmate at FDC, Laurence Holmes just an acquaintance. She had asked him if he told either inmate anything about his case. He swore he never did and said they were all friendly. She and Harrison believed the young man.

Keera suspected Tran had listed the two inmates to intimidate her and to try to force a plea deal. She didn't believe Tran would actually call either man to testify. She'd known other prosecutors who invoked the same strategy.

Now she wasn't so sure, not after yesterday's bombshell concerning Melissa Scott. She'd sat in her office late into the night wondering if that's what the two men would testify about, Michael's relationship with Scott. She wondered if she was defending a guilty man; if Michael was another Vince LaRussa, her defendant in her first case. She wondered if Michael's boyish demeanor was just a front, if beneath that façade lurked a brutal killer. She'd been fooled once. "Fool me twice," she'd said, alone in her office. "Shame on me."

"I don't like this." Harrison grimaced as if suffering a cramp. "I think they're snitches. Why else would Tran be calling them? What did the witness statement say they'd testify about?" he asked.

Keera looked at her watch. She was running out of time. "Tran was slick. She provided enough to satisfy the court order, but not enough to reveal any specifics. I have to get in there. Find out what you can."

Keera was the last to enter the courtroom, precisely at 9:00 a.m. Michael Westbrook looked at her as if for an answer, but she had none to offer. Michael was on edge, a young man struggling to hold it together. She leaned over, speaking quietly. "No matter what these two witnesses have to say, I want you to remain composed. Do you understand me?"

Michael's facial expression confirmed a man quickly unraveling at the seams.

Patel took her place on the bench and instructed her bailiff to bring in the jury. Keera noticed a subtle shift in the jurors' demeanor. They avoided eye contact with Michael and with her, never a good thing, as if they'd already made up their minds.

If this morning went as Keera anticipated, it would be even more difficult to convince them to keep an open mind until they'd heard all the evidence. Her defense case would be largely superfluous.

When the jurors were seated, Judge Patel greeted them, then addressed Tran. "The State may call its next witness."

Tran rose. "The State calls Laurence Holmes."

Patel, aware that Holmes was an inmate, addressed two correctional officers standing against the wall. "Is Mr. Holmes present?"

"He is," one of the officers said.

"Bring him in."

The two correctional officers left the courtroom and returned with Holmes between them. He entered without handcuffs, wearing FDC-SeaTac's khaki pants and shirt and white socks. He shuffled forward in plastic sandals. Holmes did not look at Michael as the officers escorted him onto the witness stand. Tall and thin, Holmes raised a long arm to take the oath, then sat, fussing with his gunmetal-gray hair and adjusting black-framed glasses. He looked to the jurors with the hint of a smug expression, as if he held the key to a long-sealed lock and would open it for them this morning.

Tran approached the lectern and had Holmes provide his full name, then asked, "Where are you currently incarcerated?"

"I'm at the Federal Detention Center at SeaTac," he said, his voice higher pitched than Keera expected and with a slight stutter.

"What crimes were you convicted of?"

"Drug running and murder in the second degree."

"One murder?"

"Two."

"Will you tell the jurors the circumstances of your conviction?"

"I was found guilty of participating in the killing of two men who tried to rob me and others I worked with."

Tran said, "Let's be clear. They tried to rob you and men you ran drugs with?"

"That's right."

"And these two men tried to rob you of drugs and cash illegally earned from the sale of those drugs?"

"That's right."

"You shot these men?"

"I did not. I was present when they were shot."

"You were convicted under Washington State's felony murder rules?"

"That's pretty much what the court said."

"When did you arrive at FDC-SeaTac?"

"About a year ago."

"Is that an identification card clipped to your uniform?" Tran pointed to a laminated card punched with a star-shaped hole over Holmes's assigned unit.

"Yes."

"To what housing unit have you been assigned?"

"Unit C."

"Do you have a private cell?"

"No. Two inmates to a cell. Sometimes more, but usually two."

"Do you know the defendant, Michael Westbrook?"

Holmes finally turned his head and looked at Michael, but it was just a passing glance. He quickly returned his gaze to Tran. "Yeah. We were both on the C Unit until he got moved."

"Did you consider Mr. Westbrook a friend?"

"Yeah, Mikey was all right."

Keera cringed at Holmes's use of the familiar.

"How did you two meet?"

"The first time? The first time we met was in the prison rec yard. I was sitting on one of the benches catching some sun, listening to the radio. Mikey approached and sat down."

"Did he say anything to you?"

"Not at first," Holmes said, shaking his head. "He sat a couple bleachers below me. If I remember correctly, I said 'Hey' and we started talking, nothing specific or anything. Pretty common, especially when you first arrive on the unit and don't know anybody. You spend time sizing people up, wondering what's their story; what they're in for; who you can trust."

"How often did you see the defendant?"

"At first? Not often. Here and there. Dining hall. Rec yard. But eventually Mike came around looking for some advice."

"Where was this?"

"The rec yard."

"What kind of advice did he want?"

"He wanted some advice regarding the drug charges the federal prosecutor had against him."

Michael had told Keera of his conversation with Holmes. Keera stood and objected. "This is irrelevant to the charges before this court."

Tran responded in that condescending tone that so annoyed Keera. "Your Honor, the defendant has been charged in the State's case with breaking and entering and robbery of narcotics and cash. I would request some leeway."

"Overruled."

Tran again engaged Holmes. "What kind of advice was the defendant seeking?"

"He said the federal prosecutor wouldn't let him plead to the drug charges so he could make bail, that the prosecutor told the court he was awaiting the outcome of possible State charges."

"Did Mr. Westbrook tell you what those State charges were?"

"Eventually."

"What did he tell you?"

"He said two people he knew had been murdered, a man and his girlfriend, but he denied killing anyone. He said he was innocent."

"What did you say?"

"Me and Glenn just chuckled, and I said, 'Don't you know, Mikey. We're all innocent in here.'"

"Who is Glenn?"

"Glenn Ellis. He and Mike shared a cell."

Michael had also told Keera this.

"Did Mr. Westbrook and you continue to meet after that?"

"Not anything planned. We were on the same unit so, like I said, I'd see him at meals and invite him to take a seat at the table, introduce him around, and I'd see him in the yard."

"Did you two become close?"

"'Close' is hard to define in prison. Everyone is on guard. I'd say we were friendly."

"Did Mr. Westbrook ever change his story about the two killings?"

Holmes now looked reluctant. If he was lying, and Keera sensed from his body language—fidgeting with his hands, avoiding eye contact, crossing and uncrossing his arms—that he was, it was a decent performance. "Yeah."

Keera subtly shifted her gaze to the right. Michael's hands gripped the table's edge, his knuckles white. She leaned toward him and spoke out of the side of her mouth. "He's lying. Let him lie."

Michael turned his head. His eyes searched her face, as if not understanding, though she had told him this morning the bolder the lie, the less credible Holmes became.

"Would you tell us about that?" Tran asked.

"He just spilled the beans one day while we were sitting out in the yard, said he'd killed the two people."

"He's lying," Michael said under his breath.

"Stay calm," Keera responded.

"Who else was present and heard Mr. Westbrook make this admission?"

"Glenn Ellis."

"Did Mr. Westbrook say how he had killed the two people?"

"He said he shot the guy in his garage, that the guy had his back to him, working on a car, with loud music playing. Mikey said he walked right in and shot him. Then he took a tire iron from the garage, and he killed the woman while she slept in her bed."

"I never said that," Michael said.

"Easy," Keera whispered.

"Did he say how many times he struck the woman?"

"He said like ten or more."

"No. I didn't say that." Michael sounded panicked.

Keera reached and touched his hand, rock solid. "Easy, Michael. Easy."

"What else did he tell you?"

"He said he got the gun, a 9-millimeter, off some guy on Craigslist, but that he'd gotten rid of it."

"Did he say where he got rid of it?"

"He said he busted it into pieces and discarded those pieces in different garbage cans as he ran back to his house. He said the cans were out in the street because it was garbage day. I think he said it was a Friday."

"I never said any of this. I never said—" Michael had increased his volume.

"Ms. Duggan," Patel said.

Keera leaned toward Michael. She again put her hand on his hand gripping the table and whispered in his ear, "Let him lie. I have this under control."

"Did he say what he did with the tire iron?" Tran asked.

"He said he cleaned it with bleach in the laundry room, then put it back in the garage under the car so it would just look like another tool the guy used."

"Did Mr. Westbrook say why he killed the two people?"

"He said the guy was dealing drugs. That he had a lot of cash in the house. He said he had a deal to help the guy distribute the drugs, but the guy had reneged on the deal, kept stringing him along, giving him a little money here and there, but not everything they had agreed on. He said he got fed up; felt that the guy and the woman were both playing him."

A twinge in her gut, one so strong it made Keera turn and look at Harrison. The night before, in the conference room, they'd formulated an argument to explain why Michael's sperm was located on the bedsheets, and Keera had postulated the very argument Holmes just voiced, that the woman was using Michael to gain his trust for Lockett.

"He said, 'Screw this, I'm getting what's owed to me,'" Holmes said.

"And the woman? Did Mr. Westbrook say why he killed the woman?" Tran asked.

"He said she'd been jerking his chain with sex, acting like she cared about him, but when he told her the guy owed him money and he asked her to help him get it, she laughed and told him to get lost. Called him a loser. He said after he beat her to death, he masturbated on the bed."

"What did you say?" Tran asked.

"I said that was sick *and* stupid. I told him the police could get his DNA from the sperm, but Mikey was cocky. He said that wouldn't happen."

"Did he say why not?"

"Yeah. He said he didn't think the police would suspect him because he'd made it look like a professional hit and robbery. He said he'd even picked up the shell casing in the garage so the police couldn't find it. He said he thought the police wouldn't give a shit about a drug dealer and his girlfriend getting killed."

The table flipped out from under Keera's hands. Her laptop and binders crashed to the floor. She fell from her chair, which toppled over sideways. Michael stumbled over the table and lunged toward the witness chair, swearing and yelling. "You liar! You Goddamned liar!"

Tran quickly stepped back from the lectern, which Michael had also knocked over. The court staff, seated in the well below the bench, retreated just as quickly. Patel descended and disappeared through the door behind the bench.

The two correctional officers who had tackled Michael struggled to pin him to the floor just short of the witness stand, where Holmes now stood looking terrified. The jurors in the front row had scrambled away from the railing, all twelve pressed up against the wall.

Michael continued to struggle and scream profanities at Holmes. Additional marshals converged and worked to get Michael's hands behind his back to handcuff his wrists. When they'd finally subdued him, the officers carried him out the door.

At some point in all the commotion, Keera got back on her feet. Minutes later, Judge Patel returned to the bench and instructed the bailiff to clear the courtroom and secure the jury. Then she said, "I'll see counsel in chambers. Now!"

Keera turned to Tina Westbrook in the gallery, but Tina had her head in her hands, weeping.

"Ms. Duggan. Now!" Patel said again.

Keera followed Tran down the narrow hallway leading to Patel's chambers. No one sat. The judge paced her spartan office, striding past a single photo, presumably her husband.

"I'm sorry, Your Honor," Keera said. "I specifically talked to my client about the possibility of Mr. Holmes lying and—"

Tran quickly turned. "I object."

Keera raised her voice. "—and advised him to remain calm, no matter how fabricated the lies."

"Counsel's statement is completely improper," Tran growled.

Patel grimaced but with an *I knew it* smile, like she'd been down this path before. Probably with Patsy. She pointed her index finger at Keera, not raising her voice. "You know better, Ms. Duggan."

"I was merely speaking from my client's perspective, Your Honor. In light of what just transpired, the defense moves for an immediate mistrial."

Tran scoffed and raised her arms as if dumbfounded.

"The defendant's actions have irreparably prejudiced this jury," Keera said. "It is naïve to think the jurors can disregard this incident and render an impartial verdict. My client can't get a fair trial with this jury."

"Your Honor, that is preposterous," Tran said. "I'm beginning to think this implosion was premeditated and planned by the defense."

"And I object to your implication that I had anything to do with what just transpired. It couldn't have been pre-planned because you didn't give us proper notice that this testimony was coming this morning."

Tran said, "To declare a mistrial would reward the defendant for his improper behavior. The jury can be admonished to ignore the outburst and to disregard it, and to focus only on the testimony."

"Your Honor, the jury can't disregard what it has witnessed. And to suggest it can is preposterous," Keera countered. "The prosecution has argued this was a crime of rage."

Patel raised her hand. "Sit down. Both of you." She gestured to the two chairs across from the desk. After Tran and Keera were seated, Patel said, "I'm not going to declare a mistrial, Ms. Duggan. If you want to make a motion on the record when we return to court, you're free to do so, but I'm not going to reward you for failing to control your client."

"Failing to control him?" Keera said. "How would you have proposed I do that?"

"I've heard enough, Ms. Duggan."

"Do you think I told him to do this?"

"I said, I've heard enough."

"I try my own cases. Don't judge me for something between you and my father."

Judge Patel's eyes shot daggers across the desk, as did her ensuing words. "Ms. Duggan, another word and I'll hold you and your client in contempt, and I'll take a bite out of your pocketbook." She paused a beat, daring Keera.

Keera was smart enough to stay silent. Her final sentence had been strategic. Were Patel to now hold Keera in contempt, it would look punitive—for some dispute between the judge and Patsy.

Patel shifted her attention to Tran. "How much more do you have of this witness?"

"Not much. Five or ten minutes."

"All right. We'll continue without the defendant."

"The defendant has a constitutional right to be present and to confront witnesses," Keera said.

"I'm well aware, Ms. Duggan, but that right is not unrestricted and subject to his complying with courtroom procedures and decorum, as I instructed him at the start of the trial. Make your motion before I reseat the jury. After the jury is brought in, I will admonish them. And I want to be clear that neither of you is to refer to this incident for any reason, not in the examination of witnesses or in closing arguments. Is that understood?"

"How long will you keep the defendant out?" Keera asked.

"The remainder of today. After which, I'll decide on the remainder of the trial. No more discussion. My jury has waited long enough."

Back in court, with the furniture righted and the parties in their proper places, except for Michael, Keera stood and moved for a mistrial. Patel denied her motion. Keera moved to have the proceedings suspended for the day and that Michael be present pursuant to his Sixth Amendment right. Patel denied that motion also.

Patel then instructed the bailiff to reseat the jury. The jurors returned to the courtroom looking apprehensive but also a bit like they'd just witnessed a climactic scene in a movie and were still buzzing about it. Patel told them to disregard what they had witnessed and not to give it any further consideration. Fat chance. She said the court would proceed in the defendant's absence.

"Ms. Tran, you may continue."

"Thank you, Your Honor." Tran resumed her place at the lectern. Holmes had been reseated in the witness chair. "Mr. Holmes, did Mr. Westbrook tell you how he arrived at the decedent's house and how he departed after the murders?"

"I think he said his car had broken down. Something like that. He said the guy gave him a lift to work, and after they got off work, drove him back to his house to shoot some pool and drink beer out in the garage. He said the guy's girlfriend wasn't around, that she was wasted and had passed out in her bed. He said he brought up the subject of getting the money owed to him and the discussion got heated. The guy told him to get the hell out of his garage. Mikey said it all worked out, that his car breaking down was fortuitous because no one could say they saw his car at the house."

Keera had refocused and made notes of Holmes's inconsistencies—and two possibly fatal flaws in his testimony.

To illustrate the trust between Michael, Holmes, Glenn Ellis, and a few other inmates, Tran displayed several photographs, the men together in the FDC-SeaTac visitors area. The inmates stood behind family members. Michael had his hands on his mother's shoulders.

"Mr. Holmes, will you tell the court if you and I met before today?"

"Yeah, we met at FDC-SeaTac, and I told you what Mike told me."

"Did I offer you anything in exchange for the testimony you have given today?"

"You said that if I testified truthfully about what Mike told me, then you would talk to my federal judge about getting my sentence reduced."

"And have you testified truthfully here today?"

"I have," he said. Then he grinned. "The truth, the whole truth, and nothing but the truth."

"Are you in any danger, coming to court and testifying against another inmate?"

"Hell, yeah," he said. "You just witnessed it. Informants aren't well liked in prison. You got to be careful, or you'll end up dead."

"Then why are you testifying?"

Holmes paused a beat like a trained stage actor. "I think the thing that got to me was when Mike said he beat that woman with a tire iron, then masturbated over her. That was sick, man. That was just wrong."

Tran waited a beat before she said, "No further questions."

Judge Patel looked at the clock on the wall. "It's fifteen minutes before noon. We'll take our lunch recess now and be back in court at 1:00 p.m."

Keera wanted to cross-examine Holmes immediately, but she also needed the time to consult with Harrison and see what more, if anything, he had learned.

After the jury left the courtroom, Keera turned to where Tina Westbrook sat weeping. She put her hand on the woman's shoulder and sat beside her for a moment.

"There's no way Michael said or did what that man said," Tina said. "Michael doesn't have it in him."

Unfortunately, the jurors had just witnessed a vivid illustration that Michael maybe did have it in him, if he got angry enough. Keera looked up when the door pulled open. JP Harrison entered the courtroom and gave her a nod.

She left Tina and found Harrison outside, further down the hall, away from the courtroom entrance.

"Holmes was indicted for first-degree murder with two others under the felony murder rule but negotiated for second degree and testified against two of his codefendants. He served the drug conviction at FDC-SeaTac."

"He has a history of this."

"He does. He also lied under oath during a portion of his testimony in that trial, and the judge called him on it."

"Did you get that portion of the transcript?"

Harrison held out a document with Post-its marking several pages. "It's the best I could do."

It wasn't much, but it was more than Keera had a moment ago.

# Chapter 30

An hour later, back in court, the jury seated, Patel asked Keera if she had questions on cross-examination. Keera quickly made her way to the podium, then stepped past it, positioning herself near the jury box so Holmes would have to face the jurors. Had Michael still been in court she would have stood beside her client and forced Holmes to look at him. "You're making quite a career for yourself as a snitch; aren't you, Mr. Holmes?"

He smiled. "I don't know about that." His tone was flippant.

"That's how you're referred to in prison; right? One prisoner who informs on another prisoner in return for a favor is a snitch. Am I right?"

"Doesn't bother me none."

"Apparently not. Nor does friendship prevent you from being a snitch; does it?"

"I'm under oath to tell the truth."

"Did you tell the truth, the whole truth, and nothing but the truth when you ratted out your two drug partners?"

Tran, Keera knew, was in a tough spot. She couldn't very well come to Holmes's defense without it looking like she was protecting him, which she did not want to do. Holmes was on his own.

"I did tell the truth."

"But the judge in that case didn't think you told the whole truth; did she?"

"I don't know."

"But we do know." Keera walked to the defense table where she'd placed the document JP Harrison had provided, picked it up, and flipped to the page marked with a Post-it note. "Isn't it true that federal judge Evelyn Harper told the jurors, and everyone else in the courtroom that day, to disregard your testimony with respect to your involvement in the importing of drugs?"

"I don't recall."

"'Mr. Holmes,'" Keera said, reading from the transcript, "'I find under the circumstances that your testimony is not credible on this topic, and I am therefore instructing the jury to disregard it.' Does that refresh your recollection?"

"Not really."

"You don't recall a federal district judge calling you a *liar*? Does this happen to you often?"

Tran stood. "Objection, Your Honor. Mischaracterizes the court transcript. Move to strike."

Keera expected Patel to sustain the objection, but to her surprise, the judge paused, then said, "Overruled."

She sensed Patel did not want to look as if she was punishing Keera for being Patsy's daughter. Whatever Patel's reason, it gave Keera a chance to dig into Holmes. "Judge Harper says, right here in the court transcript"—she held it up to the jury—"'Your testimony is not credible.' Did you interpret the judge's statement to mean that she believed you were lying?"

"I don't know what I interpreted, if anything."

"The two defendants in the case in which you testified, your *work buddies*, were sentenced to first-degree murder and given life imprisonment based in part on your testimony; weren't they?"

"Yes, they were."

"But you, because you snitched against them, were charged with two lesser crimes, murder in the second degree, and given a sentence of just twelve years; weren't you?"

"That's right."

"That's quite an incentive to testify, even lie, as the federal district court judge found; isn't it?"

"Objection. Mischaracterizes the transcript."

"Sustained."

"I just told the truth," Holmes said.

Keera pointed to Tran. "How many years did the prosecutor promise to get shaved off your sentence for testifying in this case?"

Again, Tran made no move to stand.

"Nobody promised me any years."

"But you expect to have your sentence reduced again for testifying here; don't you?"

"If I helped solve two murders, I would think a judge would find that to be substantial assistance."

"'Substantial assistance.' Wow. You do this so often you even know the court's criteria for determining if you should get your sentence reduced?"

"It was told to me."

"By prosecutor Tran?"

"I don't recall."

"You have quite an incentive to not just testify, but to solve these two crimes; don't you?"

"I'm just telling the truth," he said again, this time sounding weary.

"You considered the two defendants in your murder case to be your friends also; didn't you?"

"We were business partners."

Keera opened the transcript to another page. "In federal court you testified, quote, 'We were all friendly.' 'Were you friends?' the prosecutor asked you. You responded, 'Yeah. You could say we were friends.' Do you recall that testimony?"

"Not specifically; no."

"Being your friend is dangerous; isn't it?"

"I don't think so."

"You testified against your two friends, and they got life sentences. You're testifying here against your 'friend' 'Mikey,' and the prosecutor is seeking to put him away for the remainder of *his* life. Having a friend like you is like falling on a grenade; isn't it?"

"Objection, Your Honor," Tran said.

"Overruled."

Keera didn't need an answer. Some jurors hid smirks. She was reaching them. "The court sentenced you pursuant to the federal sentencing guidelines, which mandate a minimum range of years you are required to serve for the offenses you committed; don't they?"

"I was told by my attorney they do. I don't really know."

"Once a judge sentences you, you are required to serve the mandatory minimum sentence; aren't you?"

"That's how it was explained to me."

"So good behavior while you're in jail can't shave years off that sentence; can it?"

"I don't know."

"So really, the only way for you to reduce your sentence is to snitch on other prisoners and have the prosecutor bring a motion to have your sentence reduced; isn't it?"

"It's not that simple."

Keera smiled and looked at the jury. "You seem to be the expert here, Mr. Holmes. Please explain snitching to the jury."

More smirks from several jurors.

"It's like I said. Being a prison informant can be dangerous. Other prisoners find out and you can end up getting yourself killed."

"But that's why you were at FDC-SeaTac and not at the Washington State Penitentiary in Walla Walla, which is where your other *two friends* who you testified against are serving their time; isn't it?"

"I meant it's dangerous in this instance."

"Except it's really not dangerous; is it?"

"I don't understand your question."

"It's not dangerous in this instance because Michael has been moved out of FDC-SeaTac and you're going to be moved also; aren't you?" Keera didn't know if Holmes was or wasn't going to be moved.

"I don't know."

"You might even be set free."

"I don't know."

"Couldn't a skeptical person like myself conclude that your life has been on the line ever since you snitched against your two buddies, and your motivation for cooperating in this case is because it's the only way for you to get out of prison alive?"

"I'm not going to lie and say I'm not motivated to get my prison time reduced. Anyone in my position would be. But that doesn't mean I'm lying."

"Are you saying you suddenly found a conscience; is that what you want this jury to believe?"

"I guess you can say I did."

"Just not soon enough for the two people you and your friends murdered; right?"

Holmes got a defiant look. "We all can change, by the grace of God."

Having attacked his credibility, Keera now focused on his testimony and what she perceived as two mistakes. "Mr. Holmes, you testified that the defendant told you he bought a gun on Craigslist; correct?"

"That's what he said."

"You testified under oath that he told you he and Mr. Lockett drove to work, then, after work, Mr. Lockett drove Michael back to Lockett's house to shoot pool and drink beer; right?"

"That's what he told me."

"So then Michael had the gun on him at work and at Mr. Lockett's house while they were shooting pool; is that right?" Keera raised her tone an octave to make the argument sound ludicrous.

Perhaps realizing the potential problem, Holmes said, "I don't remember exactly. I think he said maybe he had a locker at work? I don't know. He didn't tell me what he did with the gun while he was at work."

Keera went with what she knew. "He certainly did not put it in a locker at Mr. Lockett's house; did he?"

"I don't know."

"And you're saying Mr. Lockett argued with Michael about money when Michael was armed with a gun?" she asked, her voice rising with incredulity.

"Maybe he covered the gun with his shirt or something. I don't know. Like I said, he didn't tell me what he did with it."

"And he certainly didn't change clothes while he was at Mr. Lockett's house; did he?"

"I don't know."

Several jurors in Keera's peripheral vision lowered their heads to their notebooks, taking notes.

"So his work clothes should have been covered in brain and blood spatter; correct?"

"I don't know."

"You said you met with Ms. Tran prior to providing testimony here today?"

"That's right."

"That was to tell her what you were willing to say and to strike a deal to get your sentence reduced; right?"

"She had to learn what I would say; didn't she?"

"She certainly did. So how did you let her know that you had all this information related to the two murders?"

"I wrote her a letter."

Keera looked to Tran, then to Judge Patel. "Your Honor, the defense has received no such letters during discovery, and they would certainly be discoverable. I would request Mr. Holmes's letter and any other letters from informants offering to provide testimony in this case be immediately produced."

Tran stood. "Your Honor, if they were not produced, it was an oversight by my office. The prosecution will do so."

"There seems to be a lot of oversight in your office," Keera said under her breath but loud enough for the jury to hear as she returned to counsel's table.

"Objection. Move to strike," Tran said.

"So stricken. Ms. Duggan . . . ," Judge Patel said in a warning tone.

"The prosecutor used the word 'they,' meaning *more than one* letter. Until the defense receives those letters," Keera said, staring at Tran, "I have no more questions of this witness, but the defense requests the court dismiss but not release him subject to the defense calling him in its case in chief."

"This witness is dismissed but not released from his subpoena." Not that Keera could stomach another minute of Holmes on the witness stand, nor did she have any time to consider it—not with a second prison snitch about to testify, and what he had to say could further sink Michael's ship.

# Chapter 31

Physically, Glenn Ellis was the polar opposite of Laurence Holmes. He was Black whereas Holmes was white. Holmes was tall and lean, Ellis short and plump. Holmes had a full pate of gunmetal-gray hair. Ellis shaved what remained of his hair, just nubs visible. He, too, wore glasses, but his glasses were not fashionable, almost transparent on his face. Whereas Holmes came into court looking smug, Ellis entered looking ill at ease.

It soon became apparent why.

Ellis's testimony contradicted Holmes's testimony in some key areas. As she listened, Keera wondered why. Both men had surely testified before the grand jury, which should have given Ellis and Tran a chance to iron out any inconsistencies. Her father had once told Keera the problem with a lie, even a well-crafted one, is the details are hard to remember, because they never happened. This seemed like one of those instances.

"Mr. Ellis, you testified you were, for a time, Mr. Westbrook's cellmate at FDC-SeaTac; correct?" Keera asked on cross-examination.

"That's right," he said in a soft voice. "Mike and I were cellmates until he got taken to the King County jail."

"And you testified it was in your jail cell that Mr. Westbrook confessed to you and to Mr. Holmes that he killed John Lockett and Melissa Scott; is that right?"

"That's what I remember."

"He didn't confess out in the rec yard; did he?"

Ellis made a sour face and shook his head. "No. Not out in the rec yard. There would have been a lot of other inmates around."

"You also said Mr. Westbrook told you Mr. Lockett drove him home to Mr. Westbrook's house after work; is that correct?"

"That's what I recall."

"You don't recall him telling you they stopped at Mr. Lockett's home to shoot pool and drink beer; do you?"

Ellis's eyes shifted for a moment to Tran, but her expression remained stoic. He looked uncertain. "I can't recall," he said. "But . . ."

Keera shifted her body, ever so slightly, to prevent Ellis from having eye contact with Tran. "But what?"

"Nothing."

Keera thought she knew what Ellis had been about to say, but she'd have to work her way around it so Ellis would think he was giving her the answers Holmes had given. "I'm just wondering, did Mr. Westbrook tell you when and how he got the gun that he used to kill Mr. Lockett?"

"He said he got it off Craigslist. I don't know when."

"Yes, you testified to that," she said as if recalling it. "I'm just wondering if he told you when he got the gun that night or that morning, to shoot Mr. Lockett; did he say?"

"Well, that's what I was going to say earlier. If Michael stopped to shoot pool and drink beer, then he wouldn't have had the gun."

Keera nodded as if understanding and to give the jurors time to digest this discrepancy. "So, Michael told you Mr. Lockett dropped him off at home and that's when he got the gun?"

"I think it was something like that."

Keera flipped through pages, making it look like she couldn't find what she was looking for. "And then what? Did he tell you he drove back to Mr. Lockett's home?"

Again, Ellis paused, maybe catching on to her highlighting his inconsistencies. "No. He said his car had broken down." He lowered his gaze, as if in thought. "I'm not really sure if he said how he got back." Keera was about to ask another question when Ellis said, "He ran back."

Keera looked to him as if she hadn't heard him. "I'm sorry?"

"Mike said he ran back."

"He ran back," she repeated.

"He said his car had broken down. So he had to run back to the house and then run home again."

Michael's treating physician would testify that Michael had asthma, making it unlikely he *ran* anywhere that morning and certainly not the four and a half miles round trip. Keera could now argue the two men couldn't get their story straight, and the jurors shouldn't trust either one of them. She'd argue they were opportunists who would say anything to get their sentences reduced.

Keera dismissed Ellis, but also did not release him.

Tran opted not to do a redirect to rehabilitate Ellis, no doubt not wanting to further draw the jurors' attention to his inconsistencies.

"The State may call its next witness," Judge Patel said.

Tran rose. Keera suspected she had saved Emily Carter and these two dramatic informants for last, to leave an impression on the jury during Keera's case in chief. She was right.

"Your Honor," Tran said. "The State rests."

# Chapter 32

Before leaving the courthouse, Keera, Harrison, and Tina Westbrook commiserated for a few minutes in the hallway. It had not been a good week for the defense, though Keera didn't say this in front of Tina.

"You did a great job pointing out all the inconsistencies between Holmes's and Ellis's testimony and letting the jurors know the two men had every reason to lie," Harrison said, but it sounded like he was encouraging his sister to maintain hope—as much as to encourage Keera not to lose it. They still had a case to put on.

When she arrived back at her office, the reception area was dark, and the computer at Maggie's station had been turned off. Maggie was likely starting the weekend with her new boyfriend. It only served to remind Keera that she had no one to rush home to, no date to primp for. She'd told her family Italy had been a wonderful escape, but like the darkened reception area, it had also served as a reminder that she did not, at present, have anyone with whom to share her life.

She walked down the hall, the associate offices and the staff desks empty. A light peeked from beneath Patsy's office door. She wondered if her father had forgotten to turn it off. She pushed in the door. Patsy waited at the conference room table with several white boxes, paper plates, chopsticks, and cans of soda and soda water.

"I got Thai food," he said.

She couldn't hold back her grin—or her welling tears. "What are you doing here, Dad?"

"I thought we could have dinner together, maybe talk through the good, the bad, and the ugly."

She walked in further and lowered her briefcase. "I'm afraid it's mostly the bad and the ugly. I thought you were taking Mom away for a few days."

"I was," he said. "But she has a head cold and asked to postpone our trip to Victoria."

"You should go home and take care of Mom."

"Your mother is a terrible patient. You know that. She refuses to admit she's sick and won't let me do anything to help her."

"That's true."

He smiled. "Besides, I remember what it's like when a trial isn't going well. I just thought you might like a little dinner company. Come on, let's eat before it gets cold. I got all your favorites: pot stickers, tom kha soup, drunken noodles with chicken."

"You really are trying to make me feel better; aren't you?" She removed her jacket and sat. "So, who told you the trial wasn't going well?"

"I still got a few spies at the courthouse." He opened boxes and passed them to Keera. The smells made her realize she was starving, not having eaten lunch that day. Instead, she had reviewed the transcript Harrison had brought her to prepare her cross-examination of Holmes. "Tell me about the two informants."

"Well, it's not great." She dipped a pot sticker in sauce and took a bite, nearly dropping the other half from her chopsticks. The taste was heavenly. Ground pork, sesame oil, garlic, and ginger. "They got the high points right, both saying Michael killed Lockett and Scott, but they didn't get the details accurate. I'm sure Tran will dismiss the inconsistencies as trivial, as proof the two men didn't concoct a story together, and I'll attack the inconsistencies as proof they're lying. Unfortunately, I don't have a great argument to explain Michael and Melissa Scott having an affair. That might be more difficult for some jurors to dismiss. And I'm sure you heard about Michael's meltdown in the courtroom?"

"I think everyone did." Patsy ate a piece of chicken and tried to get a long noodle to his mouth.

"It's odd, Dad." Keera put down her chopsticks and took a drink of her soda water. "It's like Tran knows where I'm going before I get there."

"Tell me why you think that?"

Keera told her father about Tran calling a DEA agent at the start of her case, though he wasn't listed to testify that day, undercutting Keera's plan to open with the agent in Michael's defense. She told him how Tran had undercut her argument that Michael had the packages because Lockett was using him, and how she'd argued that had been Michael's motivation to kill Lockett and Scott. In between the discussion, she and Patsy ate more pad Thai. "She's very good, Dad. She'd make a great chess opponent. She's smart, intuitive, and unpredictable."

"Sounds to me like you're still playing her game."

"Kind of hard not to. She seems to have figured out my game and is doing a good job of preventing me from going on the offensive."

"Why do you think she called the two informants?"

"Why?"

He nodded, unable to answer verbally with his mouth filled with a dumpling.

"Because it puts a nail in Michael's coffin," Keera said. "To disregard both witnesses, the jury would have to believe both men made up the entire story. The jury might question why they didn't get their facts right, but I don't think I can persuade them they made up the entire confession."

"Understood. But why would Tran call the two informants?"

"I don't understand your question."

"You're speculating that she called them because she wanted strong witnesses at the end of her case in chief, to put a nail in Westbrook's coffin, as you so eloquently stated. What if the opposite were true? What if she called them because she wasn't confident in her case?"

Keera hadn't thought of this.

"Maybe she's worried you poked enough holes to make reasonable doubt a real possibility. What if her using the informants—not one but two—was a desperation move?" Patsy grinned and flexed his eyebrows.

Keera had seen this look before and had heard this questioning tone of voice. Patsy never gave her answers. He always made her think for herself. "What do you know?" she asked.

He gave her that Patsy shrug and mischievous smile. "Tran didn't have someone on the other side poking holes in her arguments when she presented the case to the grand jury."

"You're saying she's worried she didn't have enough without Holmes and Ellis?"

"Why run the risk of calling both men and having the inconsistencies you spoke of? I'm saying, maybe you're scoring more points than you think." He put his arms up, like a boxer protecting himself. "You've been covering up, which is exactly what you need to do during the State's case. Now it's your turn to throw a few punches."

Keera sighed. "Thanks, Dad." She was still his daughter. Still the little girl he had trained to play chess, and she still liked to hear him compliment her. This had been a much-needed pep talk. It made her feel better than she'd felt all week.

After eating together, Keera sent her father home, which was a definite role reversal. She wanted to check her messages and clear the deck so she could enjoy a few hours off tonight, maybe watch a movie on television, a comedy or a sappy romance, then dig in again tomorrow. She went through her emails first and assigned certain associates to respond to matters that needed attention. Eager to get home, she shut her computer down and grabbed her briefcase. At the door she turned out the lights.

Her desk phone rang.

Since it was well after hours, the answering service would pick up if Keera didn't, but when in trial, an attorney didn't have the luxury of ignoring phone calls, not even late at night when most sane people had gone home. She dropped her briefcase in her office chair and picked up the phone. "Duggan & Associates. Hello? Hello?"

"Sorry. I didn't expect a live voice. I'm trying to reach Keera Duggan." A man's voice. She did not recognize it.

"This is she."

Keera listened as the man explained the purpose of his call. Her stomach got that familiar feeling, the one she got when she sensed a trial or a chess match taking a turn, maybe even a turn in the right direction.

# Chapter 33

With the evening rush hour having passed, Keera made the five-mile ride from her office in under fifteen minutes. She didn't know where Harrison had been when she'd called his cell, but just a minute after she parked in the street, he pulled up behind her in his BMW and quickly got out of his car.

"Déjà vu," he said, greeting her as they approached the door to the one-story rambler on the corner lot across the street from Tina Westbrook's home—where they had previously spoken to Jada Davis.

The door pulled open before Keera knocked. A Black man, as tall as Harrison and dressed in a blue long-sleeve button-down shirt, jeans, and slippers, stepped outside and pulled the door closed behind him. Jamar Davis introduced himself and adjusted tortoiseshell glasses. "Before we go inside, I want you to know that my daughter is nervous. She deals with anxiety, and this has piqued her anxiousness."

"I understand," Keera said. Jamar Davis was looking out for his daughter. "We'll proceed slowly."

"Michael is not a bad kid," he said, looking across the street to Tina Westbrook's home. "He got mixed up with the wrong people in high school, but he seemed to have his life headed in the right direction until all this happened. Tina has done her best, but raising a young man on her own is tough. I know. My mother did it. Young women can be difficult also, I'm learning. Jada's mother and I are upset with her . . ." He shook his head. "It's hard to accept that your daughter is an adult who can make her own decisions, especially when she still lives in your home, but all that has to take a back seat right now, given what we've recently read in the paper and seen on the news about Michael's trial. And what Jada confided in us."

"We'd love to hear what Jada has to say," Keera said.

Jamar Davis gave a tight-lipped grin, then said, "Come on in."

Davis opened the door and Keera and JP stepped into a well-kept house with hardwood floors and throw rugs. Colorful paintings of African settings hung on the walls, and wooden bowls and sculptures of a giraffe and a Cape buffalo adorned the mantel over the fireplace. Jada Davis and her mother rose from a dark-blue, L-shaped, leather couch. The young woman's eyes were swollen. She'd been crying.

"Hey, Jada." Keera shook the young woman's hand and introduced herself to Michelle Davis.

They all sat, Jamar on the couch with his wife and his daughter, Keera adjacent to them on the short side of the sofa. Harrison took a seat in a chair. The home was cozy and something smelled delicious. It reminded Keera of her home and childhood, after all her siblings had left the house. She could also feel the tension in the room, the unease of those seated.

Keera decided to let Jada go at her own pace. "Jada, your father said you have a few things to tell me."

"I didn't tell you everything that morning we spoke." Jada's eyes darted between Harrison and Keera, her voice soft. "I didn't know Michael was in so much trouble. I thought . . ." She paused and took a breath. "I thought they arrested him for selling drugs again. Then my dad told me what the media was saying, about what the two informants said in court. I'm sorry. I just . . ." The young woman lowered her head, crying. "I should have told you sooner but . . . I hope it's not too late."

"That's okay," Keera said.

Jada took another breath and let it out in a rush. "I was out that night." She glanced at her father, who had one hand on the stubble of his beard, chin pressed to his chest, his gaze on the black walnut coffee table. "I snuck out to see my boyfriend. He lives in an apartment just a few miles away. We were watching a movie, and I fell asleep. When I awoke it was four fifteen in the morning."

Keera tried not to rush the young woman or to question her. She didn't know if Jada had fallen asleep watching a movie or was just tempering her story for her father's benefit. That had nothing to do with Keera.

"I was really scared . . . I told my boyfriend I had to get home, that if my parents woke up and found out I wasn't in my room they'd freak out and think something had happened to me. And I did have a test that day in chemistry. I needed to go over the material again."

Keera waited. She could feel her heart hammering in her chest. She was anxious to hear what the young woman had to say about Michael.

"I couldn't find my keys right away, but when I found them, I hurried out to my car and quickly drove home. When I reached the corner"—she gestured—"I shut off the headlights before I turned and parked in the driveway. As I was about to get out, I saw headlights coming down the street. I don't know why, but I ducked down and waited for the car to pass. When it didn't, I looked in the passenger's-side mirror. I could see that the car had stopped in front of Michael's house. At first nothing happened. Then Michael got out. He had something in his hands. A package."

"You could see the package?"

She nodded. "It was dark out, but Mrs. Westbrook's porch light was on. Michael put the package on the roof, then bent down, like he was continuing to speak to the man driving the car."

"How long did Michael talk to the man?" Keera asked.

"He only stayed there for about a minute. Then he reached inside and moved his arm, like this."

"Like the two men were shaking hands," Harrison said.

"That was my impression," Jada said.

"Did you hear them saying anything?"

"I heard Michael say, 'Thanks for the ride.' Then he took the package, closed the car door, and went inside his house."

"You watched him go inside his house?" Keera said trying not to overreact.

"Yes."

Keera looked at Harrison and could tell they both were thinking Jada Davis's testimony further discredited Laurence Holmes's testimony.

"There's more," Jada said, and it sounded ominous. The good feeling Keera had became a twinge of nerves. She was certain Jada was about to tell her Michael came back out wearing dark clothing and ran down the street.

"I got out quietly and went inside. I told you that my room faces the street."

"I recall," Keera said.

"And my desk is pushed up against the window."

"You had to study," Keera said, starting to put it together, though still not certain what Jada was about to say.

"I sat at my desk and turned on the lamp. I was studying and periodically watching the sky. It doesn't get light out that time of year until about eight o'clock. That's when I got up from my desk and went to school to take my test."

"At any time between when you sat down and got up to take your test did you see Michael come back out of his house?" Keera asked.

Jada Davis shook her head before Keera had finished asking the question. "No. He never did. In fact, when he went inside, he turned on the light in his room. I was at my desk, and at four thirty in the morning I could see light behind his blinds. After a few minutes he turned the light off. Michael never turned the light back on. He never came back out."

"How high up is the window in your room?" Keera asked. "Did you have a clear view of Michael's house?"

"Do you want me to show you?"

"Yes," Keera and Harrison both said.

The family got up from the couch, and Jada led them all down a hallway with framed family photographs of Jada, her parents, and her brother. "Sorry, my room is a bit of a mess at the moment."

Keera smiled. "Probably looks like mine," she said.

Jada opened the door to a modest-sized room with a captain's bed, drawers beneath the mattress. To the left was a narrow closet, the door open. Clothing hung from a wooden rod. A desk was pushed up beneath the window, the blinds raised.

Keera walked to the desk and looked out the window at Tina Westbrook's home and the postage-stamp-sized yard. She sat in the ergonomic chair at Jada Davis's desk. Her eyes were above the windowsill. She could clearly see Tina's house and yard. A streetlamp illuminated the street. She tempered her good feelings for the moment and thought of questions Tran might ask to discredit the young woman.

She turned in the desk chair. "Did you get up, leave this spot for any reason . . . to go to the bathroom, to take a quick nap? Get a cup of coffee, something to eat? Any reason at all?"

Jada shook her head. "Not until I got up to take my test. I had too much to do. I'm a bit OCD, and I was cranking to get through the material. I figured I could sleep when I got back home that afternoon."

Keera turned to Harrison to see if he could think of anything else.

"Tina's house has a door at the back, off the kitchen. It leads to the backyard," he said.

"I remember it. When Michael and I were kids we used to play back there," Jada said. "His father hung a rope swing from a tree branch and put up a play structure."

Keera knew Harrison had put up the rope swing and the play structure.

"So, Michael could have gone out the back door?" Keera asked.

"He could have," Jada said, "but he'd still have to come around to the front yard."

"She's right," Harrison said. "There's no gate in the fence back there."

"He could have jumped the fence," Keera said.

"Could have, but the backyard separates the house behind it on the next street over, which is in the opposite direction Michael would have needed to go to get to John Lockett's house," Harrison said. "It wouldn't make any sense for him to go out the back, even if there was a gate."

"And you never saw Michael that morning?" Keera asked Jada.

"No. I never did," Jada said.

Keera ran all this information through her trial filter, figuring out ways to get it introduced into evidence and for the jurors to consider it. She had wanted to open the defense's case with a DEA agent, but Tran had foiled that attack.

Opening with Jada Davis, however, could be better.

She looked to Jamar Davis and his wife. "I'd like JP to take some photographs of your house in relationship to the Westbrook home, where the two are situated, as well as from the interior of this room, looking out the window, across to the house and yard. Would that be all right?"

"Can Jada clean her room first?" Michelle Davis asked.

Keera almost responded yes, then rethought it. She smiled. "I'd rather she didn't. I don't want anyone to make the argument that this was in any way staged."

# Chapter 34

Back in the conference room Saturday morning, Keera felt not quite rejuvenated but at least invigorated. She had a team of reinforcements come into the office this morning—Harrison, her father, and Ella. Even Maggie came in to lend a needed hand, though Keera suspected her father had a part in Maggie being there. Blood was blood, and he was circling the wagons for Keera.

At the conference room table, Keera and Harrison told all of them about Jada Davis, what the young woman had seen and heard. The report gave everyone a much-needed lift and a new sense of optimism. That afternoon, Keera, her father, and JP met with expert witnesses, went over direct examinations, and went through the documents and photographs Keera would seek to admit into evidence.

After she'd sent her experts home, Keera, Patsy, JP, and Ella discussed possible motions and trial strategy, as well as Keera's direct examination of Jada Davis. Ella would bring a motion arguing that the State had not met its burden and request that the court dismiss the charges. Patel would summarily deny that motion, but it would secure the appellate record.

"Let's also bring a motion to compel the two letters the prison informants wrote to Tran," Patsy said.

"I agree," Keera said. "I want the request in writing, should Tran fail to voluntarily comply."

"And make it broad enough in scope to encompass any and all statements from any and all prisoners, whether the informant testified or not," Patsy said.

"I'm also going to need you to amend the witness statement to add Jada Davis," Keera said to Ella.

Ella smiled like she used to when her baby sister did something surprising or remarkable. "I'm already on it," she assured.

"And I want your opinions on my idea to open our defense with Jada Davis."

"Tell me why you're considering it?" Patsy asked.

Maggie came in with a fresh pot of coffee and some bagels, setting them on the table as Keera told them her rationale.

"I don't want the specter of Michael confessing to the killings hanging over the jurors throughout every witness I call. I'm concerned the jurors will dismiss my case if they believe Michael confessed. Opening with Jada Davis is a strong rebuttal to both Laurence Holmes's and Glenn Ellis's testimony, proof that Michael went home and never left the house."

"I like it," Patsy said. "Come out throwing punches."

"And you've already raised questions about their veracity," Harrison said. "This will further expose them as liars."

"How confident are you in this young lady testifying?" Patsy asked.

"Confident," Keera said. "She's intelligent, though understandably anxious about getting on the witness stand and testifying in court. I think the jurors will like her—a lot."

Harrison agreed.

"Have her acknowledge her nerves up front," Patsy counseled. "The jury will empathize with her even more. It will put Tran in a tough spot when she cross-examines Davis."

"I like opening with her also," Ella said. "There's something tender about it in a violent case."

"For what it's worth, I do too," Maggie said.

"It's unanimous. I'll amend the witness list, but I won't send it over to the PA's office until Monday morning," Ella said. "What's good for the goose, right?"

Tran would object, but given her own last-minute disclosures, Judge Patel would be hard pressed not to dismiss her objection.

"Anything else?" Ella asked.

"Nothing that I can think of," Keera said.

She looked to Patsy, who shook his head and said, "If I think of something else, I'll let you know."

"Did Judge Patel issue any updates about Michael's attendance at trial going forward?" Harrison asked.

"She emailed over a three-sentence ruling last night. She will allow Michael back into the courtroom but under a no-tolerance policy. If he acts up again, he'll be removed from the courtroom permanently."

"He won't," Harrison said. "I've had a come-to-Jesus meeting with him."

"What else can I help you with?" Patsy asked.

"I'm going to need some direct examinations of our experts. Can you put them together for me?"

"I'll get it done."

"I can help with that," Harrison said.

"Mail came," Maggie said. "I put it on your chairs. Anything else?" She sounded anxious to leave.

"I think things are under control for now," Keera said. "Thanks, Maggie. I appreciate you coming in on a Saturday to help. Are you off somewhere fun?"

"Sam is taking me out."

"So this new beau actually has a name?" Patsy said.

"When are we going to get to meet him?" Ella asked.

"I don't know," Maggie said, coy as she moved to the door. "I don't want you to scare him off."

Maggie departed and Keera took a breath. With things under control, and everyone tasked with their assignments, she wanted to go for a run along the waterfront and give herself time to think further about the case she would present.

She went into her office to change into running clothes. A stack of mail waited on her chair—or more accurately awaited her assistant Monday morning. Then she recalled the informant witness statements she'd moved to have Tran produce. She checked her emails first. Not seeing anything from the PA's office, she picked up and flipped through the mail, tossing nonurgent mail back onto her chair and junk mail into the wastebasket beside her desk.

She stopped when she came to a solid white envelope with blue-gray typing. The return address on the envelope was from an inmate at the Monroe Correctional Complex.

Victor Carlos Garcia
DOC # 478532
Monroe Correctional Complex
16774 170th Ave SE
Monroe, WA 98272

Keera periodically received mail from inmates after the publicity generated from the Vince LaRussa and Jenna Bernstein trials. Most inmates were looking for an appellate lawyer to appeal their convictions. DOC stood for Department of Corrections and was included to ensure an unopened letter could be returned to the correct inmate.

Maggie had sliced open the envelope with a letter opener. Keera pulled the letter out and unfolded it. Reading the first sentence, she realized she would not be going for a run.

She hurried back down the hall to the conference room. Harrison and Patsy looked up from the table. "I need you to get us into the Monroe Correctional Complex," she said to Harrison as she handed the letter to Patsy. "ASAP."

"What's going on?" Harrison asked. He pulled out his cell phone to make a call.

Keera paced as Patsy read the letter.

> I have information related to you're case involving Michael Wesbtrook that you will want to here. Cometo the Monroe Correctional Complex to talk. Be careful who you tell about this.
>
> Victor Garcia
> DOC # 478532

"Do you have any idea what this is about?" Patsy asked.

"No. I don't recognize the name," Keera said. "Do you?"

"I don't think it's anyone we've ever represented," Ella said.

"Look at the date on the letter. He typed it a week ago."

After several minutes, Harrison disconnected his call. "Garcia is kept in the reformatory unit. Visiting hours are ordinarily Friday to Monday 12:30 to 7:30, but they canceled all visits today and tomorrow."

"What? Why?" Keera asked.

"An unplanned incident was all they would say. They anticipate opening again Monday morning."

"Can they make an exception?" Keera asked.

Harrison shook his head. "I was told they would not. It sounds like the incident was serious."

"I'll go Monday with JP," Patsy said. "And determine if Garcia has something to say, or if it's a prison con to get us to represent him. I've dealt with this before. You take care of your case."

# Chapter 35

Monday morning, Keera sat in court, anxious to get started. Around her, Judge Patel's staff discussed their weekends. Keera did her best to concentrate on the task at hand, but her mind kept drifting to the letter from the prisoner at the Monroe Correctional Complex and what possible information he could possess.

The correctional officers escorted Michael to the counsel table. Keera had met with Michael over the weekend and had told him what Jada Davis had to say, which seemed to improve his mood. She asked if he knew an inmate named Victor Garcia, but he did not. She did not tell him more, in case what Garcia had to say was just a con and he was seeking representation.

Prior to Patel bringing in the jury, Keera and Michael Westbrook stood. Michael apologized for his outburst and told Patel it would not happen again. Patel reiterated what she had put in her order about the court having a zero-tolerance policy. She emphasized she would not hesitate to remove Michael if he caused another disruption.

Patel brought in the jury, explained to them about the defense putting on its case, then turned to Keera. "Counsel, call your first witness."

Keera called Jada Davis. She prepared for a Tran objection that never came. Tran had her gaze fixed on her tablet computer, on which she appeared to be typing notes on top of notes. Interesting.

The bailiff returned from the hallway with Jada. Her mother and father followed her into the courtroom and took seats in the gallery to provide their daughter moral support.

Jada looked like a college student on her way to an important interview, a bundle of nerves in high-waisted black pants, a collared shirt beneath a light-blue cashmere sweater, and flats. She was unfamiliar with court procedure—where to go or where to stand, which was perfect. It would give her instant credibility with the jurors. The bailiff led her onto the witness stand and Patel told her to face the bench and raise her right hand, then administered the oath to tell the truth.

"I do," Jada said, lowering her hand and sitting.

Keera approached. "Are you nervous, Jada?" she asked.

"Very," Jada said, sounding like she was releasing a held breath.

"Just try to relax and answer my questions. If you don't know the answer you can say you don't know."

"Okay."

Keera ran Jada through the preliminaries, where Jada lived and how she knew Michael. Keera also brought up their conversation with Harrison outside Jada's home. Jada explained why she had not brought up the subject of seeing Michael return home early in the morning. She didn't realize the amount of trouble Michael was in, or that she could have relevant information until after she'd heard the news reports of what the two informants had said. Racked with guilt, she went to her mother and told her what she had seen that morning.

Keera introduced photographs JP Harrison had taken and had Jada verify they accurately represented the proximity of her home to Michael Westbrook's, the location of her bedroom with the window facing the street, and the view she had that morning.

"And you never saw Michael, or anyone else, leave his house that morning after he arrived home at approximately four thirty?" Keera asked.

"No. No one."

Keera thanked Jada. She had performed admirably. As she turned to Tran and passed the witness, she felt a bit like a mom about to leave her child at school alone for the first time. She knew Tran would be adept at poking holes in Jada's testimony, but she was confident the young woman could handle it. "Your witness."

Tran rose and approached Jada Davis, bypassing the lectern and moving to the witness chair. It was an intimidation technique, but one Keera told Jada she could expect.

"You're a good student; aren't you, Jada?" Tran sounded complimentary, no animosity in her voice. Perhaps she'd decided the jury wouldn't take kindly to her beating up a nervous college student.

"I try," she said.

"You testified you are in Seattle University's nursing program; is that correct?"

"Yes."

"And what is your grade point average?"

"I have a 4.0."

"Straight A's. I can see why, being so dedicated that you'd get up to study at four thirty in the morning and study for three and a half hours without taking a break."

"I didn't," Jada said. "Not one."

"I believe you," Tran said. "To achieve those kind of grades takes immense concentration and focus; doesn't it?"

Keera now realized Tran sought to use Jada's diligence against her, but she could do nothing to let the young woman know.

"It's a difficult major," Jada said.

"You have your nose in your books; don't you?"

"I guess so."

"You had your eyes down, studying the course material, maybe taking practice exams; correct?"

Jada looked like she'd caught on. "Not the whole time; no."

"No? What else were you doing?"

"I like that time of day, so I'd lift my head and watch the early morning sky brighten."

"So, you lifted your head what . . . once, twice . . . maybe three times while you were seated at your desk studying hard for that upcoming test you were anxious about?"

"I don't know how many times I looked out the window."

"Did you see any dog walkers?"

Keera stood. "Speculation. The question implies there had been any dog walkers that morning."

"I'm just asking if *she* saw any," Tran said.

"Overruled."

"Did you see any?"

"No," Jada said.

"Did you see any cars drive up or down the block?"

"Just the one Michael got out of."

"Any others?"

"Not that I can recall."

"Newspaper delivery man or woman?"

"I didn't see any."

"Did you see any of your neighbors?"

"No."

"When you arrived at home at four thirty in the morning it was still dark out; wasn't it?"

"Yes."

"And you testified that Michael got out and stood in the street for a moment, and you believed he was talking to the driver; correct?"

"He was facing the car and bent down beneath the roof."

"You didn't hear what they were saying to one another, still in your car and hunkered down so you wouldn't be seen; did you?"

"Not the entire conversation."

"So you can't really say if they were arguing or disagreeing on something."

"Michael didn't look like it. And I did hear him thank the driver for the ride home."

"But you don't really know; do you?"

"He reached in and shook the man's hand, and he thanked him. I saw that and I heard that. And I didn't see him make any other hand gestures or anything," Jada said. "And I didn't hear him raise his voice."

It was a good answer by the young lady. She wasn't going to be pushed off her testimony.

"What was Michael wearing?"

"I don't know."

"You couldn't see what he was wearing?"

"I didn't really look at his clothes."

"Could you see if it was a man or a woman driving the car with Michael?"

A pause. "No."

"You assumed it was a man?"

"I guess so."

"What was the make of the car?"

Another pause. "I didn't pay attention to the make of the car."

"How about the color?"

"I don't recall."

"You don't know the license plate number either; do you?"

"I don't. I wasn't paying attention to the license plate."

"You were fixated on getting inside and studying; weren't you?"

"I suppose."

"Now, when you got to your room, you turned on the lamp shown in this picture of your desk; didn't you?"

"Yes."

"It was still dark outside when you turned on this lamp; wasn't it?"

"Yes."

"Still too dark for you to see what Michael was wearing, or the car's make; right?"

"Michael had gone into the house. I didn't see him after that."

"I'm not surprised. If I turn my desk lamp on and it's dark outside, that light reflects in the window glass and all I can see is my own reflection. I can't see outside. That's how it is for you also; isn't it?"

Jada paused again, now looking uncertain. Not good. "I don't really recall a reflection."

"Let me show you a photograph that your attorney showed you." Tran nodded to George Thomas and a photograph appeared on the computer screens. "Do you see the desk light's reflection in the window in this photograph?"

"Yes."

Tran removed the photograph, switching gears. "Now, you testified that you and Michael grew up together; correct?"

"Yes."

"Right next door to one another; right?"

"Yes."

"You played at his house and he at yours; correct?"

"Yes."

"You also said you don't really hang out anymore."

"Not really. I'm in school and studying a lot, and he works part-time and goes to the community college. So our paths don't really cross."

"But you still consider him a friend; don't you?"

Jada looked at Michael. "Yes."

"A friend in a lot of trouble; wouldn't you agree?"

"It seems that way."

"So even though you met with Ms. Duggan and her private investigator shortly after Michael was arrested and taken away, you didn't tell them that you saw your friend come home for what . . . months? Is that your testimony?" And just like that Tran's tone became disbelief.

"I didn't know how much trouble Michael was in until my father told me what the media was saying."

"Not until you read about this trial, accusing Michael of killing two people; is that your testimony?"

"I read what the media said the two prisoners had to say and that isn't what happened. Not what I saw, anyway. Michael came home at four thirty that morning and he didn't leave again."

"You snuck out of your house without telling your parents; didn't you?"

"Yes," Jada said, looking confused by the question.

"And you also didn't tell them what you had supposedly seen that morning until months later; did you?"

"No. I—"

"But then, when you learned that your very good childhood friend was in trouble, you suddenly remembered this very important bit of information and you told your parents; is that your testimony?"

Jada looked at her father seated in the gallery, and it seemed to give her strength. She sat up. "I told you—"

"That's a 'yes' or 'no' question Ms. Davis. Yes or no. Is that your testimony?"

"Yes."

Tran looked at the jury. "No further questions."

"Redirect, Ms. Duggan?" Patel asked.

Keera stood. "Jada," she said, approaching. "Is everything you said here in this courtroom the truth?"

"Everything."

"Would you lie to protect Michael?"

"No," she said. "I wouldn't."

"Did you see him come home that morning?"

"One hundred percent."

"Did you see him leave again?"

"One hundred percent, no."

Keera sat. Tran stood again. "You wouldn't lie to protect Michael?"

"No."

"But you lied to your parents when you snuck out, and you lied to Ms. Duggan and to her investigator that morning; didn't you?"

"I didn't lie to them. I just didn't tell them everything."

Tran smiled. Her point made.

# Chapter 36

Patsy and JP Harrison arrived at the Monroe Correctional Complex at noon to begin the check-in process. Maggie had completed two visitor applications online, and had Harrison and Patsy approved and added to Victor Garcia's visitors list. They left all jewelry at home and locked their cell phones in JP's car. Inside the facility, a guard guided them and other visitors into a meeting area that looked like a cafeteria, where they sat at a table and waited. When the door opened on the other side of the room, inmates entered wearing sweatshirts and sweatpants or khaki pants and shirts. The chatter in the room increased to an almost uncomfortable level.

Patsy noticed an inmate enter and not move immediately to a table. Short but muscular, with large trapezoids that made his neck look small, he scanned the tables. His salt-and-pepper hair had been cut short, perhaps acquiescing to premature balding. Tattoos emerged along his neck above the collar of his long-sleeve sweatshirt.

When the other men found their visitors, Victor Garcia approached Patsy and Harrison by process of elimination. "I thought I was meeting with Keera Duggan," Garcia said, talking above the cacophony of voices and explaining his confusion.

"Keera is my daughter. She's in trial. I'm Patsy Duggan. This is JP Harrison, our investigator on the Michael Westbrook case. He's also Michael's uncle." They did not shake hands, per the visiting no-contact rules. "Keera got your letter. We're eager to hear what you have to say."

The three men sat.

Patsy and JP waited. Garcia continued to look between them. "Before I tell you what I got to say, I need some type of assurance."

"Assurance?" Patsy said. *Here we go.*

"My appellate attorney won't listen to me. Doesn't believe me. Won't do anything about what I'm about to tell you."

"You need a lawyer to help with your appeal," Patsy said, already thinking this had been a waste of time.

"That's right. I did some digging on my own in the law library. I know your law firm represents the accused, and I know you're good. You help me and I'll help you. And trust me, what I'm about to tell you is no bullshit. It's the God's truth. I swear it." Garcia pulled out a wooden cross from beneath his sweatshirt and kissed it, then looked up and pointed to the ceiling. He had prison tattoos of crucifixes on the back of each hand.

"Okay, how do we assure you that we'll look at your case?"

"Give me your word," Garcia said. "I don't need anything in writing. Just tell me you'll do it."

"There are no guarantees we'll find anything to appeal, or anything that would warrant a new trial, Victor," Patsy said.

"I'm in prison. There are no guarantees of anything. But I think you'll find something." He looked at JP. "If this big man is worth his salt, you'll find something that will help your nephew *and me*. Do we have a deal?"

"Deal," Patsy said.

Patsy liked to observe witnesses, look for tells the witness was lying or perhaps exaggerating. He'd once had an eidetic memory, back before alcohol put a dent in his abilities. One thing he couldn't deny, he liked being back in the trenches and digging in, especially if it would help his daughter. Keera was an accomplished trial attorney, but she'd always be his daughter, and he'd always want to help her.

"When I got pinched for drugs, I was originally sent to FDC-SeaTac for a four-year bid," Garcia said. He had a habit of squinting, as if the room was too bright. "I stayed there until after I was tried for the murder of Jesus Montoya, which I did not commit. They had no evidence I did. My attorney even said that. They had nothing but circumstantial bullshit. Then, out of the blue, these two inmates at FDC-SeaTac get on the stand and say I told them I killed Jesus, which was pure bullshit. Jesus and I were friends. And I never told anybody nothing about killing anyone, nor would I."

"Who was the prosecutor?" Patsy asked.

Garcia smiled and sat back. "Anh Tran. Same prosecutor you're dealing with now in the Westbrook case."

"What were the inmate witnesses' names?" Patsy asked.

"Angel Hernandez and Vincent Constantino."

"Go on," Patsy said.

"Okay. Fast-forward. I'm in King County Superior Court for a hearing. I can get you a date. My appellate attorney was arguing ineffective assistance of counsel and other bullshit arguments that had no chance of success."

Garcia was right. Ineffective assistance of counsel was one of a cadre of routine motions appellate lawyers picked through and brought, usually without success.

"I was waiting in the holding tank to be transferred back here, and they bring in another guy. He was all smiles, man. He said he'd just had his case thrown out, and he was being processed out. We told each other our names and he says, 'I know all about what had happened to you.' And I said, 'Yeah, how do you know about me?' And he said he knew about me because the same thing that happened to me was happening to some inmate named Michael Westbrook in the King County Superior Court."

Garcia had Patsy and Harrison's attention.

"What did he say was going to happen to Michael?" Harrison asked.

"He said FDC-SeaTac has this ring of snitches who testify in exchange for getting their sentences reduced. He said he hears that's what went down with me."

Patsy listened but remained cautious. He continued to look for any tells Garcia could be lying.

"He said Vincent Constantino and Angel Hernandez were part of this ring and so were the two guys who were going to testify against Westbrook."

"Did he give you the names of the informants who were going to testify against Michael Westbrook?" Patsy asked.

"I don't know their names."

"Do you recall his name?" Patsy asked. "The man you spoke with in the holding tank."

"I'm not sure he gave me his full name, okay. But I remember he said his name was spelled like the place of worship but pronounced like a French word, 'chapel.' Something like that."

"What did he look like?" Harrison asked.

"He was maybe as tall as you," he said. "But not built like you. Lanky. Wore these thick, black-framed glasses. Prison glasses."

Patsy asked, "Did he say how this ring got started or who was running it?"

Garcia sat up straight, as if accepting Patsy's challenge. "He said the guy running the show at FDC was an inmate named George Frazier, a convict serving a long bid. He said this guy Frazier had a job inside FDC, that he could move through the different units to recruit inmates to be snitches."

"Did this guy, Chapel, say how he knew this?" Harrison asked. "I would think the inmates would want to keep it quiet, if it is as you say it is."

"He knew of it because Frazier had recruited him to give a statement against your guy before your guy got to FDC. Said Frazier even provided him with details about the crimes Westbrook had committed."

Again, Patsy tempered his reaction.

Garcia called him on it. "I know what you're thinking. You're thinking I'm making this shit up. Or maybe Frazier made this shit up. That it's just prison bullshit. Right?"

"We need more to prove it," Patsy said.

"Okay. Chapel said he was given a written statement to sign about your guy's crimes, but then the prosecutor used two other inmates so Chapel didn't get any sentencing help."

"Where is this guy Chapel now?" Patsy asked.

Garcia shrugged. "No idea, man. Like I said. He got his case kicked out. He's out there somewhere."

"You told this to your appellate lawyer?" Patsy asked.

"Yeah. And she said what you're thinking—that it wouldn't be considered credible, and we couldn't get it into court anyway because it was speculation. She said Chapel, even if she could locate him, wouldn't likely testify to what he'd told me and get his ass in trouble. And that was it. So, I went on the library computer and found Michael Westbrook's lawyer, Keera Duggan, in an article in the newspaper and I wrote a letter directly to her."

"I need to know the name of your public defender in the State case, and the name of your appellate lawyer," Patsy said.

"What for, man? What you need is to find this guy Chapel."

"That will be JP's job. My job will be to talk to your lawyers and determine where things stand, if we still have grounds to appeal on your behalf, provided everything turns out as you say."

"I'm good with that, man. You should do that. You should make sure I'm telling you the truth." Garcia leaned forward and looked JP in the eye. "Because when you find out I am telling the truth, big man, you're going to be even more motivated to help your nephew. And the more motivated you are to get him out, the better for me."

# Chapter 37

After Judge Patel dismissed Jada Davis, Keera met with the young woman and her parents in the hall outside the courtroom.

"I'm sorry," Jada said. "I know I didn't help Michael out as much as you would have liked."

"You did fine," Keera assured her. "The jury liked you and believed you. It's the prosecutor's job to poke holes in your story, but that doesn't mean the jury believes she did," Keera said, though Tran had done so. It was almost as if Tran had prepared for the young woman in advance, though that wasn't possible.

"When will we know?" Jamar Davis asked.

Keera didn't want to say: *When the jury convicts Michael.* "We may not," she said, but she could tell from the glum expressions on Jada's and her parents' faces that they knew the answer.

After the recess, Keera recalled Billy Ford to the witness stand, and Patel reminded him that he remained under oath.

"Detective Ford, will you list for me the names of the suspects you and your partner Frank Rossi pursued for the murders of John Lockett and Melissa Scott?"

"We talked to a number of different witnesses."

"Excuse me, Detective, but can you answer the question I asked? List the suspect names you and your partner, Frank Rossi, pursued for the murders of John Lockett and Melissa Scott."

"We considered many people who we interviewed as possible suspects."

"Did you bring in Alex Cortez to Police Headquarters for questioning?"

"No. We did not."

"Did you bring in any of Mr. Lockett's neighbors to Police Headquarters for questioning?"

"No."

"Did you bring in any of his work associates?"

"Other than Michael Westbrook, no."

"Did you bring in any other suspects to Police Headquarters for questioning?"

"Not to Police Headquarters; no."

"At some point in your investigation you learned Mr. Lockett was smuggling drugs through his employer, Blue Horizon; did you not?"

"Yes, we did."

"And who did you learn that from?"

"We learned that from the Drug Enforcement Agency."

"And did you speak to DEA Special Agent Jordan Parker?"

"Yes."

"For what reason did you speak with DEA Agent Jordan Parker?"

"Once we found the drugs and money within John Lockett's house, and the two packages in Michael Westbrook's bedroom, we suspected Lockett had been running drugs. Under such circumstances, we routinely check with the narcotics division at SPD to determine if they know anything about the operation, as well as with the federal agencies, in this case the DEA."

"Mr. Lockett was a professional drug runner; wasn't he?"

"He imported drugs."

"You worked the narcotics unit as one of your rotations before becoming a Violent Crimes detective; did you not?"

"I did."

"You busted drug dealers with large quantities of drugs in their homes; didn't you?"

"Among other places, like storage units."

"You had the largest drug and money bust in SPD's history; didn't you?" Keera knew this. She'd just arrived at the PA's office when the bust went down.

"I was part of a team."

"You're familiar with drugs and drug dealing in the Seattle area; wouldn't that be a true statement?"

"Not like when I worked narcotics on a daily basis, but I'm familiar with it."

"Gangs running drugs are territorial; aren't they?"

"They can be."

Tran stood. "Objection, Your Honor. This line of inquiry is getting far afield. Detective Ford is a Violent Crimes detective. He told Ms. Duggan he is no longer on the narcotics team nor is he on the gang unit."

"Your Honor," Keera said. "This case is about violent crimes *and* narcotics, as Ms. Tran pointed out in the State's case. I'm simply exploring, with this highly experienced detective, the nature of those violent crimes as they relate to drugs."

"I'm going to overrule the objection. But . . . Ms. Duggan. Let's get to the point quickly."

"Certainly. Detective Ford, I asked you if the gangs running drugs in Seattle are territorial?"

"The difference between Seattle and other cities, like Los Angeles, is in Seattle, the gangs are not as territorial or neighborhood based. They're more fluid and tend to move from neighborhood to neighborhood."

"Isn't it a fact that the prosecuting attorney of King County stated at a summit on gang violence, that you attended, that gang violence over drug territory was, quote, 'An all-out war.' Do you recall him saying that?" Keera had been at that conference also.

"I do. Or words to that effect."

"King County currently has an estimated one hundred to one hundred twenty different gangs operating; doesn't it?"

"That sounds about accurate."

"Of that number, how many did you and your partner, Frank Rossi, investigate as possibly linked to the murder of John Lockett and Melissa Scott?"

"We did check with the narcotics unit and asked if John Lockett was on their radar."

"So how many gang members did you bring in and question about what they had heard or knew about the two murders?"

"We learned early on that John Lockett had given Michael Westbrook a ride home within the medical examiner's estimated window for the murder of Mr. Lockett and Ms. Scott." Ford then detailed how that led to the search warrant and the two envelopes.

"And you pretty much closed your investigation to find the killer; didn't you?"

"We didn't close anything, but we felt we had our man."

"Mr. Westbrook didn't confess to the crime; did he?"

"No. He did not."

"He offered to take a polygraph test to prove he wasn't lying; didn't he?"

"Polygraphs are not admissible in court."

"No. But the results could lead a prudent investigator to realize they were looking in the wrong direction; couldn't they?"

"They could."

"But in this case, we will never know; will we? Because you did not administer a polygraph test to Mr. Westbrook; did you?"

"We did not," Ford said.

"Did you make the decision not to allow Mr. Westbrook to take a polygraph test?"

"No. That decision came from the prosecuting attorney's office."

"By Ms. Tran?"

"I don't know who made the decision."

"Ms. Tran was the prosecutor in the Most Dangerous Offender Program who came out to the crime scene; wasn't she?"

"Yes."

"The attorney from the Most Dangerous Offender Program has control over the legal aspects of a case; doesn't she?"

"She does."

"You secured a search warrant to search Tina Westbrook's house through prosecutor Tran; didn't you?"

"We did."

Tran objected. "Your Honor, we've been over this with this same witness."

"We have, Ms. Duggan."

"I'll be quick."

"Be so."

"Did you ask my client, Michael Westbrook, what was in the packages found in his room?"

"I did."

"What did he tell you?"

"He said John Lockett gave him those packages when he drove him home after work that morning and asked him to hide them; that they contained birthday presents for Melissa Scott."

"The same packages that Jada Davis testified she saw from her car when John Lockett drove Michael home?"

"Objection," Tran said, rising. "Speculation."

"I don't know," Ford said.

"Sustained," Patel said a beat too late.

"Did you believe Mr. Westbrook?" Keera said.

"I just noted what he said."

"You don't know if he was telling you the truth; do you?"

"I don't know."

"If you had just allowed him to take a lie detector test, that would have been a question you could have had the examiner ask him; isn't it?"

Tran stood. "Argumentative. Calls for speculation."

Patel, to Keera's surprise, didn't immediately respond, and Keera, having learned from Patsy that if a judge wasn't ruling against you, you kept your mouth shut and didn't give her a potential reason to do so.

"Overruled," Patel said. "This is cross-examination. Does the witness need the question repeated?"

"No, Your Honor," Ford said. He looked at Keera. "Yes, that is a question we could have asked the polygraph examiner to ask Mr. Westbrook."

"You testified the distance from the defendant's residence to John Lockett's home was roughly four to four and a half miles round trip?"

"Sounds about right."

"We've established the defendant's car wasn't working that morning; was it?"

"We've established it was not."

"Did you ask Mr. Westbrook if he owned a bike?"

"I didn't ask."

"During your investigation did you note a bike anywhere at the residence?"

"No."

"A skateboard?"

"No."

"Did you do anything to investigate whether the defendant was capable of running four miles round trip?"

"No."

"You didn't seek out the defendant's medical records during your investigation?"

"No."

"You are unaware then that the defendant has severe asthma?"

Tran objected. "Your Honor, there is no such evidence before this court, and therefore she is asking this witness to speculate."

"Ms. Duggan?"

"I'm simply asking if this detective is aware that this defendant has severe asthma."

"The detective stated he did not seek the defendant's medical records," Tran said.

"He did," Patel said. "The objection is sustained."

Michael Westbrook's general practitioner would testify next, and Keera would get into evidence Michael's asthma. More importantly, the jury would know the detectives did not know this, which all but ruled out that Michael had run anywhere. Tran would argue Michael could have walked, but it was one more discrepancy in a list that Keera could argue constituted reasonable doubt.

# Chapter 38

Patsy spoke on the phone with Garcia's public defender as well as his appellate attorney. They agreed to meet Patsy at the public defender's office on Second Avenue in the Dexter Horton Building, just a few blocks from Patsy's office in Pioneer Square. Harrison used Keera's office computer to scour the Federal Bureau of Prisons' and Washington State Department of Corrections' databases looking for the prisoner Victor Garcia had mentioned named Chapel.

Patsy was escorted into an austere conference room where two women waited. They both looked to be early to mid-forties. The public defender, Margaret Tinsdale, was heavyset with short-cropped, prematurely gray hair with a two-inch-wide blue streak. She wore a long-sleeve button-down shirt and slacks. The appellate lawyer, Jenny Chin, wore blue slacks, a beige shirt, and a long, brown sweater.

"Mr. Duggan," Tinsdale said, approaching. "It's a pleasure. I followed the Vince LaRussa case, and your cross-examination of the detective in that case is already legendary. I was just telling Jenny I use it to train younger attorneys in the office."

Chin, too, introduced herself and seemed equally starstruck.

"That's kind of you, thank you," Patsy said. "And thank you both for taking time out of your busy schedules to see me on short notice. My daughter is in Judge Patel's courtroom, and I'm running down a few things for her."

"We know and we're happy to help. If we can," Tinsdale said.

"As I mentioned on the phone, I'm curious about Mr. Garcia's statement that two informants from FDC-SeaTac testified against him in his murder trial."

"That's true," Tinsdale said. "The case was going pretty well up until that moment."

"Were they credible?" Patsy asked.

"First, Tran blindsided us. She didn't release their statements until after the fact." Which Tran had also done to Keera. "I argued prejudice, but I didn't get far. The judge found nothing in the statements that the witnesses hadn't testified to in court. It was near the day's end, so I had the evening to prepare for cross-examinations."

"Judges are great about deciding when we're prejudiced and when we're not; aren't they?" Patsy asked.

"They are," Tinsdale agreed. "The two informants, Vincent Constantino and Angel Hernandez, were remarkably consistent in their testimony. I thought almost too consistent. Garcia had thought they were all friends; Hernandez had been his cellmate."

Westbrook had used similar words to describe Laurence Holmes and Glenn Ellis. "Did Tran introduce photographs of them together?"

"She did," Tinsdale said. "And they looked as thick as thieves."

"Are these the transcripts of their testimony?" Patsy stepped to a table with a two-inch-thick stack of documents. He'd asked for copies when he'd called to set up the meeting.

Tinsdale nodded, then asked, "What did your client have to say?"

"Much the same thing yours said. He never confessed to anyone because he didn't commit the crime. He said the informants lied."

"I wanted to believe my guy," Tinsdale said, looking recalcitrant. "Maybe I should have."

Patsy turned to Chin. "Mr. Garcia said he wrote to you that FDC-SeaTac was home to a ring of informants."

"He did, but he had little useful information. First, he couldn't remember the guy's name who told him. Second, it just didn't sound plausible, and certainly not grounds for an appeal. As Margaret said, the two men were consistent in their testimony, and that's all the appeals court will care about."

"You think Garcia lied?"

"Victor is looking at a life sentence. He's going to try everything he can to get his sentence shortened. And he isn't that trustworthy," Tinsdale said. "He said some things that were just flat-out fabrications, and it came back to bite him in the ass at trial."

"Plus, how do we prove FDC-SeaTac has a ring of informants?" Chin said. "I couldn't very well ask Tran about it. And those deals aren't made out in the open, and the two informants weren't going to say anything to jeopardize having their sentences reduced."

"And if there *is* a guy who told Victor Garcia this, that's only the first step," Tinsdale added.

"You'd still have to get him to testify and still prove the two witnesses lied," Patsy said.

Tinsdale said, "With two guys stepping forward to testify against your client . . . Maybe there's something more to this. Maybe it's not just inmate bullshit, as far-fetched as it sounds."

"Maybe," Patsy said. But he and Keera faced the same problems as Tinsdale and Chin. How to prove it? And maybe more challenging—how to get anyone to believe it?

Patsy left the office with a promise to keep Tinsdale and Chin apprised of anything he learned. His cell phone rang. Harrison. "What did you find?"

Harrison told Patsy he'd found several inmates named Chapel with one *P* in the Bureau of Prisons' public database, and a few others named Chappel with two *P*'s. "Several are Black. I then tried to determine if any had spent time at FDC-SeaTac during the time Victor Garcia said he was there."

"And?" Patsy said.

"I found one."

"Why didn't you lead with that?" Patsy asked.

"Edgar Steven Chapel was released from FDC-SeaTac. Doesn't say why, but he's no longer an inmate."

"What about a parole officer?" Patsy asked, thinking it a possible way to find Chapel.

"There isn't one. Which makes me believe he had his sentence overturned, which is just what Garcia said the guy told him in the holding tank."

"So how do we find him, and quickly?"

"You know these drug dealers, Patsy. They're creatures of habit. Eventually they go back to what they know best. The Chapel I found got pinched with drug paraphernalia in his car and is sitting in the King County jail. He has a first hearing at two o'clock this afternoon in district court. Sounds like maybe he could use a good lawyer."

Patsy checked his watch. "Again, you could have led with that. You still have contacts at the police department?"

"A few."

"I'll get to court and get his charging document. You get me the officer's name who arrested him. Have Maggie subpoena the officer to appear in court."

"He won't appear. He won't have time."

"That's what I'm hoping."

Patsy entered the cramped, windowless district courtroom on the first floor of the King County jail and sat alongside other private defense attorneys and public defenders. A few gave Patsy double takes, as if they knew him, or recognized him and likely wondered what an attorney of his stature was doing at probable-cause hearings.

He opened his briefcase and pulled out the charging document he had obtained from the court clerk. It was short and provided little information—the probable-cause standard to hold a suspect was extremely low and easily met—but this would not be an ordinary hearing. Patsy would make sure of that.

He scribbled notes and armed himself with Ella's hastily-put-together motion to suppress evidence due to an unlawful search and seizure of Edgar Chapel's car. The rest he would have to wing. He smiled. This was the stuff he'd lived for as a young attorney, and he could feel that thrill building again.

After the third case hearing, the prosecutor, a young female, shuffled her files, opened another, and said in a rote monotone, "The State of Washington versus Edgar Steven Chapel, case number 25-1-0172-7."

A correctional officer brought in a Black man fitting the description Victor Garcia had given them. Chapel wore the orange scrubs of inmates in general population.

"Genevieve Pierre for the State," the prosecutor said with her head down, eyes quickly scanning the charging document that she was likely seeing for the first time. She was about to get a surprise.

Patsy walked up beside Chapel. "Patsy Duggan of Duggan & Associates filing a notice of appearance on behalf of the defendant, Edgar Sean Chapel."

Chapel spun to look at Patsy with more than a little curiosity. The prosecutor also looked surprised. "Steven," Chapel said.

"Edgar Steven Chapel." Patsy handed a document to the prosecutor and the court clerk.

"Who are you?" Chapel said in a voice louder than a whisper.

"I'm your attorney."

"I can't afford no attorney."

"I'll discuss your payment later."

"But I can't afford—"

Patsy turned his head and spoke softly. "Are you the Chapel that served time at FDC-SeaTac?"

"Yeah."

"And your case got overturned on appeal?"

"That's right."

"You met Victor Garcia in a holding tank and said FDC-SeaTac was home to a ring of informants?"

Chapel, who had been gregarious, paused. "Could have. Don't know a Garcia."

"Do you want to get out of here today?"

Chapel nodded.

"Then do exactly as I say."

"Mr. Duggan, is there a problem?" the judge asked.

"No problem, Your Honor. It's been some time since Mr. Chapel and I saw one another. We're just catching up."

"Do so on your own time. I have a busy docket."

"I'm sorry, Judge, but it's about to get busier."

Patsy stepped forward and handed the court clerk a copy of Ella's motion to suppress evidence based on an unlawful search and seizure. He handed a second copy to the prosecutor, who continued to look sucker punched.

As he went back to his table, Patsy noticed Harrison enter. His private investigator gave him a nod. Patsy walked to Harrison and the PI handed him a document. "Your Honor, the defense calls Officer Allan Haggar to the witness stand. I am providing the court's clerk with a proof of service of Officer Haggar previously filed with the court documenting that Officer Haggar has been properly served and notified of this afternoon's hearing."

The clerk handed the document to the judge, who took a moment to consider it. "Is Officer Haggar present in the court this afternoon?"

No one answered.

"Your Honor, in light of Officer Haggar's failure to appear, the defense requests the court dismiss this matter for a lack of probable cause," Patsy said, knowing the judge would never do so.

"Your Honor, this says Officer Haggar was served less than a half hour ago. The State moves that the matter be held over until tomorrow when Officer Haggar can be located," the prosecutor rushed. "I had no notice he had been served."

"The defense requests the defendant be released on his own recognizance with a promise to appear for tomorrow's hearing."

"The State objects. The defendant is a convicted felon for drug-related offenses."

Patsy said, "The defendant should not be penalized for the police officer's lack of diligence. He has never been convicted of a violent crime. Moreover, the charging document alleges that an open container of marijuana and drug paraphernalia were found in a passenger's handbag inside Chapel's car. The officer's reason for pulling the defendant's car over was a nonfunctioning taillight. I'm curious to ask Officer Haggar how a nonfunctioning taillight gave him probable cause to search the passenger's handbag when nowhere in the charging document does the State indicate the owner of that bag gave permission. The defendant will promise to appear tomorrow, and I will further vouch that the defendant will be here."

"Mr. Chapel, do you promise to voluntarily appear before this court tomorrow?"

"If he's here to represent me, I will," Chapel said, smiling.

"I'll be here, Your Honor," Patsy said.

"If your client fails to appear, it will cost you, Mr. Duggan."

"Understood."

Patsy and Chapel stepped back. The correctional officers stepped forward. Chapel would need to be processed before his release. Patsy checked his watch and spoke to the officers. "Can you make it a priority?" he said. "This witness is due to appear in Judge Patel's chambers this afternoon."

"What? What for?" Chapel said looking both curious and concerned.

"To tell a jury exactly what you told Victor Garcia in the holding tank about the ring of informants at FDC-SeaTac."

Chapel now looked wary. "What if I don't?"

"Then you're going to be standing here tomorrow afternoon by yourself. And without me, you're going back to jail. I don't think you want to go back to jail, not after you agreed to be an informant. Do you?"

# Chapter 39

Keera had just dismissed Michael Westbrook's primary care doctor, who confirmed Michael's asthma would have made his running anywhere unlikely. Keera heard the courtroom door open and turned. Patsy entered, followed by Harrison and a tall, lean, Black man. Her father nodded. They needed to talk.

"Ms. Duggan," Judge Patel said, also taking notice of Patsy's presence in the courtroom. "Do you have another witness to call?"

"Your Honor, the defense requests a brief recess to review its notes and make that decision."

"You either do or you don't have another witness, Ms. Duggan."

Patsy nodded.

"The defense does, Your Honor."

"Then call your next witness."

Keera looked to her father. Judge Patel was not going to give her a recess to prepare. Patsy stepped forward. "The defense calls Edgar Steven Chapel," he said.

"Mr. Duggan, what brings you to my courtroom?" Patel asked.

"Defending *our* client," Patsy said.

"You will recall, Judge, you asked me if Patrick Duggan would be appearing when I entered my notice of appearance, and I said I did not know at that time, but I held the door open for the possibility," Keera said. "That door just opened."

Tran was already on her feet. "Your Honor, the State objects. We received no notice this witness would testify. He is not identified on the defendant's witness lists, and we have no idea what he is expected to testify about."

"Counsel?" Patel said to Keera.

"To the contrary," Patsy said. "This is no surprise witness. Ms. Tran is well familiar with Mr. Chapel, and she is fully aware of what he will testify about, a subject germane to this case." He sounded like the polished Brawler of old.

Keera couldn't resist. "And this is, after all, the nature of trials."

Patel addressed Tran. "Do you know this witness?"

"Yes," Tran said. "But the defense gave no notice he would testify."

"The defense just learned yesterday that this witness had information germane to this matter and just located him today," Patsy said.

"Have you met with him?" Patel asked Tran.

"Briefly," Tran said. "Some months ago."

Patel leaned back in her chair. For a moment she looked like she might clear the jury from the courtroom. She considered Patsy, her face as rigid as stone, and Keera wondered if their past history would influence her decision. After another moment, she leaned forward. "When did you become aware of this witness and the relevance of his testimony, Mr. Duggan?"

"We did not know he would be available to testify until about . . ." Patsy looked at his watch, ever the showman. "Thirty-six minutes ago. And because Ms. Duggan has been present in court, we did not have an opportunity to get word to her about Mr. Chapel's willingness to testify."

Patel gave this some weight. "In light of counsel's representations, I will permit the defense to call its next witness."

Tran leaned over and whispered something to George Thomas, who got up from his seat, the chair legs scraping the linoleum. He quickly left the courtroom.

"Thank you, Your Honor," Patsy said. "The defense calls Edgar Steven Chapel to the witness stand."

Chapel stepped forward with a cocky half smile that made Keera think he clearly liked being the center of attention. After the judge swore Chapel in, he sat. Patsy stepped to the lectern without notes or a laptop, and Keera realized he had no time to prepare for this direct examination, but he still looked like the picture of composure.

"Would you state your full name for the record?"

Chapel said, "Edgar Steven Chapel. But everyone calls me 'Bo.'"

"Mr. Chapel, have you ever been incarcerated at the Federal Detention Center in SeaTac?"

"I have."

"What for?"

"Drugs. I was convicted of buying and selling drugs. But it was BS."

"Just answer the questions asked, Mr. Chapel," Patel said.

"How long was your sentence?" Patsy asked.

"Initially it was twelve years, but my attorney got the conviction thrown out."

"What year and months were you at FDC-SeaTac until your attorney got the conviction thrown out?"

"I got to FDC-SeaTac right around the holidays."

"The Christmas holidays of last year?"

"Yes."

"In what unit did you serve your sentence?"

"General population. C Unit."

"Did you know the defendant at FDC-SeaTac, Michael Westbrook?"

"I knew of him before I knew him."

"Can you explain to the jury what you mean by you 'knew *of* him before' you 'knew him'?"

"I was sitting in my cell and an inmate named George Frazier came by and started talking to me."

"Did you know George Frazier before he came to your cell to chat?"

"Not really. He wasn't in C Unit. Frazier worked as an orderly, which allowed him to pass between the various units."

"When he came to your cell, did Mr. Frazier indicate what he wanted to talk about?"

Tran stood. "The State objects to this witness testifying about anything George Frazier said as hearsay."

Patsy said, "The statements to be offered will not be offered to assert the truth of those statements, only that Mr. Frazier uttered them."

"Overruled. For now. I'll need to hear these statements. Ms. Tran, you can object then."

Patsy said, "When Mr. Frazier came to your cell, what did you talk about?"

"At first just this and that; you know? Prison BS. Then he asked me what I'd been convicted of, and how long a bid I was serving, and I told him. And he told me he had like a fifty-year sentence. And I said that was rough, man. Then he asked me how I'd like to get my sentence reduced."

"Same objection," Tran said.

"Same response," Patsy said. "Not offering it for the truth."

"Overruled."

"The State would request a standing hearsay objection to anything this witness claims Mr. Frazier told him," Tran said.

"So noted," Patel said.

"What did you say to Mr. Frazier when he asked if you'd like to get your sentence reduced?"

Chapel perked up and smiled. "I said, 'Who wouldn't?'"

"Did Mr. Frazier tell you how you might get your sentence reduced?"

"Not at that time, but another time he came back and told me."

"He came back?"

"Yeah. I spoke to him maybe half a dozen times."

"Where were these conversations?"

"Always in my cell."

"Never in the courtyard or the cafeteria?"

"No. You don't want to talk about this stuff where others are present."

"What did you discuss?"

"Frazier told me an inmate was coming to FDC-SeaTac C Unit named Michael Westbrook."

"He told you this before Mr. Westbrook arrived at the detention center?"

"Yep," Chapel said.

"Did he say how he knew Mr. Westbrook was coming to your unit at the detention center?"

"Nope. Just said he was coming."

"What else did Mr. Frazier say?"

"He said Westbrook had robbed a drug dealer, that he shot the guy and beat the guy's girlfriend to death with a tire iron. He said Westbrook masturbated over the woman's body."

"What did you say?"

"I don't know what I said."

"What else did Mr. Frazier tell you?"

"He said Westbrook had a fake alibi about the dealer asking him to hide a package of drugs, and he was denying the killings. He said that if I could get Westbrook to confess, he would put together a letter for me offering to help the prosecution, and I could get my sentence reduced."

"What did you say?"

"I asked what I had to do."

"And what did Mr. Frazier say?"

Chapel shrugged. "Just get close to Mr. Westbrook and get him to confess."

"Did Mr. Frazier say where he got this information about Michael Westbrook's alleged crimes?"

"No. But it had to be from someone on the outside; right?"

Tran objected. "Calls for speculation."

"Sustained. Just answer the questions you're asked, Mr. Chapel."

"Did Mr. Westbrook come to your unit at FDC-SeaTac?" Patsy asked.

"Yeah, he did."

"Will you point him out in court?"

Chapel pointed directly at Michael. "That's Mike sitting right there."

"Did you become friendly with Mr. Westbrook?"

"Yeah."

"How?"

"Just did. Had some stuff in common. No father in my picture either."

"Did Mr. Westbrook tell you about the crime that sent him to FDC-SeaTac?"

"Guys don't talk about that stuff either. Not in the open."

"Why not?"

"Because you don't know who might be listening. You discuss those things in private. In your cell. When no one else is around."

"Did he ever say he killed anyone?"

"Not to me."

"Did you talk to Mr. Frazier again about Mr. Westbrook?"

"Yeah, he came and asked me about it, and I said, 'He hasn't confessed.'"

"What was his response?"

"He wanted me to get pictures with Mike in the visitors center, and I asked him, 'What for?' He said to make us look friendly. And I told him again that Mike hadn't confessed."

"And what did Mr. Frazier say?"

"He said the pictures would show how close we were and make it more believable Mike trusted me and had confessed."

"What did you say?"

"I said that was fucked up, man."

Patel said, "Watch your language, Mr. Chapel."

"Why did you think that?" Patsy asked.

Chapel seemed to give this a moment of thought. "That wasn't the deal. The deal was for me to get Mike to confess. I mean, if Mike did what Frazier said he did, and he confessed, then that was one thing. But he didn't confess . . . Not to me, but they wanted me to say he did. That just seemed fu . . . wrong to me."

"Were you close with Mr. Westbrook?"

"I thought he was an all-right guy after I got to know him a bit."

"Did Mr. Westbrook ever confess to you?"

Chapel shook his head emphatically. "Not to me."

"You said, 'Not to me.' Do you know if he confessed to any other inmates?"

"I don't know for certain that he did or didn't. I just know he never confessed to me."

"Did you observe other inmates spending time at Mr. Westbrook's table or out with him in the yard?"

"Two in particular."

"Who were they?"

"Laurence Holmes and Glenn Ellis."

"Did Mr. Holmes or Mr. Ellis tell you why they were getting friendly with Mr. Westbrook?"

"Objection," Tran said. "Hearsay."

"Again, Your Honor, not being offered for the truth, only that it was said."

"Overruled. The witness can answer."

Chapel said, "They said Frazier had also approached them and told them the same thing he told me. That Mike had done some sick stuff, and the prosecutor needed a confession."

"Did you know George Frazier had approached other inmates about getting Mr. Westbrook to confess?"

"Not before they told me he did."

"And what was your response?"

"I didn't want no part of it no more."

"Do you know if Mr. Holmes and Mr. Ellis took any pictures with Mr. Westbrook in the visitors center as Mr. Frazier asked you to do?"

"Yeah. They did. I did too. But I wished I didn't."

"Why did you?"

"I don't know." He paused. Then he looked to Michael. "I'm sorry I did, Mike."

"Objection, Your Honor," Tran said. "Move to strike."

"So stricken. The jury is to disregard the witness's last statement."

"Were you ever asked to testify against Mr. Westbrook?"

"No. I got my conviction thrown out on appeal so . . . I didn't need to."

George Thomas returned to the courtroom carrying an envelope. He handed it to Tran at counsel table, whispering in her ear.

Patsy turned from the podium. "Your witness."

"Does the State wish to conduct cross-examination?" Patel asked.

"The State does," Tran said. She approached the lectern. "Mr. Chapel, when did you meet Mr. Duggan?"

"He just showed up today in court for my first appearance."

"Why were you in court?"

"The police pulled me over and said I had drugs in the car. But I didn't."

"Was this the district court in the King County jail?"

"That's right."

"You were before the court on a probable-cause hearing?"

"Yep."

"You'd never met Mr. Duggan before today?"

"Nope."

"He just materialized in court?"

"Something like that."

"You hadn't hired him?"

"I have now," Chapel said with emphasis.

"Did he say why he was there?"

"He said he was there to represent me."

"Did he say why he would represent a client he had never met before?"

"After the hearing."

"What did he say?"

"I'll object, Your Honor," Patsy said. "Mr. Chapel has testified that he had retained my services. Attorney-client privilege."

"Sustained."

"Did you agree to Mr. Duggan representing you because you didn't want to go back to prison?" Tran asked.

"Yes."

"That's the reason you originally agreed to help George Frazier, so you could get out of prison early; isn't it?"

"I just said that *if* Mike confessed, I'd let Frazier know. Mike didn't."

"But you agreed to do so because you could maybe get out of prison early; right?"

"He said that was the deal. I didn't make it. He made the deal."

"You weren't always with Mr. Westbrook; were you?"

"Always? No."

"You weren't his cellmate; were you?"

"No."

"Who was his cellmate at FDC-SeaTac?"

"When I was there it was Glenn Ellis."

"You also said inmates never talked about their cases out in the rec yard or in the cafeteria; correct?"

"That's correct."

"Because inmates with big ears might overhear; right?"

"Right."

"And those prison informants might be looking to ingratiate themselves to the prosecutor to get their sentences reduced; is that right?"

"Yeah."

"You were looking to ingratiate yourself with the prosecutor also; weren't you?"

Perhaps realizing where Tran was going, Chapel said, "I was minding my own business until George Frazier approached me."

"Do you think a reason that Mr. Westbrook never confessed to you was because you always saw him in the rec yard or in the dining hall, and he didn't trust you or the people around him?"

"Calls for speculation," Patsy said.

"Sustained."

"Mr. Westbrook could have confessed to Mr. Holmes or Mr. Ellis in his prison cell where it was private; couldn't he?"

"Calls for speculation," Patsy said again.

"Sustained."

"In your time in prison, did you ever hear an inmate, perhaps incarcerated for the first time and naïve about prison life, talk about their crimes in a place like the rec yard?"

"Objection. Relevance."

"Overruled."

"I never heard anyone confess." Chapel smiled. "Everyone in prison is innocent."

"You never testified against Mr. Westbrook because he never confessed to you; correct?"

"I got out. I didn't need to take the deal Frazier was offering."

Tran walked to counsel table and picked up the envelope that George Thomas had brought to court. "Mr. Chapel, did you ever write a letter advising that Mr. Westbrook confessed to you while the two of you were seated in the rec yard?"

Chapel looked wary. "I didn't write any letter."

Tran opened the envelope and pulled out a single sheet of paper. "You didn't write a letter stating that Mr. Westbrook confessed to the killing while you were seated with him in the rec yard?"

Tran walked to Patsy and Keera and showed them the letter, then sought to have it introduced.

Keera stood. "Your Honor, the defense objects. We filed a motion asking for *any and all* letters the prosecutor had from inmates related to Michael Westbrook. This letter Ms. Tran is seeking to introduce was never produced to defense counsel."

Patel gave this some thought. "I'm going to allow the letter to be introduced. I'll take up counsel's failure to comply with discovery outside the jury's presence."

Tran moved to the clerk and asked that the sheet of paper be admitted as the prosecution's next exhibit. After it was so marked, the clerk put it up on the courtroom's computer for the jury to view, and Tran handed the exhibit to Chapel.

"Mr. Chapel, will you review that letter?"

Chapel looked less and less comfortable. "I didn't write it."

"Is that your signature attesting to the fact that you wrote it?"

"I signed it, but I didn't write it."

"Who did?"

"I don't know. George Frazier brought it to me, and he told me to sign it. And I said for like the hundredth time, 'But Mike didn't confess.'"

"That is your signature; isn't it?"

"Yeah, that's my signature."

"And above that signature it states, 'I swear, under penalty of perjury, that the statements made in this letter are true and correct'; doesn't it?"

"I told George Frazier—"

"Yes or no. That is what the letter says."

"Yeah, it says that."

"You never were asked to testify?"

"No. I wasn't."

"You were unhappy about not getting your sentence reduced; weren't you?"

"I asked Frazier what the deal was, and he told me the prosecutor said they could only help the witnesses who testified in court."

Tran looked toward the jury. "No further questions."

Patsy rose immediately and moved to the lectern. "Mr. Chapel, you started to tell the jury what you said to Mr. Frazier when he asked you to sign this letter. What were you going to say before the prosecutor interrupted you?"

"I said to Frazier that the letter wasn't accurate, and he told me Westbrook had confessed to both Holmes and to Ellis, and that they were going to testify. He said Westbrook was going to be convicted, so I might as well get something out of it too. He said that if I signed the letter, he'd tell the prosecutor that I'd also helped."

"But you didn't get any help having your sentence reduced?"

"No."

"Mr. Chapel, when Mr. Frazier told you that you weren't going to get your sentence reduced, were you upset?"

"Yeah. I was pissed, and when I saw Frazier, I told him it was bullshit."

"Language," Patel said.

"What was Mr. Frazier's response?"

"He said 'Too f-ing bad.' He told me to keep my mouth shut because word could get out that I had informed on another inmate, and he couldn't be responsible if anything was to happen to me. He said to keep my mouth shut and if another opportunity came along, he'd let me know."

"Did you take that as a threat by Mr. Frazier?"

"Yeah, I took it as a threat. I mean he had that job where he could go to all the different units, which meant he could tell anyone—an inmate who had nothing to lose, or maybe someone friendly with Mike. I'd never know when someone was coming to get me."

"Why did you sign the letter if Mr. Westbrook never confessed to you?"

"Like I said, Frazier said Westbrook was going down, that Holmes and Ellis were going to testify, and I might as well get something out of it and that's all there was to it."

"You never considered that Mr. Frazier could use the letter to threaten you with physical violence were you to ever tell what had actually happened?"

"I never did, no. I wouldn't have signed it if I had."

"Is everything you said here today in court the truth?"

"It is. I had no reason to lie here today. I'm not in prison no more."

Patsy sat.

Tran stood. "Yet," she said.

"What?" Chapel said.

"You're not in prison *yet*, but you could be, if Mr. Duggan doesn't get you off of the charges pending against you; couldn't you?"

"I don't know," Chapel said.

Tran sat.

Patsy said he had no further questions and Patel dismissed Chapel.

Patel looked at the clock on the wall, then to the jurors. "Ladies and gentlemen, we are going to conclude and resume Wednesday morning. You have tomorrow off because of a scheduling conflict on the court's calendar." Patel had notified Keera and Tran at the start of the trial of her conflict. She then went through her admonishments to the jurors before dismissing them.

"Ms. Duggan, does the defense have further witnesses it will seek to call Wednesday?"

As she was about to say *No*, something niggled at the back of Keera's neck. Instead, she said, "The defense will convene and discuss this, Your Honor. I will advise the court clerk and the State tomorrow afternoon."

"Do so," Patel said. "We're adjourned."

# Chapter 40

Billy Ford waited, hands folded at his waist, his gaze watching the jurors depart the courtroom through the door at the back. He noted how several had glanced at Michael Westbrook, as if wondering, perhaps, uncertain.

Juror number twelve, a Black man from Seattle, looked back over his shoulder, a fleeting glance at Westbrook, then at Ford. The bailiff closed the door. Ford had experienced that glance before, from other Black men. Juror twelve wondered what he'd just witnessed, and his glance summed up exactly what Ford, too, felt—a shiver of doubt.

Ford left the courtroom after confirming with Tran that the prosecutor did not need him tonight. The evidence appeared, at least, to have been submitted, though in this crazy case anything could happen. Ford wouldn't be surprised if Keera Duggan came up with another surprise witness. Barring her doing so, all that remained were the attorneys' summations before the evidence went to the jury.

Ford walked back to Police Headquarters and the elevator to his bull pen on the seventh floor. Rossi was the lone detective still there, but for the team working the graveyard. Rossi usually waited until Ford returned from court to learn what had happened, and to assist if Billy needed to do anything.

Rossi asked, "What's bothering you? I can tell by the look on your face."

"I'm not so sure anymore." Ford spun his chair to face his partner. Before sitting, he looked over the cubicles, wondering who remained at his or her desk.

"Not sure about what?" Rossi said.

Ford sat and rolled his chair closer to Rossi so they could both keep their voices soft. "You missed one hell of a day in court."

"Tell me," Rossi said.

Ford rested his elbows on his knees, leaning forward. "Patsy Duggan made an appearance."

"The Irish Brawler? For what reason?"

He told Rossi about Bo Chapel's testimony. Rossi listened attentively, without asking questions, as if absorbing what Ford had to say, and possibly also wondering if Michael Westbrook was being set up, and if so, by whom.

"He was masterful. No notes. No script. No time to prepare a direct examination of Bo Chapel, yet he was smooth as silk, as if he and the witness were just having a conversation before the jury."

"What did Tran do? Did she cross him?"

"Tran did what she does best," Ford said. "She beat him up a bit on cross-examination, made him look like a liar. Made him look like an opportunist. Made him look like an angry man looking for some vindication, an inmate who would say anything for a chance at a lighter sentence."

"But you don't think he is a liar. I can tell just by the way you phrased your answer."

"Let's just say I'm not certain Chapel is any of those things," Ford said. "And if he is an opportunistic liar, what then does that say about Holmes and Ellis and their testimony?"

Rossi waited a beat before saying, "Good point."

Ford let out a burst of air. "I was staring at the jurors, watching them depart for the day. More than one looked confused, but it was juror twelve that got to me."

"What do you mean? Got to you how?"

Ford explained, though he wasn't certain Rossi could truly understand, having never experienced what the juror had intimated by his look and his nod. Ford had. He explained that the glance of uncertainty was the juror's expression of doubts.

"Doubts about Chapel's testimony?" Rossi asked, clearly not understanding.

"Doubts about another in a long line of Black men, standing in handcuffs, at trial, and whether he really is guilty, or just another victim of the system."

"We can't dismiss the envelope of fentanyl we found in Westbrook's bedroom, or the envelope of money, Billy."

"I know. And I have doubts about Westbrook's statement that John Lockett asked him to hold on to the packages."

"And we can't dismiss Westbrook's sperm on Melissa Scott's bedsheets. How can he explain that?"

"I don't know, but Anh Tran and Keera Duggan have both argued Lockett and Scott were grooming the young man to hold packages for them, maybe serve as a courier. Duggan used the argument to explain why Westbrook had the packages. Tran used it as Westbrook's motive to kill Lockett."

"Things about this case bothered us from the start, Billy."

"Things that Keera Duggan hit hard during her cross-examinations," Ford agreed.

"It's why we told Tran the case wasn't ready to be tried, that we needed more to convict Westbrook."

"But then Tran found Holmes and Ellis, and that was that. Seemingly. But Bo Chapel and Patsy Duggan have now cast their testimony in serious doubt."

"We've never trusted inmate informants," Rossi said. "They all have an inherent reason to lie, and many are adept at it."

"Pathological," Ford agreed. "Holmes and Ellis were consistent and credible in their letters to Tran and their grand jury testimony. I sat through it. I know. But then Ellis's testimony changed in court. He said things that contradicted Holmes."

"Significant differences?"

"Ellis forgot Westbrook had not driven with Lockett to work, that he took an Uber. He nearly forgot Westbrook's car wasn't running."

"Not a big thing," Rossi said.

"He also testified Westbrook confessed in their cell, not the rec yard, as Holmes said. And he said Westbrook told him Lockett had driven him home, which—" Billy paused when they heard a noise in the room. Billy popped up and looked over the cubicle wall, then sat, keeping his voice low. "Which confirms the testimony of Westbrook's neighbor, Jada Davis, who said she saw Westbrook come home that morning and never leave his house again."

"Mistakes are possible, Billy, especially when a witness is nervous and under a withering cross-examination."

"And I was willing to give both men that benefit of the doubt, even with the inconsistencies—until Patsy Duggan walked in the courtroom door with Bo Chapel. Now I'm wondering if it was Holmes who made the mistakes. If Westbrook had gone straight to Lockett's home, then Westbrook's work clothes and shoes would have been covered in blood; wouldn't they?" Ford said.

"Not to mention the problem with the gun," Rossi said.

"So did Ellis make a mistake?" Ford asked. "Or were his mistakes intentional?"

"Intentional? Why?" Rossi asked.

Ford thought he might know. Thought it might be like that glance from juror twelve; an indication a Black man wondered if Westbrook was being unfairly charged and judged in the criminal justice system because of the color of his skin. "If Chapel is to be believed, FDC-SeaTac is home to informants willing to say almost anything to get their sentences reduced. In fact, to discredit Chapel, Tran had to get the jury to believe that very thing—that Chapel was a liar who'd say whatever he was told to get his sentence reduced. But if that's true . . ."

"What does *that* say about Laurence Holmes and Glenn Ellis?" Rossi said. "Yeah, I get it, Billy. Why should the jury consider one a liar but believe the others?"

Ford said, "And if there truly is a ring of informants, then this inmate, George Frazier, seems to be in charge, according to Chapel anyway. But Frazier couldn't have done it on his own." Billy again rose up, looked over the cubicle walls, sat again, and further lowered his voice. "Someone had to be feeding Frazier the specific details of each case so he could educate the informants, so their testimony would be convincing and believable. And someone had to be passing the inmate letters back and forth."

"Again, *if* Chapel is to be believed," Rossi said.

"And that is the stinging question; isn't it? Is Chapel telling the truth? Because if he is, it means Michael Westbrook is being set up, and that is something I just can't dismiss, Frank. I'm the father of three Black teenage sons. The prisons are filled with young Black men. Some are guilty, sure, but some are not. Each year the Innocence Project frees another inmate wrongfully convicted, and too often that inmate is Black and has spent decades behind bars for a crime he did not commit. I've experienced racism, firsthand, Frank. Know it all too well. It's the reason I went into law enforcement. Thought I could make a difference. Now I'm wondering . . ."

"Hey, Billy. You can't put this on your shoulders. You did your job."

"Yeah. I did my job," Ford said, but he didn't feel good about it. "Could Tran be behind this?"

"Tran? For what purpose?" Rossi asked.

"To get a conviction," Ford said. "That's what she's paid to do, Frank."

"But to convict an innocent man? Knowing he's innocent? Would she do that?" Rossi asked.

"Everybody wants to crown her Batwoman of Gotham City. Maybe it isn't that simple," Ford said.

"What do you mean?"

"She watched her parents die and their killer walk free, Frank. I'm just wondering: What does that do to a young kid? What does that do to a prosecutor now trying to put killers behind bars?"

Rossi didn't answer.

They sat silent for a long minute, perhaps neither one of them wanting to take that next step, knowing it could be perilous to their careers. Rossi spoke first. "I could pull some of her old cases. See what I can learn."

"And do what with the information?"

"I don't know," Rossi said. "But it might answer the questions you've posed."

"I'd like to find out if this guy, George Frazier, is at FDC-SeaTac. Chapel said he works a job that allows him access between the different units. I'd like to know what he's in for, if he's had his sentence reduced, and if so, why?" The look on Rossi's face made Ford stop. "What?" he asked.

"And if he had had his sentence reduced, by whom?"

"And by whom, you mean Tran?" Ford said.

"If Chapel is telling the truth, that would stand to reason; wouldn't it? Maybe we should look into what happened to Tran; maybe there's something more there we should know about."

"Maybe, but we've got to be careful, Frank. This could be a career ender. No prosecutor will go into battle with us if we're wrong and Tran finds out. We'd be DOA and out on our asses."

"Then let's not be wrong," Rossi said.

# Chapter 41

Following trial, Keera met with JP, Patsy, and Chapel in a private room off the courthouse hallway. Chapel was again smiling his same cocksure grin, and she wanted to find out just how reliable a witness he really was, not having had the time to talk to him before her father put him on the witness stand.

"What's motivating George Frazier?" Keera asked Chapel.

Chapel raised both hands. "Same thing that motivates all of us. He wants to get out."

"And Laurence Holmes and Glenn Ellis?"

"Same motivation, man."

Keera checked the notepad on which she had been scribbling, searching for the two other names Chapel had mentioned in his testimony. "And Hernandez and Constantino, who testified against Garcia?"

"I don't know them. Before my time."

"I'll find out," JP said.

"Why did Frazier come to you?" Keera asked, pushing Chapel a bit.

"Maybe because I'm young and Black like Mike, and he thought I had a better chance of befriending him. And, I was looking at being in prison a long time."

"He thought you'd be able to get close to Michael," she asked.

"Maybe."

"Are you aware of other inmates at FDC-SeaTac who testified to get their sentences reduced? Who were part of this ring?"

Chapel shook his head. "I don't know. I don't have specific names for you. Frazier is the guy you need to get to talk."

Keera glanced at Patsy, who had an uncertain look on his face. They both knew that was not a likely scenario. Not unless they could find some leverage. At the moment they didn't have any.

Back at the office, Maggie ordered dinner for the trial team in the conference room. Harrison was at the clerk's office but expected to arrive shortly. Ella came into the conference room looking like the cat that swallowed the canary. "Guess who in the prosecutor's office handled the Victor Garcia case?"

"Tran?" Keera asked.

"Tran," Ella confirmed. "She also filed the federal Rule 35 motions asking that Angel Hernandez and Vincent Constantino get their sentences reduced. In both cases they had their sentences cut nearly in half."

"That would motivate an inmate," Patsy said.

"I also reached Garcia's appellate lawyer, and she sent over this," Ella said, handing Keera a document.

"What is it?" Patsy asked.

"Another inmate, Armando Lopez, confessed to the killing for which Garcia was convicted. He said Garcia wasn't even present."

"What happened at Garcia's appeal when that was introduced into the record?" Keera asked.

"Lopez's statement was not found credible by the appellate court. Apparently Garcia and Lopez were both members in the same gang, and Lopez was already serving a life sentence without the possibility of parole for another murder."

"The court believed Lopez only confessed because he had nothing more to lose," Keera said.

"Another thing: Garcia was a drug dealer when convicted, just like Lockett," Ella said. "I don't know what that means exactly. I've made a request for the trial transcript, and I'll prepare a motion to compel Tran to produce her investigative file in that case."

"You won't win that," Patsy said from across the table. "No way Judge Patel allows that into evidence."

"I don't disagree, but you said you needed leverage to get this guy George Frazier to talk. Maybe we can find something in the transcript to use as leverage," Ella said.

"If we can get to Frazier, we may get to Tran," Patsy said. He had that mischievous look on his face.

"What are you getting at?" Ella asked.

"How did Tran know Chapel was upset she didn't use his letter and wasn't going to get his sentenced reduced?" he said to Keera.

Keera thought back to Tran's cross-examination. Tran hadn't asked if Chapel was upset. She knew Chapel was upset his letter hadn't been used.

"Maybe she just presumed it," Ella said.

"Or someone told her," Patsy said.

"Frazier?" Keera said. "How the hell are we going to prove that?"

"Get her notes," Patsy said. "Let's find out if she had any meetings with this guy, George Frazier."

"She's too smart for that," Keera said. "Had to be a go-between."

"Let's also argue we want to determine when she first met with Laurence Holmes and Glenn Ellis. If it was before Michael was sent to that unit, it would confirm what Chapel had to say in court today. She also likely met with both inmates to discuss what they had to say before they testified to the grand jury. Let's ask for any notes Tran kept at any and all such meetings that would reveal when those meetings occurred and what was discussed."

"We can compare them with Holmes's and Ellis's letters," Keera said.

Ella typed rapidly on her tablet computer. "I'll get on it."

"Ask for an in-camera inspection by Patel. It will prevent Tran from arguing she's giving up her work product," Patsy said, meaning Judge Patel would privately review the material to determine what could and could not be turned over to the defense.

"Let's move that Tran be compelled to turn over her entire file in this case," Keera said. "And ask Patel to decide whether Tran has met her discovery obligations to produce all discoverable material, including her notes. Tran clearly withheld the letters signed by Holmes and Ellis, and she withheld Chapel's letter. It might be enough to convince Patel to take a serious look at the file."

Harrison walked into the conference room, pulled the strap to his leather satchel over his head, and put it on a chair, digging inside. He produced the letters written by Angel Hernandez and Vincent Constantino in the Victor Garcia case, setting them on the table.

"How did you get these?" Ella asked.

"I still have a few contacts in the King County clerk's office," Harrison said.

Keera had working copies made of the letters, then set them side by side on the table beneath the letters from Chapel, Holmes, and Ellis. She used a highlighter and a pencil and circled, underlined, and made notes in the margins as they all read each letter.

"Same typos and misspellings," Keera said.

"They damn near say exactly the same thing, with only minimal differences," Patsy said.

"Somebody made slight changes to make them look independently typed, but look at the similarities in the various phrases used to describe the specific crimes," Keera said.

"The formatting and font is also identical," Maggie said, looking over their shoulders. They turned to her. "Well, isn't it?"

"It is," Keera said.

"That indicates to me the same person typed and printed these. Possibly that he or she just cut and pasted the letters together," Maggie said.

"Good work, Mags," Patsy said.

"This wasn't coming from Frazier." Keera tapped one of the letters. "He was just the messenger. Somebody had to let him know when Victor Garcia and Michael were coming to the unit. Someone had to provide the specifics of their crimes."

"Whoever did, he had to have met Frazier in person to give him the letters and have them signed," Patsy said to Harrison. "And you and I both know a person can't just walk into FDC-SeaTac unannounced."

"They have to show identification and be on the approved visitors list," Harrison said, understanding where Patsy was going with his comment.

"Can we get those visitors lists?" Ella asked.

"We can try," Keera said. "Chapel said Frazier first came to talk to him a little before Michael was sent to the unit after his arrest in December."

Harrison said, "I'll determine when Victor Garcia was sent to FDC and give you those dates as well. Maybe we get lucky and find a common name on each inmate's visitors list."

"Do you think either Holmes or Ellis might talk?" Patsy asked the group. "Have we tried?"

Keera shook her head. "Given what Chapel said about Frazier using the letters as a threat, I doubt either would."

"We don't have anything to lose trying," Patsy said.

"I doubt Holmes will talk, but I think Ellis may already have," Harrison said.

"What do you mean?" Keera said.

"Ellis and Holmes had coordinated letters." Harrison tapped the letters on the table. "And both testified before the grand jury. If Ellis had made the kind of mistakes to the grand jury that he made in court, Tran never would have put him on the witness stand."

"You think he made those mistakes on purpose?" Keera asked. "Why?"

"It's a bit like what Chapel said, how he felt about Michael after getting to know him and because Michael never actually confessed. Maybe they typed up Ellis's letter ahead of time like they did Chapel's, and they told him, if he had similar hesitations like Chapel, that he might as well sign it because Holmes and Chapel said Michael confessed."

"You think Ellis could have felt guilty the same way Chapel felt guilty?" Patsy asked.

"I'm not saying you all wouldn't understand, but for one Black man to do that to another Black man? There's a lot of history they'd have to forget."

"Do you think Ellis might talk to *you*?" Keera said. "One Black man to another?"

"I don't know. But it's like Patsy said. It can't hurt to try. Patsy and I are going over to FDC-SeaTac to look at the log of visitors anyway."

"They don't have regular visiting hours tomorrow," Patsy said. "But they have to allow for exceptional circumstances."

"I'd say this qualifies," Keera said.

# Chapter 42

The following morning, Ford walked into the A Team's bull pen early and found Rossi already at his desk, busy working on his computer. The smell of coffee permeated the cubicle along with the chatter of other detectives getting their days started. Except for different clothes, jeans and a blue polo shirt, Rossi looked like he'd spent the better part of his night at his desk. He'd strewn papers about the cubicle, and his stained coffee mug perched precariously on a stack of documents beneath his computer screen.

"Tell me you at least went home last night," Ford said.

"For a bit," Rossi said. "Couldn't sleep."

"You too, huh?"

"Got in early. Found some interesting things." He sounded like he'd been waiting for Ford to arrive.

Ford scooted his chair close to Rossi's computer screen so they could keep their volume down.

"First off, George Frazier *is* an inmate at FDC-SeaTac. And Chapel was correct that Frazier has periodically worked as an orderly and as a janitor, which does allow him to go between the different units." Rossi pulled up a file on his computer. "Victor Garcia was initially arrested in a drug bust by the ROPE team. That's how he originally ended up at FDC-SeaTac doing ten years. While he was incarcerated, he was accused of the murder of a rival drug dealer—an unsolved drive-by shooting cold case. Even from a cursory reading I'd say the file was thin, and the evidence suspect, but two jailhouse informants came forward and testified that Garcia had confessed to the killing."

"Garcia wasn't on anyone's radar for the murder before that?" Ford asked.

"Not before the informants said he confessed. I also pulled the two letters each man allegedly wrote to the prosecutor."

"Tran?"

"Tran was the ROPE team prosecutor at the time it pinched Garcia in the first place."

"So she knew him."

"Clearly. I compared the two informants' letters with the letter Chapel said was written for him, as well as the letters written by Holmes and Ellis. Take a look?"

Rossi placed the five letters on a table in the center of their bull pen. Ford moved beside him. After a couple of minutes, Rossi said, "They have the same typos and misspelled words."

"Indicating it's likely the same person wrote all the letters," Ford said.

"I thought so too. I pulled the other files in which Tran served as the prosecutor when she was on the ROPE team and during her years as an MDOP prosecutor. I've found three cases so far in which she used informants to convict a defendant of what was, until then, a cold case. All three men she convicted were drug dealers, Billy. Just like Lockett and Garcia."

"No shit," Ford said in a whisper.

Rossi bent down and picked up a stack of files from the floor, putting them on the table. He went through the files one at a time. "Pete Scalsa. A drug dealer busted by the ROPE team. While incarcerated at FDC-SeaTac, an informant named David Dixon testified Scalsa confessed to the killing of a rival drug dealer. A cold case. Scalsa got life."

Rossi closed the file and set it aside, opening another. "Henry Buck. I reached Buck's attorney and asked him about an informant Tran used to convict Buck. According to the attorney, while Buck awaited trial in the King County jail, he was put in the same cell as a guy named Anthony Hurt. Hurt later testified for Tran, said Buck confessed to the killing. Buck denies it. You seeing a pattern here, Billy? Garcia, Scalsa, and Buck were all drug dealers, same as John Lockett, and the State had little more than circumstantial evidence to convict any of them."

"Until informants said they confessed," Ford said.

"Tran is knee-deep in this shit, Billy."

"More like up to her neck."

Ford scanned over the top of the bull pen, then lowered and said, "Okay. Let's slow down for a minute. There's nothing that prevents a prosecutor from using an inmate informant; right?"

"If that inmate informant is telling the truth," Rossi said. "If what that inmate has to say is not being manufactured."

"But we don't have anything to indicate Tran manufactured anything, except supposition."

"We don't. But the go-between she was using, the one Chapel testified about in court, might have been manufacturing things for her."

"Frazier? You think Tran knew he was recruiting inmates to lie?" Ford was skeptical but intrigued.

"Nothing indicates she did, but . . . come on, Billy, it's a hell of a coincidence. All of them drug dealers? All incarcerated at FDC-SeaTac? All of their files thin until inmate informants step forward and say they confessed to murders?"

"What would be Tran's motivation?"

"Convictions? Upholding her reputation as Batwoman? Getting perceived dangerous criminals off the street."

"She's never taken a promotion," Billy said.

"What?"

"Tran. She's been asked to run for King County prosecutor. Some people wanted her to run for mayor. She's always turned them down. So we can all but rule out personal ambition; right?"

"Or maybe she didn't think she'd withstand the scrutiny that comes with running for higher office," Rossi said. "Maybe she worried someone would find out what we've found out."

"Maybe."

"We have a meeting this afternoon with Jack Thompson," Rossi said.

"Who's he?"

"He's the detective who investigated the murder of Tran's parents."

"Why are we talking to him?" Ford asked.

"See if he has anything interesting to say about the murders, or about Tran. He's eighty-two and lives on a farm in Duvall and, according to his wife, he spends much of his time golfing, caring for his horses, and fly-fishing the Snoqualmie River. If nothing else, it will be nice to get out of the office, and it will give us time to go over all this again. Maybe we'll think of something else."

# Chapter 43

Patsy made his way to FDC-SeaTac with a subpoena Ella had prepared and had signed by a court clerk first thing that morning, JP Harrison at his side. The subpoena sought the federal prison's visitor logs for certain time periods before Victor Garcia and before Michael Westbrook each arrived at the facility. Ella had also contacted the warden, Bill Erickson, and requested an exception to the normal visiting hours to allow Harrison to speak to Glenn Ellis. She said it related to an emergency legal issue that made prior notification not practical, given the trial schedule's complexities. Erickson, aware of the trial taking place, granted the request.

"Ella said Laurence Holmes has been moved," Patsy said from the passenger seat of Harrison's BMW. "Right after he testified."

"Moved where?" Harrison asked.

"The Monroe Correctional Complex," Patsy said.

"But Ellis wasn't moved?"

"Warden didn't say he was," Patsy said.

"Huh," Harrison said. "Seem odd to you?"

"It does."

Inside the prison complex, Patsy checked himself and Harrison in at the front desk, where they provided the required identification. Shortly thereafter, a female correctional officer arrived.

"The warden has asked to see you both." She led them through a security screening before escorting them to the warden's office.

Warden Bill Erickson, a Black man with a shaved head, large chest, and meaty arms stretching beneath a button-down shirt and tie, came out from behind his desk to introduce himself, then asked the correctional officer to close the door on her way out. Patsy suspected the warden was interested in the subpoena—what they wanted and why.

"Sorry for the change in plans, but we've had a hell of a morning. We're on lockdown. Glenn Ellis was stabbed early this morning on his way to the dining hall."

"Is he dead?" Harrison asked.

"No. He was treated here in the medical facility, then taken by ambulance to Harborview."

"Do you know *who* stabbed him?" Harrison asked.

"We're investigating, but as you might imagine, no one saw or heard anything, so far. As you might also imagine, I'm more than a little curious, given your request to speak to Ellis this morning, if you know what this might be about. It seems more than a coincidence."

"Does seem like more than a coincidence," Patsy agreed. "But we didn't make our request to speak to Ellis public, only our request for the visitors log," Patsy said. "The better question is, if Ellis's stabbing is more than a coincidence, how did someone in here find out we wanted to talk to him? And why wasn't he moved from the facility when Holmes was moved?"

"I don't know," Erickson said. "I've been asking myself the same questions."

"Who issued the order to move Laurence Holmes?" Harrison asked.

"It came down from the Department of Corrections," Erickson said.

"But no order was given to move Ellis?" Patsy asked.

"None," Erickson said, shaking his head.

"I may have an answer," Harrison said.

He explained to Erickson what had happened in court, and his theory that maybe Ellis had made mistakes in his testimony on purpose, that he had second thoughts about wrongfully convicting another young Black man.

"And somebody didn't want you to find out from Ellis if that was the case?" Erickson asked.

"Let's call it a working theory," Harrison said.

Patsy told Erickson about George Frazier's threat to Bo Chapel about making his witness letter common knowledge inside the prison. "I'd start with him."

Erickson said, "Okay, we'll get on it."

"I know things are busy this morning," Patsy said. "But it's important we see those visitors logs today."

"I've had the digital record copied for you for the two time periods you requested," Erickson said. He handed Patsy a USB flash drive. "I think you'll find them self-explanatory."

"Does it include the digital log from yesterday?" Patsy asked.

"It does not," Erickson said, though Patsy could tell from the look on the warden's face that he understood why Patsy had asked the question. Inmates could not receive calls from outside the facility. If someone had leaked that Patsy and Harrison were coming to speak with Glenn Ellis, some person had to have delivered the message.

"I'll have yesterday's log pulled and send it over to you today. But I'd like a little quid pro quo here," Erickson said, confirming Patsy's suspicions the warden was not happy about what had happened in his prison, and he hoped to nip it in the bud before it became public.

"Anything we learn we'll let you know," Patsy said. He thanked the warden and exited, the same correctional officer escorting them back to reception.

Outside the facility, Patsy asked, "I don't suppose you have a laptop with you?" He wanted to plug in the USB drive.

"Unfortunately, no," Harrison said.

"Then let's get a move on and get back to the office," Patsy said.

# Chapter 44

Frank Rossi and Billy Ford made the hour-long drive to Duvall, the picturesque town nestled in the Cascade Range's foothills, seemingly a world away from the clamor of Seattle.

"You ever been here?" Rossi asked Ford, who had been quiet in the passenger seat as they passed open fields and marshland.

"Me?" Ford said, glancing over. "No."

"You should bring Allysia out here for a weekend. Go to a B and B. It's quaint, has some good restaurants."

"You want to babysit three young boys?"

"No, thank you," Rossi said.

Rossi had visited the town several times, mostly on his way to local golf courses. He had stopped at a local brewery for lunch and checked out what had been the train depot and now served as a museum. He'd learned that Duvall had at one time been a logging town. The Snoqualmie River was the only access in and out until the state constructed Highway 203 and tourists came calling. Following the directions Jack Thompson provided, Rossi drove through Main Street. The buildings had been renovated but maintained their original façades. Just past downtown Duvall, Rossi turned left toward the river, driving across fields of what looked to be hay. They eventually came to a circular drive in front of a yellow, multistory farmhouse with white trim, built on stilts.

Rossi parked and the two detectives stepped from the car into bright sunshine, just the hint of a breeze on which Rossi could smell the hayfields. Three horses in a pen adjacent to the house lifted their heads and watched them with curiosity.

Rossi and Ford climbed the tall staircase to a wraparound porch. The Snoqualmie periodically overflowed its banks during heavy rains, necessitating the piers, hidden with decorative lattice sheets.

"Not a bad place to retire, if you like peace and quiet," Rossi said.

"I can only dream about peace and quiet at this stage in my life," Ford said. "And climbing these stairs every day would be a killer."

Rossi knocked on the front door, which caused dogs inside the house to bark. An elderly woman and two yellow Labs answered, the dogs continuing to sound the visitors alarm until the woman assured them everything was all right.

"You must be the detectives from Seattle." She pushed open the screen door. The two dogs bounded out, tails wagging, circling the detectives.

"He doesn't like to talk about his cases much," Emma Thompson said after introductions. "He doesn't like to go back there."

"We understand," Rossi said. "And I promised him on the phone we wouldn't overwhelm him. Is he home?"

"Not if the sun is shining. Beautiful day like today, he's either fishing the river or hitting golf balls. Today he's fishing the river, expecting you, though." She stepped out onto the porch and pointed. "Take that path there about fifty yards. You can't miss him. That's his honey hole. Never gets skunked, though I think he just keeps catching the same fish over and over."

"Catch and release," Ford said with a smile.

"Always," she said.

They thanked her, descended the steps, and slipped on sunglasses as they walked the path. "You know fishing?" Rossi asked. He'd never heard Billy talk fishing before.

"Growing up in Texas, I did more fishing than I cared to. We didn't catch and release, though. We caught and ate."

The path narrowed, trees and foliage pressing on each side. Rossi smelled fragrant, flowering bushes, along with the hay, and heard the river's flow. Approximately fifty yards down the path, the river came into view, the sun glistening on the ripples like sparkling lights. Getting closer, he noticed a sandbar and, about ten yards off it, a tall man in waders in knee-deep water. Thompson wore a vest with many pockets over a long-sleeve sun shirt, and a floppy sunhat. He rhythmically brought the fly pole up, the fishing line arcing behind him. Then he flicked the tip forward and the line snapped and landed gently on the moving current near the opposite bank.

"He's good," Billy said. Rossi was about to call out, but Ford put a hand on his forearm. "Has a fish on," he said.

They watched as Thompson played the fish, stripping in line. The pole flexed, the line skimming across the water's surface.

"Doesn't appear to be in a rush," Rossi said.

"No reason to be," Ford said. "That's the fun of it."

After several minutes, Thompson moved toward shore, netted the fish, popped the hook, and gently set the fish free.

"Nice fish," Ford called out as the two detectives approached.

Thompson turned, took notice of them, and made his way to the bank with a proud grin on his face.

"Cutthroat?" Ford asked.

"Yeah. Good size too," Thompson said.

"Had a lot of fight in him," Ford said.

"You must be the detectives from Seattle. I told Emma to send you down. Too nice a day to sit inside."

"It's a beautiful spot," Ford said, looking about the honey hole. "The bank provides the fish good shade to hide in. What are they hitting, nymphs?"

"Started with nymphs, but that one hit on a hopper. You fly-fish?" Thompson asked.

"No time at present," Ford said. "I have three teenage boys. Took them once. They caught tree branches and bushes, and I caught a headache. Haven't tried again."

Thompson laughed. "I remember those days well. It can get expensive." He looked at Rossi.

"Not me," Rossi said. "I don't have the patience. Spend most of what little free time I have golfing."

"I remember those days well also, being so busy you don't know if you're coming or going. Don't like to go back often."

"We won't take up too much of your time," Ford assured. "Have to fish while the fish are biting."

"I think the bite might be over for the day," Thompson said.

He leaned his pole against a picnic table on the bank. On it rested a small pack of lures and a cloth cooler. He opened the cooler and removed a Coors Light, holding out the silver can. "Can I offer you one?" They both politely declined. Thompson sat on the table, his feet on the bench, popped the tab, and took a sip. Then he said, "So what can I help you with? You said this has to do with a case you're trying with Anh Tran?"

"Hoping to get a little bit of information about the case involving her parents," Ford said.

Thompson took another sip of his beer and shook his head. "That was my last homicide case. Couldn't do it anymore after that one. Moved upstairs with the brass."

"Can you tell us about it?" Ford said.

Thompson took his time, seemingly uncomfortable with the memory. He told them Tran's parents owned a jewelry store in Little Saigon, Anh the only child. He told them her parents' hands had been bound behind their backs and they'd each been shot once in the head, execution style. "It was gruesome. I had a young partner at the time who I was showing the ropes. He was a Marine. Served in Vietnam. Tough guy. Nearly lost his breakfast when we walked into the store that afternoon."

"I read somewhere that Anh Tran witnessed the murders," Ford said.

"That was the worst part," Thompson said. "The store had a living area in the back where they locked up the jewelry in a safe at night and cleaned and polished it and fixed clasps. That sort of thing. Anyway, that's where we found the two bodies. I noticed a garment under the bed. Turned out to be Anh. Her mother had told her to hide. She had a clear view of the executions."

"Shit," Ford said.

"Yeah." Thompson took another gulp of beer. "Now you know why it was my last homicide." Then he said, "The worst of it, though, was we couldn't get enough hard evidence to convict the killer."

"He walked?" Ford asked.

"Yes and no," Thompson said. "We arrested Andrae Ollson, a drifter with a record for drugs, burglary, that sort of thing. He was seen near the store on several occasions prior to the killings. But we didn't have enough hard evidence." He leveled his gaze on both of them, and Rossi could almost feel the withering stare Thompson had likely once used on suspects. "It killed me to do it, but we had no choice. We put Anh on the stand." Thompson looked and sounded choked up. He took a moment, then another sip of his beer.

Rossi and Ford gave him time to recover.

"How did she do?" Ford asked.

Thompson smiled but it had a sad quality to it. "She was a real trouper. I can still remember her up on that chair, legs swinging." He used two fingers to imitate legs swinging. "So little. So brave." He shook his head. Blew out a breath. "She identified the defendant. When I went through it with her, showed her photographs, she had no doubt it was Ollson. Did great on the stand too. She did great . . . but . . ." His voice trailed off again. He looked to them both with moist eyes. "The defense lawyer was good. Did what he was paid to do."

"Made her look unreliable?" Ford asked.

"Ollson walked," Thompson said. "And the case went to cold cases when I moved upstairs and remained there when I retired. No sense pursuing it any further. We knew the killer." Thompson paused. "Can I ask what's your interest?"

Rossi and Ford had talked about this on the drive over and decided it best to not get too specific. "We have a murder case in Seattle. The evidence sounds a lot like your case. We don't have a lot of direct evidence," Ford said.

"But . . ."

"But two jailhouse informants came forward and testified. Grand jury indicted. We have some questions about the informants. Things seem not . . . all together," Ford said.

Thompson looked to the river and took another sip of beer as he watched the water ripple past. Rossi sensed he had something more on his mind. Something else he debated saying. He obviously cared for Tran, at least the little girl. Rossi had heard it in the tone of his voice. The words he used to describe her. Ford looked about to speak, but this time Rossi touched his arm and slowly shook his head.

Thompson looked back at the two of them. "Informants, huh?"

"That's right," Ford said.

Thompson exhaled. "I guess it doesn't really matter anymore."

"What's that?" Rossi said.

"Ollson's dead now."

Rossi and Ford waited. Patient. They let Thompson wrestle with whatever demons tormented him.

"I used to have nightmares that I was that kid under that bed, seeing those two murders." He smiled, though it was more of a grimace. "I can't imagine what it was like for her. The reality of it. The dream was bad enough. It would only be natural for her to want justice; wouldn't it?"

"It would be," Rossi said. "Certainly." What was Thompson justifying?

Thompson again looked out over the water. "Ollson was in and out of prison, as is normal for those guys. Eventually he got convicted . . . It was for a robbery, I believe. Anyway, while he was in prison he was charged in a double homicide in Seattle. A cold case. The Newsome killings." He looked to Ford and Rossi again with that withering glare. "I was understandably interested."

Rossi and Ford both nodded. "Of course," Rossi said.

"We had little direct evidence. But the prosecutor had a witness. A jailhouse informant named Tommy Phan, a drug dealer in a large Southeast Asian drug ring who had testified against others in that ring and received a reduced sentence. Phan testified that Ollson confessed to the Newsome killings . . ." He paused before adding, "And to having killed the Trans. The latter was the reason for my interest. Double jeopardy, I know, made it water under the bridge. Couldn't retry Ollson. Still, it would have pleased me to know I was right."

Rossi picked up on Thompson's use of "would have." "Was Ollson convicted of killing the Newsomes?"

Thompson nodded. "Sentenced to death, later commuted to life. Died in prison."

"But you had doubts about the conviction?" Rossi said.

"I had doubts."

"About whether he killed the Newsomes? About the informant . . . Phan?"

"Both."

"Who arrested Tommy Phan?" Rossi asked. "Was it the ROPE team?"

Thompson looked at Rossi, but he didn't say another word. He didn't have to. His eyes, tearing up, told Rossi he wasn't about to say anything more.

Rossi and Ford had enough to figure out what happened on their own—or to get close enough. Tran had been the prosecutor on the ROPE team. She'd put Phan in jail, and he'd cut a deal with her, testifying against others for a lighter sentence. So she knew he had, at least, a proclivity to inform—and how powerful a jailhouse informant could be in getting a conviction.

It wasn't too large a leap to conclude Tran had likely gone to him again later, when Ollson was sent to prison on a robbery, perhaps persuaded Phan to testify against Ollson in the Newsome killings, and she could finally see the man who murdered her parents get convicted.

Rossi was sure of it. And from the look on Ford's face, so was he.

# Chapter 45

Keera was in the conference room going over motions with Ella when she saw Patsy and Harrison round the corner from reception and hurry down the hall. Patsy pushed open the door.

"Glenn Ellis was stabbed early this morning on the way to the dining hall," Patsy said. "He was treated and taken to Harborview. Somebody had to have leaked that JP was coming to speak to Ellis."

"Wait. Slow down. Repeat that," Keera said.

Patsy did, with interjections by Harrison.

"Did Frazier stab him?" Keera asked.

"Don't know yet," Harrison said. "They're investigating."

"But inmates can't take incoming calls," Patsy explained. "And all outgoing calls are monitored and limited to specified time periods, which was not last night. So whoever leaked the information had to have appeared at the prison in person; we're assuming he or she did so to let Frazier know." He handed Keera the flash drive.

"What's this?"

"It's the log of visitors for the two time periods we requested—just before Victor Garcia and Michael each arrived at the facility. The warden is going to send over the log from yesterday, so we can see if anyone visited George Frazier."

"You think it's the same person who visited before Garcia and Michael showed up?"

"No idea. But let's find out."

Keera put the flash drive into her computer. It took a moment to load, the computer humming. Harrison and Patsy stood behind her, looking over her shoulder, like expectant fathers. Within moments a blown-up document appeared on Keera's computer screen, though too large to fit in the margins. Keera zoomed out to bring the document into focus, and they familiarized themselves with the various columns: Each visitor's name. The time each visitor arrived. The visitor's form of identification. The inmate's name and DOC number. The time the visitor departed the facility.

"Focus on the column with the name of the inmate visited," Patsy said. "Look for George Frazier."

Keera centered that column and scrolled down through the visitors' names.

After several seconds, Harrison said, "There. There. Go back. Go back." They'd found the name George Frazier.

"What's the date?" Patsy asked.

Keera scrolled the mouse to her right and the column containing the date of the visit.

"Too late. Go back further, to December," Patsy said.

"Who was the visitor?" Harrison asked.

"Looks like a family member," Keera said. "Same last name."

"Continuing scrolling," Harrison said.

"Hang on. Let me do a search for the name."

They found Frazier's name a few additional times, but the time period was again off. They wrote down the visitors' names anyway, not knowing if they could be important. Keera eventually found Frazier's name for an entry date in December, before Michael was sent to the facility. She ran her finger across the row to the visitor's name. "Sam Vo," she said and looked up at Patsy. "Does that name mean anything to you?"

"No," he said, shaking his head. "Anyone?" Patsy asked the others.

They all shook their heads.

Harrison said, "Go to the next entry for George Frazier. Hang on. I got an idea. Can I use your computer in your office?"

"Sure," Keera said. Harrison departed.

Patsy's cell phone rang. He checked caller ID. "This could be the warden." Patsy answered and put the warden on speaker.

"You were right," Erickson said after brief pleasantries. "George Frazier had a visitor last night named Sam Vo." Patsy looked to Keera and Ella. "We've alerted the authorities."

"Do you know that name, Warden? Did he serve time at FDC?" Patsy asked Erickson.

"I didn't know it personally, but we ran him through the Department of Corrections, and he's got a record for dealing, burglary, aggravated assault, among others. And yes, he spent time here."

*Which meant he could have known George Frazier*, Keera thought.

Patsy advised they had located Vo's name earlier in the visitors log, and that he had also visited George Frazier just before Michael Westbrook was brought to the prison.

"Well, that is interesting," Erickson said.

Patsy agreed to call the warden back after they finished reviewing the visitor logs, and if they found Sam Vo's name on other dates. He asked if Erickson would let him know if the police picked up Vo.

"I will, though simply visiting an inmate is not an offense," Erickson cautioned.

*He was right*, Keera knew. They'd need more.

Patsy disconnected the call, and those listening silently digested the information. Harrison returned to the conference room with documents in hand. "Sam Vo has a record," he said, holding up a photograph of a young Asian man.

"We know. I just got off the phone with Erickson," Patsy said. "Vo visited George Frazier last night."

"That doesn't really answer the question, though; does it?" Harrison said.

"Which is what?" Ella said.

"How would Vo have known we were interested in talking to Glenn Ellis?" Keera said.

They looked between one another, and Keera asked, "Who, other than the people in this room, even knew you were going to talk to Glenn Ellis this morning?"

Harrison shook his head. "I didn't tell anyone." He looked at the others. "Did anyone say anything—to anyone?"

They each shook their heads.

"So how could this guy Sam Vo have known?" Keera asked. "*If* he knew." When no one immediately answered, she suggested, "Maybe someone suspected from the mistakes Ellis made while testifying, as we did, that Ellis was getting cold feet, that he made the mistakes on purpose. Maybe someone figured it best to not take the chance that Ellis could be turned."

"We weren't the only ones in the room after trial yesterday," Ella said.

Keera turned to where Ella sat at the conference room table. Ella looked pale. She glanced at Keera, then Patsy, as if hesitant to say anything.

Keera knew why. "Maggie was in here. She brought in dinner and ate with us while we were going over what happened in court, what we wanted to do, including you and JP talking with Ellis."

"She said she had a date," Ella said.

"And her new beau's name is *Sam,*" Keera said, finishing her sister's sentence.

"Shit," Patsy said.

"You know Maggie," Ella said to Keera and her father, her voice sounding as if she didn't believe it could be true. "She's never been able to keep a secret. If she knows something, she plays it like it's the nuclear codes." Ella rose to her feet and reached across the table for the speakerphone and dial pad.

Keera covered the speakerphone before Ella could press the button. "Wait. If we accuse Maggie, she's just going to get defensive and think we're ganging up on her. I think it should be me and Dad who talk to her."

"Maggie will not like *you* questioning her most of all," Ella said. "You know that."

"Let me do it," Patsy said. "I'll talk to her in private in my office." He held out his hand to Harrison. "Let me have the picture." He took it and moved toward the conference room door.

"I'm going to head to Harborview, see if Ellis will talk to me," Harrison said.

"Ellis will be protected by police officers; won't he?" Keera asked. "They are not going to let you anywhere near him."

Harrison exhaled. "So what do we do? How do I get to him?"

Keera let out her own burst of air. "I'm not sure you can, but maybe someone else can talk to him. Another Black man who might also understand what you're suggesting—that Ellis got to know Michael and felt guilty about what he'd put in the letter. That Michael didn't confess to anything."

# Chapter 46

Back in the office, Rossi and Ford divided the work. Rossi had the Andrae Ollson murder case and the Tommy Phan drug case files pulled from storage. The department had not inputted its criminal investigation files into the computer system until May of 2019, when they replaced their records management system to improve the efficiency and accessibility of their reports and other records.

Ford had Tommy Phan's file open on the desk. "Thompson's memory was accurate. The ROPE team busted Phan as part of a Southeast Asia drug ring, but he cut a deal and testified against two others for a reduced sentence, and Tran was the prosecutor who cut that deal."

Rossi leaned back. "So Tran knew Phan would inform if there was something in it for him."

"Seems she did," Ford agreed.

"But did she know he'd lie? Did she know he'd say Andrae Ollson confessed to the two Newsome cold case killings?"

"For a chance to get out of prison? I'm betting she thought it likely he would," Ford said. "And if he would lie, Tran likely saw it as a chance to finally put her parents' murders to rest."

Rossi's personal cell phone rang. He looked at the caller ID, then looked at Billy.

"Who is it?" Ford asked.

# Chapter 47

Patsy took a deep breath and thought again about how best to handle Maggie. Had it been Ella, he would have been straightforward, ripped off the Band-Aid, and asked her if she'd told anyone about their going to see Glenn Ellis. If Keera, he would have employed a gentler touch but still been direct. Maggie, though, was like a bomb that needed to be carefully defused. He'd have to be cautious that he disconnected the correct wires in the correct order to keep her from exploding.

He pressed the speakerphone button for reception. "Maggie, can you come to my office for a minute?"

"Now? I was getting ready to leave."

"It will only take a minute."

"Okay. Coming."

A moment later, Maggie knocked on the door and stuck her head in Patsy's office. "What is it, Dad?" She sounded rushed.

"Come on in, hon. Take a seat."

Maggie didn't move right away. She looked concerned, even a bit timid. "I'm not being fired; am I?"

Patsy smiled. "No. Of course not. Besides, Ella would have to fire you. She's the managing partner now." When Maggie hesitated to sit, Patsy smiled. "I'm kidding. Come in. Sit."

She lowered into the chair, facing his desk. "What is it, Dad? Is everything all right? You're not sick? Mom's not sick?" This was Maggie, a bit paranoid and always anxious.

"No. Your mother and I are fine." Patsy came around the desk and sat next to her. Not something he could remember the two of them ever having done.

She raised her palms, as if surrendering. "Okay, Dad. You're starting to freak me out."

"I'm sorry. I'll get to the point. Yesterday, in the conference room, when we all ate dinner together, we were talking about Keera's case. Do you remember?"

"Yeah." Her brow wrinkled.

"We were talking about me and JP going to the Federal Detention Center this morning to talk to a witness, Glenn Ellis. Do you remember us talking about that?"

"Vaguely. I'm pretty busy, Dad. I can't remember what everyone else around here says." Deflecting. Also Maggie.

"I know you're busy, Maggie. I know. It's just . . . the person we were going to speak with was stabbed this morning in prison, and the warden seems to think that is an awfully big coincidence. JP and I do also. We're wondering how anyone in prison could have found out we intended to talk to Ellis."

"I don't know how," she said.

"We don't either. So we're asking everyone who was in the conference room if they might have mentioned it to anyone." He paused. "Did you mention it to anyone, Maggie?"

She quickly dismissed him. "Anyone in prison? No, of course not."

"Not someone in prison, Maggie. Did you mention it to anyone at all?"

"Why would I bring that up?" Maggie said, getting her hackles up. "Why would I talk about work? I'm here enough as it is."

"Okay," Patsy said in a calm voice. "We're just trying to be . . ." He stopped because Maggie got a look. The same look she used to get when, as a young girl, she realized she'd done something wrong and feared punishment. She looked like she was watching a movie in her head. Her eyes were open, but unfocused.

"What is it, Mags?" he asked.

Now she looked scared. She had difficulty swallowing. Not like Maggie. "I . . . I mentioned it to my boyfriend," she said. "But . . ."

Patsy tried to remain calm. Inside, his stomach churned. He was most afraid for his daughter. "What's your boyfriend's name, Maggie?" Patsy asked. "You said it was Sam something. Is it Sam Vo?"

"No. No, it's Sam Chen. He's in computer tech sales."

Patsy felt some relief, but not completely. He looked at the mug shot on his desk that JP Harrison had pulled from the Department of Corrections. "This isn't your boyfriend then, right?"

Maggie's face went blank, her mouth open.

"Maggie?"

"Where did you get that?"

"The Department of Corrections. Is this your Sam Chen?"

"It can't be, Dad."

"But it is him; isn't it?"

"Who is he?"

"First, what did you tell him about the trial?"

She looked and sounded stunned. "We were just talking about our days; what we did that day. I told him the trial has pretty much been all-consuming in the office and was the reason I had to work late."

"Had you done that before, told him about the trial?"

"Well, yeah. I mean, we always talk about our days."

It explained, perhaps, why Tran had opened the State's case with a DEA agent, as Keera had intended to do in her case in chief, and perhaps also why Tran had not looked concerned when Jada Davis was called to the stand, how Tran could have prepared for that cross-examination.

"How did the subject of Glenn Ellis come up?"

"Sam said he'd read about the two prisoners in the newspaper; that they had said Michael Westbrook committed the murders. He said it sounded like Michael was guilty."

"And did you respond?"

"I just told him he shouldn't jump to any conclusions."

Ella had been right. If Maggie had information, she would have played it like she was intimately involved.

"What else did you tell him, Mags?"

Maggie's eyes watered, also something Patsy rarely saw. Maggie didn't cry. She got upset. She got angry. But she did not cry. These, he deduced, were tears of embarrassment.

"I told him not to underestimate Keera. I said she was a bulldog, that she thought one of the inmates was lying."

"What did he say to that?"

She took a breath, and it shuddered in her chest as the realization hit home. "He said something like 'Yeah, but they can't prove he was lying.' And that's when . . . Oh God, Dad. That's when I said Keera was sending an investigator to talk to the witness to find out. I said it was my idea. I . . ."

Just wanted to be relevant; also Maggie.

Patsy took her hand. "He's been lying to you, Mags. He's been using you to get information about the trial, about Keera's strategy. It's why Anh Tran has been so well prepared in court each day. He has connections to an inmate at FDC-SeaTac, likely someone he met while incarcerated there on drug charges."

"What? No, Dad. He's in tech sales."

"He isn't, Maggie. It's a lie. He works for a Southeast Asian drug dealer. His name is on the log of registered visitors to the prison last night. We think he's been feeding information to someone inside, and that person was providing the information to the informants who testified against Michael Westbrook."

"Oh God. Keera is going to hate me more than ever."

"No, Mags. Your sister doesn't hate you."

"I feel like such an idiot, Dad. Why does this always happen to me? Why can't I have a normal relationship for just once?"

"You were used, Maggie. This is not your fault."

"I'm such an idiot," she said again, this time more vehemently.

"No, Mags. You're a victim here."

She let out a long sigh. Patsy handed her the Kleenex box from his desk, and she pulled a tissue to dry her tears.

Now Patsy's only thought was protecting his daughter. "Do you have any plans to see Sam Chen today?"

Her gaze focused on her hands in her lap. She shook her head. "He said he would be busy for the next few days with work."

"If he calls, don't tell him you know who he is. Don't take the call. In fact, don't go home to your apartment."

She stopped wiping the Kleenex beneath her nose and looked up at him. "You think he's dangerous, Dad?"

"I do, Maggie."

Maggie's eyes widened and she put a hand over her mouth. Now the tears rolled freely down her cheeks. Fear.

"Has he been in the office, Maggie?"

"Once. No, twice."

"I'm going to ask JP to get an off-duty police officer to take you back to our house. I want you to stay with me and Mom for a few days."

"What are you going to do, Dad?"

First, he'd ask JP to sweep the office and determine if Vo had planted listening devices in places where Keera would have discussed the case, starting in the conference room.

# Chapter 48

A short while later, Keera had just slid into the Paddy Wagon's private booth behind the dining area and bar when Frank Rossi appeared in the dim light of the candle-shaped wall sconces. The room smelled of beer and deep-fried food.

"Déjà vu," Rossi said, giving Keera that familiar smirk.

Rossi and Keera met in this same booth during the Jenna Bernstein trial. She had provided Rossi information explaining why her client was not guilty and who had killed Sirus Kohl. The booth had a history of such clandestine meetings, once used by Seattle's powerful and corrupt in the days of prohibition and bootlegging. Photographs on the walls surrounding the booth depicted much of Seattle during that time.

"You know I can't talk to you about the case," Rossi said, but he slid onto the brown leather to her right. Liam, a waiter and Keera admirer, had put two glasses of water and a basket of potato chips on the table.

"I would never ask that of you, Frank. I would never take advantage of our friendship." She'd leave it at that, for the moment.

"Sorry," he said. "I know you wouldn't." He looked around and his lips parted, just the hint of a smile. "So, why are we here, again?"

"I'm just asking you to listen."

"I'm all ears."

Keera took a breath. She'd thought of several different ways to begin this conversation and ultimately decided to jump in feet first. "Anh Tran called two witnesses to testify against Michael Westbrook. Billy was in court. I'm sure he told you of their testimony."

"He did."

"Glenn Ellis's testimony deviated from Laurence Holmes's testimony in several significant areas."

"But not in the most important area—that Westbrook confessed."

She paused. She did not want to imply that Rossi and Ford's investigation was insufficient, a rush to judgment, or just plain wrong. She didn't want to make him defensive by arguing with him. He and Ford needed to come to the conclusions her team had reached, but on their own . . . Though she hoped to lead them there.

"Ellis signed a letter detailing where, when, and what Michael said. It matches, almost verbatim, the letter Laurence Holmes signed . . . And the letter Edgar Chapel signed. Even the misspellings and the typos are the same."

Rossi looked as if he'd been about to say something, then didn't. Had he also made this deduction? He was a good detective. One of the best she had worked with while at the prosecutor's office. After his pause, Rossi said, "You're saying the same person wrote and typed the statements for all three?"

"If you haven't already, look at the three letters side by side."

Again, Rossi did not immediately respond, but Keera knew his tells, how his gaze shifted down and to the right when trying to avoid acknowledging something. He had already compared the letters side by side and he had noted the same things she had.

"Go on," he said.

"I can see where a witness, in the heat of a trial, under cross-examination, gets his facts mixed up. It happens."

"It does."

"But Tran tried this case before the grand jury." She raised her palms. "I don't know for certain, but I'd be shocked if she didn't put on both inmate informants as witnesses. If she did, then she had to be confident they each had their stories straight."

"You're saying one of them didn't tell the truth in court?"

"I'm saying there's no way Tran puts on one witness to contradict the other and gives me the opportunity to argue reasonable doubt to the jurors."

"So," Rossi said with a shrug. "She didn't know Ellis was going to make those mistakes . . ."

"What if they weren't mistakes, Frank?"

Rossi paused again. This time it seemed genuine. "What are you saying?"

"I'm saying Ellis wrote a letter and he testified before the grand jury. What if the discrepancies he made when he testified in court were intentional?"

Rossi got an inquisitive look. "Why would Ellis do that?"

She shrugged, gently. "Because Michael never confessed, Frank. Maybe when Ellis was told by George Frazier that Michael was coming to the unit, Frazier neglected to tell him Michael was Black. Maybe that was important to Ellis, especially if Michael didn't confess."

"You're saying he had what? Doubt?"

"Or guilt."

Rossi seemed to give that consideration. "He didn't want to be responsible for convicting a Black man of a crime he may or may not have committed?"

Keera wondered if Rossi was just summarizing what she had led him to, or if he was repeating something Billy Ford had said. "Or of a crime that, at the very least, Michael didn't confess to having committed," Keera offered, again not wanting to imply their investigation wasn't thorough. But she added, "That's JP Harrison's take on it."

"Why wouldn't Ellis just refuse to testify in court?"

"I assume Billy told you about Bo Chapel's testimony."

"He did."

"So you know how George Frazier threatened Chapel with the letter he'd signed, said he'd let others in prison know Chapel was a snitch."

"And you're suggesting Ellis knew if he refused to testify, Frazier could have made the same threat." Rossi leaned back into the leather booth. "How can you prove that, Keera?"

"By talking to Ellis."

"What makes you think Ellis would say more?"

"JP thought he would." She sighed. "JP and Patsy took a drive out to FDC-SeaTac this morning. JP had intended to talk to Ellis."

"And?"

He didn't know yet. Rossi didn't know. "And the warden intercepted them. Ellis was stabbed early this morning on the way to the dining hall, Frank. He was treated and taken to Harborview."

Rossi's eyes widened. "He's still alive?"

"Far as I know."

"Does the warden know who stabbed him?"

"No, but the visitors log from last night indicates someone named Sam Vo went to the prison to talk to George Frazier. Vo has convictions for running drugs and spent time at FDC-SeaTac."

"The same George Frazier who Bo Chapel testified went from unit to unit recruiting jailhouse informants?" Rossi asked.

He and Billy Ford *had* talked about the testimony. "Same one. Also, the DOC moved Laurence Holmes after he testified."

"But they didn't move Ellis?"

Keera shook her head. "Sam Vo also came to see Frazier before Michael Westbrook arrived at the facility. He's also been dating Maggie since just before this trial started, though he told her his name was Sam Chen."

Rossi sat up. "And Maggie told him about JP going to talk to Ellis?"

Keera did not want to throw her sister under the bus. "JP found Vo in the Department of Corrections, and he called a contact at the DEA's office and asked if Sam Vo has been on their radar. He's a foot soldier to a Southeast Asian drug runner in Seattle and Vancouver named Tommy Phan."

What Keera had said had hit home, and it hit hard. Frank's eyes widened. He looked as if he'd just found the key piece to a jigsaw puzzle and a dozen other pieces suddenly fit together.

He slid from the booth. "Thanks for the information, Keera. I'll let Billy know." He started to turn.

"Frank?" He stopped. "I'm sorry I didn't tell you I was going to Italy for a vacation."

"You don't owe me any explanation, Keera," he said, and it sounded sincere.

"No. And you don't owe me anything. It's . . . I just thought . . ."

"It could get complicated?" Rossi said, his lips again rising to that faint smile.

"Yeah," she said. "It could be complicated." She almost stopped there but continued. "That's not to say that I didn't think about it."

"About telling me?"

"About asking you to go with me." It was the most vulnerable Keera had allowed herself to be since her breakup with Miller Ambrose in the prosecutor's office.

"It would have been nice . . . to be asked."

She wanted to ask the next question. She wanted to ask, *Would you have gone?* But she knew that wouldn't be fair to put him on the spot.

# Chapter 49

Billy Ford's dress shoes snapped against the linoleum as he and Frank Rossi walked into Harborview Medical Center's surgical unit. They made their way toward the nursing station, hearing the pinging of bells and a cacophony of voices from the doctors, nurses, and staff attending to patients. It made Ford wonder how anyone slept in a hospital. At the corner nurses' station, Ford displayed his detective badge and asked for the room number for Glenn Ellis. The young man gave him directions to a room down the hall, where a young officer stood talking to a nurse. On the floor beside the officer's chair was his clipboard with, presumably, a log for visitors.

The officer alerted when Rossi and Ford approached, looking embarrassed. He bent down and retrieved his clipboard. The two detectives presented their credentials and signed the log. "Has anyone else tried to get in to see him?" Rossi asked.

"You're the first."

According to Glenn Ellis's doctor, whom Rossi had spoken with on the telephone to determine whether he could answer questions, Ellis had been stabbed in the back, but the wound had not impacted his vital organs or arteries. The doctor told Rossi he believed Ellis was stable enough to answer questions.

Ford had also called JP Harrison, at Rossi's suggestion. He asked Harrison why he believed Ellis had deliberately made mistakes in his trial testimony. After disconnecting that call, Ford told Rossi they needed to take a drive.

"Let me ask the questions," Ford said to Rossi.

"You're the lead detective," Rossi said, hiding a grin.

"Yeah. And I won't ask where you got this piece of information that Ellis might have screwed up his testimony on purpose."

"Just good police work, Billy," Rossi said.

"Let's hope Ellis is willing to talk, and Harrison is right about why he thinks the two testimonies differ."

"Harrison's reasoning sounds similar to yours."

"I know."

Ford pushed open the door, and they stepped inside the room. Ellis lay in a hospital bed propped up on several pillows, his right wrist handcuffed to the bed railing. He had his head back but his eyes open. He turned to the door opening, took in Ford and Rossi, then returned his gaze to the ceiling.

The detectives stepped to his bedside. Ellis was attached to a monitor that emitted blips and pings and showed his pulse and his heart rate. He wore a hospital gown and a hospital wristband. His glasses rested on a side table.

Ford introduced himself. Rossi stayed several steps back.

"I know who you are," Ellis said. "Both of you. You were in court when I testified."

"How do you feel?" Ford asked.

Ellis shrugged.

"You up to answering a few questions?"

"I don't know who stabbed me or why."

"Fair enough," Ford said. "And I will respect that. But that's not really why I'm here or what I want to know."

Ellis glanced over at Ford but did not speak.

"I have three sons," Ford said. "I worry about them. They're good boys. Their mother is more responsible for that than I am. I worry about them because I grew up in the South."

Ellis turned his head. "Yeah? Whereabouts?"

"Texas. Small town not far from the border with Louisiana."

Rossi be damned, but he could almost hear a Texas twang in Ford's voice.

"I'm from Houston," Ellis said.

"So you understand why I worry about my boys."

Ellis glanced over again. "I understand. I have a son of my own."

"You understand when I say I don't want to be part of any system that convicts a young Black man of a crime he did not commit. Don't get me wrong, Mr. Ellis. I'm colorblind when it comes to this job. I don't care if you're white, black, green, purple. If you're guilty, I will see you convicted. *If* you're guilty." Ford paused. "I was at the grand jury proceeding also."

"I recall."

"And I remember your testimony at that proceeding conformed with Mr. Holmes's testimony and with the letter you wrote to the prosecutor, Anh Tran. So it makes me wonder why the testimony you gave in Superior Court differed. Why it left room for reasonable doubt. I have to ask if it was intentional."

Rossi admired Ford's patience. He didn't rush.

"I don't have anything to say about that," Ellis said.

"Are you worried that word could get back to other inmates that you snitched?"

Ellis shrugged.

"We can have you moved. Someplace out of state. I'd do what I could to have you moved to a facility in Houston, closer to your family."

Ellis chuckled. "After Anh Tran prosecuted me for perjury?"

"Frank and I could explain to Seattle's prosecuting attorney why he wouldn't want to do that. Let him know that it could be embarrassing to the office if what I believe you have to say came out in court. If the media got ahold of it."

"I'll need some assurances in writing," Ellis said. "No perjury charge, and you'll have me moved, to Houston . . . if you can. And I want my trial attorney to approve of any agreement before I say anything."

"Give me your attorney's name. Better yet," Ford handed Ellis his cell phone. "Get your attorney on the phone. If we're going to do this, we need to do it now."

An hour later, Ford and Rossi walked back into the hospital room, this time with King County prosecuting attorney Daniel Butcher and Isabel Martinez, Ellis's public defender. They'd hammered out an agreement giving Ellis immunity from prosecution for anything he was about to say. They also agreed to have the Department of Corrections move him to a federal facility outside of the state, and to do what they could to move him to a facility in Houston. With the agreement signed off, and a court reporter present to take down what Ellis had to say, he sat up and put on his glasses.

Butcher had agreed to let Billy Ford, who knew the case and the circumstances that had led them all to this hospital room, ask the questions.

After reading the agreement into the record and asking everyone in the room to identify him- or herself, Billy asked Ellis questions about how his testifying all got started.

"They told me Westbrook was guilty. They said he'd killed those two people."

"Who told you he was guilty?" Ford asked.

"George Frazier."

"Was this before Westbrook arrived on your unit at FDC?"

Ellis nodded. "That's right. Frazier said he was coming to the C Unit, and that he'd shot a guy, then beat his girlfriend to death and masturbated over her. He said the guy had some flimsy alibi. He said that if I could get this guy Westbrook to confess, Frazier knew someone who would get my sentence reduced. I figured a guy that sick . . . he deserved to spend the rest of his life in prison. And I wanted to get my sentence reduced. I wanted to go home to my wife and kids. So, I signed the letter. Then Mike arrived on the unit, and Frazier told me to get to know him, to get him to confess to the things they said he'd done, that they'd put in my letter. Only Mike didn't confess, and the more I got to know him, the more I began to believe him. Mike didn't have it in him to do the things they said he'd done. Frazier kept coming around asking me if Mike had confessed, so I finally told him I didn't think he did it, and I wasn't going to testify that Mike confessed when he hadn't. That's when Frazier said that Mike was going down, that he had already confessed to Larry Holmes and to another inmate, Bo Chapel, and I might as well get something out of it also. I told him to use Holmes and Chapel if Mike had confessed to them, that there was no reason to use me. That's when Frazier said he had the letter, and if I didn't testify, like I said I would, that letter might find its way around the FDC and there wasn't any place I'd be safe."

"Did you take that as a threat?" Ford asked.

"Hell, yeah, I took it as a threat. Frazier was free to roam all over that facility. So I testified before the grand jury."

"Why did you change your testimony in the King County courtroom?"

Ellis gave a small shrug and blew out a breath. "I knew Holmes had testified, because he talked to me about it. And they told me Chapel had testified, but then I heard that Chapel got out on appeal, which meant he didn't have any reason to testify at the grand jury proceedings. He was already going home. So, the next time I saw George Frazier, I asked him about it, and he told me not to worry about it. Said they had enough with me and Holmes testifying." Ellis shook his head. "He just smiled at me. Gave me this shit-eating grin that I took to mean I'd better keep my mouth shut. And I did. But every time I saw or spoke to Mike I thought of my own son." Ellis glanced at Ford. "And I felt guilt, man. I felt guilt. Because I was telling myself what everyone else was saying, that Mike did it. That he was guilty. But as I said, the more I got to know Mike . . . He just didn't seem to me to have it in him to do what they said he did. He kept saying he couldn't make bail because the prosecutor was going to charge him with the murders, and that he didn't kill anyone." Ellis paused, sucked in a breath, exhaled. "I don't know anymore, not for certain. Guilty. Not guilty. I don't know. I just know Mike didn't confess." He turned his head and looked at Ford. "Not to me. So, it's like you said. I didn't want to be the reason Mike spends his life in prison if he didn't commit the crime." Ellis fought back emotion. "Do you know? Is he guilty?"

"What you put in the letter wasn't true then?" Ford asked. "Michael Westbrook did not confess to committing the two crimes."

Ellis shook his head. "No. Not to me he didn't."

"He didn't confess to you and to Laurence Holmes in your prison cell?"

"That never happened."

"Do you know where George Frazier was getting his information before Michael Westbrook arrived at FDC-SeaTac?"

Ellis shook his head. "No."

"Have you ever heard the name Sam Vo?"

"No," he said, offering another headshake. Then Ellis said, "Can I ask you a question?"

"Sure," Ford said.

"What happens to Westbrook now?"

Ford glanced over at Daniel Butcher, who stood in the corner, listening intently, his hand rubbing the stubble of his chin. "I'm not sure."

# Chapter 50

Keera watched Harrison pace the carpet behind the conference room table, passing back and forth in front of the view of Puget Sound through the windows. He was anxious, and it was making Keera anxious. Harrison had previously scanned the conference room and Keera's office for bugs, not finding any. Sam Vo had got his information the old-fashioned way. He'd conned it out of Maggie.

"You're going to wear out the carpet, JP."

Harrison was aware that Keera had spoken with Frank Rossi, and that Rossi and Billy Ford had gone to speak to Glenn Ellis in the hospital. Harrison had also spoken with Alexander Kuznetsov, who said, late that afternoon, the DEA, the FBI, and the Department of Justice had been called to a meeting with two Seattle Violent Crimes detectives, Billy Ford and Frank Rossi, and Seattle's prosecuting attorney, Daniel Butcher.

Something was going on.

"How long can this take?" Harrison asked Keera.

"To unravel this whole thing? It could take months to get Michael out of prison. Why don't we go over what you found out again?" Keera said, hoping to distract him. "Give the floor a rest."

Harrison stopped pacing, but he did not sit. He repeated what he'd told Keera earlier, what he had further learned about Tran, and how it could relate to Lockett and to Michael. Ford hadn't exactly told Harrison the information, not with a criminal investigation still open, but he'd given Harrison enough that the former police officer knew where to look and whom to talk to, including Kuz. What Harrison had learned had been a revelation, for him and for Keera. "Tran convicted a drug dealer named Tommy Phan back when she worked for the ROPE team. Tran then made a deal with Phan, who testified against two others in that drug organization and, for his testimony, Phan received a lighter sentence. While Phan was in prison, it is suspected that he came into contact with Andrae Ollson, the same man tried and acquitted of murdering Anh Tran's parents. We suspect this because Phan then came forward and testified for the prosecution that Ollson confessed to the Newsome cold case murders."

"Though there existed little direct evidence he killed them," Keera said.

"Correct," Harrison said.

"But Phan also said Ollson had confessed to murdering Anh Tran's parents, though that also seems unlikely given Ollson had already been acquitted. We don't know for certain whether Anh Tran solicited Phan's testimony—"

"But Ford and Rossi suspect she did, given her prior interaction with Phan through the ROPE team, and his having turned State's witness once before."

"Ollson was convicted of the Newsome murders and ultimately died in prison. And for his testimony, Phan was released," Keera said.

"According to Kuz, the DEA was investigating a drug smuggling operation out of Southeast Asia for which John Lockett worked, but it had never determined the head of that organization," Harrison said. "Kuz said the DEA now suspects that person is Tommy Phan."

"We, meaning me and you," Keera said, "were postulating that John Lockett was skimming product and profits from that organization, and received some warning his bosses suspected him of doing so."

"Which is why he gave Michael the two packages to hold. He didn't want it in his house," Harrison said. "And if we're correct, then Phan had the motivation to have John Lockett and Melissa Scott murdered, and to do so in a way that sent a message throughout his organization."

"And Michael was just in the wrong place at the wrong time," Keera said.

Harrison stopped pacing. "Why would Anh Tran solicit prison snitches if she suspected they were lying?"

Keera had also given this some thought. As upset as she was, she tried to give Tran some grace, as Keera's mother had so often instructed her children, given Tran's tragic childhood. Keera didn't know the depth of what Tran had gone through, and she could only imagine it had been horrific and had left deep scars, scars that had never healed, perhaps in part because Ollson walked. Maybe Tran's using Phan as an informant had started with good intentions. Maybe she was motivated to take down big names in the drug smuggling world. Maybe the urge to go back to Phan to finally convict Ollson was just too tempting for Tran to let go—the pull to finally put her parents to rest too strong. But once she'd made that deal, once she'd let Phan lie on the witness stand to her benefit, she'd made a deal with the devil, and the devil wasn't about to let such a valuable asset walk away without getting something in return.

She told Harrison this, and he said, "And once she made that first deal, Phan had his hooks into her. And wasn't about to let her go."

"But it isn't an excuse for what we think happened here, JP. It isn't an excuse to pin the two murders on Michael and discourage further investigation that might have led back to Phan's organization. That can't just be dismissed."

Keera's cell phone rang. She looked at the caller ID, then Harrison. "Billy Ford," she said.

# Chapter 51

***May 2013***
***Monroe Correctional Complex***
***Monroe, Washington***

Tommy Phan entered the area of the prison with the attorney-client meeting rooms. He'd been told an attorney had requested to speak with him. He hoped Tuấn Le had good news about his appeal.

The correctional officer opened the door to the room and Phan stepped to the threshold but hesitated and did not immediately enter. It was not Le sitting at the table, waiting for him. Phan looked at the guard, then back to Anh Tran, uncertain.

"You can leave us," Tran said to the guard.

After Phan stepped in and the guard closed the door, he said, "Did you come here to gloat?"

"Gloat? Hardly. I gave you a hell of a deal."

He scoffed. "Fifteen years? That's a hell of a deal?"

"Could have been a lot more. Would have been a lot more if you hadn't taken the deal."

"Maybe, but I gave you something also."

"We would have convicted Huỳnh or Bùí eventually without you."

"Maybe. But I've seen the newspapers. I made you a rock star in Seattle. What did the paper call you? Batwoman?"

"I didn't ask to be labeled."

"I read the articles. I never knew about your parents. Tragic." Tran's expression remained impassive.

"And I'm not looking for sympathy."

"The guy who killed them walked; didn't he? Despite you testifying, is what Le told me." He studied her face. Again, her facial expression revealed nothing, but she was here in this room for a reason, and Phan suspected he knew her reason. "That's the way it goes sometimes; isn't it? The guilty walk free."

"Sometimes," she said.

"I guess even Batwoman has to accept fate sometimes."

"Maybe not."

"No?"

"No," she said.

"What did you have in mind?" he asked.

# Chapter 52

Billy Ford awaited Keera when the elevator doors opened to the seventh floor of Police Headquarters in downtown Seattle. She stepped from the elevator and detected the familiar strong odors of coffee and microwave popcorn.

"Thanks for coming over," Ford said.

Keera felt ill at ease and nervous. She had no idea why Tran had asked to speak to her, but she felt compelled as Michael's attorney to find out. "Got a minute before I talk to Tran?" Keera asked.

Ford nodded and led her to an unused office on the outer portion of the bull pen. He shut the door.

"You said Tran was forthcoming in talking to the feds?" Keera asked.

"To an extent."

"Did she say why she wants to talk to me?"

Ford shook his head. "Didn't say. Maybe she wants to explain. As I said on the phone, I don't know. Just asked to meet with you."

"My primary concern is my client, Michael Westbrook."

"I understand. We've picked up Sam Vo. We're in the process of bringing in Tommy Phan. I doubt either man will say much, but we have the visitors logs at FDC-SeaTac, and Frank and I are going out to confront George Frazier. Maybe he'll be a little more forthcoming if we threaten him with attempted murder. We'll find out soon enough. As for your client, I've spoken to Daniel Butcher," he said. "And he is now intimately aware of the situation. I think it's highly likely the charges against your client will be dismissed within the next twenty-four hours. Without Ellis's or Holmes's testimony, they don't have enough to convict."

"Michael Westbrook is innocent, Billy. No offense to you or to Frank, but he's innocent, and I'm going to insist on a complete exoneration."

"The PA's office is going to need to save a little face here, Keera."

"Not at Michael's expense. He has to live his life." Keera sighed. Then she asked, "What will happen to Tran?"

Ford shook his head. "That's above my pay grade. But what I've been told is she's looking to cut a deal if she comes clean. I expect they'll do it. Tough to get a prosecutor, as you know. The standard of proof is very high."

Prosecutors had near absolute immunity for actions related to their duties in the courtroom. That immunity prevented them from being sued for trial misconduct such as withholding evidence, coercing witnesses, or presenting false testimony. The legal standard to convict a prosecutor for misconduct required clear and convincing evidence the prosecutor intentionally violated her legal or ethical standards and didn't simply commit a harmless error.

Ford continued. "Tran denies knowing the informants were lying when they got on the stand."

"Do you believe her?"

Ford shrugged. "Can we prove otherwise?"

Keera knew that would be tough.

Ford shrugged. "Even if Phan says she did know, he's a drug dealer."

"Not the most credible source," Keera said.

"It will be a 'he said, she said' situation," Ford said.

"But you think she knew."

Ford paused, as if considering his words carefully. "I think sometimes people start out doing things with the best intentions, and don't realize or don't care that what they do will make them susceptible to people who do not have the best intentions."

Keera had come to a similar conclusion. Hearing Ford say it confirmed for her that Tran, steeled by what she had witnessed as a child, made a conscious and honest decision to prosecute criminals.

She had seemingly risen above the trauma to do well enough in college to attend one of the most prestigious law schools. She also seemed to have a refined sense of priorities, and she had likely passed up lucrative private practice offers to work for the King County prosecutor and put away criminals like the one who had taken her parents' lives.

Then an opportunity had presented itself in the form of Tommy Phan. Keera believed Tran had realized the power of an informant's testimony when Phan first testified against two powerful Southeast Asian drug dealers. She believed Tran had decided such an informant was the only remaining chance she had of putting Ollson away for life.

Had Tran not fully thought through the ramifications of making a deal with Phan? Had she not realized she'd left herself exposed to blackmail and manipulation? Keera found that unlikely. But at some point Keera believed Tran decided she didn't care, that the desire to put the man who killed her parents away for life was too enticing to pass up.

Keera doubted anyone, other than Tran, would ever know the truth.

But the truth didn't matter. What mattered now was Tran had not been Bruce Wayne, aka Batman—far from it—and her actions now cast doubt on every conviction she had won using an inmate informant.

"I have to advise you that if you talk to Tran, you could become a witness, should the Department of Justice or the FBI seek to pursue her," Ford said.

"But that isn't likely; is it?"

"Probably not," Ford said with resignation in his voice. "I think it more likely Tran will be given the option to retire and go away, quietly."

Keera agreed, but what she cared about was getting Michael exonerated and not just released for a lack of evidence. And now she saw a path to ensure that happened.

"And Butcher and the powers that be really don't want someone going to the media with an embarrassing story that their Batwoman went rogue; do they?" she said.

Ford smiled. "You really are becoming a chip off the old block; aren't you? That's the kind of subtle persuasion I could see Patsy using, in his prime. If I were a betting man, I'd say that's a safe bet."

Keera shrugged. "What about her other drug cases, the ones Tran won with the help of inmate informants?"

Ford sighed. "That's going to be a very big job for a team within the Department of Justice, I would assume. Simple enough to look for cases in which she used prison informants. Rossi and I have found three so far. But it's not so simple to look for cases in which other evidence might have been manufactured, or exculpatory evidence withheld, *if* she's guilty of that. I don't know. I don't think she is, but we don't have the luxury of assuming that's the case. Not now."

"Michael Westbrook could have been convicted and spent the rest of his life in prison. I understand everything Tran has been through, but it doesn't justify what she's done; does it?"

"The judicial system isn't perfect. We both know that. But it did work. In this instance anyway. Westbrook *isn't* going to spend the rest of his life in jail. Then again, not everyone is going to be defended by the Irish Brawler's daughter." He looked at his wristwatch. "Come on. It's getting late. I'll show you in."

Keera followed Ford to the soft interrogation room. He pushed open the door to the small, dimly lit space. Keera stepped inside. Tran sat in a plastic chair at the conference room table, her hands folded atop it. She looked subdued, maybe even broken, but not necessarily beaten. Tran knew better than anyone that she had the law on her side and had no doubt figured out what Keera had figured out. The PA would want to keep what transpired quiet and out of the media.

"I take it there are no cameras or microphones in here," Tran said to Ford.

"There are not," Ford said. Then he closed the door.

Keera pulled out a chair and sat across the table from Tran, keeping her eyes on the prosecutor. She wondered how many young female prosecutors looked up to Tran as a role model. How many would she let down?

"I meant what I said about being disappointed you left the prosecutor's office," Tran said. "When it happened, I thought you didn't have enough fight in you, that you let Ambrose get the better of you. I was wrong. You have a lot of fight in you."

"You asked to see me," Keera said, not interested in Tran's backhanded compliments.

"When your name, and your father's name, showed up on the notice of appearance . . . some people wanted assurances Michael Westbrook would be convicted."

"Tommy Phan?"

Tran did not answer.

Keera tempered her anger because she wanted to get more information. "I'll let Patsy know his name still carries some weight."

"I'm not talking about your father's name. I'm talking about *yours.* After the Vince LaRussa and Jenna Bernstein trials, people in the office have taken notice. The public as well."

Keera remained silent. She wondered if Tran wanted something of her.

"For what it's worth, I believed your client to be guilty. I wouldn't have brought the charges if I hadn't."

"You manufactured evidence."

"I didn't," she said.

Ford had been right; Tran wasn't about to fall on her sword and admit to anything.

"The PA's office intends to drop the charges against your client tomorrow morning. Without the confessions, which Patel will throw out, we don't have enough to go forward."

"I'll deal with Butcher about that. Michael deserves to be fully exonerated."

Tran smiled, but it had a sad quality to it.

Keera waited for an apology that never came, and she couldn't hold back, not completely. "You'll understand if I tell you that all of this rings hollow . . . after everything Michael Westbrook and his mother have been put through. What you put them through."

"I understand," Tran said. "Better than most people."

Keera shook her head. "Was your entire reputation just a fraud?"

Tran gave the question a moment of thought before answering. "Some will think so. But to be honest, I never really cared about my reputation. The whole Batwoman thing was not of my doing, and I never sought to capitalize on it. I'd like to think that I started with good intentions, but . . ." She shrugged.

"My mother used to say, 'When you dance with the devil, the devil changes you.'"

Tran nodded. "Your mother must have been very wise."

"She was referring to liquor and my father's alcoholism."

"My parents didn't live long enough to give me such advice. I doubt we'd be having this conversation if they had. They wanted me to be a doctor."

Keera was struggling to give Tran the grace her mother taught her every person deserved. She would not take any pleasure in kicking the woman while she was down, but . . . "I'm sorry you had to go through what you did as a child, but it doesn't justify what you did to get Andrae Ollson convicted."

Tran looked as if she was about to say something, then caught herself. She raised her gaze to meet Keera's, and what emanated from her was nothing short of defiance. "You're not in a position to lecture me, or to know if it was justified. When I see my parents again, I'll ask them if it was justified. Until then, I'll have to find a way to live with it. The way I've had to live with their murders."

"The difference is their murders weren't of your doing; the conviction and incarceration of innocent men is."

"The men I convicted were drug dealers. They were far from innocent."

"Not Michael Westbrook," Keera said.

"The evidence indicated otherwise."

"If it did, you wouldn't have needed the two informants."

Tran didn't respond.

Keera had heard enough. She stood and moved to the door. "I suspect your conviction of innocent men will be a far worse demon to live with. But as you've said. Time will tell."

# Chapter 53

Keera left SPD and started down the hill to her office. She called JP and told him the charges against Michael would be dismissed in court in the morning. Tran would not be present, but the prosecuting attorney, Daniel Butcher, would be. Keera would push for a full exoneration, and she told Harrison she believed Butcher would agree. Harrison's voice choked with emotion over the phone.

"I'll call Tina," he said. "And I'll let Michael know. I was going to stop by the jail on my way home. Unless you want to be the one to tell him?"

Keera thought about it. "You and Tina tell him. Take some family time. I'll see them in court in the morning."

"You sure?"

"I'm sure." She didn't need any accolades. She thought of what the accolades had wrought on Anh Tran. They were a double-edged sword. She thought of Tran's comment about Keera's reputation getting noticed, the way her father's reputation had once been. Keera could no longer fly under the radar, and the firm certainly could use the publicity, but Keera didn't have to crash her plane into it either.

She didn't want a moniker like Batwoman or the Irish Brawler. She just wanted to do her job and do it well. When Keera was young and started winning chess matches and gaining some fame and notoriety, her mother used to say fame was like a candle. It burned bright, but eventually the candle either burned out or was blown out, and then the person had to find their way in darkness. Not everyone could.

"You want to go out, get a celebratory drink? Dinner?" Harrison asked.

Keera was tempted. Not by the celebratory drink, but the dinner. She hadn't eaten since breakfast. She was about to answer Harrison when she spotted Frank Rossi further down the hill, leaning against a building, watching her with his boyish grin.

"I'm good, JP. We'll celebrate another night. All of us. When Michael is free."

"Okay. What do you have planned for the evening? Something good, I hope."

"I hope so too," she said.

She disconnected and walked down the hill. "Are you stalking me, Frank?"

Rossi pushed away from the building. "Billy told me Tran asked to speak with you."

When he didn't continue, she said, "And you're what, out here waiting for a bus?"

He smiled. "No. I was waiting for you. I was thinking about your question."

"My question?"

"Whether I would have accepted your invitation to Italy."

"I never asked you that question," Keera said.

"No. But you wanted to." Rossi smiled. "Every attorney thinks about the question she didn't ask; doesn't she?"

"And?" Keera said.

"And?" Rossi mimicked.

She suppressed a smile. "Are you going to make me ask it?"

"I would not have gone with you."

His answer surprised her. "Oh." Keera couldn't help but feel a little hurt, though she also knew that wasn't the end to this conversation. Rossi wouldn't be out here, leaning against a building waiting for her just to tell her he would not have gone.

"As I said, I don't want to complicate your life."

"Chivalrous," she said.

"It's the truth."

"I've been thinking too," she said.

"About?"

"I'm a grown woman, Frank. I can decide for myself whether I want to complicate my life."

"Fair enough. Do you?"

"Want to decide for myself? Yes."

He laughed at her avoiding his real question. "Answered like a true lawyer. You really are the Irish Brawler's daughter; aren't you?"

She thought again about what Anh Tran had said about Keera gaining notoriety. "There's only one Patsy Duggan. Besides, I wasn't talking about my decisions in the courtroom."

"No?"

"No."

"Speaking of which, do you have to be in court tomorrow morning?"

"I do. The PA is going to dismiss all charges against Michael."

"So, then you don't have to go back to your office and prepare a closing argument tonight."

"Doesn't appear I do. Did you have something in mind?"

The boyish grin returned. "I did miss out on a trip to Italy. I thought maybe we could have dinner. There's an Italian restaurant in Fremont that another detective's son owns. It's supposed to be very good. It's called Fazzio's."

# Chapter 54

The following morning, Keera appeared in Judge Patel's King County courtroom. Across the aisle stood Daniel Butcher. Anh Tran was not present and would not, this day, be making a dramatic entrance. The gallery was nearly full. The reporters and spectators had, perhaps, expected to hear closing arguments this morning, but it was more likely rumors had spread from the courthouse to the media that the State intended to dismiss the charges. The families of John Lockett and Melissa Scott were not present, having been advised of the circumstances and the new direction of the police investigation into the two murders.

When the jury was reseated, they looked more than a little curious about what was going on, not seeing Tran seated at the State's counsel table, but instead a short man with thinning red hair and a beard flecked with gray.

"Let's get started," Patel said.

At the judge's instruction, marshals escorted Michael Westbrook into the courtroom, his smile spread from ear to ear. He nodded to his mother, again seated in the first row beside JP Harrison. Tina cried tears of joy.

Butcher stood. He seemed an unlikely politician. Everything about him—from his height to his looks—was inconsequential. You'd walk past him without giving him a second look.

"Your Honor, King County prosecuting attorney Daniel Butcher on behalf of the State. In light of recent events, and after reviewing the remaining evidence, the State has decided to dismiss the charges against Mr. Westbrook with prejudice, and to fully exonerate him of the crimes for which he has been charged. We believe proceeding with this case is not in the interest of justice."

"Thank you, Counselor." Patel turned to Keera. "Does the defense have any objections?"

Keera stood. "No objections, Your Honor. We appreciate the prosecution's decision. It is the right course of action."

"Very well. The charges against the defendant are hereby dismissed, with prejudice. Mr. Westbrook, the marshals will take you back to jail for processing and the recovery of any personal effects. Afterward, you are free to go. This court wishes you the very best moving forward."

Michael stood. "Thank you, Your Honor."

Patel turned to the jurors. "Ladies and gentlemen of the jury, I want to thank you for your commitment to your civic duty. You, too, are free to go. The attorneys may try to speak to you about the trial. You are under no obligation to speak to them. It is up to you. I'm sure many of you have questions, and Mr. Butcher has informed me that he is willing to answer what questions he can. With that, this court is adjourned."

The buzz in the room started even before the judge had finished rapping her gavel. The jurors were clearly perplexed and intrigued, as were many in the gallery.

Keera turned to Westbrook. "You're a free man, Michael."

Michael gripped her in a bear hug, tears flowing down his cheeks. JP Harrison and Tina joined them. The marshals gave them their space. When Michael released his embrace, the marshals took him to be processed, and JP and Tina went to greet him when he walked from jail a free man. They all intended to meet at the Paddy Wagon to celebrate.

Keera turned at the sound of Judge Patel's voice. "Ms. Duggan. I'd like to speak with you in private."

Keera made her way behind the bench and down the hall to Judge Patel's office, not knowing what to expect. Patel had removed her black robe. She looked far less imposing in a blouse and slacks and no longer peering down at Keera from atop the bench.

"Take a seat," Patel said, gesturing to the two chairs across her desk.

Keera did so.

"I wanted you to know that when this case initially was assigned to me, I intended to recuse myself because of my history with your father, of which I assume you are aware."

"My father said you had some legendary battles when you were with the prosecutor's office," Keera said, choosing her words carefully.

"'Wars' might be a more appropriate term," Patel mused. "I decided to take the case because I had heard about your defense of Vince LaRussa and of Jenna Bernstein. I was intrigued. And now I am impressed. Despite the incident that led to our meeting in my chambers during trial, I owe you an apology. You are not your father."

"I don't know if that's a good thing or not," Keera said, displaying the wisp of a smile.

"I can understand that. So let me say that you are every bit the attorney he was. He fought tirelessly and passionately for those he defended, and he didn't care if he ruffled feathers, mine included."

"Sounds like my father," Keera said.

"I brought you back here because I wanted to say congratulations. The deck was stacked against you, but you persevered for your client, and against a formidable adversary."

"Thank you, Judge."

"And because I hope you realize this is only the beginning for you."

"The beginning?" Keera asked, uncertain of Patel's intent.

"Your reputation is growing, and that can be lucrative, and it can be intoxicating if not kept in perspective. Never forget that while your responsibility is, first and foremost, to your clients, it also extends to the integrity of judicial system in which you participate."

Keera didn't know if the judge was referring to Anh Tran and what she had done, or if she had intended to take a not-so-subtle jab at Patsy, his alcoholism, and the many indiscretions he'd likely perpetrated in his career.

"I'm not interested in fame, Your Honor."

"And yet it has found you, nonetheless. Fame can be difficult to handle when it arrives without warning, Ms. Duggan. The entertainment business is littered with the spent carcasses of those who were unprepared for it. Better to expect it, and to be prepared for all that comes with it. The good and the bad."

# Epilogue

The line of cars outside Tina Westbrook's home stretched down the block and around the corner. Harrison had parked his BMW at the end, safe from any possible dings or nicks. The man was nothing if not OCD about that car.

Keera parked behind him, stepped out into a bright fall afternoon, then reached into the back seat to retrieve the large plate of chocolate chip cookies she'd baked for Michael Westbrook's welcome home party. She'd used her mother's recipe, which was a lot of butter and even more milk-chocolate chips.

Tina had waited to have Michael's party. She wanted to give her son some time to decompress, and to contemplate what had nearly happened to him. She wanted him to learn from it. Keera thought it a wise thing to do.

Following the dismissal, Keera had held a brief press conference to reiterate Michael was innocent, that he had simply been in the wrong place at the wrong time and had agreed to hold the two packages thinking they were Lockett's birthday presents to Melissa Scott. She said Michael had made mistakes, like most young people, but he was not a murderer or a drug dealer. As for who had killed Lockett and Scott, Keera directed all further questions to the DEA, the FBI, and Billy Ford of the Seattle police.

She did not say that Sam Vo and Tommy Phan had been arrested, and the FBI was operating under the assumption that Vo, upon

Phan's orders, had killed Lockett and Scott. She also did not say that the Department of Justice was beginning the time-consuming task of reviewing Anh Tran's convictions to determine further improprieties. It would be a tall task, but one they could not ignore.

Tran was said to be cooperating, though not in Seattle. She had left the state of Washington and the public scrutiny she likely never wanted and never would have received but for the horrific murder of her parents.

As Keera neared the gate to the cyclone fence surrounding the Westbrook home, she recognized some of the people standing on the lawn to be Tina Westbrook's neighbors. As she walked through them, they thanked her for what she had done for Michael and for Tina. She accepted their accolades graciously, but she kept moving, looking for Tina, Michael, or JP.

She spotted Harrison in the corner near a billowing barbecue that brought a sweet smell of roasting meat. He wore an apron streaked with barbecue sauce and held tongs in one hand, a small brush in the other. Darned if he didn't look good, even in the apron.

"You look like you belong," she said. "Maybe this is your true calling."

He smiled. "I'll have you know that I've tended many barbecues, and you won't find better-tasting ribs than right here."

"Someone has had a couple of beers," Keera said. "And has gotten cocky."

"A few, but no one is counting," Harrison said. "I'd give you a hug but I'm afraid I'd get barbecue sauce all over your nice clothes."

"I'm in jeans and a pullover fleece. Save me a couple of those famous ribs, will you? I need to find your sister, and Michael."

"Inside," Harrison said, using the tongs to point to the front door. "But first, let me have one of those." He reached and snatched a cookie.

Keera wound her way through the guests inside the house. It wasn't as crowded as the yard. Most were outside enjoying the weather. In the kitchen, Tina filled trays with hors d'oeuvres. Keera greeted her, and the two women exchanged a warm hug. She handed Tina the plate of cookies.

"Homemade," Tina said. She removed the plastic wrap and smelled the cookies. "Where did you find the time?"

"My father is trying to get me to better balance my time," she said. She'd driven her father and mother to the airport a few weeks ago for a monthlong trip to visit relatives in Ireland. Before leaving, Patsy told her not to be a workaholic, as he had been. "Don't wait to see the world, Keera. Remember, no one looks back on their life and wishes they had more time to work."

Maybe not, but Keera's notoriety was bringing more work to the firm, more than they could handle, and finding time off was more difficult.

"I'm glad you and Mom can enjoy it together," she had said.

"You'll have somebody someday too," he'd said.

She thought of Frank Rossi. They'd managed to keep things casual, mostly dinners. A movie. An occasional play at the 5th Avenue Theatre. He'd kissed her but he had not spent the night, though she'd thought about it. She enjoyed his company. They'd put boundaries in place to keep things aboveboard. Frank didn't talk about his cases, and Keera didn't talk about hers. It was liberating—two people not talking about their work. They had to come up with other topics and were learning a lot about one another. They did jigsaw puzzles and board games. Frank refused to play chess with her, knowing that if he were ever to win, she would have let him, and that would be too damaging to his ego.

"Michael was asking about you," Tina said. "I saw him out back. He has a surprise. Go on. He's eager to see you."

Keera stepped to the screen door leading into the backyard, Michael stood in the center. Behind him, a sign hung on the cyclone fence. **WELCOME HOME, MICHAEL.** He spoke to Jada Davis and, again, from a lifetime of studying body language, Keera thought she detected something between the two. Jamar and Michelle Davis were also present, and Keera greeted them on her way to Michael.

Michael smiled and gave her a hug. "Ms. Duggan," he said. "Thank you for coming."

"Of course. I wouldn't miss it," Keera said. "And now that the case is over, you can call me Keera. I'm not that much older than the two of you." She greeted Jada Davis.

"I'll let you two talk while I get more ribs." Jada stepped aside.

"I got you something," Michael said.

"You didn't have to get me anything, Michael."

"It isn't much, but I talked to JP about it." He reached into his pocket and pulled out what looked like a fifty-cent piece. It had been engraved. "It's a challenge coin," he said.

Keera knew law enforcement and military personnel gave the coins to select people to recognize those people's accomplishments and to serve as symbolic acceptance into their organization. Receiving one was considered the ultimate compliment.

"JP helped me design it."

On one side, Michael had inscribed Keera's name and the scales of justice. She flipped the coin over and read the words inscribed on the back. Honor. Bravery. Integrity.

"I have one too." Michael pulled a coin from his pocket and showed it to Keera. "To serve as a reminder of what happened. I'm done with all the dumbshit stuff I was doing. I learned a valuable lesson that I want to carry forward. I want something good to come from all of this. I've set goals for myself. I'm going to finish my prerequisites and go to a university. And I'm thinking of maybe becoming a lawyer, helping out people who need it, like you."

"You'd be a great lawyer, Michael." Lord knew he'd had a ringside seat to a trial unlike many others—and a view she hoped he never had again, unless he was standing at the lectern asking the questions.

They spoke for a few more minutes, but Keera now had ribs on her mind. "JP promised me a plate with ribs. I better get back there before they're all gone."

Michael reached out and hugged her again. "I'll never forget what you did for me, and for my mom. I owe you my life."

She held up her coin. "I'll remember."

As she stepped away, Keera considered the young man's words. *I owe you my life.* In a way, Michael Westbrook did. And it was an enormous responsibility her father had passed to her; one she would do her best to honor.

She made her way back to the barbecue. JP had indeed set aside an enormous plate of ribs, as well as potato salad and two ears of corn. "I can't eat all of this," she said.

"No, but you and I can." He handed her a napkin and a soda. They sat across from one another at a picnic table covered with a red-and-white-checked tablecloth. Others sat at the table as well.

Keera took a rib and bit into it. The meat was so tender it nearly fell from the bone, the sauce spicy and sweet. "These are good," she said. "Wow."

"Old family recipe passed down for generations."

"I'm honored."

"I'm kidding. I got it off the internet."

"Is nothing sacred to you?"

JP laughed and wiped the corners of his mouth with a napkin. "How's Maggie?" he asked.

Keera licked her fingers. "You know Maggie. She's back to being as ornery as ever."

"And how are you doing?"

"Me?" Keera asked.

"Don't give me that 'Me?' like this was another walk in the park. I know this trial took a lot out of you, especially with Michael being my nephew. I'm indebted to you. I just want to be sure you're okay."

"I'm okay. When I drove my mother and father to the airport to catch a flight to Ireland for a month, my father told me not to be a workaholic like he'd been."

"Good advice. So, what's your plan?"

"I'm working on it, JP. Just taking it a day at a time and seeing where life takes me."

"Don't be so laissez-faire. You'll wake up and be in your fifties and wonder where the years went."

"Are you getting nostalgic, Mr. Harrison?" She took another bite of her rib.

"I'm just thinking; you know. Maybe I should find somebody."

"You? The confirmed bachelor?"

"This old dog can learn new tricks."

"Anyone in mind?"

"Well, I was thinking . . ." He set down his rib. "Maggie is back on the market; right?"

Keera threw her rib bone at him. It hit his chest and slid down the front of his apron. "You jackass. Don't even joke about that. If Maggie heard you say that we'd have to pry her hands off you."

Harrison laughed and wiped the sauce with a napkin, tossed it on the table, and nibbled at another rib. "By the way, I talked to Frank the other day. It didn't work out."

"What didn't work out?"

"The woman he was dating; he said she was too clingy."

"Yeah?" Keera hid her smile behind an ear of corn.

"I don't think that was it, though. Not the reason they broke up."

"No. What do you think?"

"I think he has his eye on someone else. Someone not clingy. Someone independent." He smiled at her.

"Like I said, JP. I'm just taking it a day at a time."

# Acknowledgments

My mother suffered a massive stroke a month ago, February 8, 2025. She is dying and won't be alive when this book is published. I write this anticipating my loss. Mom was ninety-two, led a good life, lost a husband twenty years ago, and was ready to go. But as my wife has said before, dying is toughest on the living.

How I will miss her.

She meant the world to me. She encouraged me to read, and she encouraged me to write. I wrote *The Extraordinary Life of Sam Hell* in many respects to honor her and everything she stood for. If you read the final scene between Sam and his mother, Maddie, I was fortunate to have that scene with Mom, before her stroke. I told her everything she meant to me, and she told me she was so very proud of me. After her stroke, when she still had some cognitive ability, she would struggle to speak, and I could see the frustration on her face when no words would come. I would touch her cheek and tell her, "We don't need to talk, Mom. We've said everything we needed to say. I love you and I know you love me. Rest, Mom. It's okay to go. Dad is waiting for you."

My mother had unconditional love for God, his son, and his mother, Mary. Her faith helped her get through so many difficult periods in her life. She told us kids once, "I had a good life, but it wasn't an easy life."

She deserves to die with dignity. She deserves peace. She deserves to be with her husband, married fifty-four years.

May the road rise to meet you.
May the wind be always at your back.
May the sun shine warm upon your face;
the rains fall soft upon your fields and until we
meet again,
may God hold you in the palm of his hand.

Godspeed, Patricia Joan Branick,
Godspeed, Patty Dugoni,
Godspeed, Mom.
I will miss you.

These recent novels have been tough for me, with Mom ill. Luckily, I have a kind and understanding team supporting me. As usual, they gave me time and encouragement and helped me to write the best book possible. This third novel in the Keera Duggan series came from an article I stumbled upon about the most powerful people in the judiciary. I would have said "judges" but was surprised when the answer in the article was "prosecutors."

Prosecutors make the decision whom to charge and what charges to bring. They make the decision on plea bargains and negotiations. Like most lawyers I know, they have to be competitive to be good. They like to win. Those I've met also have a strong sense of justice and believe when a crime is committed, justice must be served for the victim and the victim's family.

But what happens, I wondered, when that power is abused?

I was surprised I found so few articles on the subject matter and learned that is in part because prosecutors are protected for their acts as prosecutors. It is a very high standard to prove a prosecutor guilty of misconduct and didn't just make a "harmless error." I think it is also, in part, because like in most professions, the large majority of prosecutors do their jobs well and for the right reasons; it is the outliers who misuse and abuse their power.

But what if one does?

That "what if" and those "outliers" are what we fiction writers focus on to create tension.

I've come to truly enjoy Keera Duggan and the Duggan family and all its dysfunction. I've enjoyed it so much, I have a great idea for the next edition, a prequel of sorts I'm excited to start on soon. All I can say is, stay tuned.

Years ago, now, when my editor Gracie Doyle and I sat down and discussed the idea of a legal thriller, I wanted something a little different. I wanted a novel that blended legal thriller, police procedural, and family dynamics. Gracie was game for the idea, and Keera and the Duggan family were born inside my head and later committed to paper in *Her Deadly Game*, and *Beyond Reasonable Doubt*, and now, *Her Cold Justice*.

Keera is an accomplished chess player. I am not. I'm grateful for the help of National Master Elliott Neff, who has been instrumental in helping me create the chess games within this series.

For the police procedural elements of these novels, I have relied upon dozens of hours of help from Scott Tompkins of the King County Sheriff's Office, deceased, and Jennifer Southworth, retired, Seattle Police Department, Violent Crimes Section. Alan Hardwick, a retired law enforcement officer, has also made himself available to answer questions, and more recently, Carl Kleinknecht joined the team and has helped me with guns and shooting. I've also met with and kept notes from meetings with forensic experts who have been instrumental in my characters solving the case. To the extent there are any mistakes in the police aspects of this novel, or the forensics, those mistakes are mine and mine alone.

In the interests of telling a story, and hopefully keeping that story entertaining, I have condensed certain timelines, such as the time it now takes for a case to go to trial.

Thanks to Meg Ruley, Rebecca Scherer, and the team at the Jane Rotrosen Agency. They have helped me with every aspect of my career, including my time away from writing to recharge and refresh. I rely on them so much.

Thomas & Mercer, Amazon Publishing, is also a great team of individuals. I've written a number of books and series in various genres, and they adapt with each novel to bring it to its fullest potential. Their assistance promoting my work allows me to focus on what I do best, writing novels. I work nearly every day, and I love what I do. The team at Thomas & Mercer has made each novel better with their edits, comments, and suggestions. I take each seriously because I know it will make the novel better.

Thanks to Angela Elson, production manager; and Jarrod Taylor, art director. I am anxiously awaiting the cover art for *Her Cold Justice* because they do such a spectacular job finding just the right fit. The Amazon PR team, which now includes Megan Beatie at Megan Beatie Communications, has done a fabulous job promoting me and my work. Thank you, Megan, for everything that you do for me. I am grateful.

Thank you to the Amazon marketing team working on my novels—Andrew George, Erica Moriarty, and Andrea Mendez—for all your efforts and creative ideas. Thanks to Amazon Publishing's publisher, Julia Sommerfeld, for creating a team who believes in my work. It shows.

I am especially grateful to Amazon Publishing's associate publisher, Gracie Doyle. Gracie is busier than a one-armed paperhanger, as the saying goes, but still manages to find time for me and my work and has been a terrific support during these weeks as my mother's health has failed.

Thank you to Charlotte Herscher, developmental editor. Charlotte has edited nearly all of my books with Amazon Publishing. She picks up the storyline quickly and ensures I don't drop something along the way. Thanks to Scott Calamar, copyeditor, whom I will miss when he moves on to new horizons. I wish you the very best.

Thanks to Tami Taylor, who creates my newsletters, and creates some of my foreign-language book covers. Thanks to Pam Binder and the Pacific Northwest Writers Association for their support.

Thanks to you, tireless and loyal readers.

Thank you to my family. We stand by one another in each of our endeavors, during the good times and the bad. We are there for one another. I'm so grateful to you all, and so proud of you.

I couldn't do this without all of you, nor would I want to.

# About the Author

*Photo © Douglas Sonders*

Robert Dugoni is the *New York Times, Wall Street Journal, Washington Post,* and Amazon Charts bestselling author of several series, including Tracy Crosswhite, Charles Jenkins, David Sloane, and Keera Duggan. His stand-alone novels include *A Killing on the Hill, Hold Strong* (coauthored with Jeff Langholz and Chris Crabtree), *Damage Control, The 7th Canon, and The World Played Chess. The Extraordinary Life of Sam Hell, a Newsweek* magazine staff pick for favorite books of all time, was *Suspense Magazine's* 2018 Book of the Year and won Dugoni an *AudioFile* Earphones Award for his narration. The *Washington Post* named his nonfiction exposé *The Cyanide Canary* a best book of the year. Dugoni is the recipient of the Nancy Pearl Book Award for fiction and a multitime winner for best novel set in the Pacific Northwest. He has been a finalist for many other awards. Dugoni's books are sold in more than twenty-five countries and have been translated into more than thirty languages, reaching over twelve million readers worldwide. He lives in Seattle. Visit his website at www.robertdugonibooks.com.